"The ultimate final girl. Bruised, battered, bleeding but never broken. Dark Mill South has no idea what he's hit. Delivering characters as riveting as an axe to the face and surprise reveals like body blows, *Don't Fear the Reaper* is another bloody triumph."—**A. G. Slatter**, author of *All the Murmuring Bones* and *The Path of Thorns*

Praise for Stephen Graham Jones

"Stephen's writing is a chainsaw and every sentence in this book drips with blood, every paragraph is clotted with skin, and every period is a bullethole. He makes me feel like an amateur."—**Grady Hendrix**, *New York Times* bestselling author of *The Final Girl Support Group*

"A homage to slasher films that also manages to defy and transcend genre. You don't have to be a slasher fan to read *My Heart is a Chainsaw*, but I guarantee that you will be after you read it."—**Alma Katsu**, author of *The Hunger* and *The Fervor*

"Brutal, beautiful, and unforgettable, *My Heart Is a Chainsaw* ... a bloody love letter to slasher fans, it's everything I never knew I needed in a horror novel."—**Gwendolyn Kiste**, Bram Stoker Award-winning author of *The Rust Maidens*

"Stephen Graham Jones can't miss. *My Heart Is a Chainsaw* is a painful drama about trauma, mental health, and the heartache of yearning to belong... twisted into a DNA helix with encyclopedic Slasher movie obsession and a frantic, gory whodunnit mystery, with an ending both savage and shocking. Don't say I didn't warn you!"—**Christopher Golden**, *New York Times* bestselling author of *Ararat* and *Red Hands*

"An easy contender for Best of the Year ... It left me stunned and applauding."—**Brian Keene**, World Horror Grandmaster Award and two-time Bram Stoker Award-winning author of *The Rising* and *The Damned Highway*

"Jones masterfully navigates the shadowy paths between mystery and horror. An epic entry in the slasher canon."—**Laird Barron**, author of *Swift to Chase*

"An intense homage to the classic horror films of yore."—***Polygon***

"At once an homage to the horror genre and a searing indictment of the brutal legacy of Indigenous genocide in America, Stephen Graham Jones' *My Heart Is a Chainsaw* delivers both dazzling thrills and visceral commentary... Jones takes grief, gentrification and abuse to task in a tale that will terrify you and break your heart all at the same time."—***Time***

Also by Stephen Graham Jones and available from Titan Books

THE ONLY GOOD INDIANS

MY HEART IS A CHAINSAW

DON'T FEAR THE REAPER

STEPHEN GRAHAM JONES

TITAN BOOKS

Don't Fear the Reaper
Print edition ISBN: 9781803361741
E-book edition ISBN: 9781803361758

Published by Titan Books
A division of Titan Publishing Group Ltd.
144 Southwark Street, London SE1 0UP
www.titanbooks.com

First Titan edition: February 2023
10 9 8 7 6 5 4 3 2 1

A CIP catalogue record for this title is available from the British Library.

Printed and bound in the United Kingdom by CPI Group (UK) Ltd, Croydon, CR0 4YY.

For Wes Craven: we miss you

The killer is with few exceptions recognizably human and distinctly male.

—Carol J. Clover

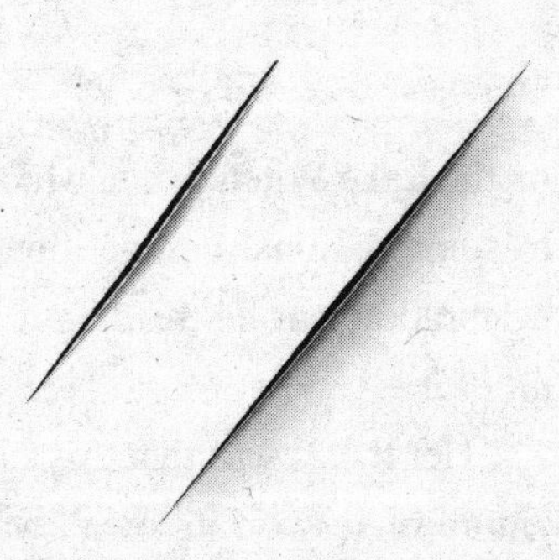

MOTEL HELL

It's not really cool to play Lake Witch anymore, but that doesn't mean Toby doesn't remember *how* to play.

It started the year after the killings, when he was a sophomore, and it wasn't a lifer who came up with it, he's pretty sure, but one of the transplants—in the halls of Henderson High, those are the two main divisions, the question you always start with: "So… you *from* here, or you'd just get here?" Did you grow up here, or did you move here just to graduate from Henderson High and cash in on that sweet sweet free college?

If it turns out you're from Proofrock, then either you were almost killed in the water watching *Jaws*, or you knew somebody who was. Your dad, say, in Toby's case. And if you're the one asking that question? Then you're a transplant, obviously.

The reason Toby's pretty sure it was a transplant who came up with the game is that, if you'd lived through that night, then the whole Lake Witch thing isn't just a fun costume.

But it is, too, which is what the transplants, who had no parents dead in those waters, figured out.

The game's simple. Little Galatea Pangborne—the freshman who writes like she's in college—even won an award for her paper on the Lake Witch game, which the new history teacher submitted to some national competition. Good for her. Except part of the celebration was her reading it at assembly. Not just some of it, but *all* of it.

Her thesis was that this Lake Witch game that had sprung up "more or less on its own" was inevitable, really: teenagers are going to engage in courting rituals, that's hardwired in, is "biology expressing itself through social interaction"—this is how she talks. What makes Proofrock unique, though, is that those same teenagers are also dealing with the grief and trauma of the Independence Day Massacre. So, Galatea said into the mic in her flat academic voice, it's completely natural that these teens' courting rituals and their trauma recovery process became "intertwined." Probably because if life's the *Wheel of Fortune*, then she can afford all the letters she wants.

What she said did make sense, though, Toby has to admit.

The game *is* all about getting some, if you're willing to put in the legwork. And, as Galatea said to assembly, the elegance is the game's simplicity: if you're into someone, then you do a two-handed knock on their front door or the side window of their car or wherever you've decided this starts. You have to really machine-gun knock, so you can be sure they get the message, and will definitely be the one to open that door. Also, knocking like that means you're standing there longer than you really want, so you might be about to get caught *already.*

But, no, you're already running.

And?

Under your black robe, you're either naked or down to next to nothing, as the big important part of the game is you leave your clothes piled in front of the door. Galatea called this the "lure and the promise." Toby just calls it "pretty damn interesting."

Which is to say, just moments ago he got up from the ratty, sweated-up queen bed at the Trail's End Motel at the top end of Main Street, his index finger across his lips to Gwen, and pulled the dull red door in to find a pair of neatly folded yoga pants and, beside them, one of those pricey-thin t-shirts that probably go for ninety bucks down the mountain.

He looked out into the parking lot but it was all just swirling snow and the dull shapes of his Camry and Gwen's mom's truck. Idaho in December, surprise. One in the afternoon and it's already a blizzard.

"Who is it?" Gwen creaked from the bed, holding the sheets up to her throat just like women on television shows do. Toby's always wondered about that.

Another part of the game is that, if you don't give immediate chase, then this particular Lake Witch never knocks on your door again. "Message received," as Galatea put it, because "menacing the object of your affection while disguising your identity is... kind of creepy?"

It was the first laugh she got at assembly that day.

"Message received..." Toby mutters to this Lake Witch, kneeling in his boxer briefs to touch these yoga pants, this expensive shirt, as if his fingertips can feel the body heat from whoever was just wearing them. Who was just standing right here where he is, slithering out of her clothes under cover of a robe—and in minus whatever the temperature is.

The question, of course, is does he leave Gwen in the room to chase another girl through the snow?

It's not really a question, though. This is the game, isn't it? It's not about convenience. It's about opportunity.

"Gonna get a coke," he mumbles back into the room, and steps out, just managing to reach back in for his letterman jacket. It's against the rules—you have to give chase exactly as you are, no tying your laces, no brushing your teeth, no pulling your good pants on—but he's already freezing.

Gwen calls something to him but the door's already shutting, catching, latched.

Now he's alone under the second-floor balcony or walkway or whatever it's called. Galatea would know. "Parapet?" Toby chuckles, zero idea what that word's doing swimming around in his head. English class, maybe? Some movie?

Doesn't matter.

What does are the footsteps in the snow, already rounding off in the icy wind.

"This better be worth it!" he calls out into the parking lot.

It feels like he's the only person in the world, here. Like he's standing on *top* of the world.

Everybody smart, which is everybody but him and this Lake Witch, they're inside where it's warm. Anybody outside, they probably have their winter gear on, and, for this kind of storm, goggles, and maybe a defibrillator.

Toby thrusts his hands up into his armpits, hunches his head as deep into the no-collar of his jacket as he can, and steps out into the cold.

When he doesn't come back with a coke fresh from the machine, Gwen'll know something's up, sure. But Toby's already got his lie ready: he thought he had change in the jacket. Just... Gwen's not exactly stupid. Granted, she just moved here this year, for the scholarship, and the Lake Witch game had pretty much run its course by then, meaning she didn't recognize its signature knock, but still.

If he's got a line of shiny-wet hickeys coming down from his neck? If his mouth is smeared with some other girl's lipstick?

Gwen's big city, but she's not *that* big city.

If you're a shark, though, you keep moving, don't you? Keep moving or die. That's been Toby's mental bumpersticker ever since the massacre—a strict policy of constant movement means that bad night in the water gets farther away with every day, with every swish of the tail. Or—this is the motel—with every *piece* of tail. Galatea should write something about *that*, really. The principal's basketball-star son landing on "shark" as his spirit animal? "Really? Is this, pray-tell, maybe the same shark that was on-screen when your principal-dad was dying in the water?"

Probably, Toby knows.

You do what you have to do.

And you keep moving, from Penny last week to Gwen this week. And now… now whoever this Lake Witch is going to be.

Wynona F, emphasis on that last initial?

Oh yeah. Yeah yeah yeah.

He's *glad* this game is back. Who cares if it's already old. It's also forever new. And no, Henderson High, having a Terra Nova princess read it to assembly didn't quite kill it, thanks. It did pull it into the spotlight, but it didn't wither.

Neither is Toby—though he does reach down, check to be sure.

Good to go.

The cold doesn't matter to a lifer, does it? To someone born to this elevation, to these winters?

He does have to turn his back to the wind, though, to keep it out of his jacket, and whoever the Lake Witch is tonight wasn't expecting that, evidently—a ragged black form slips out of his peripheral vision, into the white.

Too fast to tell for sure if it's Wynona.

"Here I come!" Toby calls out all the same, and like that the chase is on.

Galatea's explanation to assembly was that all the running after each other is foreplay, is hunter-prey seduction: the blood's flowing, the breathing's already deep, and, if this Lake Witch knocked at the right time, then the one who finally catches them is probably in some state of undress. Just like they are under that slinky robe.

"Convenient, yes?" Galatea said to assembly—her second laugh.

As always, there were bowls of no-questions-asked condoms at the two doors out of the auditorium that day.

As always, someone had already dropped an open safety pin into each bowl.

Hilarious.

And, speaking of: Toby pats his pockets, comes out with... Visine, of course. A blue pen, okay. His wallet, damnit. Unless he stashes it out here, Gwen'll know he had money for the machine.

In the other pocket, though—yes. Three rubbers.

He counts in his head, and... yeah. That's how many he should have left.

He puts everything back into his pockets, just catches a hooded face watching him from the vending machine hall.

He's there in a flash, his feet ten degrees past numb, but this Lake Witch, who *did* keep her boots on, it looks like from her tracks, has run all the way through to the other side of the motel.

Instead of falling for that like a noob, Toby backs up, jogs to the front, because that's the only way you can come back, if, say, you think your pursuer is coming up the vending machine hall.

"This better be worth it, it better be worth it!" Toby calls out into the storm, but he's grinning wide, too.

Until Gwen opens the door of their room.

"My money blew away!" Toby says back to her, bending like trying to catch a dollar scraping across the snow.

"I'll give you another!" Gwen calls back, hugging herself against the cold.

And… no.

But yes: she's seeing the yoga pants and shirt she's nearly stand-ing on.

"What?" Toby thinks she says. It's what her body language is saying anyway. What her eyes are beaming across.

You don't understand, he wants to explain to her. *I have to see who this is. She won't come knocking again.*

All of which translates down to *I'll never be this eighteen again,* he knows.

He takes a step toward her, which is when he becomes aware of… of some *massive* shape in the parking lot. Like a great black wall fell out of the sky, planted itself across the lines.

"What the hell?" he says to himself, and looks over his right shoulder for the chance of this Lake Witch slashing up beside him, touching his side before slipping away again.

And there's Gwen, holding those clothes up now, inspecting them.

Recognizing them? Girls can do that, can't they?

And—and… and now this whatever-this-is in the parking lot?

It's too much.

Toby doesn't want to get too far from the motel, but this is a mystery he can solve in four or five steps, he's pretty sure.

He shuffles out, his teeth starting to chatter, and it's… a *trash truck*?

A big gust swirls hard little crystals of snow up into his face, his eyes, his lungs, and he spins away from it all, shakes his head no, that he's just going to go back to the room, back to Gwen. That if Wynona's into him, great, fine, wonderful. But another time, girl, please. Can't she see he's otherwise occupied?

Doesn't she know how freaking *cold* it is?

He balls himself as small as he can to take less punishment from the wind, which is when… something hot happens. Hot and fast.

At first it doesn't even make sense to his primitive shark brain.

Part of the game, the "advanced version" as Galatea had called it, making it all super boring and academic, was the Lake Witch dashing past, "counting coup" on her or his intended's shoulder—"part of the dance," Galatea called it, getting zero laughs, this time.

"Coup" is a Native American thing, she then slowed down to tell them all, being kind of judgy about it, like she was insulted that this even needed to be said out loud.

In the parking lot two months after that day at assembly, Toby looks up to the blinking neon sign, the giant dying Indian on his giant tired horse, and then, to be sure he felt what he thought he felt, he looks down to his hands, opening at his waist.

They're not just red with the light leaking down from the Indian, they're red with his blood, and they're holding his, his—

He shakes his head, falls back.

He's holding his intestines, his insides, his liver and pancreas and gall bladder and whatever else there is, and his hands are so numb they don't even know what it is they've caught.

He pushes them away as if getting them out of his vision will mean they're not really happening, but that just pulls more out, and they're glisteny and lumpy and slick and getting away fast, and he feels a warm hollowness inside that he's never felt before—it's the wind, blowing *into* him for the first time, because his gut is now an empty cavity.

He falls to his knees, trying to gather himself to himself, and when he looks up again, the giant neon Indian is looking right down at him.

It flickers once, comes back stronger, redder, and then it dies all the way out.

Toby Manx goes with it.

DARK MILL SOUTH

In the summer of 2015 a rough beast slouched out of the shadows and into the waking nightmares of an unsuspecting world. His name was Dark Mill South, but that wasn't the only name he went by.

Cowpoking through Wyoming, working the feedline as they used to call it, he'd been the Eastfork Strangler. Not because he ever hung his hat in the Eastfork bunkhouse or rode their fences, but because he'd somehow come into possession of one of their 246 branding irons, and had taken the time with each victim to get that brand glowing red, to leave his mark.

For that season he'd been propping his dead up behind snow fences, always facing north. It wasn't necessarily a Native American thing—Dark Mill South was Ojibwe, out of Minnesota—it was, he would say later, just polite, after all he'd put them through.

His manners extended to six men and women that winter of 2013.

Come spring melt, the Eastfork Strangler lobbed his branding iron into the Chugwater and drifted up into Montana, where the newspapers dubbed him the Ninety-Eye

Slasher. It was supposed to have been the "I-90 Slasher," since Dark Mill South's reign of terror had extended up and down I-90, from Billings to Butte, but the intern typing it into the crawl on the newsfeed had flipped it around to "90-I." By that evening, "Ninety-Eye" had gone viral, and so was another boogeyman born.

The "slasher" part was close to right, anyway: Dark Mill South was using a machete by then. With it he carved through eleven people. He was no longer being polite with them. According to the one interview he'd ever supposedly given, Montana had been a bad time for him. He didn't remember it all that clearly.

Next it was the Dakotas, where he was known as the Bowman Butcher, responsible for eight dead at Pioneer Trails campground over a single weekend, and then two weeks later in South Dakota he became the Rapid City Reaper, who didn't use a bladed weapon at all, but hung his five victims by the neck, one per month.

It was those five victims who got the authorities piecing his history together—what could be his history. The campground this "Butcher" had sliced through in Bowman, North Dakota, was 160 miles directly north of Rapid City, and murders happening two and a half hours from each other, with major arteries connecting them, and on successive months… this couldn't be the same killer, could it?

At which point someone probably unfolded the map, to see what roadways fed into Bowman. To the east it was smaller and smaller farming communities, and no major highways or interstates until I-29, which was nearly Minnesota. And there had been no unaccounted-for bodies turning up over there. Nothing to suggest a killer prowling the rest stops and truckstops.

U.S. Route 12 west out of Bowman, though, connects with I-94 just over the Montana state line, and, although called "94," it's really what I-90 should be, if it hadn't taken a sharp turn south. And there were definitely bodies piling up alongside I-90. Or, there had been. Two months had gone by since the last one turned up in pieces. Either the Ninety-Eye Slasher had been locked up for some minor offense or he had hung up the white pantyhose he'd been using as a mask and moved on to other pastures, other victim pools.

A campground in North Dakota, perhaps? And then Rapid City?

While Dark Mill South hadn't used a machete on those eight campers, the felling axe he did use to deadly effect that weekend had, according to forensic analysis, been swung from the left, not the right. Just like the Ninety-Eye Slasher's machete. And those brands the Eastfork Strangler had burned into his victims were all deep, mortally deep in most cases, but autopsy showed that they were just a smidge deeper on their right side.

Since only ten percent of people are left-handed and less than 0.0008 percent are serial killers, then, statistically speaking (ten percent of "0.00008"), it was less likely that the Eastfork Strangler and the Ninety-Eye Slasher and the Bowman Butcher all just "happened" to be left-handed than it was that they were actually the same killer, adopting different methods and rituals with each change of location, so as to not attract an interstate task force.

That task force was forming all the same.

However, this Rapid City Reaper wasn't using a bladed weapon or a branding iron that could give away his handedness. And instead of a sustained killing frenzy involving stalking and masks and campgrounds, he seemed more deliberate with his victims, as if he was feeling out a way to extract more meaning from the act.

How he staged his series of hangings through the suburbs of Rapid City from December 2014 through April of 2015 was to allow his victims metal stools to stand on, so as to take their body's weight off the rope around their neck. But these stools, which the Rapid City Reaper was bringing with him, were all metal with rubber feet, so he could open up an outlet on the wall—always the north wall—and splice into that current, leave this stool circulating with blue fire.

The result was that the stool these people could stand on to take the pressure off their neck was sizzling hot, would arc up and down through their hanging bodies. Without shoes or socks, just touching that stool would cook the soles of their feet, a show the Rapid City Reaper would observe while eating cold leftovers from the victim's refrigerator, the crumbs of which he was leaving either carelessly or due to overconfidence.

Since there were no wounds on these hanging victims other than their cooked feet and crushed windpipes, where the authorities had to look for the telltale signature they needed was the splices in the wires used to pass the current. As it turned out, these copper unions had all been twisted counterclockwise instead of what would be natural to a right-hander—and so were the murders all connected, and the various media-bequeathed epithets collapsed into a single name.

This is when Dark Mill South became sensationalized as the "Nomad," a term dialed back from the throwaway "nomadic" the authorities used to explain his interstate peregrinations, but also stemming from the "Indian" silhouette the surviving camper from North Dakota insisted wasn't her imagination—traditionally, before incursion by wave after wave of settlers, Plains Indians had been nomadic.

At this point, all indications were that this Nomad was responsible for the violent deaths of some thirty people.

Which is perhaps when Dark Mill South himself started counting.

The couple he killed in their car just outside Denver, Colorado, in June 2015 had "31" and "32" burned into their torsos with the cigarette lighter from the dashboard. They'd evidently been alive for this hours-long process, and it hadn't quite killed them—a car lighter is no red-hot branding iron. What did kill them were the headrests of their seats, which had twin metal posts with adjustment notches in them. Dark Mill South lined those two metal posts up with this couple's eyes and then pushed them in to the last notch. When found, the murdered couple had their seatbelts on, the car had been positioned to face north, and the radio was tuned to an oldies station high up on the AM band. One responding officer claimed that, while he'd once had a taste for what he called "Poodle Skirt Music," he now preferred silence on patrol. The quieter the better.

The next three victims were in Elk Bend, Idaho—a 767 mile drive by the most direct route, which crosses Caribou-Targhee National Forest here in Fremont County. In Elk Bend, Dark Mill South took on the guise of Dugout Dick, the local legend, and stalked and eviscerated volunteer firemen with a railroad pickaxe. Finally, pushed to her limit and beyond, one of those firemen's wives—Sally Chalumbert, Shoshone, technically a widow by this point—stalked this "Dugout Dick" back, and, in a final confrontation, bludgeoned him with a shovel. After Dark Mill South was down, though, Sally Chalumbert's fury was still far from spent. Screaming, she continued beating him with her now-broken shovel, dislodging most of his front teeth, fracturing the bones of his face, and then using the blade of the shovel to neatly remove his right hand. The only reason she stopped there was that her husband's brother tackled her away, trying to, as he said in his statement, "save her soul."

He was too late.

The dark place Sally Chalumbert had to go to was a place she couldn't come back from. Thus her continuing institutionalization.

Dark Mill South came back, though.

The good ones always do.

When he tried to swim the Salmon River and get away into his next killing spree, one of the remaining volunteer firemen rammed the county firetruck into a utility pole, dropping its transformer into the water. Before that power line shorted out, it killed every trout, muskrat, duck, and beaver in that portion of the Salmon, and apparently scalded a young moose as well.

Dark Mill South floated in to shore face down, his wrist and face seeping blood, and when he woke weeks later, he was strapped to a reinforced hospital bed, the charges against him accumulating fast, every federal agency wanting a piece of him, every state he'd passed through angling for extradition. The Nomad was a nomad no more.

In that one muttered and variously reconstructed interview he supposedly gave, recorded by a nurse who had been given questions she'd had to crib onto her inner forearm, Dark Mill South claimed that he wasn't done yet. Thirty-five dead wasn't thirty-eight, and that's the number he was going for.

The media followed this number back to his home state of Minnesota, where thirty-eight Dakota men had been hanged in 1862—the largest mass execution in American history. Dark Mill South's claim, then, the media surmised, was that he was merely taking lives to balance the scales of justice. Whether this had been his mission all along or if it were just something he picked up along the way was anybody's guess. Either way, the effect was to permanently associate this 1862 atrocity with Dark Mill South's seven-year, multi-state "rampage," as it was now being called.

And so the Eastfork Strangler, the Ninety-Eye Slasher, the Bowman Butcher, the Rapid City Reaper, Dugout Dick, and the Nomad had their day in court, as Dark Mill South. Specifically, as he'd been arrested in Elk Bend, Idaho, Dark Mill South's "day" was down in Boise. Since those three killings were the most recent, had the most evidence directly associated with him, even including cellphone footage of surprisingly good quality, it was felt that conviction was guaranteed in this case.

Dark Mill South was a media sensation by then, and nearly a celebrity—not just another serial killer after a half century of them, but the West's favorite new boogeyman, a, according to one account in Montana, "latterday Jeremiah Johnson." At an imposing six and a half feet tall, with shoulder length hair he never tied back but wore like a shroud, with a hook attached to the stump of his right wrist and a sly grimace permanently etched into the knotted scar tissue of his face, the public couldn't look away. Fan fiction surfaced of him escaping his holding cell, making his way to the local lovers' lane, and, with his hook hand, "giving precedent after the fact to all the urban legends, and making some new ones in the process."

Because the so-called trials of the thirty-eight Dakota in 1862 had been as short as five minutes in some cases, Dark Mill's day in court went for years, as every *i* needed careful dotting, every *t* the most patient crossing, and he had to get a new set of teeth installed besides. The Elk Bend Massacre, as it came to be known, had been July 3rd and 4th, 2015—a fateful day in the history of American violence, to be sure—but Dark Mill South's much-negotiated plea deal wasn't entered until mid—October 2019.

His claim was that he could show the officers of the court more of his north-facing dead if they were interested in that kind of thing, and had enough bodybags.

They were interested.

And of course nobody doubted that Dark Mill South could lead them to leathery body after leathery body in Wyoming, in Montana, and down through the Dakotas, across to Colorado. There could even be some in southern Idaho, on the way to Elk Bend, right? After all, there had been a sensational death along that path that had garnered national attention in the summer of 2015, and it very well could have been a murder, not just an animal attack. Better yet, if it could be established that Dark Mill South had passed that holy bodycount of "38" well before getting to Elk Bend, that would serve to mitigate the continuing outrage over all those Dakota men Abraham Lincoln had hanged in 1862, as they wouldn't be people anymore, but simply an excuse a wily killer had used to rally public sympathy.

Social media dubbed this circuit The Reunion Tour—the killer reuniting with his victims.

The convoy of armored vehicles left Boise on Thursday, December 12th, 2019. Dark Mill South's shackles supposedly had shackles, he had been doped to the gills besides, and the blacked-out SUV he was strapped into was one of four identical vehicles, each of the others mocked up to appear as if they too were carrying him. The fear was that the victims' families might attempt an ambush, or—worse—that Dark Mill South's ever-expanding fanbase might stage an escape.

There was air support, state troopers both led the way and rode drag, and local constabulary closed the roads ahead of this convoy when possible. And in what was surely a strategic slip, the speaker at the press conference laying all this out went "off-script" to whisper into his bouquet of microphones that there would at all times be an armed guard assigned to sit directly behind Dark Mill South, for "any eventualities," which was of course wink-wink code for the last resort being a bullet to the back of the Nomad's head, halting his murderous peregrinations once and for all.

If, indeed, a bullet would even be sufficient.

All of America poured a stiff drink and settled into their most comfortable chair to ride this out with the grim men and women assigned this task, but then the hour got late, the channel got changed for a quick look at the game, and… attention waned.

Which was just how the convoy of armored SUVs wanted it.

Better to travel in anonymity, well out of the camera's eye. And, though they hadn't counted on the weather helping them stay off the national radar, the weather was a boon in that regard all the same. When visibility is nil and the temperature's in a nosedive, journalists can't deliver progress reports to the world. The convoy ceased to be a blinking blue dot on a map over an anchorperson's head. Instead, there were special reports interrupting the usual programming to warn viewers about this winter storm, this once-in-a-century whiteout.

The first of the interstates along the convoy's route to shut down was I-80 across Wyoming, which was no surprise to anyone familiar with that stretch of highway. The convoy shrugged, went to their Plan B: the old stomping grounds of the Ninety-Eye Killer—Montana.

Retracing their route, they picked their way through Pocatello, then Blackfoot, intending to follow the I-15 north to Idaho Falls and then all the way up to Butte, ideally in a single push.

The blizzard rocking their SUVs didn't agree: I-15 shut down as well, and wouldn't open even for badges.

Now this convoy had no recourse but to either register at a hotel they hadn't vetted or attempt a northern passage up Highway 20, which would spit them out just west of Yellowstone, right at the Montana state line.

When the call went out for a snowplow to clear the way for them out of Idaho Falls, three class 7 trucks showed up, each of them the size of a garbage or cement truck. The drivers let it be known that if that judge down in Boise needed someone to pull the switch on Dark Mill South's electric chair or gas chamber or lethal injection, they could probably find an open slot in their schedule for that as well.

Or if, say, he were to accidentally fall out the side door of an SUV, then… well, it was slick, and snowplows are heavy, and that big blade's gonna do what it's gonna do, right?

There was much manly handshaking, many shoulders patted, and so began the slow grind up the mountain, the swirling gusts of snow revealing only greater blackness beyond and, every few miles, old billboards touting Proofrock, Idaho, as "The Silver Strike Heard 'Round the World!" and Proofrock's Indian Lake as "The Best Kept Secret of the West." By 2019, of course, these billboards had been defaced—a shark fin spray-painted onto the glittering surface of Indian Lake, along with the obligatory "Help! Shark!" dialogue balloon, the miner making that world-famous silver strike given overlarge eyes and a leering grin, since there was now the cartoon of a screaming woman painted in between his pickaxe and that seam of foil.

It's probably safe to assume that Dark Mill South, seeing this graffiti through the storm, chuckled to himself with satisfaction. Just as the Marlboro Man would feel right at home walking into a forest of cigarettes, so would the Nomad recognize the country his convoy was broaching into. He was even, at this point, facing north.

As were his drivers, his guards, his handlers.

The individual flakes of snow crashed into the windshields and the wipers surely batted them away, smeared them in, fed them to the heat of the defrosters on full blast, but still the safety glass had to be icing over, making it tricky to stay locked on the taillights of the phalanx of snowplows leading the way, flinging great but silent curls of snow over the guardrail, out into open space.

Had air support been able to stay aloft in this storm, they would have had to hover so close over this crawling black line that their rotor wash would have only made visibility worse. But the two helicopters had retreated to the private airports hours behind, were handing the convoy off to Montana pilots, already waiting at their pads.

So, by 11 a.m., possibly 11:30 a.m., the convoy was out of the media eye, it had no air support, and it was being swallowed by the snow, by the blizzard, by the mountain. There was a team of snowplows carving a route, there was thermos after thermos of coffee for those drivers, but there was also Dark Mill South, perhaps already testing the limits of his shackles' shackles—handcuffing a prisoner who only has a single hand is a tricky proposition, and some metabolisms burn through sedatives so fast you can almost see them steaming away.

It was like the West was calling him back. Like the land needed a cleansing agent to rove across the landscape, blood swelling up from each of his boot prints, his shadow so long and so deep that last cries whispered up from it.

Or so someone might say who believed in slashers and final girls, fate and justice.

But we'll be getting to her later.

And everyone else as well.

First, though, this convoy lost in the whiteout, this Reunion Tour slouching toward a Bethlehem already swimming in blood.

Fifteen miles up Highway 20 is where accounts of that night begin to differ, Mr. Armitage, but where they converge again is a pier jutting out onto Indian Lake here in Proofrock, 8,000 feet up the mountain. In the offhand words of Deputy Sheriff Banner Tompkins—the sound bite that came to characterize this latest series of killings—"If we were looking anywhere for more bad shit to go down, we were looking out onto the lake, I guess. Not behind us."

"Behind us" would be U.S. Highway 20.

Dark Mill South's Reunion Tour began on December 12th, 2019, a Thursday.

Thirty-six hours and twenty bodies later, on Friday the 13th, it would be over.

As Martin Luther says on that poster by your chalkboard, "Blood alone moves the wheels of history."

Our wheels are moving just fine, thank you.

Just, don't look in the rearview mirror if you can help it.

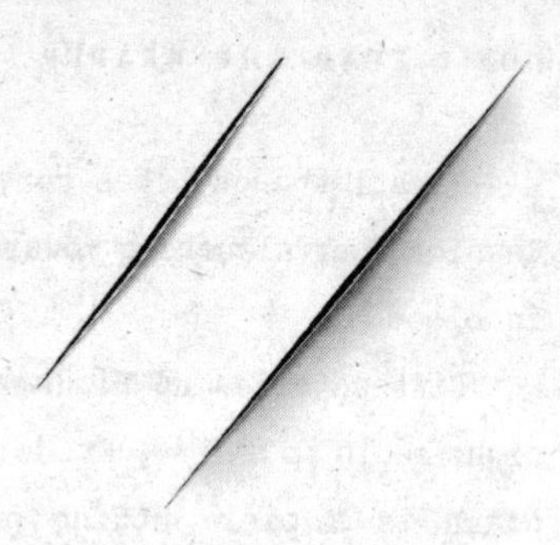

SCREAM

This was so much easier when she was seventeen.

Jennifer Daniels looks to her left, out across the vast expanse of Indian Lake, then to the right, that long drop down and down and down, and she has to take a knee, tie her right boot tighter.

Her fingernails aren't painted black, and her boots are the dress-ones her lawyer bought for her. The heels are conservative, there are no aggressive lugs on the soles, and the threads are the same dark brown color as the fake, purply-brown leather.

She stands up, is still kind of unsettled by all this open space, like it might swallow her, disappear her.

Her bangs blow into her eyes and she threads them away, and they don't make that dry sound they always did. She's still getting used to that, too: healthy hair. Long hair.

The jacket she's wearing is from the sheriff's office, because she didn't have one. The jacket was balled in the backseat of the county Bronco. It's Carhartt brown, with bright yellow conspicuity stripes down the arms and around the waist. It's too big, fits her like a tunic. Her hands don't reach the bottoms of the pockets. It makes her feel like a little girl, like she's come out into the big bad cold with her dad and he's wrapped her in his jacket because the wind doesn't bother him, a lie that makes her even warmer.

When she buries her face in the lapel it smells like cigarettes.

"You can do this, girl," she says to herself, and steps out onto the narrow concrete spine of the dam.

Why there's still not any safety rails here, she can't begin to imagine. This is walking a tightrope. If it were summer and she started to overbalance to her right, into that long silent fall, she could just fling herself the other way, fall back into the water, try to swim over to the rusty ladder there specifically because this is a drowning place. But this deep into winter, Indian Lake's frozen. She would burst on its icy back, just be a splash of red for the wolves to come lick in secret. Scuffling out here across its wind-scoured surface, the safety cones all scattered, there were ice skate carvings back and forth like giant spiders dance there at night, and, farther out, there were wide tire tracks—the firetruck Proofrock always eases out, the second week of December, to show that the deep cold's really and finally here.

Like anybody could ever doubt that. Still—and she'd never tell a soul this—it's sort of good to be home. All through high school, her dream had been to blast off, escape down to Boise. She couldn't get out of there fast enough, though.

Submitting her bare hands to the ten-degree chill, she holds her arms out to the side, places one foot in front of the other, no longer sure whether to watch where she's walking or to fix her eyes on the control booth.

The silence out here is a pressure, almost. It makes her feel like her hearing's been snatched from her.

Proofrock is so far down there it looks like a toy town, like a person in a Godzilla suit could step down through the drugstore, the bank, the post office, the motel. Not Dot's, though, please. These last two days since Rex Allen ferried her back, slipped her the jacket and a couple of twenties, Dot's coffee has been the only good thing.

In every place Jennifer Daniels puts her feet, there's peg holes in the crusted snow, as if some daredevil of a clown's been out here with a pogo stick.

She can't let herself get distracted, though.

Halfway to the booth, she stops, is having a sort of panic attack.

Worse than anything, she wants to look behind her, so sure there's going to be a trash bear standing there, leering at her.

She makes her lips into a wide oval and pants air in and out to try to calm herself. *You can do this*, she says inside, now. She has to. She at least owes him that.

On cue, then, the wind gusts from her right and she doesn't know if she *has* to drop down to her hands and knees to keep from being blown off, but she does. Shaking and freezing and near throwing up, she crawls the rest of the way to the control booth, the heels of her hands and her knees burning with cold.

This is home, all right. Goddamnit.

At least there's railing now around the little bulge of platform the booth occupies.

Jennifer stands, clamps onto it, and, just to be touching home base, keeps one frozen hand to the wall of the control booth.

Finally to the door, she bangs the side of her fist against it. Her whole forearm, really, all the way to the elbow. There's still a divot in the metal at eye-height. It's from the point of an axe, swung as hard as she could swing it.

It's rusting now, and some joker with a marker's scrawled *5 July 2015* beside it, and then, below that, in parentheses, *jade*.

Jennifer Daniels looks away from that.

One by one the door's locks disengage, and then it pulls in, exhaling warmth around her.

Jennifer Daniels finally brings her eyes in from the lake, looks through the hair blowing across her face. She's already blinking too fast.

"Well well well," Hardy says, smiling one side of his mouth.

He's leaning on a walker—the source of those peg holes out in the snow—and he's gaunt, drawn, colorless. Losing feet of your intestines will do that to you.

Jennifer Daniels rushes forward all the same, buries her face in his chest.

Instead of closing the door, the former sheriff wraps the arm he can around her, pats her back while she sobs. He needs the other hand to stay on his walker, so they don't both fall forward.

"This is my old jacket," he says with wonder, down into the top of her head.

Jennifer Daniels tries to tell him she knows that, she remembers, she remembers everything, but she can't exactly make words right now, can only press her face harder into his flannel shirt.

It smells like cigarettes too.

"Rex Allen could have chauffeured you up here the back way," Hardy says over the dam version of coffee.

His second-best deputy is the sheriff now.

Torches were made to be passed, he figures.

Badges too.

Except, he only had two deputies, meaning Rex Allen was also the worst deputy.

But—not his headache anymore.

All he has to do is keep Indian Lake Indian Lake, the valley below them mostly dry.

Well, that and smoke cigarettes.

His skin is going yellow and drawn from being locked up here in this smoky cell, but it's not like he ever planned to live forever, right?

He shouldn't even really be alive *now*, he knows.

"He would have Banner do it," Jade says—no: *Jennifer*. Jennifer Jennifer Jennifer. She's already told him that's who she is again. That "Jade" is dead. That she died that night in the water.

"'Deputy Tompkins,'" Hardy says with a chuckle, adjusting the flow a smidge in the #2 tube. Not because it needs adjusting, but old men like to feel necessary.

"He always wanted to play college football," Jennifer says, her eyes that kind of checked-out Hardy recognizes.

"Probably what he should be doing," Hardy tells her.

Instead of grinning or even smiling, this new Jennifer stands, holding her coffee close for warmth, and studies the Terra Nova side of Indian Lake.

The trees are naked and black for about two acres into the national forest.

"You did that," Hardy tells her, and when her eyes come back to him about that, he adds, "It would have *all* burned, I mean. You and Don Chambers, the valley owes the two of you. Maybe all of Idaho."

He's trying to build her back up, give her something to stand on, but she just shrugs it off, takes another drink, holding the mug with both hands. The sleeves on that jacket are long enough that she's had to roll the cuffs back.

Hardy remembers another little girl who wore this same jacket, and has to look away.

"I'm living in my old house again," Jennifer says, trying to make it into a sick joke. "My old bedroom, even."

"Camp Blood," Hardy says, commiserating.

He was down the mountain in surgery after surgery those first couple of years, but he was still getting reports. After that night in the water, all the murder tourists and horror junkies had come through Proofrock, and the Daniels house was one of the main stops. Then, when that finally died down with winter—snapshots for social media are fun, but not at twenty below—the high schoolers had jimmied the back door, made Jennifer's old house into a party pad. Camp Winnemucca had always been that for them, but the lake was still spooky those first couple of years, the shore still haunted.

So: the Daniels house. And, because it kept them in out of the cold, kept them from starting bonfires that could get out of control, Rex Allen looked the other way. Which Hardy guesses is what sheriffing has come down to, these days.

Pretty soon some punk left "Camp Blood" spray-painted in red across the front of the house.

"It fits," Jennifer says.

"You haven't had hair like this since, what?" Hardy says, reaching forward to lift some of it up. "Fifth grade?"

"Sixth," Jennifer says, blinking something away. She leans back, taking her new head of hair with her.

"*Indian* hair," Hardy says, watching her eyes to see how she takes this.

He could have said her hair was like her dad's, but he has a pretty good idea how that would go down. Anyway, she's not saying anything about Trudy, so he's not going to be bringing Tab Daniels up.

Neither is Ezekiel, he wants to add, except that last part, about her dad, wasn't out loud, so adding anything *to* that would be awkward, to say the least. Spending all his time up here alone, it's easy to lose track of what's in his head, what's not.

Which he guesses is the idea.

Jennifer doesn't answer about her Indian hair, just chucks her chin out the bulletproof glass, says, "Everybody down there has PTSD, you know?"

Now it's Hardy's turn to duck the question. But yeah, he does know. When he first came back, was still in the wheelchair, it had given him a better angle on everybody in town. If you watch their faces, their eyes, then it's business as usual, they've already put that night behind them, are just thinking about the future, or the moment, not that night in the water. But don't fall for those poker faces. Instead, watch them sitting at the outdoor tables at Dot's. Watch them leaning against that chipped blue pole at Lonnie's while their cars gulp gas in. Watch them sitting on Melanie's bench for the last little bit of the sunset.

They'll make it three minutes, five minutes, their book distracting them, this phone call taking all their attention, this bite of omelette so perfect. But then, when their mental discipline slips—you can see it happen: a shoulder will twitch, a hand will clench into a sudden fist. A chest will fill with air as if the lake is washing over them all over again.

Better to sit up here on this impossible cliff of water and smoke a thousand cigarettes.

Speaking of—

Hardy thumbs his pack up from his shirt pocket, packs them, and shakes one up for Jennifer.

She shakes her head no, thanks.

"Good," he says, taking that lead smoke himself. "You're a stronger person than I am."

"If I start, I won't be able to stop," she explains. "And I can't afford them, right?"

"I can make a call or two," Hardy tells her, digging for a match. "I might have lost three feet of my gut, but I still throw some weight around down there, can get you on the clock somewhere."

Jennifer closes her eyes, nods thank you, her eyes filling with either gratitude or regret, it's hard to tell. Either way, Hardy gives her her privacy, falls into his coughing routine, the one that makes him feel hollow inside.

"You good?" Jennifer asks, real concern in her voice, but a concern tinged with something a lot like anger, like this damnable cough is something she can fight—that she *will* fight.

She's still in there, all right. Somewhere. Under everything that's happened to her, everything that's been piled onto her. Everything she's still carrying, or trying to.

She's only twenty-two years old, Hardy reminds himself.

The world is shit, to not have treated her better.

She should be on a full-ride scholarship at some school far away. All she should be worried about is a test, a date, a party.

Instead, her only friend is an old man dying in a concrete box at the top of the world, and her only memories are stained with blood.

So as not to be a complete insensitive, Hardy guides his cigarette from his lips back into the pack, sure to turn it around upside down so it won't lose its place in line. It's stupid being superstitious like that, he knows, but if you don't have private little rituals, the days can lose their meaning real fast.

"How long you got up here?" he says to her.

"Why?"

"You'll see," he says, nodding down to the lake.

It's three in the afternoon already, and dark at four, and she probably isn't watching the barometer—kids—doesn't know that that storm that's stalled out down the mountain isn't stalled anymore. With dusk the temperature's going to plunge so fast it'll punch the bottom out of the thermometer.

Hardy palms his radio, holds his finger up for Jennifer to be quiet, and squelches Meg in.

"Sheriff," she says, and Hardy can just about see her back straightening to prim and proper now that the *real* boss is in the room.

"Gonna need a car up here in about forty-five minutes," he says.

"You're already on the schedule for *six*," she reminds him in her clipped way, but that just means she's flustered, he knows. The distinct sound of shuffling papers comes through her mic.

Because driving's complicated for him, and because he is who he is, the sheriff's office sends someone the back way to ferry him home each night. Meaning he only ever sees Proofrock at night, now. It's becoming a shadow town for him, which, taking into account all the ghosts, is about right.

"You make it happen, Meggie?" Hardy asks. "Don't want to get caught up here when it starts in blowing good."

"Already doing it," Meg says.

"And don't send that kid," Hardy adds with mock seriousness, holding Jennifer's eyes about that.

She shakes her eyes like this is all so stupid, and she's not wrong.

Hardy grandly clicks off, reseats the mic. It takes two tries to get it to stay.

"You don't have to do that," Jennifer says about him calling them a ride.

"I'm not sending you out there after dark," he tells her, pointing through the window out to the lake, the night, all of it. "You step onto that soft spot, you're gone, goodbye, world."

"I saw the cones, I know where it is."

"The cones that are blown to hell and gone?"

"I can leave now, it won't be—"

"You'll want to see this."

"There's something in this valley that can still surprise me?" she asks.

"Glad you made the trip," Hardy tells her, lifting his mug in appreciation.

"Sorry I was such a… such a handful, back when," she tells him, like maybe that's the reason she made the long walk all the way up here.

"Was always interesting," Hardy says back. "That time you wore those knife hands to school?"

"They weren't real."

"You still believe in all that?"

"In slashers? That was a long time ago. I was a—a different person, I don't know."

Hardy shrugs sure, and Jennifer shrugs back, says about all the space out the window, "You ever think about him?"

Hardy looks out into the grey sky with her.

"Bear," he adds, obviously.

Mr. Grady "Bear" "Sherlock" Holmes, because one name would have never been enough for him.

"I do," Jennifer says, all the muscles around her mouth tight. "I—it's stupid."

"So am I," Hardy says with his stupidest grin.

Jennifer looks down into her mug, says, "I was… my lawyer said it would look good for the court if I took a lot of correspondence courses from the community college. Doing all that writing papers, reading history books, sometimes I would forget he was—he was—"

She leans her head back, working her throat to keep from crying again.

"I would forget what happened," she goes on. "I would think how surprised he was going to be when I came back, had all that course credit."

Now it's Hardy who has to press his lips together, study the window glass.

"You *did* always have it in you," he finally says. "I'm not surprised at all, Ja—Jennifer."

She flicks her eyes up about her old name almost slipping in here, but doesn't call him on it.

"Listen," she says, setting her mug down, "I should—"

"Right on schedule," Hardy says, leaning forward.

Jennifer tracks where he's directing.

It's the ruins of Terra Nova.

"I think they bed down over in Sheep's Head," he says about the small herd of elk picking their way down through the burnt houses and charred trees.

"But the lake's frozen," Jennifer says.

"They're not drinking," Hardy tells her. "It's—that's where the construction crew's bank of port-a-johns were, remember?"

Jennifer narrows her eyes, dialing back, it looks like.

"Two blue ones and that wide grey one," she says, nodding.

"After the… after what happened," Hardy says, "nobody came and picked them up for that first year. But they were just plastic, couldn't make it through winter. They cracked up, spilled. It's like… you wouldn't know, growing up in town. But the grass over a septic tank is always the greenest, the best. It's the same there, and for the same natural reason. The grass was lush right there. Last summer, this little herd couldn't stay away."

"But it's all gone now," Jennifer says.

"Elk are hopeful, and they have good memories," Hardy says, and directs her down there again, to the big bull pawing at the snow, to see if the good days are here again. And to… to the other one, stepping lightly down from the trees, fully aware of how obvious he is. How conspicuous.

"Oh," Jennifer says, steepling both her hands over her mouth and drawing her breath in. "It's—he's *white*."

"Snake Indians would have called him a spirit elk," Hardy says. "And he doesn't show himself for just anybody."

"It's the—it's the storm," Jennifer says.

"It's you," Hardy corrects, gently, and the way he can tell that Jennifer feels this is how the muscles around her mouth tighten her lips into a line. Like she's trying to keep them from trembling.

Her chin is a prune, though.

Hardy gives her her privacy, doesn't intrude on this moment anymore, and four or five minutes later, the elk pick their way back up the slope, fade into the trees, the white elk the last to leave.

"Thank you," Jennifer says.

Hardy nods once.

Skirls of snow are swirling across the ice of Indian Lake, meaning things are about to pick up again.

Hardy bundles up, offers his scarf to Jennifer, and then he's reaching his walker out along the dam's icy backbone and pulling himself to it, the girl's hands holding tight to the back of his jacket, and he kind of suspects that, with her letting him lead her like that, and take the brunt of the wind, he could maybe walk across all of Idaho.

Deputy Sheriff Banner Tompkins is drumming fast on the steering wheel of the snowcat when the old man materializes out of the storm, his edges blurry like he's an oil painting leaking sideways.

Banner slows that drumbeat to more like sixty per minute, leans forward.

The ponderous single wiper on the cat is good enough to keep it between the sidewalks in town, but, facing the wind like this, the slush has been trying to freeze on the windshield. Banner wipes at the fog on his side of that glass but the forearm of his jacket sops up exactly nothing.

Step by walker-assisted step, then, the oil painting gaining resolution, Hardy goes from six legs to… eight? Him, his aluminum walker with the tennis ball feet, and—

He isn't alone? What the *hell*, old man? Taking hitchhikers here, at the top of the world?

Banner checks the still-tight catch on his sidearm, because his every last nerve is frayed: with Rex Allen gone up the highway in the county Bronco for the big manhunt, and Francie, the other deputy, tagging along, that leaves Banner to hold the fort down. Never mind that he's still on probationary status—come April, his contract either will or won't be renewed, depending on performance. Never mind that he's still mostly in the ride-along phase of being a deputy, where either Rex Allen or Francie watches from the car while he rousts tourists or tags out-of-state vehicles parked too close to the lake.

Not that there's been much of that since the snow set in.

All the same? Banner has a two-year-old daughter back at what used to be his parents' house, and he hasn't seen her now for nearly thirty-six hours—the longest he's gone without her so far, he's pretty sure. Being law in a town of three thousand is supposed to be mostly about getting cats out of trees and finding lost kites, then making it home by dinner.

Not today.

And, technically, he doesn't have permission to take the snowcat out of the county garage. Even more technical than *that*, it's not the county's cat at all, but Lonnie's. Just, as Rex Allen explained on the big walkthrough in October, Proofrock leases it from Lonnie at a good rate.

"And we also pay him for maintenance on it?" Banner had asked, studying the far walls of this cavernous garage.

In all his years coming up, from Golding Elementary to Henderson High, he'd never once been inside this place. Why hadn't there been tours in fourth grade, like they did up at the dam, the library, the post office?

"Not your concern," Rex Allen had told Banner about Lonnie charging whatever he wanted for oil changes on his own machine, and Banner had nodded once, trying to be a good soldier. One who doesn't see or hear or, most importantly, say anything.

Before today, every time somebody's got to loop around through the creek to collect Hardy from his post at the dam—"somebody" always being the least senior deputy, as this is a shit-run—that order's come with the keys to the county Bronco, the inside of which Banner *did* already know, from Hardy running him back to his parents a time or two in the wayback, when he was stupid.

But nothing to mar his record, keep him from qualifying to carry a sidearm.

Just, the last couple of weeks, that order to make the climb has always come twenty minutes earlier, so Banner can chain up. Not for the creek—it's been frozen over for a month—but for the series of steep switchbacks that lead up to Glen Dam.

Along the way are the rusting husks of at least three trucks that didn't make the climb. One's got Model A–looking fenders, no rubber on the wood-spoke wheels, the wheels down to splinters themselves, one's a still-green-in-places Dodge Power Wagon that *should* have made it—"driver error," Banner was informed—and the third's a wrecked Grand Prix that Rex Allen says had been pulled that far on a *chain*, of all things. Apparently a couple of miscontent idiots from town had been trying to tow the car up to the dam just to push it off, watch it fall, maybe flip it off on the way down.

With snowchains on all four tires, in powder like this… the county Bronco *might* make it. Depending on the driver, and luck.

It doesn't matter, though: the Bronco's with Rex Allen. And no way would the cruiser Banner's been assigned make it, even with chains. He hasn't even tried backing it out of its slot at the cop shop, has just been walking the two blocks in.

So, the only option left to get up to the dam had been the snowcat.

Because he doesn't have the first idea about how fast it burns through diesel, he's got two sloshing-full jerry cans strapped to the bed railing. And the cat, while not fast, it does sit you high like in a tractor seat, and the four tracks churn through the snow like magic.

If this whole deputy thing doesn't work out, Banner figures, maybe he can sign on with whatever outfit will let him drive one of these things on a daily basis.

That is, if he lives through these next ninety seconds: Hardy having two extra legs means that... that someone's walking behind him, right in his tracks. Someone who could very well have a snubnose pistol snugged against the former sheriff's back, meaning that—that that second person's the Joker, is going to hold the whole valley hostage with some grand scheme involving the dam, the lake, who knows.

"Except you're not Batman," Banner has to remind himself.

Batman and *Joker* are his default settings for hero and criminal. Which neither Rex Allen nor Francine ever needs to know, thank you.

Whoever this second person is, they're shorter than Hardy, slighter, and—

Wait, Banner tells himself.

"*Her?*" he hears himself saying, incredulous.

He cocks the door open, stands up over the cab to see better, the cold nearly taking his breath.

"Holy shit," he says.

By the time Hardy hauls the flimsy passenger door open, Banner's got his chest to the steering wheel, is already looking over at this least likely person to be up here on the mountain.

"*Jade Daniels?*" he says.

"What the hell?" she says back to Hardy, about Banner.

Hardy guides her up into the relative warmth of the cab.

The cat's got seats for two people, and a little green half-size cooler between, with a much-battered white lid. Jennifer has no choice but to sit there, in constant contact with Banner.

"Serious?" Banner says to her, still not completely believing this is happening.

"It's Jennifer now," she says back, staring straight ahead, her hands already holding onto the unpadded dashboard, which is really just gauge cluster housing and instructional decals.

"Tompkins," Hardy says in greeting, his walker stowed in the bed.

"You bungee'd it down?" Banner confirms.

"Just drive," Hardy tells him.

"You said it wouldn't be him," Jad—*Jennifer* says, like lodging enough objections can change what's happening.

"Got a sleeping bag up there," Hardy says, hooking his head back up to the idea of the control booth.

"I'm the only taxi left," Banner says, pulling the complicated, many-bends stick shift deep into the one single spinning notch that means "reverse." It brings that stick deep between Jennifer's legs, along with his hand. She backs up a smidge.

"Haven't called you 'Jennifer' since elementary," he tells her.

"Haven't called you 'deputy' since my worst nightmare," Jennifer says back.

"When did you get back?"

"Rex Allen picked me up two days ago."

"But he didn't—"

"Guess it was need-to-know," Hardy explains, "and you didn't."

Banner gets the cat turned around, and churning back down the road is using about a tenth as much diesel, it sounds like.

Good.

They can't get mired up here. Or, *he* can't get mired up here with a girl and an old man he's responsible for. Not when he's responsible for the whole town.

"So where is my former deputy this fine evening?" Hardy asks. His hand is holding the oh-shit handle up by his head, exactly like he doesn't trust Banner's driving.

"Probably looking for his jacket," Banner says, eyeing Jennifer's bright stripes.

"He gave it to me," she says back.

"Didn't even know they let you *out*."

"I didn't do anything wrong."

"Says you."

"Kids, kids," Hardy says, apparently amused by this.

"You really don't know where Rex Allen is?" Banner says to him, leaning forward to say it across Jennifer, like now the adults are talking.

Jennifer leans back and crosses her arms in disgust.

"Your scanner not working up there?" Banner asks.

"Excuse me, son?" Hardy says.

"Your scanner not working, *sir*," Banner corrects.

It's their usual stupid little insulting game—Hardy's way of reminding Banner that it's hardly been any time at all since he was just a punk kid, still wet behind the ears.

"'Sir,'" Jennifer repeats, just loud enough for Banner.

She's loving this.

She's also not remembering the time Banner found her in the band supply closet, crying in the dark, her black eyeliner running all down her face. And how he just shut the door back like it was, found another place private enough for him and Amber.

But those days are over. No more Amber, or Bethany, or Tiff—he's a dad, now. And a deputy.

He shifts even though he doesn't have to, just so Jennifer will have to make room again for that obnoxious stick.

"Whoah, whoah," Hardy says, holding that handle by his head for real now, it looks like.

Banner grumbles inside, slows. Hardy can't give performance ratings anymore, but Rex Allen is still thirty years his junior.

Such bullshit.

"Scanner's been quiet all day," Hardy says.

"Oh yeah, guess it would be quiet," Banner says, hand-over-handing the steering wheel to crawl them around the sharp, steep switchback by the mound of snow he knows is the Grand Prix.

"Because of the holiday?" Jennifer chimes in.

"Christmas?" Banner says back, incredulous. "That's still—What are you even doing up here?"

"Waiting for a knight in shining armor to come carry me down the big bad mountain," she says, all fake-wistful.

Everybody's a Joker.

Banner takes them around another sharp turn, rides the transmission.

"It's been quiet because there's nobody to talk to," Banner explains, sliding them across the creek now, the ice too hard to even crack. "Sheriff's down the highway, with Francie."

"Wreck?" Hardy asks.

"Oh," Jennifer says. "It's that Dark Mill South, right?"

Of course she'd know.

"They're trying to find his motorcade, convoy, prisoner transport, whatever it's called," Banner explains for Hardy.

"'Reunion Tour,'" Jennifer quotes.

"Here," Banner tells her, giving her the wheel before she can protest.

Jennifer takes it, keeps them straight, giving Banner hands enough to dig in his clipboard case for…

He unfolds it, passes it across to Hardy.

"You really don't watch the news?" Banner asks, impressed.

"Get to be my age, you figure out it's the same shit, different package," Hardy says, studying the faded clipping, the grainy mug shot. He looks up over it to Jennifer, then to Banner.

"She already told you," he says across to Banner, some scold to his tone now, like he might really mean this. "The court found in her favor, Deputy."

"*What?*" Banner asks, taking the wheel back, Jennifer holding her hands high like she never wanted it in the first place.

"What, *sir*," she mutters, just loud enough.

Because they're in town now, Banner turns all the cat's lights off except the front ones—no need to be casting shadows in folks' living rooms.

"You telling me that's not Tab Daniels?" Hardy says.

"My *dad*?" Jennifer says, looking at the mug shot of Dark Mill South now as well, even though she's probably got his poster on her bedroom wall.

"Put your glasses on, sir," Banner says.

Hardy does, sees his mistake.

"Sorry, Jennifer," he says. "Didn't mean to—it's just, they're both Indian, and that… his face."

"*Bad* face," Jennifer repeats, then adds, "Win-ne-muc-ca," hitting each syllable.

"You remember," Hardy says, clapping his big hand on her knee.

His house is only at the end of the block now.

Banner slows, mostly so Hardy won't have to tell him "here" like he always does.

"Remember what?" Banner asks.

"Camp Winnemucca," Hardy says. "In Snake, that means 'Camp Bad Face.'"

"I don't even know what we're talking about anymore," Banner announces grandly, stopping in front of Hardy's place.

"Dark Mill South's transport is missing," Jennifer says, saving Banner the trouble.

Banner nods.

Hardy opens his door, the wind taking it, slapping it against the front fender exactly how Lonnie would probably hate.

"Well if his rolling jail cell went off the road," Hardy says, stepping down, collecting his walker, "then this prisoner is a Popsicle by now, you both know that, right? He might turn up come spring, and he might not."

"I'm sure you're right, sir," Banner says—whatever it takes to make this go over, please.

"You two don't stay out too late, hear?" Hardy says with an evil smile, then shuts the door before either of them can say anything.

Banner starts to grind the cat away but Jennifer's hand is on his forearm, stopping him. She's still sitting right beside him, not in the empty seat.

"Make sure he makes it," she says, a little bit of *please* to her voice.

Banner crunches the stiff clutch back in, waits until Hardy lifts his whole walker from the porch to farewell them.

"I'm going to have to bring him back up there tomorrow morning, first thing," Banner says. "Because I don't have anything else to do, evidently."

Jennifer slides over into Hardy's seat, tries to figure out the harness Hardy refuses to strap into. Her doing this is, of course, an insult to Banner's driving.

"Thought you were the horror girl," he says about her safety concerns.

He's chugging them down Main Street, going faster than absolutely necessary.

"Ghost town," Jennifer says, about Proofrock.

"Know why he took that job at the dam in the first place?" Banner says.

"You remember my house?" Jennifer asks back.

Banner doesn't dignify that, just makes the turn.

"*Why?*" Jennifer asks. "He's… he's old, and hurt. Can't be sheriff anymore."

"You know what happened to his daughter?" Banner asks.

"Melanie?"

"Oh yeah, you would know," Banner says, stopped in front of *her* dark house now.

"What are you trying to tell me, Deputy Dewey?"

"Your mom, your dad," Banner says, barely giving it voice. Which makes it even louder.

Jennifer just stares straight ahead, her almost-smile gone, her "Jennifer" mask back on.

"Yeah, they were there when she—when Melanie drowned," she says. "So what? They weren't the only ones."

"Up there by the dam's where it happened," Banner says, doing a rimshot with his hands on top of the steering wheel, like showing off this high-level town lore he's privy to, now that he's deputized. Or, almost deputized. Practically deputized.

But, "*No*," Jennifer says. "My mom told me. It was… it was right here at the pier. They were swimming, it was summ—"

"It was summer, yeah," Banner says. "But they were up by the dam."

"That's restricted."

"She's why that ladder's there now," Banner says. "So nobody else will drown. That's what Rex Allen says. It's Melanie's ladder."

"Just like Melanie's bench."

"And that airboat," Banner adds, winning this little one-up game. The airboat had been in the county garage as well, waiting for summer.

"So…" *Jennifer* says, "so you're saying that Sheriff Hardy—"

"*Mr.* Hardy."

"That he took the job up there just to be close to where his daughter *drowned*?"

"Kind of sick, yeah?" Banner says. "Figured that'd be right up your alley."

"I know why you're playing peace officer, Banner Tompkins."

"Playing?"

"That night," Jennifer says, not having to explain which night. "It's when you picked Letha up from the water. You felt like a hero, like you were saving her life. And now you want some more of that. It makes sense."

"Mr. Holmes always said you were smarter than you came off."

"Keep his name out of your mouth."

"That's a county jacket you're wearing, you know."

"Tell your pretty wife to call me, we should—" Jennifer starts, her door already open, but the radio unit at Banner's belt interrupts her:

"Deputy Tompkins, Deputy Tompkins," Meg's saying.

Banner holds his finger up for Jennifer to be quiet here, thumbs the mic at his shoulder open, says, "Tompkins here. What is it, Mrs. Koenig?"

"Where are you?" Meg asks back. "No, no, I mean, I'm—I'm—I'm patching her through, patching her through."

"Who?" Jennifer asks, and Banner slashes his eyes up to her.

"Cinnamon Baker," Meg answers.

"She's still *here*?" Jennifer says, way too loud.

Banner glares her quiet, and then the distortion coming through the speaker at his belt dials up higher.

"*Banner, Banner!*" Cinnamon's saying, shrieking, crying.

"Not 'Deputy'?" Jennifer mouths.

Banner's foot slips off the clutch and the cat jerks forward, stalls, throwing Jennifer against her safety harness.

Her eyes never leave Banner, and Cinn's voice coming through.

"*I don't know!*" Cinn screams in response to Banner asking for her location.

Then she's sobbing and sort of hyperventilating.

"We're coming," Banner says.

It's a lie, though. How can he know where she is?

Then another voice comes through this staticky connection. A girl, a woman: "What's the last thing you remember? What were you doing?"

"What were we *doing*?" Cinn asks. "They're dead!"

"Who, who?" this girl-woman says.

"Deputy Tompkins, is your line clear?" Meg asks.

After a pause, "It's Jennifer Daniels, Mrs. Koenig," Banner says. "She's with me."

"*Jade?*" Meg says, something dready about how she says it.

Cinn screams into the phone as loud as she can, because they're not understanding the urgency, here.

Number one, she's just in a bra and panties and snow boots, because that's the rules.

Two, she's slathered in blood.

Three, Toby's body is leaned against the glass, the one eye he has left staring through at her.

"He didn't even break the windshield," Cinn says, kind of in wonder.

"Windshield, windshield, good," Jennifer Daniels says. "So this is a wreck. Where were you going? Where were you coming from?"

"No!" Cinn says. "It's not—we were. Oh god. Gwenny, she's… she's…"

She lowers the phone to her collarbone.

Just past this hood, Gwen Stapleton is hanging by her neck from a tree limb.

She's been slit up the front. Her insides are spilling down and down, harsh red against the falling snow, and her tongue's been pulled out too, a screwdriver pushed down through it, to keep it sticking out.

"No, no, no," Cinn says into the phone. Or, just "says," really, but she's still holding the phone.

Banner or Jennifer or Meg is saying something into the sensitive skin at the side of her neck, but Cinn's just sobbing, and trying so hard to breathe.

Finally, she pulls the phone back up.

"I was just—it was the *game*," she says, speaking now as if from a dream, one that's happening to someone else. "I didn't know Gwen would, would…"

"That's Toby Manx and Gwen Stapleton," she hears Banner saying in some background. "Meg, you got that? Can you call, see where they're supposed to be?"

"*How* is he dead?" Jennifer asks, evidently holding the radio—she's much closer, much louder.

"His—it's his stomach," Cinn says, or tries to. "There's… there's nothing there anymore."

"'*He*,'" Jennifer repeats. "He-*who*, Cinnamon?"

"How do you know my name?"

"Who did this?" Jennifer asks back.

"A—he was a monster…" Cinn says, barely pushing enough air across her voice box to make the words.

"One you know, or one you don't know?" Jennifer asks.

"I don't—what do you mean?" Cinn asks. "We were just—and then—I can't—no—"

"And Gwen?" Jennifer asks, then mutters something the mic can't pick up, probably to Banner.

"He hung her from the tree!" Cinn screams into the phone.

"Okay, okay. And—did he also—?"

"He cut her *open*, okay! What else do you want!"

"Casey Beck—" Jennifer says, maybe forgetting her mic's open, which is why she swallows Casey Becker's last syllable.

"No!" Cinn says, switching her phone to her other ear for emphasis, and volume. "*Gwen Stapleton!* And he did something to the doors! I can't get out!"

Meg comes back, breaks in: "I talked to someone at the Manx household."

"What already!" Banner yells, still not holding the mic.

"She says her brother and—and Gwen Stapleton, they're at Trail's End. The motel."

This makes Cinn cry harder into the phone.

She lets it slide away, down her front, meaning it's got blood on it now.

She sucks snot in as deep as she can, she tries to center herself, and, using both feet at once, she kicks the windshield.

Toby bounces away from the windshield, then slumps back to exactly where he was.

"I'm sorry, I'm sorry," Cinn says, and kicks again, and again, until the windshield cracks under her heel, over Toby. Two kicks later, one of her snow boots crunches through, pebbles of glass cascading back onto her. She pushes them away, sure they're going to cut her, leave a thousand and one scratches.

Shaking and shaking her head no, she crawls through the hole she's made, which is also crawling directly over and right up against Toby.

"Sorry sorry sorry," she says, directing his dead eyes to the side, then sliding off the hood, catching the step-up by the hood with her knee and crashing into the powdery snow like the ragdoll she is.

She stands, looks back to, back to—

The huge tall truck, a crusty snowplow reaching out from its front bumper.

It's driven into the wall of trees as far as it could, which wasn't very.

Cinn turns to Gwenny, spinning slightly in the wind, her trailing intestines kind of anchoring her.

"No," Cinn says, and falls to her knees.

Then she makes herself stand, the cold cutting into her, the blood tacky now, and she runs forward four fast steps but the snow's so deep already, the sky so white all around her, the cold needling right through.

She falls, slides on the heels of her hands. Stands again.

In this way she hitches across the parking lot screaming for help, motel window lights coming on, but she can't stop, she won't stop, she has to get away.

She stumbles out onto Main Street, holds her right hand up for the headlights she's standing in to stop, please, to not run her over.

It's not a car or a truck, though.

It's the town snowcat, the one that usually plows up and down the streets.

It stops without sliding, and Banner—thank you thank you—is already vaulting down, his gun out and everywhere all at once, and the girl, the woman—Jade fucking *Daniels*?—is coming in from the other side, leading with a brown jacket that's already open.

She wraps Cinn in it and hugs her tight, and that's when the shaking really gets started.

Along with everything else.

HER NAME WAS JADE

Dark Mill South wasn't the only killer in town that December, either.

Two days before his Reunion Tour, Jennifer "Jade" Daniels was starring in what you could call her Comeback Special, following a four-year ordeal in state court. Her legal difficulties stemmed from what she claimed were the Lake Witch Slayings—the Independence Day Massacre to the rest of us.

Jennifer was born to Henderson High seniors Junior "Tab" Daniels, Jr., and Kimberley Ledbetter on July 31st, 1998. And, just to be sure you don't think that's a mistake, Mr. Armitage, the "Junior" at the beginning and also at the end of her father's name must not have raised any county or administrative eyebrows, as it's the same name associated with his missing photo in the 1997 class annual; it's the one hand-written on his birth certificate in Records; it's the caption under his thumbnail photo in the obituary edition of the *Proofrock Standard*; and it's the one that was entered into evidence against Jennifer down in Boise.

Perhaps they named people differently in 1980?

But it's the charges against Jennifer that are

important, here, and I'm sure you've got access to Henderson High's legendarily thick file on her anyway, so there's no need for me to dredge that up. Suffice it to say that her career as a student in Proofrock was, in keeping with her post-graduation life, tempestuous.

However, without Tiffany Koenig's Instagram blowing up, Jennifer's last four years might have unfolded… differently. Though Tiffany's Instagram account had, before the Independence Day Massacre, fluctuated between seventy-five and eighty followers, most either local or family, the afternoon of July 5th one of her "story" posts was liked 2.78 million times. This was her shaky, low-light, poorly-framed phone recording of the Independence Day Massacre, captioned with "I can't believe this really happening n my hometown!"

The skipped verb and abbreviated spelling only contributed to the rawness of her video, which, by the time her account was suspended (it was both "intense" and "violent," neither of which Instagram allows), had been downloaded and reposted all over the internet, with various overlays and filters, and no small amount of slow motion, spotlighting, and loops.

The cat wasn't just out of the bag, it was all over the world.

The result was that on July 6th, responding to accounts from media helicopters, a SWAT unit ascended Glen Dam and apprehended Jennifer Daniels. She was sitting on the flat roof of the control booth, her arms hugging her knees, and she needed immediate triage for her injuries, including intravenous fluids for dehydration.

Just like Dark Mill South then, and perhaps even on the same afternoon, Jennifer woke handcuffed to a hospital bed. She was in Idaho Falls. The charges against her were murder and evading arrest.

In Tiffany Koenig's eventually subpoenaed recording, five people are killed in the shallows of Indian Lake alongside the town pier, six more are seen after having been killed, and one last one dies deeper out in the water, almost past the limit of Tiffany's phone.

During that grainy melee, Jennifer is seen wearing a distinctive set of custodial coveralls. She is also newly bald, her scalp paler than her face and neck. The light from the screen identifies her clearly, as if Tiffany were looking for the calm at the center of the carnage. And then it smears away to a paddleboard gliding unmolested through the thrashing bodies while Tiffany screams urgent advice to someone, the recording bouncing with each of Tiffany's jumps, which were most likely emphasis or punctuation to her advice (in her time at Henderson High, Tiffany had been on the varsity cheer squad).

By the time the recording settles down again, the focus is a curious canoe drifting away from the pier. Tiffany claims she was looking out there to see if any children had tried to swim to safety, where they might now be in need of assistance. Who she found was someone spinning around on the canoe's bench to swing a machete into the neck of a man conclusively identified as Tab Daniels.

This someone is wearing Jennifer's custodial coveralls,

has a bare scalp not yet tanned, and testimony surfaced that Tab had evicted Jennifer from his house earlier in the week, leaving her homeless.

It was damning evidence.

The only other person in Proofrock with those coveralls at the time had a radically different body type, Jennifer's scalp was still shaved when she was carried down from Glen Dam, and bodycam footage from the SWAT team has her looking calmly down from her rooftop perch and saying it took them long enough, didn't it?

As she had yet to be Mirandized, Jennifer's legal team was able to keep this spontaneous outburst from being used against her—she was injured, dehydrated, traumatized, nearly naked, and supposedly not in her right mind, as confirmed by her attempt to struggle her way off the dam when she was being led away in handcuffs. As a result, she was put on suicide watch for her recovery, though it's not clear whether she had been trying to jump off the dry side of the dam that day, or into the lake.

During her convalescence, she was tried in the court of social media, which generated enough theories and explanations and outrage that her attorneys petitioned for, and were eventually granted, a change of venue. Their argument was that Proofrock and its immediate environs had been polluted by prejudices regarding both Jennifer's lifestyle and heritage, and a larger, less biased pool of potential jurors was needed.

By this point Jennifer is eighteen, can be tried as an adult.

While cameras and videos were banned from the courtroom, a telephoto did surface of federal marshals chaperoning her at a graveside service in Swan Valley. In this telephoto she's wearing an orange jumpsuit and is shackled at the wrists, waist, and ankles—this is the image of her everybody knows. It's how I first saw her.

The funeral service she had been allowed to attend was for Grade Paulson, the only non-local victim of the Independence Day Massacre. As he had been employed as unskilled labor by the Terra Nova Project, the Project donated $25,000 to his mother, seen at the edge of that telephoto's frame.

This would be the last photograph of Jennifer Daniels for the next three and a half years. It's just sketches and descriptions from here on out. In those sketches, Jennifer is wearing the tasteful skirt and blazer of the wrongfully accused, but her posture gives away her attitude concerning these proceedings: she goes from combative, always ready to rise from her chair, to more and more resigned, as if just sitting through another class in high school.

As I was saying: she was digested by the court for four years and four and a half months—long enough for her to, at the urging and expense of her defense team, earn an associate's degree via correspondence, in the hopes it would show her looking to the future, and her plans there.

Her initial defense was that the party responsible for the Independence Day Massacre was the local lake legend, Stacey Graves, which prompted the prosecution to put on display the birth certificate associated with the "Stacey Graves" in question, born in 1912. This would make her 103 years old on that fateful July Fourth, and, according to lake lore (no death certificate exists), either 95 years dead or 95 years not *quite* dead.

Jennifer's team's next line of defense was testimony from survivors of that night. But there, accounts varied in the extreme. The two things they all agreed on was that the person perpetrating these acts of violence was A) "feminine" and B) in "some sort of costume."

At which point a series of photographs of Jennifer Daniels in an assortment of Halloween get-ups was entered into evidence, establishing a long and troubled history of dressing up to scare.

In the sketch of this particular afternoon in court, Jennifer is leaned back in her chair with her arms crossed, glaring at the state seal above the judge's head.

Most harmful to Jennifer's proposition that it had actually been a 103-year-old dead girl committing these acts was the deposition read to the court by Jennifer herself, under duress from the prosecution. This was deposition instead of testimony, as the witness here was 9 years old—the daughter of Misty Christy, Proofrock local, successful real estate entrepreneur, and victim of the Independence Day Massacre.

This daughter's deposition documented Jennifer being there precisely at the moment of Misty Christy's death, and then leaving the daughter with the mother's corpse as a sort of cruel joke.

Which begins a months-long period of Jennifer ceasing to participate in her own defense.

Working in her favor whether she wanted it or not, however, were two things: the low quality of Tiffany's recording, which allowed the barest sliver of reasonable doubt as to who had been in that canoe, and… the lack of a murdered body.

A year after the Independence Day Massacre, Tab Daniels had yet to surface. He was the sole unrecovered victim from that night. He had apparently, in the lingo of Pleasant Valley and Proofrock, sunk down to "Ezekiel's Cold Box"—the waters of Indian Lake are cold enough that bodies dropped into it often don't go through normal decomposition. This means that the gasses usually produced by decay aren't present to buoy the corpse up to the surface, so it hangs suspended near the bottom of the very deep reservoir, in cold storage. Tab Daniels not having turned up was rumored to be why the prosecution was making Jennifer's trial last as long as it was: every week was another week the body could potentially get hooked by some random fisherman, or delivered to the surface of the lake by water circulation dynamics the dam controlled.

The defense, of course, tried to pivot this to their advantage, claiming that, without proof of murder, how could these spurious murder charges hope to stick? The prosecution came back indirectly, through the media, claiming that the defense was arguing "no harm, no foul," which completely dismissed the proof right there on Tiffany's verified-authentic recording, and the undeniable fact that Tab Daniels had been missing-presumed-dead since that night. Never mind, the defense said back through the newspapers, that the murder weapon, that movie-prop machete, had not yet been recovered either. Never mind that Jennifer's coveralls had washed up later in July, allowing the possibility that some other recently bald person had imperfectly disposed of that evidence.

At which point Jennifer's legal defense shifted again, via an outburst on her part.

Instead of casting Stacey Graves as the guilty party, Jennifer claimed that the "actual real killer here" was Theo Mondragon, heretofore of Mondragon Enterprises.

If she'd had a mic, this would have been the spot in her trial to drop it.

Her rushed testimony that same afternoon was that, surveilling Terra Nova the day before the Independence Day Massacre, she had seen another massacre-in-process—not the killings on the yacht, which she claims to have woken in the midst of, but Theo Mondragon disposing of the murdered bodies of two construction workers and attempting to kill a third, all to hide his culpability in the wreck of a certain history teacher's ultralight he had a history *with*. The proof, she claimed, would be the nails embedded in the bodies of those construction workers, which should have been recovered by now from Sheep's Head Meadow on the Caribou-Targhee side of Indian Lake. These golden nails, she claimed, would match the nails extracted from the back of Grade Paulson, who died swimming two of Terra Nova's children across the lake to safety, following the killings on the yacht the night of July 3rd.

The prosecution's response to this was, "*Nails*?"

Their next response was, "Bodies?"

While the fire that nearly burned Pleasant Valley was identified as having an origin point in the meadow adjacent to the Terra Nova construction, the lake, which had started rising on July 5th, had done what water does, and found the first drain it could, taking any debris suspended in it along. What this meant, the experts testified, was that any bones that survived the fire, elk or human, had most likely been deposited in one of the caves evidently hidden under that meadow, which collapsed into sinkholes before the lake could recede in the following weeks. Legal translation: the two construction workers Jennifer claimed Theo Mondragon had killed with a nailgun were fantasy unsupported by fact. And, if there had ever been nails in the body of Grade Paulson, X-rays taken before his burial didn't show them, and exhumation would cause undue emotional strain on his surviving family.

While Jennifer's defense to this point had been funded by the Terra Nova Project, allowing Jennifer the exclusive services of Mars Baker's storied law firm, after these aspersions concerning Theo Mondragon, Jennifer's defense would be state-appointed. The Baker Firm's official statement regarding this was that it would be a conflict of interest for them if they had to both defend Jennifer Daniels and continue to act as executors for Theo Mondragon's estate.

At this point, Letha Mondragon, Theo's daughter, who had been listed as a witness for the defense, stepped away as well, citing medical reasons.

Jennifer's state-appointed attorneys' strategy, then, after months of regrouping, was to *enhance* Tiffany's recording, which involved stipulating that that was indeed Jennifer on the canoe, with the machete.

What this enhancement showed was that the Tab Daniels who had risen behind his daughter to drag her down was already suffering a mortal injury. A large portion of his face had been ripped away, including his left eye. Medical experts testified that he appeared to have suffered a massive trauma to at *least* the zygomatic process and supraorbital foramen of his eye orbit, and, without immediate medical attention, could not possibly have survived. And, yes, he looked to have been in the process of drowning when he came up from the water behind that canoe.

When asked if she knew how her father had suffered such an injury, Jennifer's attorneys relayed flatly that "it was a bad night," she had no idea. Why would she?

The media's running commentary on the trial now opined that Jennifer's new defense was that Tab Daniels had been dead already, practically, thus her killing blow was actually not "killing" at all. Does shooting a person already falling from a building still count as murder? Does the doctrine of intervening causation count in this instance? And, further, when Jennifer's seating position on the canoe is taken into account, her defense argued—this is toward the end of the second year of her trial—then any resentments or bad history she had with her father didn't matter at all. As far as Jennifer was concerned, she was now being attacked by whoever had just killed so many of the people she'd grown up with, a scene she had narrowly escaped herself, thanks to the providential placement of this canoe, and her own instincts.

Her state of mind was then argued to have been "survival," not recompense or revenge, nothing personal like that, and photos scavenged from social media documenting the celebration in Proofrock leading up to the Independence Day Massacre showed that same machete in the hands of Mason Rodgers, a graduating classmate of Jennifer Daniels, and another victim of that night.

At which point common opinion was that her defense had planned to rest, but then one last witness wheeled into the room.

Retired Sheriff Angus Hardy.

His testimony was that there had been a moment during the Independence Day Massacre when he actually shot the killer. Four times. In the chest. On cross-examination, when faced with slide after slide of autopsy reports of each victim (save Tab Daniels), and pressed on why none of them had bullet wounds, Hardy remained steadfast: as a peace officer of forty-one years, he had no doubt shot whoever it was dressed up as the Lake Witch Stacey Graves, and Jennifer Daniels had been in his field of view at that moment, meaning it wasn't her.

Sketches that ran along with reports of Sheriff Hardy's

testimony show Jennifer Daniels crying in court for the first time.

And so public sentiment turned.

As did the jury's.

One month later, on Valentine's Day, Jennifer Daniels was found not guilty of killing Tab Daniels, and that afternoon she was released.

Only to be arrested again, this time by federal authorities.

The charges this time concerned the damage to Glen Dam's control booth, which, since it was under government contract, was considered government property, making her subject to all laws associated with that willful destruction.

This was February 2019.

By the second week of December, Jennifer's state-appointed attorneys had negotiated her provisional release, the conditions of which were that if she could refrain from the destruction of all county, state, and federal property for the next six months, then the charges concerning Glen Dam would be dropped, as there was some evidence that her efforts had mitigated the Terra Nova Fire's damage. If she *couldn't* resist that sort of property destruction, though, then she would be subject to the full sentence of three years, with no chance of any time served counting in her favor.

At which point Sheriff Allen of Proofrock was summoned to Boise to collect Jennifer Daniels Tuesday the 10th of December, as her mother couldn't be reached at the time, and Jennifer Daniels had, and has, no other family.

But, if you will, let me go back to that iconic photograph, taken graveside, which I know is why you initially gave me permission for this special project. In addition to the orange jumpsuit and leg irons, Jennifer Daniels is also clearly wearing safety glasses and a black cap for this funeral service. As we've all seen prisoners in similar get-ups, of course the assumption would be that this "disguise" was a measure to guard against anyone recognizing Jennifer, public sentiment at the time being that she was solely responsible for both the Independence Day Massacre and the killings on the yacht in Terra Nova the night before.

As for where she got those pale yellow glasses, which did as little as the cap to hide her distinctive Native American features, perhaps the same chaperone who had that featureless cap in his car was able to supply those glasses. They're of a type used at shooting ranges, which federal marshals must frequent.

But there's more to them than that. Had I not been working through my own situation when that photo ran, I could have explained to the court that those glasses weren't meant to hide Jennifer Daniels's identity. She was wearing them in honor-of, actually.

This pertains to those nails she claimed should have been in Grade Paulson's back.

They *were* there, Mr. Armitage.

I know because, for the whole long cold swim across from Terra Nova to Proofrock, from the yacht to *Jaws*, my teeth chattering so hard that I chipped three of them, my lips and fingernail beds blue, I held onto one of those nails in his back as if they were there specifically for me, so I wouldn't drift away.

$25,000 wasn't nearly enough for this general laborer's effort.

Actually, I owe him my life.

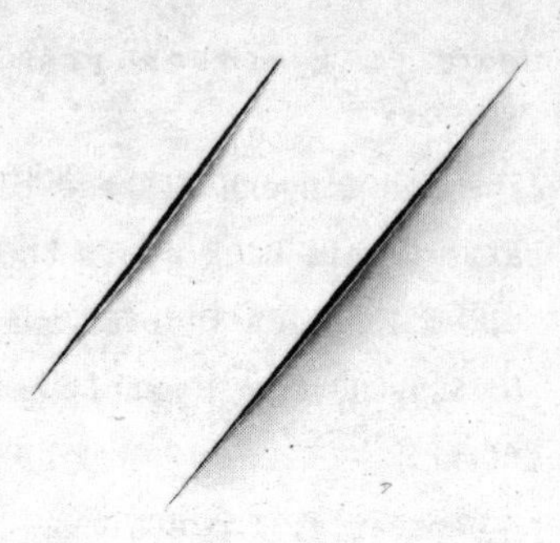

FRIDAY THE 13TH

This was so much easier when she was seventeen.

Back then, it was mostly about eyeliner and lipstick.

God, those were the days, weren't they?

Letha leans closer to the rearview mirror, working the stippling brush along her jawline, insisting on the blend that's refusing to take.

It doesn't matter, she reminds herself, looking this way and that to check the angles, the scars. She shouldn't complain. Yes, her reconstructed jaw is eighty percent synthetic. No, even four years later, she still can't eat solid food.

But smoothies are good. Shakes are filling enough.

And the alternative to all these surgeries, all these pills to keep her body from kicking the plastic?

You don't have it that bad, she tells herself.

For the ten-thousandth time.

It could be worse, right?

Before she can spiral back to that night in the water, get trapped in its sucking vortex, she does as her therapist has conditioned her and retreats to a chair in her head. The chair is simple, wooden, straight-backed, is in a featureless room, and if Letha sits there with her hands in her lap she can choose what thoughts and memories and hopes and fears she projects onto the walls around her—there's an old-fashioned sewing machine pedal under her right foot that starts and stops this image, that voice, and the cable leading from that pedal is stark and clear and undeniable, because you have to envision every little detail if you're going to intellectually and emotionally invest in the reality of a place. As her therapist tells her, you can't live in fake places, only real places, places you believe are real.

Letha nods, is there.

She moves her right foot on the pedal and her father dissolves onto the screen in front of her, the wind in his face, his sunglasses cocked up on his forehead even though it's impossibly bright out on the lake. He's teaching her to drive that boat they used to have—the *Umiak*, yeah. Whatever even happened to that thing?

"You're focusing on things that don't matter," she reminds herself out loud, in her therapist's voice.

When her father is right there in front of her.

Letha doesn't turn the sound on, just watches him squinting at all the water ahead of them, to make sure they're good.

They *were* good, she remembers. They were great that day. The whole summer was theirs. The whole world.

Letha lifts her foot, fading that image out, the sparkling water of Indian Lake all around her now, on every wall. In her head, in this room, on this one wooden chair, she can smile if she wants, and it won't feel like her face is tearing open.

And she has reasons to smile, she knows. All the reasons in the world—but one in particular.

She starts to turn around in the driver's seat but stops when she's not alone.

Her heart flutters, her breath catches, but—but this isn't the killer from the news reports, out in the broad daylight. He would be taller than the truck's passenger-side window, wouldn't he?

And he wouldn't be just waiting in the cold, either, as Ja—as *Jennifer Daniels* is.

In the mental snapshot Letha accidentally takes before feeling for the door-lock button, Jennifer's framed by the front of her house, "Camp Blood" spray-painted across it at an angle.

She could have knocked, tapped the glass to announce herself, but of course she didn't. Because it's creepier just to suddenly *be* there.

Letha keeps her face relaxed and pleasant, just as it was in the mirror, and, after checking up and down the street to be sure they're alone—Dark Mill South could be anywhere—she clicks the door locks open, and that's right when Jennifer's trying the handle.

"Wait, wait!" Letha says as cheerily as she can, holding a finger up so Jennifer can watch that finger descending to the unlock button again.

The thing about the apparatus in Letha's mouth is that, being titanium, it vibrates the slightest bit when she says anything—a tuning fork keeping her teeth wired together, so the second round of Kevlar in her jaw hinges can become part of her.

"Get in, get in," she says, waving Jennifer in out of the blowing snow.

Because the truck's tall and Jennifer isn't, it's more of an awkward clamber than an elegant step, and it takes long enough that the cab fills with swirling flakes.

The instant Jennifer's settled, Letha locks the doors again.

"I didn't mean for you to have to—" Jennifer starts, then takes another angle: "I mean, I could have walked, it's not that—"

"Cold? Deep? Dangerous?"

The little laugh Letha follows that with is high and fluttery.

"You're nervous," Jennifer says.

"I'm safe," Letha corrects, chipperly, and drops the truck into gear, steeling herself for this next part, the part nobody seems able to keep from doing: the inspection. Sneaking looks at Letha's reconstructive surgery.

To make it easier, which is code for "go over faster," Letha studies the dim outline of the glow-plug indicator under the gauges, her profile right there and drinkable for at least three seconds, maybe four.

At which point she looks over, says, "Seatbelt."

"I trust you," Jennifer says, but when the bell won't stop dinging, she straps in.

"Your hair," Letha says, pulling away. "I never knew."

"What happened to yours?" Jennifer asks.

Letha tilts her head into the truck's backseat to explain why having long hair got to be a hassle.

"Oh, *shit*," Jennifer says, cringing away. "That's yours?"

Letha nods.

"How old?" Jennifer asks.

"One," Letha says about Adie, just watching this stranger. "One and ten months."

"When do the months stop mattering?"

"Never?"

"I just—wow. I thought you were… you know."

"This?" Letha says about her teeth, her braces, her whole jaw situation.

"Sorry," Jennifer says. "You don't need me reminding you."

"We haven't seen each other for four years," Letha says, making the slow turn left. "But you're still you. Different name, same girl."

"I don't know about that."

"I never thought you would come back."

"You and me both."

"And I never thought we'd get another… one of him."

They're almost to the sheriff's office.

Jennifer's just sitting there on her side of the truck.

"Nothing to say about that?" Letha asks, trying to soften her voice, not making this any kind of confrontation. "No movie quotes? No trivia? 'The night he came home,' maybe?"

"Dark Mill South never lived here."

"You—used to, I would picture you hiding in a video store in your head. Running from aisle to aisle, ducking behind this shelf, that rack."

"Old me," Jennifer says. "High school me."

Letha steals another look at the cab, has to swallow down the memory of Ja—of *Jennifer* in that old bathroom at school, the first time they saw each other.

The Skank Station, god.

Nobody should ever have had to stand at that mirror. Or: nobody else *would* have.

Nobody except the most contrary girl in the history of Idaho.

"What?" Jennifer asks, because evidently Letha's stalling out, here.

She bats her eyes to keep them from spilling over, changes direction: "So it's really happening again?"

Jennifer shrugs, looks away, is tapping the side of her left index finger against the knee of her jeans, now.

"Last time I was the girl who cried slasher," she says. "Gonna let somebody else ring that alarm this time."

Letha stops at the curb in front of the sheriff's, not sure if she's pulled across the handicapped spaces or not. The whole little parking lot's under two feet of snow.

She puts the truck in park.

"I really could have walked," Jennifer says, her hand to the door. "Banner didn't have to call in reinforcements. No reason to get a baby out in this."

"Proofrock owes you," Letha tells her, holding her eyes. "You should never have to walk anywhere again."

Jennifer presses her lips together, blinks fast, and covers it with, "What's her name?" She tilts her head to the backseat.

"Adrienne," Letha says as clearly as she can, through her wall of teeth. "She can walk now."

"Adrienne," Jennifer repeats, nodding to herself. "That's good. Pretty."

Letha's just watching her, now.

"You really are different, aren't you?"

"What? How?"

"The old you would have opened up a can of trivia about that name."

"Family?" Jennifer asks, either innocently or fake innocently, Letha can't quite tell.

"Adrienne King played Alice in *Friday the 13th*. That's still buried in your head. In your heart. I know it is."

"You must be thinking of some other girl."

"Sorry. I just... you look just like her. Like who I always knew she could be."

Jennifer stares into the floorboard.

"So you—you named your daughter after Alice," she outlouds. "You're telling me it's *you* that's into slashers, now?"

"I finally did all my homework, yes."

"That's… good," Jennifer says, looking out over the hood, now. "The big test is probably coming soon."

"For who, though?" Letha asks. "We've already… *taken* that test. Haven't we? In high school?"

"Cinnamon Baker?" Jennifer says. "She survived the first… round. At the motel last night. And she looks—she's got the look, I mean. Like she can fight. The white-girl version of you, four years ago."

"She used to be such a doll," Letha says.

"It's *her* friends who are dying," Jennifer says. "Not ours. Those two dead kids weren't anybody to you, were they?"

"That doesn't mean they don't matter."

"And she's—I mean," Jennifer goes on, fumbling through this mine-field. "She's got *issues* to work through, I'm sure. Her mom and dad were… you know."

Letha blinks that night away, or tries to.

"It *can't* be starting again," she says, shaking her head no. "We've already lost too much, here. I think Proofrock would… I don't know."

"Adrienne," Jennifer says again, dialing them back to where they were.

"I had to be off meds and surgeries the whole time I was carrying her," Letha says. "And feeding her, too. That's why it's taking so long to get me put back together."

She touches her jaw ever so lightly, to show what she means is taking so long.

"Oh, that's why?" Jennifer says, with almost a grin. "Thought you were saving up, like. That you had a new jaw on layaway until you got the money together."

Both of them have to laugh at this.

"I am sorry it happened, though," Jennifer says. "You didn't deserve it. And I should have stopped it in the first place. Been louder, made more sense."

"It wasn't just me who got hurt," Letha says, reaching across the console for Jennifer's left hand. She turns it over, looking for the teeth marks on the fingers, but all that's there is that line of knotty scar tissue on the inside of Jennifer's wrist, suddenly trying to be part of this conversation.

Jennifer pushes the rolled cuff of her county jacket down over it, offers her right hand instead. The index, middle, and ring fingers are, literally, chewed between the knuckles and first joints.

"They don't open all the way," Jennifer says, and shows how far they do open. "And I don't have to paint these fingernails black anymore."

"But you can probably still eat solid food," Letha says, approximating a grin.

"*Thought* you were skinnier than high school," Jennifer says, almost smiling back. "Figured it was yoga or something."

"In Proofrock?"

"Oh yeah," Jennifer says. "Almost forget where we are."

"We do have a video rental place now," Letha says, hooking her chin over to Main. "Right by Dot's."

"Thought video was dead."

"The senior class is doing it," Letha explains. "A small-business project."

"Have they never heard of bonfire parties?" Jennifer asks with a devious grin.

"Last one I went to—" Letha starts, but then can't make light of finding that dead boy in the lake.

"I was there," Jennifer says.

Letha studies her, paging through her mental photo album of that party, and coming up with no Jennifer.

"I was watching from the trees," Jennifer explains.

Letha nods.

"Will things ever be normal between us, you think?" she asks.

Jennifer shrugs, no eye contact.

"Here," Letha says. "A beginning."

"A wha—?"

"I want you to be *Aunt* Jennifer," Letha says, and Jennifer looks directly away from that idea, but Letha can still see her face, reflected in the window. Her chin is pruning once, twice, her lips pressed tight together. "Come over whenever," Letha goes on, trying just to fill the cab with words, so Jennifer won't feel bad for feeling feelings. "The—" Letha breathes in, starts again: "Adrienne's doctor—"

"Not Doc *Wilson*?" Jennifer says, coming around fast, ready to fight, already being the aunt Letha knew she could be.

Letha shakes her head no, says, "Dr. *Morton*. Wilson's retired. But she says… I mean, she's concerned that Adrienne might develop a speech impediment, since I'm the one around her the most, and I—I talk like this."

"It's not that bad," Jennifer says.

"Thank you," Letha says. "But I can hear it too. Just, if Adrienne had another female voice, it might… help her?"

"I mostly just know horror stories."

"Good," Letha says. "I want her to be tough like you. *Strong*, I mean. A fighter."

"Guess she *is* going to need to learn to cuss right," Jennifer says, flashing her eyes up to Letha's.

"Fuck yeah," Letha says immediately, before she can stop herself. Then she sits there, proud, beaming.

"See what I mean?" Jennifer says.

"I did it right, didn't I?"

"It's not about how you say it, it's about your eyes when you say it. And your eyes… you're still you. No offense."

"Then you probably should come over."

"Did y'all change the furniture, at least? It used to be all bowling trophies over there."

"God."

"See, that's better. You said it with your eyes."

"It's all different now, yeah," Letha says, about the decor at her house. "Not all '1984' anymore."

"Think you can update the rest of this town while you're at it?" Jennifer asks with a grin. "'1984' would be nice, really. Compared to… 1965?"

She opens her hand to snow-shrouded Proofrock.

"It is quaint, isn't it?" Letha says, draping herself over the wheel to study the town. "I can see what Mr. Samuels saw, I mean."

"Same thing Columbus saw, from his ship."

Letha looks over for explanation.

"Something that wasn't his," Jennifer clears right up.

"Maybe *that's* why it's happening again?" Letha broaches, at which point a traitorous tear tumbles down her right cheek, in full view.

"Mr. Holmes," Jennifer says then, giving that sacred name a moment to settle. "Why would he give us the same quiz twice, do you remember?"

Letha closes her eyes to conjure up sad Mr. Holmes at the front of history class, passing quizzes out one by one instead of letting the students pass them back and back themselves.

"Because—" Letha sputters, mumbles, "because we failed the first time?"

Jennifer nods a maybe.

"'Without memory, there can be no retribution,'" Letha recites then, her affect flat like she's possessed.

"Mr. Holmes?" Jennifer asks, something timid to her voice.

"*Popcorn*," Letha tells her, apologetically. Then, quieter, but she has to: "1991."

"Now who's hiding in the video rental store?"

"It's the smiles that keep us going," Letha says, evidently, by the *thunking* sound, either unlocking or relocking the doors with her padded left elbow when she shifts in her seat. "The bits of giggles and good cheer."

"Always clocked you for a Bible girl," Jennifer says, undercutting it with a halfway grin. "What's it from, Psalms?"

"You're serious here?" Letha has to ask.

"What?"

"*Exorcist III*," Letha says, pretty much ready to cry over this too—how can Jennifer have forgotten who she is?—but before she can smooth this awkwardness over, the back passenger-side door wrenches open, snow swirling into the cab, and she whole-body flinches.

"Speak of the devil," Jennifer says, glaring into her side mirror.

"Oh, sorry," Banner says, sitting up by the car seat now, clapping the door shut behind him.

"You did that on purpose!" Letha says.

Banner holds his key fob up, to show how *he* unlocked the doors.

And then a small hand reaches over from the car seat, for those shiny-jingly keys.

For the thousandth time, he lets Adrienne take them, then lowers his face to nuzzle his forehead against hers. She giggles a little-kid giggle.

"Clean them!" Letha says, passing a wipe back.

Banner takes it, cleans the keys while Adrienne's holding them, making a game of it.

"Thanks for bringing her," he says.

"She loves her daddy," Letha explains.

"I mean—her, yeah," Banner says. "But"—nodding to Jennifer—"*her*, I mean."

"I could have walked," Jennifer says again, in her sullen, put-upon way.

"Leeth was coming up anyway," Banner tells her. "Safer up here."

"Any news?" Jennifer asks.

"Cinn?" Letha adds.

"Sleeping since three or four," Banner says, a deputy again, one who's taking careful stock of all the open space around them.

"Gwen, Toby?" Letha says, quieter.

"Rex Allen and Francie will be back soon," Banner says. It was his mantra for the three hours he was home last night.

"You didn't leave them in the parking lot of the motel, did you?" Jennifer says, incredulous. "It's just *called* Trail's End, it's not actually—"

"They're—" Banner starts, then gives himself a do-over: "The nursing home has a… it's not a morgue, but they, you know."

"Have to deal with dead people all the time," Jennifer fills in.

Banner nods, keeps nodding.

"You don't have to go after him," Letha says, reaching across the car seat to hold Banner's hand, her eyes pouring across to him. "He's too… he's killed so many people already."

"It's not like last time," Banner says. "This is—it's two kids. Rex Allen will get back and—"

"Have you talked to him since he left?" Letha asks.

"I left a voicemail," Banner mumbles. Then, even quieter, "about a thousand voicemails."

"Francie too? They can't *both* have forgot their chargers."

Banner nods: Francie too, yep.

"It's just us, then," Jennifer says, facing front again—facing the swirling snow. "Us and him."

Letha's expression doesn't change, but she does follow where Jennifer's looking, and, as her conditioning dictates, she presses the pedal under her foot to change the scenery around her, make it summer again, erase "Dark Mill South" from Proofrock, but the truck's engine just revs, and the storm doesn't change, just gusts and sighs.

In one of those lulls, Banner's keys jangling to the floorboard, meaning his head is low for the moment, Jennifer leans forward, says, "Are those footprints?"

Letha leans up against the wheel to see better, and—they are. Rounded from the wind, indistinct on their own, but in a line, they add up to footsteps. Someone's definitely walked there.

They track either to or from the general area of the sheriff's office.

"You?" Jennifer asks to the backseat.

"Parked around back," Banner says.

"Last time you checked on her?" Letha asks.

"Her?" Banner says back.

"Cinnamon Baker," Jennifer says, already stepping down.

"*Shit*," Letha says, and knows her eyes are saying it just the same.

Banner hasn't really *considered* having a heart attack at twenty-two years old, but he has the distinct feeling that, pretty soon here, he's going to be clutching his chest and falling sideways, hopefully into some less stressful place.

With the luck he's having this week, though, he'll just loop back to yesterday, when Rex Allen and Francie pulled alongside where he'd been standing on the sidewalk, told him not to let the place burn down while they were gone, yeah?

Yeah.

Sure.

No problem.

Ha ha ha.

Ha.

Sob.

And, office support?

As of this morning, Meg's snowed in at her new cabin on the other side of the highway, which is as far as she can get from the lake and still be close enough to town for work. Banner could have taken the truck out to get her if he chained up, except he doesn't want to leave Letha with just the Prius—that would be the same as locking her in the house, and with the lake frozen over, her and

Adrienne could be approached from any direction, from *all* directions, and how is Banner supposed to keep everyone in town alive if he's swinging by the house every five minutes?

He could get up to Meg in the snowcat, of course, let her handle the flood of calls about no power, no phones, the cell tower being in and out, let her manage the paperwork for murder victims *plural*, except the cat's already sitting under half a tank, and clopping up to the diesel pump to refuel would be the same as announcing that Lonnie's treasured snowcat is now the deputy's own personal ride.

Banner hadn't parked around back because it's more an employee entrance, but because there's less chance of Lonnie seeing his precious snowcat back there. All the same, though, Lonnie's going to be coming around soon enough. Aside from charging for the cat's maintenance, he also has the contract to keep Main Street plowed, a contract paid for with a kitty the bank and the drugstore and the quilt shop and the seniors and Dot's all pay into, to stay open for business during inclement weather.

So, when they all get to calling Lonnie here in a bit about why their customers don't have anywhere to park, Lonnie's going to come knocking, and Banner's going to have to explain that he has two murder victims to deal with, a witness to protect from *getting* killed, oh, and also? That big bad killer from the news is in town somewhere, and probably isn't done hanging people from trees yet. And no, Banner hasn't announced this *or* the murders to the town yet, mostly because everyone will ask questions he has no answers to, but also because if he just waits a little bit longer, another hour, another two hours, then… Rex Allen will be back, won't he? Or at least Francie?

Then Banner can have someone telling him what to do, instead of having to make all these bullshit decisions himself.

Trial by fire his *ass*, he says in his head, hauling Adrienne's car seat out the back door with him, the top already covered with her blanket like Letha's taught him to do. It's to keep Adie warm, of course, but it's also to keep all the idiots in Proofrock from leaning over and saying how she's so cute, with her "coffee" skin, her "caramel" cheeks, or the worst, "café au lait" and "café con leche," which Letha had to explain to him: it means some white in the brown, some milk in the chocolate, which is this or that idiot making a thing of Adrienne being "mixed," which is how you say it up here at eight thousand feet.

Just let her be a goddamn baby, Banner hissed to his mom and dad when they came back up the mountain either to see their first grandchild or so his dad could comment on the state of the lawn, the trees that needed cutting back, the drive that needed the gravel raked even. Or so Banner's *mom* could say all her passive-aggressive shit about how Letha had redecorated.

As if Letha hadn't let them both retire early, and bought their retirement pad up on Pend Oreille, so his dad could fish every day of the rest of his life.

They didn't come down for Adrienne's first birthday, and that's just fine with Banner, thanks. And no, Dad, he *hadn't* let Letha pay for their truck. That's coming from his county paycheck, and will be for seventy-one more months, if he gets on permanent.

Taking a job when he didn't exactly have to felt like a point of pride in October.

Now he's reconsidering that.

One of the games he likes to play with Adrienne on the living room floor before supper is that he's the Banner who turns into the Incredible Hulk: he shakes and slobbers and "transforms," pulling his work shirt open in the front.

If only.

And the whole time Letha's in the kitchen keeping dinner on-track, the flat-screen mounted in there mindlessly cycling all the horror movies she says calm her.

Banner figures he knows what that's about, though: Letha's paying penance for not having listened to Jade—*Jennifer, Jennifer*—back when she was the girl who cried slasher. Banner had *tried* explaining that Jennifer had been crying "slasher" ever since junior high, but Letha still feels guilty.

So, she dials up movie after movie like the machine she is, and he's pretty sure she's even leveraging this or that in her dad's holdings not to maximize profit or whatever, but to keep rights to this or that group of horror movies, so she can stream them in the kitchen, watch masked killers carve up high schoolers while she's carving up zucchini with the same exact knife.

Sure, why not.

What that all means, though?

It actually *wasn't* Banner's idea for Letha to come up to the office, man the front desk in Meg's absence, it was Letha's. According to her, the only killer who came through the front door of the police station was the Terminator—okay, once that guy from *Halloween*, sort of. So, she and Adrienne would be safer up here than buckled down over at the house.

Just—now she's going to be here without him, isn't she?

Sure, the diaper bag is pretty much a bugout bag, meaning

Adrienne and Letha can live out of it if they need to, but if the Terminator *does* choose to drive some stolen car through the front door?

Banner shakes his head, tries to take the brunt of the wind for Adrienne, and shoulders his way through the first set of doors, Jennifer right behind him, holding the door for Letha to huddle through.

Before pushing through into the office proper, they each sweep what snow they can off, their fingertips not quite hitting each other even though this is a glass phone booth, pretty much.

When they're dry enough, Banner steps in, holding the door open with his boot, his eyes sweeping the place to be sure nothing's changed: first is the tall reception counter, which Rex Allen says was Meg's idea, to get people to stop there instead of barreling right in to stand over her; past it is Meg's desk, sideways to the front, probably so Meg can emphasize how annoying it is to have to look over to whoever's just walked in; and then, back in the left corner by the copy machine and the water cooler, the desk he and Francie share. Well, the desk he gets to sit at when she's not there, so long as he doesn't mess with any of her stuff.

It's all just as he left it, though, and that's the important part.

Because it's too quiet, Adrienne starts in crying, the water cooler burbles hello to them all, and then, all at once, every phone in the place starts in ringing, like the calls build up whenever they can't get through.

"Where is she?" Jennifer's already asking, her head on a swivel, then just calls out: "Cinnamon? Cinnamon Baker?"

Banner tilts his head down the hall to the right, past Rex Allen's office.

"The *supply* closet?" Letha says, offended.

"Records," Banner tells her, shrugging because he knows Records isn't just super ideal either. "It's across from the ladies'."

Jennifer brushes past him, beelines Records like she knows—oh, but she would know, wouldn't she?

"You used to mop up in here, right?" Banner says from behind her.

"Just what she wants to be reminded about," Letha says, bringing up the rear, Adrienne out of her carrier now, her hand up in her mom's, her toes barely touching the floor, her sobs tamped down by the urgency she can probably feel.

"Well shit," Jennifer says from the doorway to Records.

Not only is it open, which it shouldn't have been, but Cinn's bunk is empty.

"She took the clothes," Banner says, not even really meaning to.

"Clothes?" Letha asks all the same.

"Gal delivered them, so she wouldn't be..."

"Mostly naked, from the motel?" Jennifer says, looking around. Then, "There didn't used to be a cot in here."

"Francie was having difficulties with her marriage," Banner explains, for some reason putting a black bar over "Seth Mullins," her husband.

"Galatea... *Pangborne*?" Jennifer asks, trying to keep up. "Why would she—?"

"Maybe she's in the—" Letha says, tilting her head at the restroom they're bunched in front of.

Jennifer pushes it open without bothering to knock, Banner cocks his hand up on the molded grip of his Glock, Letha turns so that Adrienne's behind her, but—

"Y'all should really get that fixed someday," Jennifer says

about the open bathroom window, the stiff plastic that had been taped over it flapping, snow swirling in, collecting in the sink.

"Why would she run?" Banner asks.

"Because she didn't feel safe?" Jennifer asks back, obviously.

"Because the police guarding the final girl always die," Letha says, her eyes filling. "No offense, Deputy. But she probably just saved your life."

"She doesn't need to," Banner says. "Rex Allen left *me* in charge, not her."

"This isn't a pissing contest," Jennifer says. "Anyway, if she's a final girl, then you lose that one, sorry, Ban."

"*Is* she a final girl?" Letha says, both hopefully and full of regret.

Before Jennifer can answer, Banner sees the thin skin around her eyes flinch just the slightest bit, almost a tic. Nothing voluntary, but speaking volumes all the same: she's terrified.

The girl she used to be would have been thrilled about all this, would have had her black pompoms out, to cheer it on.

She's different now, though. This isn't exciting to her anymore. It's exactly as terrifying as it should be.

"Well, she's leaving *tracks*, isn't she?" Banner says, and both Jennifer and Letha fix him in their eyes.

You don't have to be doing this, Jennifer is telling herself, as she's doing it: riding shotgun in Banner's snowcat, holding tight to the oh-shit handle by her head, her lips peeled back from her teeth so she doesn't bite them the next time she goes weightless.

To be sure they don't lose the post-hole footprints, which are round-ing off fast, will be gone soon, they're going the town version of cross-country, not following the streets, just chugging across grass and landscaping and whatever. The unstated but bitterly obvious excuse for this kind of rampant destruction of town property is that this is life and death: no way can Cinn make it out here in this cold very long.

"There," Jennifer says, directing Banner a little more to the left.

He nudges the cat that direction.

"If you flatten a bench or something," Jennifer says, "that's not on me, right? I can't destroy any more property for a while."

"Can't *what*?"

"I'm on probation," she explains.

"You're not even really here," Banner says. "I don't think our liability covers civilians. I'm not even sure it covers this—" The snowcat.

"What did she say last night?" Jennifer asks then, trying to spring it on him while he's distracted, since he wouldn't let her come back to the station after the motel.

Banner flashes a look over to her side of the cab that means he knows exactly what she's trying to do, here.

Still, "It's him, don't worry," he grumbles, shifting down and leaning forward to pick Cinn's tracks out from whoever's are crossing. "Her—her description, it's just the same."

"As what?"

"As on the news," Banner says, watching his mirrors and the tracks for a distracted moment.

"Which spice girl *is* she, even?" Jennifer asks.

"The Cinnamon one?" Banner asks back, slowing even more when a bike rack is suddenly there.

"I mean which twin is—"

"She's the one who made it across," Banner says, hauling the steering wheel over.

Jennifer nods, dials back to a skinny twelve- or thirteen-year-old being guided up from the water onto the pier, people screaming and dying all around, *Jaws* playing overhead.

"Who even names their kids Cinnamon and Ginger?" she says.

Banner huffs air out in agreement.

"And she calls you by your first name?" she asks, then.

"She was at the house a lot after Adrienne was born," Banner says, shrugging like it's nothing.

"Where do they even..." Jennifer says, trying to put it all together. "I mean, her mom and dad, they're both dead, right?"

"Donna Pangborne built a big place at the top of Conifer," Banner says, chucking his chin that direction. "Evidently they all had some deal... I don't know. If something happened to one of them, the other would raise the kids left behind? That kind of thing?"

"Oh, okay. They all live at the same house, that's why Galatea could bring clothes up to Cinnamon."

"She goes by Gal, like Wonder Woman."

"The comic book superhero?"

"She's a movie star now. Forget it, it was while you were... you know."

"'Gal,' got it."

"We're not supposed to talk to her, though," Banner says, looking over again like to be sure she hears this. "Sheriff's orders."

"But she *can* come up to deliver clothes?"

"It's—there's this new history teacher, right? Rex Allen thinks he only hired on to, like, write a book on the Independence Day

Massacre. So he's got his class doing all these projects that are really legwork for his book."

"He's got them picking at scabs."

"And they're not even hard yet."

"The *scabs*? Gross, Banner. Even for you."

"Says the horror chick?"

"There," Jennifer says, her hand already to the doorhandle.

Banner stops a few feet in front of the huddled, stumbling form of Cinnamon Baker. She's in a blanket, at least, but it's pretty much exactly the blanket Jennifer would expect to find on a cot in the back room of the sheriff's office. And Cinnamon's tall enough that it doesn't even cover her head to toe. Her blond hair is stiff, frozen in tangles, and the snot on her face is icy, her red-rimmed eyes the kind of blank that means she's just been putting one foot in front of the other, that she's already given up on actually getting anywhere. It's the kind of walk that's really just a long, slow fall.

"Here, here," Jennifer says, hugging Cinn to her for the second time in the last twenty-four hours, guiding her up into the cat and sitting alongside, trying to give her whatever bodywarmth she can.

"Shit, Cinn," Banner says. "You *trying* to die?"

"Where were you going?" Jennifer says.

Cinn opens her mouth but no words come out, just a creak.

"Point, point," Jennifer says, and Cinn's hand comes up from the stiff folds of the blanket, her finger extending the direction they were going.

Jennifer looks from where she's pointing across to Banner.

"*Pleasant Valley?*" he says for both of them.

The nursing home. It's the only place this street goes.

"Warn-warn-*warn* them," Cinn finally gets out.

"Warn *them*," Jennifer repeats. "About him?"

Cinn nods, keeps nodding.

"Who is 'them'?" Jennifer asks across to Banner.

He shrugs, runs the cat up onto the curb for a few yards, hauling the wheel over.

"No, *no*," Jennifer says.

"We have to get back to the *station*," Banner says. "Where the big guns are?"

"Can we warm her up like she needs, there?" Jennifer asks. "Or will they have actual medical staff at Pleasant Valley? I mean, do you want her to live, or do you want her to die?"

Banner considers, considers some more, hating this.

"Batman would save everyone," he mumbles. "He didn't have to choose like this."

"We're playing with action figures now?" Jennifer asks.

Banner lets the clutch out, jerking them ahead.

In Jennifer's arms, Cinn is shuddering and shaking, and starting to cry.

"Hurry," Jennifer says, trying to breathe warmth into the top of Cinn's head, and Banner opens the cat up, has them there in a minute and a half.

"I'll just—" he says, idling the cat under the drop-off overhang, and not bothering to open the door on his side.

"Go," Jennifer says. "Check on them. But your wife can take care of herself, too. She doesn't need any tall guy with a big gun to keep her safe."

"Marriage advice from the perpetually single," Banner says.

The instant Jennifer's got Cinn down from the cat, Banner's churning away, the swirling snow swallowing the red of his taillights before the whirring clank of his tracks is even all the way gone.

And nobody's coming out to meet Jennifer, take Cinn.

Because this isn't an emergency room, Jennifer reminds herself.

"Well," she says, and half carries, half walks Cinn in, hitting the door opener with her hip.

Two minutes later, three nurses have Cinn in a wheelchair and a better blanket, are wheeling her back into the bowels of the facility.

The high school boy working the front desk brings Jennifer a disposable cup of the most bitter, wonderful coffee.

"Thank you," Jennifer says, then raises a boot, realizes all the snow she's wearing is melting into a puddle around her. "Um," she says, by way of apology.

"Oh," the high schooler says, seemingly impressed, and not much of a problem solver.

"Maybe a towel?" Jennifer prompts, obviously.

"You could stand on the mat back there," he says.

They both inspect this industrial doormat together. The fake plant by it is waving in the wind slipping in around the doors Jennifer just came through.

"Maybe I'll just—" Jennifer says: *stand here, make a mess*.

"I can't leave my post," the kid says, by way of some sort of explanation. "If I do again—" He pulls his index finger across his throat.

"This probably is a gravy job," Jennifer says, looking around.

The lobby is mostly empty, just one small, old woman in a wheelchair by the fireplace. One small, old woman with a shawl wrapped around her shoulders…

"Christine Gillette," Jennifer hears herself saying, in absolute wonder. She turns to the kid, says, kind of whispering, kind of not, "She's still *alive*?"

"We don't generally leave them out here when they're not," the smart-ass says back.

Jennifer feels her face warming.

"I interviewed her when I was a—a freshman or sophomore," she says.

"Was Sheriff Allen for me," the kid says.

"*He's* a historical personage now?" Jennifer says, insult rising in her voice.

"Just twenty percent of my grade."

"Used to be more," Jennifer says, taking a drink that's still way too hot.

"School was uphill too?" the kid adds.

"It sucked in ways you'll never know," Jennifer says. Then, "Really, there's no towels around here? In this whole freaking place?"

"When Mark and Kristen get back I'll get one. But, like I said—"

"Can't leave your post, yeah." Jennifer looks around, nods, is going to do it, is going to walk right over and risk Christine Gillette not remembering her, screw it, but— "Mark? Kristen?" she says, like just registering those names.

"They're on break," the kid says.

Jennifer looks at him, weighing each of his words, and the disappointed way he said them.

Finally, "This *break*," she says, "how long it supposed to go?"

The kid shrugs, meaning what Jennifer thought: Mark and Kristen's break was over thirty minutes ago. Longer.

"Mark and Kristen are… an item?" she asks.

"An 'item' is what you scan at the grocery store," the kid says back, by way of non-answer.

"Did they need a condom for this break, then?" Jennifer asks. "How's that?"

The kid smiles, shrugs, says, "Two or three, knowing them."

Jennifer sets her coffee down, some of it sloshing out on the fake granite countertop.

"My station!" the kid says, reaching over and down, for a tissue.

Jennifer keeps her face pleasant while he cleans the splash up, but slides her hand across to embrace this cup, show how easy the rest of it could spill.

"Mark and Kristen," she leads off, "I take it they're friends with Cinnamon Baker?"

"Nobody calls her that. Just 'Cinn.'"

Jennifer swirls the coffee, the kid's eyebrows V'ing up with concern.

"And… where would Mark and Kristen go for *privacy*?" she says.

"I can't."

"You can't get a towel either," Jennifer says. "But, what if there's a spill at your station? What kind of… *conundrum* would that create?"

"So it's either I get fired, or Kristen kicks my ass."

"Not Mark?"

"I can handle Mark."

Jennifer takes a sip of her coffee and sets it back down roughly, jarring a second sip out.

"Four-twenty-eight," the kid mutters, no lips involved. "Don't tell them I sent you."

Jennifer toasts him bye with her coffee, spins on a wet heel, and squelches down the east wing, her skin crawling already: another institution. Which is what the holding facility in Boise was.

But you can leave this one whenever you want, she reminds herself.

Still, her legs go stiff, and now, again, she's a robot, mechanically walking past so many doorways, every resident watching her, it feels like—Christine Gillette too, probably.

"I'll come back, talk to you however long you want," Jennifer promises her, at the same time wondering what a promise no one hears is really worth.

But she *will*.

And… no, she actually *can't* leave whenever she wants, she realizes. Or, she can, but inside two hundred yards she'll be as frozen as Cinn was—which is when she finally registers that, while breathing all her warmth onto the top of Cinnamon's head, she'd been idly watching out the side window of the snowcat, and seen *other* footprints, which Cinnamon had probably been stepping into. Well, staggering into, numbly.

Whoever that had been, though, they probably had better clothes, warmer boots.

As-is, Jennifer's going to have to wait for Banner to cruise back by, scoop her up. Which should happen right about when he remembers to, meaning: never.

Of course.

Proofrock, man. Nothing ever changes.

But she's at least encouraged by the room number, "428." Not because it's one digit away from Elm Street—she's not that girl anymore—but because four times two is eight. And that's sort of comforting. Or, in the absence of anything actually comforting, it's enough.

Jennifer does an about-face at the door, looks both ways down the hall to see who's watching—it's no small thing, giving away the place's most private mattress—and, when she's alone, she knocks.

No answer.

Again.

"Coming in!" she announces like a nurse pushing a tray, and backs in through the door.

The first thing she hears is running water.

It's coming from behind the bathroom door.

"Hello?" Jennifer calls.

The water doesn't stop.

"Um," she says then, about the sheeted body on the bed.

What, is this the morgue Banner was talking about? Is this the dead kid from the hood of that snowplow truck? Would high schoolers seriously want to screw bad enough to share a room with a corpse?

Jennifer nods yes, probably they would want to that much.

"Sir, sir," she says to whoever's lying on their back under this sheet. The sheet pulled all the way over their *head*.

"Kristen?" she calls out. "Mark?"

And this is definitely 428. It was right there on that brass plate, five inches from her eyes.

"Sir, sir," Jennifer says again, taking what feels like the hugest risk of her life by reaching out to this foot, shaking it. "Hey, you."

No answer, but this does tighten the sheet, which makes something too sharp to be an Adam's apple poke up from the throat.

Then, slowly, that point becomes a single dab of red.

"Banner, you idiot," Jennifer says. "I need you, come back."

Moving slowly because she doesn't want this to be real, meaning the longer she delays it, the longer she can deny what she knows to be true, Jennifer gathers the bright white sheet in her hand, her fingers spidering it into her palm inch by inch.

The top hem catches on that point, though.

Jennifer shakes her head no, no, please, but she has to know, has to see.

She shakes the sheet from the foot, where she is, so that it billows out, going magician-high for a moment, then settling down halfway up this white guy's chest.

"Mark," Jennifer says.

There's what looks like a metal arrowhead pushed up through his throat, probably through the mattress.

"Not Mark," Jennifer hears her younger self saying, "*Jack*."

Kevin Bacon's character from *Friday the 13th*, dead with an arrow shoved up through his awkwardly long throat.

Meaning…

Jennifer backs to the bathroom door, finds it by touch, pulls it open.

It's the sink that's running.

Slumped back against the floor between the toilet and the accessible shower is—what's that girl's name?

"Kristen," Jennifer says like an exhalation.

She has a fire axe lodged in her face.

Her eyes are still open on either side of that axe. Only, if Mark, dead on the bed, is Kevin Bacon's Jack from *Friday the 13th*, then…

"Marcie," Jennifer mumbles, because who cares.

But she can't deny that this is how Marcie, who Jack just had sex with, dies.

"What is happening," Jennifer says, and turns when she senses she's not alone.

It's Cinn, standing in the doorway, her inner left forearm seeping thin blood—she dragged her IV out, staggered down here without permission, to warn her friends that Dark Mill South was coming for them.

She steeples her hands over her mouth, collapses to her knees, and then, though she looks too weak to even breathe in, she screams, her anguish filling the room.

Jennifer rushes out into the hall to wave help in.

The staff brush past her, some collecting Cinn, some checking the vitals on Mark and Kristen, which is really just confirming what they can already see.

"This isn't happening," Jennifer says to the kid from reception.

"Wish in one hand..." the kid says with a shrug.

They're standing on the opposite side of the hall now, out of the way. Jennifer still has her cup of coffee, somehow.

Cinn's being wheelchaired away again.

"I—I thought she was going to see her sister," the kid says.

Jennifer hears this, plays it back again, and then steps away so she can look this kid right in the face, give him every last bit of her attention.

"*Sister*?" she says.

THE SECOND COMING

Yes, I can speak on the case of Ginger Baker, Mr. Armitage, but you can't talk about Ginger Baker without first discussing Joss Peasun. As O. W. Holmes, Jr., says on the poster by your chalkboard, *History has to be rewritten because history is the selection of those threads or causes or antecedents that we are* interested *in*—my emphasis.

Yes, Ginger Baker's case is intrinsically interesting, is the kind of fabulous that brings Hollywood sniffing around. But of even more interest, in that it would seem to provide context or at least precedent for Ginger Baker's ordeal, is Joss Peasun's, which would seem to have provided a model for what Ginger went through.

In short, Mr. Armitage—and my research suggests I'm the first to notice this—after their respective traumas, both Joss Peasun and Ginger Baker, perhaps in a fugue state they retreated to to protect their psyches, went missing for an extended time.

Joss Peasun, sole survivor of the Pioneer Trails Slaughter in Bowman, North Dakota, is an enrolled member of the Sicangu Lakota. She's the one who, six weeks after those campground killings, first tipped the authorities off to Dark Mill South's Native American heritage. Those who push back against the claim that Dark Mill South is or was vulnerable to face-offs with Native American women are quick to cite that Joss *didn't* take him down, did she? *Did* she?

Disregarding this highly sophisticated argument for the moment, the reason Joss Peasun's recollection of Dark Mill South's "Indian" silhouette wasn't factored into the mounting evidence for two months was that, after crawling up from the pit he had been disposing of her friends in, instead of running to the campground's main office or alerting the authorities or doing any one of the other practical things she could have, she effectively disappeared, somehow becoming part of the indigent population of Bismarck, three hours to the east. When she was finally discovered, it still took weeks to get her to remember what she'd endured, and relay any telling particulars.

Where this lines up with Ginger Baker's ordeal is that after Jennifer Daniels and Letha Mondragon escaped the yacht and made their way across the lake to *Jaws*, a certain closet door deep in the bowels of the yacht opened.

It's the one Cinnamon and Ginger and myself had hidden in when the screaming started. We had just ventured timidly out into this new and bloody world when Grade Paulson found us, covered our eyes, and led us off the yacht, into the water, to swim across to the movie.

Note here that I say he "covered *our* eyes," Mr. Armitage.

How would he do this, with only two hands?

It's because Ginger was having one of her panic attacks, and Cinnamon gave her a handful of pills, a paper bag to breathe in, and her favorite hair-tie, after which she promised she'd come back for her, that Ginger should just close the door again and stay there, stay there, be safe, we'd be right back.

Ginger stayed as long as she could. I have to believe this. But finally, just as Joss Peasun had done, perhaps as a result of the yacht taking on water, she climbed up from this mass grave and navigated the halls and stairways, always moving up, up. Not having anyone to cover her eyes, she had to see it all, and—her doctors warn—sear it into her memory.

Instead of swimming the lake after us, she went the other way, into Caribou-Targhee National Forest.

It would be four weeks before Game Warden Seth Mullins found her, but by that time she'd been spiraling deeper and deeper into her increasingly frenetic cycle of trauma for so long that, in order to subsist on what berries and dew she could find, she had retreated into her own mind, and effectively gone feral.

With patient work, trained personnel were able to eventually lure Joss Peasun out of the protective shell she had retreated to.

That effort continues with Ginger.

John W. Gardner says that *History never looks like* history *when you're living through it,* yes. What does it look like when you can't stop living through it, though? When it's not even history to you yet?

The blood-dimmed tide is loosed, yes, *and the ceremony of innocence is drowned.*

Would that Ginger Baker weren't caught in that tide. Would that her innocence hadn't been drowned.

"But this," the girl Jennifer Daniels had been in high school would have said, "this is how it works, in a slasher cycle."

Just, never mind all the people who have to die along the way.

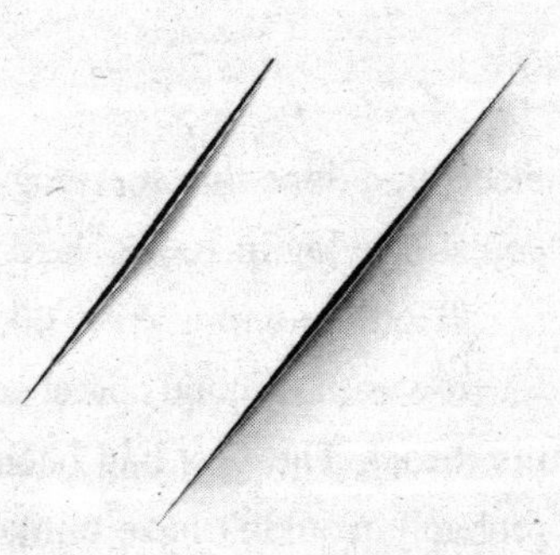

SILENT NIGHT, DEADLY NIGHT

At first it had left him dizzy in his chest, watching two television screens at once, but Rexall found out pretty quickly that he could modulate that floating feeling with just the right amount of beer.

The beer didn't make him feel any less like he was in a lawn chair tied to a clutch of weather balloons, but it did make him kind of like it, like the floor of his living room had dissolved and he was hurtling forward through some vast space, and the two televisions stacked one on top of the other were actually colossal, and he was going to get right up to them eventually, and they'd be so big he wouldn't even be able to see the edges, could maybe even touch the glass, a blue spark jumping from it to him and bringing him alive in a way that would take his breath but also swell his chest near to bursting.

Back when, he'd had the little console one stacked on top of the grandaddy of all console televisions because the picture only worked in the top one, while the sound only worked in the bottom one. So, together, with both of them clicked to the same channel, he could see and hear just fine, thanks.

But then Clate, standing in the living room and looking around like he was about to rub a white glove over every flat surface in the place, had done that sneering thing he always used to do. "What, you still living in 1996?" he'd asked, killing his longneck.

"Nothing wrong with '96," Rexall had said back.

It was the second comeback that had rolled up into the back of his throat. The first had been "I ain't mad at cha," which Clate probably wouldn't have blinked at. Tab would have, though, and he'd been there that day as well. And he wouldn't have just blinked; he would have stopped the bottle on the way to his mouth and zoomed his eyes down onto Rexall. Not because he knew that was a Tupac song *from* 1996, the year He died and the world somehow didn't collapse in on itself, but because he knew Rexall was always pulling shit like this—"betraying his race," Tab called it, more disgusted each time he had to say it.

But? Was Rexall supposed to just listen to people with the same skin color as his own? Who would that leave him, Merle *Haggard*?

Anyway, if Tab had held himself to that standard, all he could have listened to would have been recordings of Indians dying in John Wayne movies. And maybe Gordon Lightfoot. That was an Indian name, wasn't it? And he said some Indian words in his songs. Rexall knew because his dad always had a Gordon Lightfoot 8-track thumbed into the player screwed up under the dash of his work truck. Which Rexall is thankful for, really—it made him run so far to the other end of the dial that he ended up riding dirty with 2Pac, but in a way that made his soul cleaner.

In his leather easy chair, in the glow of two television screens, Rexall lifts his beer to Pac and then holds it up long enough that it can be for Tab as well, goddamn his idiot ass.

But Rexall will find him again, he knows. If he watches the top screen close enough. If he just doesn't sleep.

Grudgingly, he tips the top of his beer to Clate as well. Though, at the same time: good riddance, right? Sometimes a boat's bank of props finds the right person. Dude was always showing up and drinking all the beer in town, and he had a way of… the things he could say about Rexall, Tab would smirk and maybe even laugh at their trueness. Shit Tab never said word one about without Clate's dumb ass to give it voice. Like the televisions. Rexall and Tab had watched a weekend's full of tapes on them, no problem, but then Clate's standing there being all judgy, pretty much calling Rexall a freshman in high school—the "1996"-thing.

That was the year Rexall missed homecoming, because he'd stolen his dad's rifle and truck, headed down to Vegas on his own, to go after the fools who'd shot Pac down. Two thousand years before, he'd have also gone after that king or whoever who did the same thing to Jesus. What he never understood was why it was just him driving those roads at night. Why he wasn't part of a brigade, a swell, a *flood* of trucks collapsing in on Nevada?

When the state cops delivered him back to Proofrock, his dad turned that rifle around, used it on Rexall, broke his collarbones on both sides so he couldn't even use his arms right until Christmas. His ass had got so infected from not being able to wipe right that he had to take horse pills that just made him shit more.

But, Clate.

The thing about him was that he would piss and moan about this and that, sure, make six different kinds of fun about Rexall's stacked television sets, but Clate also liked to show off. That had always been the thing with him. It's why he was front and center under the dock that night the lake turned into his own personal blender—he was going to show how he could still barefoot it across the water, just hold onto the ski rope with one hand, his other in a fist above his head, in victory, like that dude at the end of *Breakfast Club.*

Him and Tab were going to walk on water one last time, to show that nothing had really changed.

Or, that was the plan.

Rexall's part in it that night was Kimmy's old job: keep watch, whistle a headsup when the time was right. When your collarbones never healed right, you don't do things like tie onto a fucking giant-ass *boat*, and try to hold on.

It was best he didn't try, too, wasn't it? This momma's boy knows better than to let himself get turned into chum. Or, really, if he's being honest: you don't disrespect Pac and then expect things to always go your way, *Clate*.

Still, up *until* Clate bought it, Rexall had always had to put up with his shit, with his superiority, with his strutting around like the cock he was.

Back to the stacked television sets: after being an ass about them that time—you can be a cock and also be an ass—Clate followed through on it, and showed up at three in the morning on a workday. Rexall found him out front, kicking the side of his truck to try to get it to finally *die*.

"Vacuum locking," Rexall had called out from the porch.

"Think I'm an idiot?" Clate had snarled back.

Rexall stepped back, hands held high, not so much in apology but because he could tell Clate was flying high, probably on some of his girlfriend's kid's Adderall. That had been his favorite, lately. Said it gave him focus, but didn't make his teeth fall out like meth would. The shop he worked at didn't have a dental plan. Jobs where you don't want the tax taken out usually don't.

That was the one thing Rexall always had over Clate and Tab: benefits. The county even gave him sick days. No way was he ever letting go of whatever mop they gave him.

When Clate's truck finally clattered down, he waved Rexall out and the two of them lugged in the two flat-screen televisions Clate had in the back of his truck, face down on some horse blankets, with pine boughs under them.

"Join the twenty-first century," Clate grumbled, and then, with all the concentration the Adderall gave him, he took the tubes out of Rexall's two console sets and replaced them with the flat-screens, then spliced them both into the stereo speakers Rexall had by his chair, for when he wanted to listen to "Dear Mama" and cry, hitting the top of his leg with the side of his fist the whole time, sometimes until he was black and blue.

Since Clate wired *both* sets to the speakers, the sound could get muddy, but the bottom set's audio was just hiss, really, and Rexall had traced back the gossamer speaker wire, snipped it.

It was better to watch it silent anyway.

With Tupac talking through the speakers—the stereo was still wired in, through a switcher—it was like watching a music video. Not to take anything away from Tupac's *own* videos, of course, but Him narrating over these scenes from Proofrock, it brought Him up the mountain, let Him provide the soundtrack for all this bullshit.

And?

If Rexall watches closely enough, constantly enough, he'll see a certain shape again, he knows.

It sucks being the last one left is the thing. Clate got sucked into a wall of spinning blades, Tab bought it from a *single* blade, and now it's just Rexall, snowed in for the week. The *plan* had been to do a deep clean of the cafeteria, then line all the tables up in the second-grade hall so he could spin a few layers of wax onto the floor. Not enough that it would get gummy, and he'd polish it until it shone like glass, of course, but enough that all the shit the kiddies spilled would mop up better.

But, too, sitting here and *not* having to do that isn't bad either. Not at all.

And he can submit a timecard correction in January, right when school's open again and everything's hectic, and get paid all the same. Like Harrison'll ever know he *didn't* do that deep clean? Like he's going to steal some kid's geometry compass and go out onto the floor between the tables, drill that sharp point in to see how deep the wax is?

Shit. Work's easy. Work's cake.

It's not as easy as it was when he was seventeen, had just hired on, but when you're a kid, you don't need to sleep as much.

But it's not like he can't still stay up all night watching his two screens, and then fuel this morning's viewing with beer for breakfast, and one for dessert too.

Rexall cashes his current one, ferrets another up from the cooler on the right side of his chair.

What Tab told him after his big wreck senior year was that Indians never really die. That you can tell that by how he was still there, when that Grand Prix should have killed his ass. You can tell by how there's still Indians everywhere, after the cavalry had been trying to kill them ever since Columbus—ever since the *Vikings*. Ever since that cold windy walk across from Russia, even.

Tab's other proof of this was how he said that one night over at Camp Blood, he'd been standing by the fire after nailing Kimmy again and he'd looked over to the national forest, seen a line of bow and arrow Indians on that shore, all just sitting there on their painted ponies, holding their staffs with feathers and scalps all tied to them, and the chief of them had looked over, nodded once to Tab, and Tab had nodded back, and then he knew that he could never really die, that he would always come back.

Rexall's proof of this was that Tab had never floated back up to the surface.

What this meant was that he was going to step up onto shore himself one fine day, and things could be like they were before. Just, now, no Clate. Which is fine by Rexall.

But, when Tab finally comes back, he's probably going to be weak, and confused. And need a beer, too.

So, Rexall keeps watch.

The top screen is tied into his VCR and DVD player, and his bottom screen is wired into the PC he scavenged from parts, at work. And the PC is spliced into some co-ax he buried in sections along a water main over two months of nights. The image is a bit fuzzy and jerky from too many junctions, and from not having an inline amp, but it's better than trying to jack it through Wi-Fi—someone else would eventually tap into that.

It gives Rexall access to all his cameras.

Used to, he was always smuggling SD cards back and forth from home to work, but this is *live*.

His thinking is that when Tab comes back, his head's probably going to be dialed to when he was a kid. Meaning he'll probably go to homeroom, which anybody else would think is Golding, as there's no "homeroom" in high school. But the elementary Rexall and Tab went to, it was *in* Henderson High, back when Henderson and Golding were one school, one building—before the new elementary got built, with that bond everybody hated.

But, just to be sure not to miss Tab, Rexall had also climbed the light pole in the parking lot by the pier, sneaked a lens up there so he could see any wet, mostly dead people stumbling up from the lake.

Right now, though, it's just Sheriff Hardy with his walker, struggling through the snow, probably trying to find the right ice floe to die on.

And? Really, with the lake frozen hard, he isn't just super sure how Tab is supposed to get up from his watery grave. Or, he'll have to feel for a weak spot—probably that soft spot out by the dam, where the intakes keep the ice thin—then trudge across all the ice, not even bother walking onto the end of the pier. Just walk alongside it, up into Proofrock. To what used to be homeroom.

Rexall clicks back to Henderson High.

The top screen is blank, fizzled, who knows why. The cold? And every time the gennie in the backyard sputters, the bottom screen wavers a bit. But it hasn't died yet.

Neither has the juice his cameras are all tapped into. It's emergency electricity, which the school doesn't even need right now, but screw it. Rexall could suit up and go over there, turn it off, but then the yellowy-orange lights in the hall would go black, and he'd have nothing at all to watch.

Two beers later, Rexall nods off a bit, comes back with a snap, he isn't sure why. The cycle he has the cameras on is in the girls' locker room now, the down-angled one he's had to reposition with each class, depending on who's standing where, but… is that what woke him? The memory of good times past?

Rexall grubs for the keyboard, does the key combo that tiles all the cameras across the screen instead of cycling through.

If anything's moving—anyone—he'll see them, now.

He hates that one of the tiles is Hardy, since his slow, stupid motion keeps drawing Rexall to it, instead of the other tiles.

But then, way down at the end of the lockers, there's a shadow.

Trying to get that camera's feed front and center, Rexall fumbles the controls, has to right-arrow ahead through five other cameras before getting to the one he wants.

He leans forward, the chair creaking, is looking through the high antlers of that north-facing elk at the end of the hall—*not* his favorite angle, but the hole had already been in the wall from the first time he tried hanging that bull, before he took into account how far up those tines reached.

It's not Tab, it's… oh, it's her.

Rexall doesn't know her name, but he does know what she looks like without her shirt. She's one of the new ones, he's pretty sure, one of the seniors who just moved in to get the free college.

It's the gift that keeps on giving.

She's still dressed, but that can change in a heartbeat.

And behind her is another girl, a slighter one Rexall's been watching since she was in elementary, and then a scrawny boy who keeps lifting his chin, like trying to puff himself up.

"What have we here…" Rexall says into the silence of his living room, ready for whatever this night's about to deliver to him not on a silver spoon, but on a silver line of co-ax.

The better to record them with.

Rexall hits the key he's dabbed fingernail-red, which records all his inputs, but screw it. He can go back, scrub the useless ones.

Like always, though, hitting record makes the whole system shudder, which is a continuing mystery—something to do with power, he's pretty sure.

The annoying part is it dumps Rexall's screen back to the first in the cycle: the new lens, down at the pier.

"Yeah, you're who I want to see, *Sheriff*," he says, and is tapping his index finger on his knee, waiting for the screen to dial back to the high school and whatever's about to be happening there, when—

"What," he says.

Who he's talking about is the dark shape striding so close under this camera that it disappears for a couple of steps. But then it's—*he's*—back. Moving away from town instead of towards it, and not stopping to deal any justice to the old sheriff, who still has his back turned to sweep that bench, but, it's undeniable: Tab Daniels is in the world again. What does Pac say? His only fear of death is reincarnation?

Sure, He's right; He's *Tupac*. But still, later in that same song, He'll probably be a mystery to many, but a legend to some.

That's what Rexall is seeing right now: the legend.

And, "You're *bigger*," he says, in wonder.

And Tab's face, for the fuzzy instant the camera sort of almost had it—being dead hasn't fixed it. But that's right, that's proper. Otherwise, nobody would know it was him.

Rexall comes close to the screen, is on his knees now.

When his fingers touch the bottom monitor, a blue spark arcs between him and this, and it—it starts his heart again.

Start at dawn, reach and pull, reach and pull, and an old man can get from his front porch to the pier by lunch. If he's determined, and has his Sorels on, and this godforsaken ushanka pulled down tight over his head, covering his ears.

When he got the goofy hat—it's real sable—for a retirement gift, he'd thought it was just something to lovingly inspect with everyone watching, then throw in a closet after they're gone. But those damn Russians, they know the cold, you got to give them that. There's not a warmer hat in the world, he knows now. Sure, it looks like a marmot's humping his head, but… like there's anyone else out here braving the elements?

It's just one old man, his walker, his retirement hat, and a scarf to clean Melanie's bench with. Because rituals are important. Or, really, because he can't bear to see her bench look like it's been forgotten.

Not while he's around to maintain it.

What Hardy's *been* doing is having the Tompkins kid swing him by here on the way down from the dam. The kid sits in the Bronco and does stuff on his phone while Hardy brushes Melanie's bench off, and maybe has a smoke or two, watches the sun go down one more time on a world where his only daughter's dead and gone.

He won't be coming back from the control booth today, though—this morning, no one was waiting in front of his house, to ferry him up there. Which Hardy plans on having words about with Rex Allen. No, the lake isn't going to drain or come up too high from a day or two of inattention, it's not that. Hell, in the winter like this, it can probably go a week unattended.

But this storm can't last that long, can it?

No, what he's going to have words with Rex Allen about is whether Tompkins is cut out for this line of work. What kind of deputy sits up there behind the wheel playing on his phone while he's on the clock? Part of enforcing the law, it's letting it be known that you're there, and you're always watching. While Hardy smokes on the bench, the kid could be moseying up Main, say, and taking stock of the storefronts, showing that there's a badge in the area, everybody behave, now.

Leave your phone in the glove box when you're on duty, that's the ticket.

But, too, it gives Hardy some small consolation, seeing how, without him, things are generally falling apart. He doesn't *want* it all to fall apart, but that it is means his forty-one years on the job mattered. He was holding the line, keeping people safe.

Just, that somehow didn't include Melanie, did it, Angus?

He winces, whips the scarf from his neck a second time—the snow is constant—and balls it around his right hand again, a numb action, what with the thick gloves.

Hardy brushes back and forth, staying upwind to keep his face from catching the powder. Halfway through, breathing deep, he has to lean back on his walker, use the crossbar as a stool, his back to the lake so he's looking right up Main.

How many times did he patrol up and down it?

He's not looking for a number, he's reaching back for a feeling.

And—hell. That time Don Chambers brought the lake all the way up to the fifth brick by the bank? It's still the most amazing thing he ever saw in this valley.

He asked around, too, and after that last night at the movies, when the water came up for the second time in memory, nobody thought to watch if it got as high as that fifth brick. If Ja—if *Jennifer* brought it up that high or not.

Her saving Proofrock still makes him look away and grin.

From the least likely, right? Isn't that the way it always goes?

And nobody in town would have crossed the street to piss on her, had it been *her* burning.

Not that she would have had it any other way.

For the hundredth time, counting just the past couple of weeks, Hardy wonders if Melanie would have been the same, had she got to grow up. It's natural for kids to rebel, to push back, to hate everyone and everything.

Hopefully she would have.

Or, no—she'd have *had* to, wouldn't she? The sheriff's daughter? If the sheriff's daughter doesn't raise six different kinds of hell, then her classmates never accept her, always thinks she's a rat.

With a dad like Jennifer's, though… did she feel like she had to outdo him? Out-*bad* him?

Hardy remembers Tab too, though. Seven years old, running down Main with a toy gun, shooting all the cars and rolling away from the mushroom cloud explosions he was seeing. Just being a kid, not yet a full-blown idiot.

He did one thing right, though. Well, two, counting not floating up to the surface of Indian Lake, as evidence in a homicide trial.

But Hardy knows not to start thinking like that.

If you open those gates, start mulling over the dead and what they're doing now, then you fall into what he calls the Trudy Hole.

She was never all the way good after Melanie, but she went through the motions, even kept smiling from her bed in hospice. The good thing about hospice was that it was wheelchair accessible, which matters for a retired sheriff who's had his guts unspooled in the lake. And the facility didn't have one of those death cats, that only come into your room when it's "time."

But, close to the end, Hardy had gotten some laughs from Trudy about that, holding her hand in his. He'd gone on about how he'd heard of this *one* hospice where it wasn't a cat that padded into the room when the hour was near, but a sorrel gelding, "The Blaze Reaper" they called it, because of the white star on its forehead. Whenever that horse clopped down the hall, nosed this or that door open, then shut it after walking through, those residents always turned up dead, with, you know, hoof prints all over them, and their bed all smashed to flinders.

It was stupid, but it had made her look away and grin. And that was everything.

It was only after she'd gone on that, collecting the things from her nightstand, just piling more and more in his lap, saving every little thing since there'd never be any more, Hardy'd wheeled over to the window.

There was a horse way on out there, just chomping the tall grass. But it looked up, quirked its ears as if sensing him.

Hardy flipped it off, then lowered his head and cried and cried at last, and the nurses just let him do that all afternoon.

And now here he is, still tending his daughter's bench. Here he is, having outlived the two women of his life. But, given the choice, that's exactly how he'd want it. He'd rather it be him here at the end instead of either of them. Well, instead of Trudy, anyway.

Melanie might have her own family by now, though.

Yeah, she would.

That's the way the cycle works. How it's *supposed* to go.

Hardy pushes up from the damned walker and sweeps the other side of the bench clean. If he had a hair dryer and a few hundred feet of extension cord, he could do it right, get it pristine like Mel deserves, but the storm hasn't even peaked yet. The bench will be a sparkling mound of white again by evening.

It's the effort that counts, though. The attention.

It's clean enough now to sit on, at least.

Hardy lifts his walker to shake it off and reparks it within reach for when he'll have to get back up, but then he lifts it higher, to be sure what he's seeing: he's down to one tennis ball. Figures.

There aren't more back at the house, either. Meaning? Whenever the so-called deputy turns up, he's going to have to send him down to Dollar General for one. The kid'll hate the errand, Hardy'll hate that him getting through the day has come down to a tennis ball, and… fuck getting old, right?

No, no: fuck getting your gut cut open. Fuck having your large intestines floating in the lake beside you. Fuck colostomy bags and walkers and all of it.

But neither would he trade any of it.

Or, no, that's not quite true. He would trade the last twenty-six years, even including all the walks and meals and moments with Trudy, to just have been out by the dam with Melanie that day.

He's been around long enough to know that every father's most basic wish is to sacrifice himself to save his kid, that there's no better way to cash out, and that him wishing that is just… he's one dad in a sea of dads, all of them perfectly willing to walk open-eyed into a buzzsaw if it means their kid doesn't have to.

But being one of many doesn't make him wish it any less.

And now, of the kids out there with her that day, Tab's gone, Misty's gone, Clate's fish food, Lonnie's more or less checked out, Kimmy's pretty much the walking dead, Rexall's life without Tab to lead him around is punishment enough, probably, and… none of that matters like Hardy thought it would. It's not about guilty parties suffering. It's about his little girl breathing in lake water, and reaching her hand up for someone to haul her up, and her dad not being there.

The booth he sits in day after day on top of the dam, it's not a vantage point, it's not a job; it's a cell. He's serving his sentence, doing his time.

The only moment over the last couple of decades that felt even a little bit like redemption was—it was her again. Jennifer, when she was Jade. When she was throwing her life away, or trying to, her left wrist not just seeping blood, but *spurting* it with her slower and slower heartbeats.

One possibility Hardy never even told Trudy was that when he was carrying Jade in that night, her lips blue, her chin not even shivering anymore, her eyes glassed over, he'd whispered a secret deal to the lake, that if this girl could live, then anything else could happen, bring it, it didn't matter: everything for her. Just don't goddamn let her die. Don't take her away too.

The Independence Day Massacre was just a few weeks after that, wasn't it?

It could all be his fault, Hardy knows.

And? He might make that same deal all over again.

There was a moment when she knocked on the door of the control booth where he thought—where he thought…

But no.

Melanie's not hand-over-handing it up her ladder to see you, old man. She's gone on to her reward. To somewhere better, where she never has to grow up.

And if you sit here much longer talking to yourself in your head, you're going to stiffen up, not be able to rise at all.

But maybe that wouldn't be the worst thing?

Freezing, after a certain point, is supposed to be just like falling asleep.

Hardy looks down the pier, dials back to something better, trying to give himself a reason to creak his old bones up. Where he lands is all the kids from town lining up on the pier whenever it got hot enough for him to whip his airboat around, spray them with water.

Where's Rex Allen got that old swamp machine, anyway?

It's a lot of boat, can get away from you, but that's no reason to mothball it. Out on the ice, though… Hardy guesses he understands. When the lake's icy slush, the airboat's golden, like it was born to this. But when it's frozen hard like this, there's no steering. If you have two people, then one can act like ballast, moving to the right side to weigh it down, make the boat tend that way. Forget about braking, though.

It's a good enough time, if you've *got* the time, and are dressed for the cold, but, in his time behind the badge, Hardy had usually left the airboat in the county garage for the duration of winter, too. Lonnie's cat's the real ticket for the snow, and if you need to go out onto the lake to pull in an ice skater with a busted knee, somebody in town's usually got a snowmobile fired up.

Hardy takes his right glove off, paws inside all his layers for his smokes.

He packs them, shakes one up, takes it with his lips, and then squints when he draws close to the match, more from the memory of smoke than the stinging presence of it—the wind's sucking it away almost before it even happens.

That first draw is always the sweetest, too.

Hardy holds it, holds it, can feel his lungs opening in that way he needs.

He blows it out in as tight a line as he can, like he's deliberating here, trying to figure something out, but he's not. Old men don't have to figure *shit* out. They just have to sit on a bench in the bitter cold and smoke their death sticks, and consider the white form taking shape out on the ice.

Hardy's been watching it a full ten seconds before he registers that it isn't just fog. Somebody's out there on the lake.

"What the—?" Hardy creaks, his heart thumping once, hard, in agreement.

This how it is, at the end? Not a horse, come to stomp you to death, but some reaper here to lead you away by the hand.

Maybe after opening your throat.

Or, Hardy surmises, maybe that's the version your dying mind kicks up, right? To make dying make sense. Probably he's just having a stroke or a heart attack.

Bring it, then, he says to the figure out there, gaining sharper edges now. And… swinging its arms like the Winter Olympics?

What kind of bullshit death dream is this supposed to be?

Hardy leans forward like that'll bring this into proper focus, and, sure enough, he wasn't hallucinating those arms, going back and forth like pendulums, like this shape, this person, this *thing*, is rushing toward him.

But something about the motion isn't right, too. At first Hardy thinks this is an ice skater, out long after they should be, but then he gets it: "Skis," he says, shaking his head about it, impressed.

Some idiot's out in this storm on cross-country *skis*. And in a white jacket and pants, at that. Even the helmet's white, like they want to be sure that when they get in trouble, nobody's going to be able to see them.

Hardy takes another drag and turns his head to the side to blow it out, his eyes never leaving this figure.

It's coming right at the pier, reaching out with poles to pull itself along. When it gets there it tucks like a downhill racer, whatever contraption that is in its backpack too tall *not* to duck. Whatever idiot this is slips through the posts then carves left, slides up onto shore right in front of Hardy, cocks purple goggles up on his helmet. Not to look at Hardy, out here freezing to death alone, but like to see what might have been chasing him, marvel at the trek he just made.

And that's a sleek recurve bow in his pack, Hardy can see now. It's even strung, for some fool reason.

"Ho!" he calls out.

The skier flinches, comes around fast, and—shit.

It's that goddamn history teacher, isn't it?

Figures: nobody actually *from* Idaho would be doing such a fool-headed thing as cross-country skiing on the lake in the middle of the worst storm in fifty years.

"Sheriff," Mr. Armitage says, lifting his left hand in greeting.

It's what this Claude Armitage still calls Hardy. It's what he calls him every time he comes around asking for an interview, and every time he leaves without one.

Hardy takes another drag.

Armitage poles over, opens his gloved hand to the bench beside Hardy, and Hardy shrugs.

Armitage sits. He's breathing hard, smiling with satisfaction, his long sandy hair falling down over his eyes when he takes his helmet off, clops it down onto the bench between them.

"You the cat that got the canary or what?" Hardy asks, offering the pack of cigarettes he's pretty sure is frozen to his glove.

Armitage just looks out over the lake like he owns it now that he's skied it.

It doesn't make Hardy revile him any less.

It's not because he's not Bear, it's… how can someone not even born in the state teach state *history*? And, would he even be here if the Independence Day Massacre had never happened?

He's a short-timer, as far as Hardy's concerned. No, worse: he's a *tourist*. Just, he's a tourist who happened to have a teaching certificate, at a time when there was a vacancy at the high school. But he's not about the kids. He's about the thrill of what happened right out here by the pier.

Hardy knows about the book this new history teacher's writing, yeah.

On the one hand, by the time it gets all the way written, Hardy'll probably be with Trudy. And Melanie.

On the other hand, the man's a scavenger.

Worse, Rex Allen explained on one of the times he had to come up himself to haul Hardy down, Armitage had been in the peanut gallery for the whole first year of Jennifer's trial down in Boise. Just taking notes and grinning, soaking it all in.

"Ready for that interview?" Armitage says, his voice all about good cheer and hopefulness.

Hardy chuckles. Armitage already knows what the answer is.

"Not really fit for humans, you know?" Hardy says, chucking his chin out to the lake, the weather.

"It's thick enough, isn't it?" Armitage says back about the ice, playing innocent, which is to say: working his way into Hardy's trust.

Or, trying to.

"Just don't come over by the dam," Hardy says, turning his head to blow smoke.

"Why, she back?" Armitage says then like an ambush, and Hardy can feel his face being watched so, so closely.

When he doesn't confirm or deny, Armitage bites his glove off, and, going slow like for permission, reaches over for the pack of cigarettes ice-welded to Hardy's glove.

Armitage pinches one up carefully, pulls the matchbook up from the cellophane, and lights up, holding it in deep just like Hardy did, even squinting when he lets it back out.

"I quit this six years ago," he says.

"I quit every day," Hardy informs him.

"Right there's where it happened," Armitage says about the pier then, as if still impressed—no: like he's in *church*. "Did you… I know you fired your service revolver four times that night. But at what? Can you tell me that, at least? At *who*, Sheriff? Who were you shooting at? Tell me that and I quit pestering you."

"There's blood on your glove, there," Hardy tells him back.

Armitage doesn't understand at first, then raises up the glove he took off.

It's spattered red.

"Unless you were painting a fire hydrant out there," Hardy adds.

"Hunh," Armitage says, turning the glove this way and that. He tilts his face up and stretches his lips down, showing the skin under his nose to Hardy. "I freeze up enough to have a nosebleed?"

Hardy snatches a look, shakes his head no.

"Oh yeah, oh yeah," Armitage says then, slipping back into the glove. "I *was* touching up a fire hydrant over there, how'd I forget?"

Hardy can't help but look where Armitage's meaning.

"Terra Nova," he says out loud, for both of them.

Armitage shrugs sure, Terra Nova, and Hardy—once a lawman, always suspicious—registers that across the lake's where this history teacher wants him looking.

Not back into town.

"Here," Armitage says, standing all at once, clomping around on his skis, which is a complicated enough maneuver that Hardy gets a good long look at his backside. His pack.

"So you hunt?" Hardy asks, already not believing it.

"*What?*" Armitage says, spinning around to what Hardy means: the oddball recurve, just as snow-white as the rest of his gear. "No, no—didn't even bring any arrows."

"Francie's husband'll write you up if you're hunting," Hardy warns.

"I would never—vegetarian," Armitage explains, holding his hands up as if to prove his innocence. "This is… you know the biathlon?" When Hardy doesn't dignify this, Armitage goes on: "It goes all the way back to the sixteenth century, Norway, which kind of makes sense. You cross-country it from point to point on a course, and there's these small little targets there. This is—I'm just trying to get used to having it on my back, like."

"Wheelbow wouldn't be so tall."

"Except the cams would freeze up. And there's no time to pack and unpack a rig, or take it apart and put it together."

"It's a timed event?"

"And points, and penalties… it's a whole thing. You watch the Olympics?"

Hardy takes a drag.

Armitage shrugs, looks around. "Here," he says, kind of

starting over, but extending a hand now. "I'll help you get back to… I don't even know where you live, do I? Pleasant Valley Assisted Living?"

Hardy lets his smoke seep out, like he's on fire inside.

He looks up the hill, to the nursing home, says, "Not yet, no."

Jennifer comes out of the restroom on the east wing, is opening and closing her hands by her thighs, telling herself over and over that this isn't happening, this isn't happening.

And, even if it is?

"It doesn't involve you, girl," she mutters to herself, to make it real. To get herself to believe it.

And, anyway, that senior hanging from the tree at Trail's End? She doesn't have to be Casey Becker, dying at the front of *Scream*. And these two kids down the hall, maybe it's just coincidence that their deaths line up with *Friday the 13th*.

Maybe Jennifer's remembering those movies wrong, too, right? The girl who believed in slashers, that was somebody else. This Jennifer doesn't even wear eyeliner anymore, and all the videotapes she used to have had to have been burned in a bonfire years ago already, just to watch that iridescent tape writhe.

Jennifer glares across the wide empty floor of the nursing home's lobby, at the other wing.

Because the phones are down, the kid who *was* working reception's gone on the snowmobile he evidently came on, is supposed to be coming back with the cavalry. Meaning: Banner.

That was five minutes ago, now. After probably an hour and a half of every nurse and administrator pinballing around, pulling their hair out, trying to find a manual for what to do in case of two teenage volunteers being slaughtered.

Nobody asked Jennifer what to do, of course. Her orders are just not to leave—like she could? But at least Cinn isn't her responsibility anymore. Presumably, competent medical staff have her tucked away in some safe part of this facility. If they're smart, they'll just give her a medical-grade roofie, so she can forget the last twenty-four hours, and maybe have a normal life from here on out.

But it'll take a lot more pills than that for Cinnamon to forget her parents, dead on the yacht, along with the rest of the Founders. Her dad was torn in half, wasn't he? No, no—Mars Baker was half in, half out of that window, maybe?

Cinn had to have walked past that. She has to still be walking past that every time she closes her eyes. It's a lot to lay on a kid.

And, "Founders," seriously? Jennifer hasn't thought that word in… god, *how* long? And, what, did they write the Constitution? Lay down the Oregon Trail? Drive the last spike into the intercontinental railroad?

All they "found" was a little girl who didn't know how to die, over on a shore they never should have broken ground on.

And, rich as they were, it was Proofrock that paid the price for that.

That was years ago already, though.

This is now. This is where Jennifer can prove that this isn't all happening again, that she's just falling back on old ways of thinking—ways that don't apply anymore.

Who can prove that to her, she's just down that opposite hall, too.

Jennifer retrieves her mostly empty coffee from the top of the water fountain, fake drinks it to mosey across the lobby, then sets it onto the front desk's high counter, having to really jostle it to get any of it to slosh up and out.

"Oops."

She reaches over the counter for a napkin but isn't as tall as the reception kid, so, thinking only of cleaning up this accidental mess, she steps behind the counter, uses a tissue to dab up the coffee. After which she's politely looking for the trash—she doesn't know this place, this is all so new.

It's all about frame of mind.

Then she leans forward on the counter again, wraps her hand around the coffee, and… nobody's even watching her little charade.

She sits down into the tall chair, and, after checking all around, presses the control that sinks the chair, bringing her head down to where it can hardly be seen anymore.

Perfect. Submarine girl. The human alligator.

If anybody steps up, asks what she's doing, she just needed an out-of-the-way chair to sit in? After seeing what she *saw*? Maybe she can even manufacture some sudden tears, if need be.

Already certain she won't be able to navigate Pleasant Valley's computer system, she pulls the big blue binder into her lap, which is going to be trickier to explain.

So: be fast.

Ninety seconds later, beside an exquisite drawing of a drum kit, she finds "Ginger Baker" in room 308W, "W" for "West." Which is good, since the east wing is where Mark and Kristen still are.

The keys are in a cabinet that has a lock on it, but, because this is Proofrock, not the Boise holding facility, that little key to the cabinet's on a hook up under the counter.

Jennifer rolls in the chair to the end of the counter and walks up from it smooth-criminal style, the key tight in her right hand, her coffee abandoned.

Easy as that.

You *can* do this, she tells herself, making time across the wide lobby.

"Oh, oh!" some woman says behind her, though.

Jennifer licks her lips, gets her eyes ready—Bambi, Bambi, you're Bambi—and, still walking, she turns around.

It's Christine Gillette, in her wheelchair.

"Your hair is different," she says, reaching for it.

Jennifer feels her face warm.

"Stacey Stacey Stacey Graves," Christine Gillette says, that jumprope lilt right there waiting, "she'll—"

"Put you in your grave," Jennifer finishes, not even really meaning to.

It's a spike in her heart, in her life.

Christine Gillette is the first person to have told her about Stacey Graves—used to, she was the only living person to have seen her.

If only it would have stayed that way.

"Did your history teacher give you a good grade?" Christine Gillette asks in her wavery grandma voice, lifting an ancient hand as if reaching to touch Jennifer.

"I'm sorry, I'm—" Jennifer says, trying to back away, escape this moment, not let it get her caught going down a hall she's not supposed to be in.

"You told me you would come back," Christine Gillette says. "And you did. You're here."

Jennifer blinks, her eyes heating up, her heart trying to escape her chest.

Girls without mothers fall apart on the inside when someone like Christine Gillette remembers them, notices their new hair.

But Jennifer's on a mission, here.

"I think—you've got me… I'm not—" she says, backing away, Christine Gillette's hand still raised, waiting. Jennifer wants to run to her, to fall to her knees, lay her head in the old woman's lap, let her pet her new hair down, but—

"Can you?" she says to a passing nurse. Then, quieter, just between them, "I think she… she thinks she knows me."

The nurse slows, looks between Christine Gillette and Jennifer.

"I knew you would come back," Christine Gillette says, and then the nurse is there between them, muttering to Christine Gillette like she's a child, asking who she thinks this pretty girl is, and Jennifer turns, isn't walking anymore, is scurrying, that key gouging into the skin of her palm, her knees knocking into each other, her heels hardly leaving the ground.

It's not easy, being a terrible person.

I'll come back, though, she tells Christine Gillette.

For the second time in ten years.

But right now, right now she has to get down the hall without anybody else stopping her.

"Ma'am, ma'am?" the nurse calls after her, but Jennifer pretends not to hear.

Twenty seconds later she's to 308, her head still jumping rope with that old rhyme:

Stacey Stacey Stacey Graves
Born to put you in your grave
You see her in the dark of night

And once you do you're lost from sight
Look for water, look for blood
Look for footprints in the mud
You never see her walk on grass
Don't slow down, she'll get your ass

But Stacey Graves is gone, Jennifer reminds herself. The lake finally took her.

Jennifer closes her eyes, makes herself say it the way it really happened: Ezekiel took her down to his holy church in Drown Town.

And that's that.

And she wasn't a monster any more than Jennifer was, when she was Jade. She just didn't understand.

So you had to do what you did, Jennifer tells herself.

She had to hug Stacey Graves's tiny body to her own and hold her under the lake that was poison to her, until they both drowned.

She had to.

And that doesn't make her like all the other Proofrockers who closed their doors to this hungry little girl, living like a cat in their dirt streets. It doesn't make her like the boys who threw that little girl out onto the water to prove she was a witch.

She's more like Stacey herself, she knows.

I would have bounced too, Jennifer knows.

She would have found the water hard, she would have stood up on it too, and run away on all fours, because balancing on top of the lake has to be a new thing, a scary thing, the scariest thing.

And where Stacey was running?

To find her mom.

Jennifer shakes her head, trying to quit this thinking.

What she needs now worse than anything is a cigarette, to fill her mind with delicious smoke, let her only think about inhaling, exhaling, all her capillaries opening up under her skin like some network of mushroom fibers struggling to the surface for a drink of moonlight.

"Okay, okay," she says, and, after checking both ways again, keys the door open and slips inside, shuts it soundlessly behind her.

This room is the twin to the one Jennifer talked to Christine Gillette in four years ago: hospital bed, nightstand, visitor's chair, wheelchair parked under the wall-mounted television, a tall, narrow door that must be a bathroom. The only difference is that now the television's a flat-screen.

Ginger Baker isn't watching it.

She's sitting in the window well, her back against the right side, her feet bare, the soles cracked, her hospital gown just a limp nothing. And her head, her hair: she's bald.

Out her window is Indian Lake, the frozen version. She's framed against it like she's the pastel foreground of the saddest postcard. And, except for the baldness, she might as well be her twin sister.

"You're early, it's not even prickly yet—" she says in a floaty voice, rubbing her palm over her smooth scalp, stopping because she's turned around, and Jennifer's not who she's supposed to be.

Story of her life.

"Hi," she says, kind of grinning apology, she hopes.

Ginger tilts her head over an evil little bit, taking Jennifer in.

"Who—who are *you*?" she finally asks, and there's something recite-y about the way she delivers it, like she's the computer version of a court stenographer, reading back words.

"Letha's friend," Jennifer mumbles.

This is exactly the back and forth she had with either Cinnamon or Ginger in the tight hallway of the yacht, right outside the bathroom—right after Jennifer'd shaved all *her* hair off.

"Does her dad know you're spending the night?" Ginger asks, liking that Jennifer knows her lines, it seems.

Ginger's legs come down from the window well, her feet finding the floor exactly as a spider's might.

"He—he ordered us that movie," Jennifer says, suddenly very aware that the door behind her is locked tight, and that no one knows she's here.

"No, no," Ginger says, coming over the bed instead of around it. Not stepping up onto it, but keeping her eyes locked on Jennifer's, and at the same level, her arms and legs crawling her across the mattress.

Jennifer sucks her breath in and then Ginger's there.

"He ordered us *a* movie," she says, her breath hot on Jennifer's lips, her eyes unblinking, boring in. "That's what you said, remember? What was the movie? Letha doesn't remember."

"K-K-*Kristy*," Jennifer says, stepping back, her elbows right against the door now.

"The bathroom's not even steamy," Ginger says, about the lie Jennifer—*Jade*—had told that night, with the towel around her head: that she had just been taking a shower.

And no, Theo Mondragon *didn't* know she was there.

"Who did you think I was, just now?" Jennifer asks. It's all she can think of, but it's better than the crackly silence.

Ginger spins, overplaying like a dancer on stage, and walks a straight line back to the window. But she's not looking out it. Not really. She's watching Jennifer in the reflection.

"My sister," Ginger says. "She cuts my hair for me. If anybody else tries, I bite them." She clacks her teeth as if Jennifer needs that sound. "It keeps them on their toes," Ginger adds, and Jennifer can see one side of her mouth grinning in the reflection.

She can also see that Ginger *wants* her to see this.

She spins, leans back against the ledge, her hands on it, and the way she's standing now is showy, like she's playing for the back rows.

"They have to cut it all off because if they don't I *pull* it," Ginger says, batting her eyes, her delivery more childlike, now—more fake innocent, emphasizing that this is a game.

And nothing she's said has told Jennifer which twin she was in the hall that night.

"I'm sorry about your parents," she says.

Ginger shrugs one shoulder like surely Jennifer can do better than that.

"It's happening again, isn't it?" Ginger says flatly.

Jennifer refocuses her eyes to stare out across Indian Lake, and all at once she gets why access to Ginger Baker is limited: What is there to say to her that won't compound her situation? Make it worse?

Does Jennifer tell her there's two dead high schoolers down the hall, or does she lie that everything's fine? Will news of another killer in Proofrock send Ginger spiraling, or will it confirm whatever she's already thinking?

"It's her," Ginger says, pooching her lips out in what feels to Jennifer like a junior high way. Which she guesses must be about how old Ginger was the night her parents were killed on the yacht.

What she wants to ask is what Ginger lived on those weeks in the national forest, what she saw, what she was thinking, but, first—

"It's not Stacey Graves," Jennifer says. "I killed her."

Ginger stares right into Jennifer's soul about this, and finally the dry corners of her sharp lips quirk up.

"Pronoun antecedents," she says. "We're talking about two different people, aren't we?"

Jennifer slows her thinking down, dials all around Proofrock's history, trying to come up with what other "she" there could be.

Ginger is amused with this, it seems.

"Stacey Graves's *mom*?" Jennifer tries at last.

"Her mom?" Ginger says back with an insulted sneer.

"She was—" Jennifer starts, then starts again: "Her husband killed her, probably stashed her over on the Terra Nova side of... in the national forest. Before Stacey Graves, she was the boogeyman of Indian Lake."

"You've seen her?"

"She's just a story."

"Like her daughter."

Jennifer doesn't have any answer for this.

"I don't know this one's name," Ginger says at last.

"'This one,'" Jennifer repeats, tasting it, then spitting it out. "You don't—it's this guy named Dark Mill South. It's *definitely* him. We found his truck. The truck he stole, I mean."

"That's a good name," Ginger says, nodding as if she's liking it more and more each time she re-hears it in her head.

"Names don't matter," Jennifer says. "It's what they do that matters."

"They."

"Killers."

"Slashers."

"Whatever."

"You're different now."

"So are you."

"Why are you here? Why did you steal that key?"

Jennifer looks down to the key pinched between her thumb and index finger.

"Because it's starting again," Ginger says for Jennifer, then stands all at once, alert in a new and excited way.

"What?" Jennifer asks, looking around, ready to run.

"That's locked?" Ginger asks, about the door.

Jennifer nods slowly, not exactly loving this.

Ginger bounds across the room, reaches up behind the flat-screen television, her back to Jennifer, and pulls… *some*thing down, leans her face to it.

When she turns around, Jennifer nearly screams: Ginger's wearing a Hannibal Lecter mask over her lower face.

Jennifer shakes her head no about this, but Ginger's already nodding yes, yes, yes.

"They let me do crafts with kindergarten scissors," she says, her voice hardly muffled, because… this mask isn't leather like the one in the movie. It's dummied together from construction paper, it looks like.

But the effect is the same: it erases the mouth, gives those dead X-ray eyes just the right laser focus.

"I can be your, your, your *insider*," Ginger loud-whispers conspiratorially. "The one who tells you things you would never know on your own. Never figure out."

"I don't—"

"For quid pro quo, of course," Ginger adds.

"What would you want?" Jennifer says, already sure the

answer is going to be the key in her hand. Because that's just what Proofrock needs: a girl in a Hannibal Lecter mask skulking around.

"*Revenge*," Ginger says, though.

"Against who?"

"My sister, my mother, my sister, my—" Ginger covers her masked mouth politely, somehow conjuring dimples. "No, just my sister," she goes on flatly. "My mom's already—"

She conks her head over to indicate "dead."

"That's not very respectful," Jennifer says.

"She isn't?" Ginger says back. "Is yours?"

Jennifer doesn't answer, just stares.

Ginger shrugs, sashays across the room and back again like she's a model, like this is a runway.

"You don't want revenge on your sister," Jennifer tells her.

"She, um, *left* me over there in that floating coffin for four *weeks*?" Ginger says, her intonation one-hundred-percent sorority girl now—she's Cici from *Scream* 2. Who's really Buffy 2, Kristy Swanson being Buffy Prime, but—

Jennifer shakes her head, doesn't go down those rabbit holes anymore. Not even just to hide.

"I thought you were supposed to be catatonic," she says.

"Caught me on a good day."

"Believe me, it's not a good day."

"It *can* be..." Ginger says, and takes a knee, reaches up under her bed, then reaches farther. When she comes back, it's with... a handful of pills. She sifts them down onto her bed.

"You take the blue pill, the story ends," she says, doing her best Laurence Fishburne. "You take the *red* pill, though, then you stay in Wonderland and I show you how deep the rabbit hole goes."

In her head, Jennifer's screaming right now. How did this girl know she was just *thinking* about rabbit holes?

No, she does not want to play quid pro quo, here, thank you. She doesn't even really want to be here anymore.

"Listen," she says. "You've got a lot going on, I just—I only dropped in to—"

"Apologize?"

It hangs between them, then hangs between them some more, Ginger drilling it home with her oh-so-innocent eyes.

"For what?" Jennifer finally has to ask. Which isn't to say she isn't already listing her crimes against Ginger Baker in her head: not stopping Stacey Graves from killing Mars Baker and Macy Todd; leaving Ginger down in the bloody bowels of that yacht; not coming back to save her. And then there's the one everybody blames her for: the Independence Day Massacre.

How's one "sorry" supposed to cover all that?

"For not coming to see me when you got back to town," Ginger says, peeling out of her mask, thank you. "We survivors have to stick together, don't we?"

Is she looking for another sister, now that she's aligned against Cinn?

"Natural color?" Ginger asks then, lifting some of Jennifer's hair. "I remember you used to keep it all..." She explodes her fingers from her own naked head, meaning "every color," Jennifer guesses. Which is just about right. "And," Ginger goes on, "I can see your eyes now, without all that make-up. You're kind of a stunner, aren't you?"

Jennifer shakes her head slightly: no, she isn't.

"Listen, I really—" she starts, lifting her right hand to show the key, signal that this was a mistake, she shouldn't be here.

"But we still haven't cracked the Big Pronoun Mystery," Ginger says, sitting down in the wheelchair. She offers the visitor chair to Jennifer then expertly backs up, stopping with a little wheelie that she maintains.

Jennifer shakes her head but takes that chair, says, "Why do you even have that in here?"—the wheelchair.

"The meds can leave me groggy," Ginger says, already dismissing it with a shrug. "Staff are 'very concerned' about their star patient falling and hurting herself."

"Star patient?"

"My dad's firm owns this place now."

"So that means *you* own it."

"Cinn and me, yeah. You could say that. But it's for me, really. Until I'm, you know, compos mentis."

"You seem pretty with it to me."

"I have my moments. But I change channels really fast. And I suffer from 'delusions.' My version of reality isn't the 'consensually agreed upon' one."

"Or you just didn't want to go to high school."

"You want to ask how I survived over there," Ginger says—the national forest.

"I want to solve this Big Pronoun Mystery."

"Good, good," Ginger says, letting her front wheels down so gently. "So it's not that little dead girl, and it's not her dead mother either—oh, speaking of."

"The mom?"

"The girl." Ginger tilts onto her back wheels again, the veins on her forearms standing out, making her look carved from stone. "We—me and Cinn—we used to leave little trinkets on shore for her."

"For *Stacey Graves*?"

Ginger smiles to finally have all of Jennifer's attention. "We thought she was a raccoon at first. Until we, you know, set up one of our dad's trail cams."

"When was this?"

"May, June? I'd have to look at the timestamps."

"Plural?"

"'Plural,' 'pronouns'... this is kind of *like* high school, isn't it?"

"You two knew she was there?"

"We knew somebody was taking the treasures we left on the shore. Then Cinn thought to clear the gravel out, so we could be Nancy Drew, cast an impression in the sand. We were expecting a raccoon. We got a bare human foot."

"No."

Ginger shrugs like this doesn't matter.

"But you got her on video?" Jennifer says, ready to come up from her chair, lodge an objection to the judge down in Boise—*here's* some evidence, Your Honor.

"It was all, you know," Ginger says. "Shadowy? But yeah, you could see her. I don't think she understood cameras and technology. Why would she?"

"Did you tell your parents? *Any* of the parents?"

"Would you have?" Ginger asks. "We had a secret new playmate." She shrugs. "We didn't know how mad she could get, though."

"How did you live over there, Ginger? You should have starved the first week."

"Maybe it was communion wafers," she says, turning this way and that on her rear wheels now, the grey rubber squelching against the tile. "Manna from heaven, right?"

"Where are these recordings?"

"We put them on our phones—oh, oh. Graduation? When Letha graduated? We were huddled over our phones, watching that little girl. She was the best secret ever."

"Cinn knows about this too?"

"She doesn't remember it the same anymore."

"Can I see?" Jennifer asks.

"You really want to?" Ginger asks. *"Again?"*

"Please."

"So you can know you're not crazy, I get it."

Jennifer just stares at Ginger's aquamarine sternum.

"But, you know," Ginger says, wheelieing back again, having to grab hard at the hand rims to keep from tipping over. "That was a wet night, wasn't it? July third? Did *your* phone survive?"

Jennifer shakes her head no, of course it didn't.

"Cinn's either," Ginger says, like apologizing. Except she's loving this.

"Yours?" Jennifer asks.

"I was a wild girl living in the trees," Ginger says. "Wild girls don't bring their phones with them."

"And by the time you got back… it was gone, wasn't it?"

Ginger shrugs it true.

Jennifer sits back, disgusted.

"You really still want proof, though?" Ginger asks. "Do you think that the rest of the world seeing her would be… what? Redemption?"

"So who *are* you talking about, then?" Jennifer asks back. "Who antecedes that pronoun?"

"Big word."

"Important stuff."

"Maybe I'm just lonely for conversation," Ginger says. "I'm a spider, and this is my web, and—"

"Cut the crap."

Ginger grins into her chest, caught.

When she looks back up, she's got a different mask on, now—it must have been tucked in behind the Lecter one.

This one's Phantom of the Opera: half her face in white.

"You like masks," Jennifer says.

"You used to," Ginger says back.

"How would you know?"

"Your file in the main office," she says, shrugging one shoulder.

"Pleasant Valley has a file on me?"

"Henderson High does."

Jennifer nods. That tracks. "Well, that's not me anymore," she says. "I used to be all… horror, slashers, masks, all of that."

"Now?"

"Now I'm not."

"You grew out of it?"

"More like it nearly killed me."

"It did kill a lot of other people, didn't it?" Ginger says, kind of slyly.

Jennifer knows not to take that bait. "The Big Pronoun Mystery," she says instead. "It's your sister, isn't it?"

"Cinn?" Ginger says, trying not to laugh. "Bzzt, no, sorry."

"My mom, then."

"Your mom's out chopping necks and taking names?"

"You think bringing her up will hurt me, I mean."

"Why would I want to hurt you?"

"You're disconnected from reality."

"Well—granted, yeah, guilty as charged," Ginger says, offering her wrists for Jennifer's cuffs. "But… you saved us all that night."

"You know?"

"Letha told us."

"You and Cinn."

"And Gal, yeah. Lemmy was too young to… you know."

"The children of Terra Nova."

"You make it sound like a horror movie."

"It wasn't?"

"I mean, I thought you were over all that."

"Maybe it's you," Jennifer says then. "Maybe it's you out there chopping heads and taking names."

"Not the Reaper, the Bowman Butcher, the Ninety-Eye Killer?"

His name falls flat between them.

"Cinn told you?"

"Haven't seen Sister Dear since Monday," Ginger says, rubbing her shaved scalp as if in memory of a haircut. "According to this"—the television above her—"Dark Mill South's transport went missing yesterday, right?"

"Cinn'll tell you all about it," Jennifer mumbles. "If she lives."

Ginger hears this but doesn't respond. Just lets it settle, the crow's feet she doesn't really have crinkling with thought.

"I say *she*," she finally says. "But maybe 'it' would be more accurate."

Jennifer looks up, waiting this out. Trying not to seed any more distractions for Ginger to cultivate, trace out.

"After the…" Ginger says, doing her fingers like pulling gossamer threads from the air, "after the—"

"*Jaws*," Jennifer fills in.

Ginger nods, says, "Not like *right* after, but... weeks? After they found me. September, I guess. There were still people coming to town and taking selfies out on the pier. But my doctors thought... they wanted me to, like, finally, symbolically, *therapeutically*, come across the lake like Cinn and Gal did?"

"With Shooting Glasses."

"What? No, that—'Grade... *Paulson*,' that was his name, right?"

Jennifer just glares.

"Anyway, my dad's firm got the lake shut down for the day. Including the pier. And then Security—they ran any lookyloos off, right? So we had... where it happened all to ourselves. I mean, me and Cinn, and Gal, and Dr. Trin. We didn't re-inflate that screen, but Dr. Trin played the movie through some speakers, so it was kind of like the movie was playing."

"She played *Jaws*?"

"It was what was playing that night, right? She was—she said that I was still stuck over on the other side of the lake, in my head. But Cinn wasn't. So she had Gal like lead me out into those shallows until I couldn't touch, and—"

"Not your sister?"

"I *was* my sister, yeah?" Ginger says, obviously. "And, you know, we swam for it, for the pier. So I could climb up, reclaim my sanity, whatever."

Jennifer doesn't say anything, is just watching.

Ginger lowers her face into her left hand, leaves the mask there, looks up as herself and swallows, like being serious here. Earnest. Real.

"When I went to grab up onto it, though, I kind of got swept under, right?"

"Under the pier."

"They got me back out fast, it was no danger, but, while I was under there, I… I saw something."

"No," Jennifer says.

"Yes," Ginger says back. "It was up under the planks, the part of the pier everybody walks on. It looked like a… like a tumor, I guess? Like a big wad of bloody bubble gum. But with tendrils, to hold onto the wood."

"Hold *on*?"

"It probably got sloshed up there during the… you know. Movie. Some piece of somebody."

"But this is September."

"Yeah," Ginger says. "And it was, like, not pulsing, but kind of writhing, maybe? I saw it twitch, I mean. And then Gal was pulling me back into the sunlight, to complete my therapy. But I got Cinn to sneak me out—this is back when my door didn't lock—and we went out there at night, and stole those two boards that whatever it was had been attached to. And hid them back in that little bay."

"Devil's Creek," Jennifer fills in.

"I guess so? Not all the way over to Letha's."

To the Tompkins place. Jennifer nods: Devil's Creek.

"There's, like, an old barge or something there, right?" Ginger says. "It's kind of part of the shore now, I don't know."

Jennifer nods, remembers it: before it got all grody, it's what the projector used to sit on for the Fourth of July. Back when she was in elementary.

"It needed *water* is the thing," Ginger says.

"*It*," Jennifer repeats.

"Her," Ginger corrects. "I couldn't go out anymore, they

started locking my door after that, but Cinn told me. It was growing. She found a cat collar in the water under it, meaning it had probably *eaten* that cat, so she started feeding it. Like, roadkill and stuff. It got bigger and bigger, and finally—"

"No."

"You're probably right," Ginger said. "I'm the crazy girl from Terra Nova. The mad sister in the attic."

"Why would Cinn lie to you like that, though?"

"You're sure she was lying?"

"You're saying it grew into a *girl*?"

"Cinn gave her one of Gal's old nightgowns."

"Why not one of her own?"

"She's tall and glamorous. Runs in the family."

She holds her arm out straight and rolls her hand as if luxuriating in her own height, her glamorous length.

"Galatea was in on this?" Jennifer asks.

"She's got so many clothes," Ginger says, shaking her head no.

"This is bullshit," Jennifer says. "Where is she now, then?"

"All she does is stand on shore and look out across the water," Ginger says, turning to look out across Indian Lake herself.

"It's not Stacey."

"The Lake Witch," Ginger completes. Then she shrugs. "If it's not her, then it's probably just some… a *different* dead girl? They're kind of what we're known for around here, right?"

"So Cinn has her? Is that what you're saying?"

"She's keeping her over in one of the houses," Ginger says.

Jennifer considers this, comes back with, "Terra Nova."

Ginger nods, looks at the door of her room as if hearing something Jennifer isn't.

"Why?" Jennifer asks.

"She got loose, didn't she?" Ginger says. "I heard everybody running past. They think I'm oblivious in here, but… *Someone's Watching*, 1978. John Carpenter."

"It's actually *Someone's Watching Me*," Jennifer says, hitting the "me" just hard enough. "And you probably want his *Eyes of Laura Mars*, really. Same year."

"Because I'm looking out my sister's eyes?" Ginger asks, raising her lips. "Yuck! No thank you!"

She clops the Lecter mask on, makes the lip-sucking sound behind it somehow.

"Now the quid pro quo part," she says, "since I solved the Big Pronoun Mystery, I mean."

"That was only a mystery because you made it a mystery."

"Girl's gotta have her fun."

"And it's a bullshit story," Jennifer goes on. "Somebody's seen *Hellraiser* too many times."

"*Hellraiser*?"

"That thing growing between the boards. That's Frank. That's how he comes back."

"Sorry."

"You know John Carpenter's deep cuts, but not Clive Barker's big one?"

"Clive who?"

Jennifer closes her eyes in pain. Stands.

"This has been fun," she says. "Or something."

"Will you be coming back to see me?"

"So you can make more stuff up?"

"You'll be just troping around, then?"

"What?"

"You don't even know—" Ginger says, shrugging it off, taking a different direction, it feels like. She stands, her back straighter, more "male" somehow. Something about her shoulders, her sudden new carriage. "What's wrong?" she says in a voice not quite her own. "Something you might have heard about mixing Pop Rocks and soda?"

"I don't play these games anymore," Jennifer says.

"Don't you guys get it?" Ginger says in a now-*different* voice. "Come on, it's just like that *urban legend*." Then, in yet a different voice: "I ain't gonna bite you."

"What are you getting at, Ginger?"

"That you've gone from being the final girl to..." She has to stop to cover her laugh with the back of her hand, then shake her head in apology for that slip. "Now you're the adult who doesn't believe this is really happening. And, what always happens to that adult? Do you still remember, or do you forget all the true things when you grow up, Peter Pan?"

"Fuck you, little girl."

"Yeah, no," Ginger says. "That's what you have to say, I get it now. I thought I was talking to a believer, but... you've changed, *Jennifer*."

"I deal in facts," Jennifer says, stepping in. "And the fact is, Dark Mill South is definitely in town. Last night he almost killed your sister. Two hours ago, he killed two of your classmates down the hall."

"Not *my* classmates," Ginger says. "I don't go to high school, remember?"

"Your sister's classmates, then."

"Which... does that tell you anything, ex–final girl? Or—you're Velma now, aren't you?"

"You're too young to know *Scooby-Doo*."

"I was also too young to see my parents torn to pieces."

Ginger glares this home.

Jennifer spins away, strides across to the door.

"You're just trying to pit me against your sister," she says, feeling for the keyhole.

"Why would I do that?" Ginger asks back, oh-so-sweet again.

"Because she left you over there."

"Oh yeah," Ginger says flatly. "That."

"And now she's getting to go to high school and have dates and everything else."

"You really think I want to go to *Henderson High*?" Ginger asks, hitting the name hard enough that it's an insult.

Click.

The door sighs back.

"*You* want to go back, though, don't you?" Ginger says, from the window well again, as if the room's resetting now that Jennifer's on the way out. "Your better self is buried back in those halls, isn't it? Jade the fighter. Jade the survivor. Jade the final girl."

"It's good you're locked up," Jennifer says back to her.

"Better get to class," Ginger says, speaking into her reflection again. "Don't want to miss first bell."

Strip-HORSE with Wynona and Abby is everything Jensen hoped it would be.

He's down to the shorts he had under his ski pants, and all around the gym floor it's cast-off clothes, like they're shooting baskets in a laundry hamper.

When Wynona missed her first shot, she could have taken her headband off, she could have stepped out of a shoe, she could have rolled her bracelet off her arm, even. But, by the time the ball was on its second bounce, she was peeling her t-shirt up and off.

Yellow bra.

"Get out…" Jensen had told her, not meaning that at all.

Even better, Wynona's a *volleyball* player. Meaning she doesn't know hoops, is going to be down to nothing in no time.

Abby's smoking them both, though.

When Jensen swung by Wynona's on his snowmobile to show off the Henderson High metal shop key he wasn't exactly supposed to have, though, Abby had been there, and it wasn't like he could ask Wynona to climb aboard without taking Abs as well.

What color will her bra be?

And, will it even matter?

The shot she's trying now isn't just from the three-point line where it flattens out over on the side, but she's only got one foot inbounds, meaning she's shooting from behind the backboard a bit, is going to have to hike that ball in a rainbow arc to get it up and over.

Girls aren't really supposed to have the upper body strength for that kind of fling, either, are they? It's not like Abs is tall or solid, even. She's lucky if she's five-six, and she probably wouldn't push the scale past a hundred.

Jensen's never really considered her before—all those long skirts, her hair always tied back in a severe bun—but, now…

It's just because she's beating you, he tells himself.

Wynona, though. Goddamn. Even Jensen's dad has to avert his eyes when she's over to play video games or whatever. Jensen's not sure if she's Mexican or Indian or half-Black or all-Black or Brazilian or Mayan or Egyptian or what, but it doesn't really matter.

What does is her bright yellow bra, with the delicate scallops at the top. And how it's just barely enough to cover all she's got.

As if Jensen can possibly focus on making Abs's impossible shot?

But he's got to try.

"Like this?" he says, balancing on one foot, the other hovering past the baseline like the gym floor on that side's lava.

"Except you're falling too," Abs tells him, bouncing the ball more *at* him than to him.

"Last three seconds!" Wynona yells, and then jumps with both feet into either a mockery of some cheer or a real cheer.

Again: hardly matters.

What does is the way she's jogging in place now, shaking pompoms she doesn't have over her head.

Thank the dark gods for this storm.

And thank them as well that Kristen was at work, that nobody answered at Cinn's house on the hill, that Gwen's… Jensen isn't sure what was going on at Gwen's. Just, through the window, her mom was walking around the living room, turning all the mirrors around to face the wall.

Who cares.

If any of them *had* been home?

Then this game of HORSE probably doesn't happen.

Too? If Jensen can trade his actual soul to make this shot, then Wynona's going to have to make it just the same.

At which point things are going to get real interesting.

Never mind that they're playing by candlelight—Yankee candles Abs somehow knew were in the Chemistry supply closet.

Never mind that Jensen's sport is actually football, that basketball's always been kind of stupid—you can't even hit other players? Never mind that, after walking in through the metal shop's ventilation door, he'd sparked up a little "mood emollient," as the football team calls it.

It went into his lungs hot, smoked his brain, and shot capillaries through his eyes: perfect.

According to his dad, back in the day they called weed the "anti-elastic," because of its effect on girls' panties, but Jensen's mom hits him on the shoulder with the back of her hand when he says that.

Jensen knows, of course, that she was pregnant when she walked the stage for her Henderson High diploma, though, so: Dad's probably right.

And, while this strain of mood emollient makes dribbling a syrupy enterprise at best, and kind of essentially amusing, it's gifting Jensen some Adderall-level focus right now, as he's falling out of bounds—which is to say, everything's moving *so*, so slow. He's the only one at normal speed here. He's got enough time to zero in on the basket, so far away, and to also sneak another look at Wynona in her yellow bra, bouncing through her cheer, about to surge up *out* of that bra, and he even clocks Abs, using her foot to nudge one of the Yankee candles back an inch or two, so the fifteen little sources of light oval'd around them can be more of an OCD half-oval.

Mood emollient, Jensen says in his head, for luck. And: *Yellow bra, yellowbra, candelabra—*

And now he's waited too long, is sort of really falling, shit.

"Ha!" he says, and cranks the ball up and out, out and up, more of a fourth-grade Hail Mary than an actual shot, he has to admit, but it's not like he was in a position to choose, either.

While the ball hangs in its impossible arc, rotating sideways, it looks like, which can't be right, can't be good—fucking *basket*ball—he sneaks another look over at Wynona, since her eyes are going to be tracking this shot.

Instead he finds Abby Grandlin, staring right at him.

In her eyes, he can read everything: she knows she's the third-wheel here, she knows she's the interloper, the unwanted party, the party *killer*, so she's going to step into that role with both feet, no matter how naked Wynona gets.

Nothing's gonna be happening up here except a little harmless, candlelit nudity.

And some HORSE.

How did you even make *this shot?* Jensen asks her back, with his eyes.

I can ride a motorcycle too, Abby says back, with her sneer. *I can shoot a gun, I can play poker—I even wear boxers when I sleep, how's that?*

Jensen's going to think something back to that sneer, something good, something perfect, except… now he's thinking about Abs in boxers and a little half-shirt, getting ready for bed, sneaking a look in the oval mirror probably in her bedroom, and—

Shit.

Isn't there something else going on?

The shot, yeah.

It hangs, hangs, it wobbles a bit, and, still not fallen all the way down, Jensen holds both fists up in victory.

Of the ball clanging off the back of the backboard.

He falls without his hands there to catch him, without his brain to remind about things like gravity, and his head slings down, rebounds off this stupid hardwood floor, which—"hard, wood," ha.

The pain cuts that short. The pain and the heat.

"Game over, game over…" he mutters, and it's like his mouth is far away from where he is.

The candlelight from the *non-candelabra* doesn't help. The mood emollient doesn't help.

But Wynona is bounding to him, so… there's that, yeah.

She leans over him, *all* the way over, holding his head in her hands, then shifting to come around, let him rest in her lap.

For a flash he sees her hand and it's dripping red.

From him?

But he just fell down shooting a stupid basketball, didn't he?

This isn't even a contact sport. It's for wimps who don't want to catch a shoulder to the gut, a spear to the ribs, a secret elbow to the throat.

"What?" he says.

"Your ear, your ear," Wynona's saying.

Abby Grandlin is standing over him. Judging him. Isn't her dad an ex-preacher or something? He can see that in her, now.

"It's getting on your—" she says, flinging her hand to Wynona.

"Oh!" Wynona says, and something shifts behind Jensen.

The next thing is Wynona's yellow bra, floating through the air to Abs.

"Can you?" she says.

"Seriously?" Abs says.

But she's going to do it, Jensen can tell. Because girls like her don't tolerate needless stains.

The best blood I've ever spilled, Jensen tells himself.

And: he's got to keep bleeding, here.

Abs steps away, out of the light, and then Wynona's thin t-shirt comes sailing out of the darkness. It splats on Jensen's stomach and his head jostles again when the formerly naked—*mostly* naked—Wynona slithers into that terrible, terrible invention, that… that "shirt."

"I don't care about this one," she says, her face right down to Jensen, her hair shrouding them both.

"I'm sorry about your, about your—" he says, trying to untangle *yellow* from *bra*.

"It just needs cold water," Wynona says, then she turns her face up, calls after Abs: "And hydrogen peroxide! That's what my mom uses!"

The door out in the hall closes a moment later.

"She knows," Wynona assures Jensen. As if he cares about stains.

Her uncontained breasts aren't just inches from the back of his head at this perfect moment in time. They're poking into him. Smushing into him. He's making contact at last.

This is the best snowstorm ever. The best game of HORSE. The best day, period.

If he dies now, then everything else was so worth it.

He's a man, now.

And he'll even have the scar to prove it.

He feels up for where the blood's seeping, and… it's not his ear? He thought surely that's what he'd split.

He flinches from the dryness of his fingertip, though.

It's whatever that part of the skull is behind his ear. The skin there's thin, and there's no meat between it and the bone.

So what. Screw it.

He'll bang his head on the gym floor again if it means lying like this one minute longer. His brains can start oozing out and that'll be just fine. Who needs them.

All he needs is Wynona.

Before this exact moment, too, he hadn't really been committed to college, even though it was free. More school? Why?

But? If this is the kind of action on whatever college campus takes him and his guaranteed tuition dollars, then sign him up, please.

This is exactly why he was born, one hundred percent: to have Wynona's sharp, heavy breasts just a thirty-secondth of an inch of ringspun fabric away.

"*What?*" she says then, shifting under him. Becoming more alert.

Jensen lifts his head as much as he can while still playacting weak and hurt.

It's one of the Yankee candles on the other side of the court. It's rolling on its side?

Oh: because of the basketball that just hit it.

The ball crosses the top of the key, takes another candle out. This one stays lit, makes the shadows crazy.

"Abs!" Wynona calls out. "This isn't funny!"

"Wh-what?" Jensen says, his hand coming up to circle Wynona's right wrist, so as to keep her pressing into him.

"She told me not to come up here," she says down to him, still studying the shadows. "That you only wanted one thing."

"I just wanted… to play basketball," Jensen says, going for the Oscar.

"Not me," Wynona says with an apologetic grin, giving Jensen a glimpse of what could have been, what almost was, and it's painful enough that he feels his split skin contracting in defeat, baring ever more of his skull to the air.

"We still—we still can," he creaks out to the idea of Abby, Abs… his thoughts are gumming together, slowing him down.

Or maybe it's just that all his blood is elsewhere, as his dad likes to say.

Ha ha ha.

But then Abby's back from the water fountain approximately eighty-two hours too soon, and, apparently, even though she's never a blurry face at the parties, she did about eight shots of Fireball in the hall, because, man, she's everywhere, she can hardly walk a straight line anymore.

"Abs?" Wynona says.

It doesn't stop Abby from stumbling into the arc of candles she was so worried about, and kicking through them on her way down to the floor.

The shadows lunge this way and that, stabbing darkness all over the gym.

"You're going to—!" Wynona says, pushing back from Jensen, his head clopping the hardwood again.

He rolls over, away from the dull pain behind his ear, and the basketball is a giant boulder coming for his face. He reaches up through the thick, thick air to bat the ball away, but it taps into his face all the same.

When a scream pierces the dark gym, his hand that failed at stopping the basketball continues on its slow path, feeling his rubbery lips now, to see if it's him making that noise. If it is, then that ball hitting cheek must have hurt more than he's registered yet.

It's not him screaming, though.

Wynona.

Because, because—Jensen can see why now. It's Abby. She's fallen with the hurt side of her face up, like her neck knew to protect it from more injury.

Like that matters anymore, shit.

The left side of Abby Grandlin's face is wreckage, is trash, is… it's been caved in, the sinus on that side open to the air, her left eye bulged out, flopping on what's left of her cheek. On what's *gone* of her cheek.

This can only mean someone was driving a car down the main hall, and Abby was bent down to tie her shoe, and looked up a moment too late, into the headlight inches from her face.

That tracks, to Jensen.

Until he sees the white shards embedded in Abby's skin, and meat.

That's not bone.

"John glass," he mutters, sputtering up frothy blood of his own. From a *head wound*? What?

John glass is what his dad, a wannabe flint knapper, practices on, since real flint costs a penny or two. John glass is shards of broken toilet that can be shaped into arrowheads, spearpoints, handaxes.

Somebody smashed Abby in the face with a part of a toilet. Probably the lid?

Well, maybe they held her in front of a toilet and slammed her face into the bowl, who knows.

Either way, Jensen had it right: game *over*.

The blood that's supposed to be inside Abby Grandlin is just seeping out now. Which is fairly bad news. You don't have to go to college to know that.

The real question Jensen needs answered here, he figures, still processing through the mood emollient, is… *who?* Kind of related, he guesses: *why?*

He tries to crank up high enough to see the dark doorway that opens onto the hall Abby stumbled in from, which is the first step in solving this small mystery, but then Wynona's screaming again, from deeper down, and what the football team says about her is so, so right: girl's got a serious set of *lungs* on her.

"I think—she probably just needs to lie down a bit," Jensen hears himself saying, trying to get Wynona to believe, but her footsteps are already padding away somewhere behind, behind.

And then… stopping?

"Seriously?" Jensen hears her say. Or, she says most of it. He's not sure exactly what's happened to the very end of the word, though. Not until he rolls his numb body over.

Wynona is on her knees, and, shoved into her mouth, as near as he can tell, and standing straight up above her, is—

"No fucking way," he says, with sort of a chuckle.

It's the Regionals trophy from the case by the main office, from the year after the massacre, when the team was dedicating every game to the victims, so went through the whole season charmed. The trophy's two feet long, or tall, or high.

More, when you add Wynona under it.

Well, not anymore. She's slumping over, to the side. When the hard, square, sharp-edged base of the trophy whips into the hardwood, Jensen winces. Coach is *not* going to like that chip in his gym floor.

And then things speed up all at once, like all the sensory intake he's had on delay is crashing the gates at once.

"*Tilt, tilt*," he mumbles—another Dad standby, from when he's drinking—and it gets Jensen vertical, more or less. Falling again, but he can direct this fall into a run, can't he?

Oh, he can.

And not towards Abby, because if he tries to vault over her, he'll end up splatting *into* her. Instead he stumbles toward the stands, because... whoever deep-throated Wynona with that trophy has to have done it inbounds, yes?

Meaning, get *out* of bounds, Jensen.

Go north, young man. Up, up, up.

And, as luck would have it—when you're charmed, you're charmed—the one thing Jensen's always best at in practice, that he's always a natural at, it's running bleachers. It's something about, as Coach says, being able to "commit to the flop," that being the only way to get into the wrongfooted rhythm of these long concrete steps.

Trying to hold his brain in with his right hand, he slithers up through the rails, is in the stands, his legs pumping like the machines they are, the gym floor and all its dangers falling away behind him. He doesn't run higher, he *crashes* higher.

At the top, then, in the blackest darkness he's ever known, he keeps one hand to the cinderblock back wall and runs hard for the other side of the gym, the dangerous armrests each touching the side of his knee, but none of them conking into it, quite.

About thirty feet shy of that other wall, he vaults down *through* the seats, and it's parkour all the way: the seats he needs open with his coming weight, then bottom out and *stick*, let him launch another few rows down.

If he wasn't stoned and concussed, he'd never know about this kind of movement, he knows—he'd never in a thousand years try it, as it's got to be certain death. But it's not. And there's not even anybody here with a phone to record this.

Halfway down, which is only about four suicide vaults through the air, he grabs onto the railing over the stairwell that leads *under* the stands and slings himself down, his bloody hand betraying him only at the last moment, slipping on that blue metal so he splats on his back on the concrete just past the first step of the stairs.

It doesn't even hurt, though.

He's numb, and loving it.

More than that, he's *fast*.

"Metal shop, metal shop," he says out loud, so he can be sure to follow that directive, get to the one door in the school that he knows opens to the outside, to his snowmobile, and then the rest of his life. College, even, Mom, sure, why not. All of it and more, please.

His feet slapping the floor are loud and echoey in the emergency-lit hallway, and if he had time or money he'd stop for something to drink at the concessions window, but he's got to keep moving, can't right now, sorry, Boosters.

He crashes through the back door, into the men's locker room, and slides through it, explodes out into the science hall.

It's so quiet here that he holds his breath, quiets his run to a walk.

But he keeps looking behind him, too.

This is making it, though. This is surviving.

He walks faster, legs stiff, and almost actually screeches when the full-cape bull elk at the far end of the hall is watching him, waiting for him.

"Goddamn it," he mutters.

When Banner Tompkins's mom and dad moved out, his dad had donated his record-book elk to the school, to lord it over all the students.

So that's all it is.

What? Did Jensen think it was a whole elk? That it was going to step forward through the rest of the wall, the cinderblock crumbling around it?

"Idiot," he says to himself.

And now he's jogging.

And then he's spinning around to either a sound or the ghost of a sound: a door opening, a locker closing, a ceiling tile moving over just enough to look through.

He reaches up, dabs at the split skin behind his ear and flinches away from that stinging touch.

He's going to *fly* on his snowmobile.

He's got to make it to the metal shop, though. That's the only door out.

And he can't help it, he's running now, and stumbling—what is wrong with him? His balance? His feet?

It's the weed, probably.

It's Wynona's yellow bra still drifting through the air, the whole world drained of color for its tumbling passage.

Jensen smiles, slows, and that's when something arcs out from beside him, like a giant hand to push him along even faster, only this hand, it's—

He grins inside, to at least get to solve this mystery: it's the flat white lid of a toilet tank.

It catches sort of in the back of the head, sort of on the neck, sort of on his shoulders, and is just the oomph he needs to go flying forward, past the turn he needed to make to the metal shop, right into the brow tines of this trophy bull elk, kind of sitting in a high, fancy basket the rest of the antlers make.

Jensen sees those tines coming in the same slow motion he watched his flung basketball floating through the air, and he has enough left to manage to spin around, keep that sharpness from his face.

The result is that those brow tines catch him on either side of his spine, splash out just under his collarbones.

But he's still alive.

And now he can see behind him.

Someone's standing in that darkness, and stepping out of it now, that toilet tank lid clattering to the floor, shattering into a thousand arrowheads.

"Oh," Jensen says, kind of pleasantly surprised, and his mouth stays open like that, shaped like a scream.

A HISTORY OF VIOLENCE

In 2016, not even a full year after the Independence Day Massacre, the senior class's numbers ballooned by an unprecedented twenty-new students, their families only recently residents of Proofrock, never mind the violence associated with it. Four years of paid-for college was worth any sense of risk. And, anyway, lightning would never strike twice, would it?

Had these families been familiar with Pleasant Valley's unfortunate past, I warrant that a higher percentage of 2020's graduating class would be utilizing that scholarship fund this fall. But, as Aldous Huxley warns, *That men do not learn very much from the lessons of history is the most important of all the lessons of history*.

In Pleasant Valley, there is a lot to learn. Proofrock's history of violence starts well before December of 2019. A hundred and forty-one years before, actually, and then moving, episode by episode, up to July 2015:

- 1878: Glen Henderson's murder of Tobias Golding, and the resulting legend of the "Golden Pickaxe"—never mind that the motherlode these two had struck it rich with was actually silver, or that gold isn't nearly hard enough for such a mining implement. Other accounts have it that, before his trial and hanging, Glen Henderson coated the guilty pickaxe with gold he melted down from his wife's jewelry (his wife having been the source of his disagreement with Tobias Golding) and then dropped that pickaxe into a deep pool of what was then Indian Creek, with the idea that the gold over his best friend's blood would preserve each of their crimes for perpetuity. And note that this murder is some nine years after "The Silver Strike Heard 'Round the World!" Before 1878, though, and in spite of much digging on the part of the internet, there are no Native American legends of a haunted valley, a chief's lost daughter, an abducted widow, or any water monsters, and there are no legends of disturbed burial grounds, disastrous raiding parties, inexplicable hunting accidents, lost tribes, ancient ruins, lights in the sky, caves holding strange visions, unaccounted-for fires, momentous births, or other goings-on strange enough to pass down in oral tradition. In short, what we now call Pleasant Valley was just another part of the Northern Shoshone and Bannock hunting territories—both, because the valley wasn't even rich enough in game to be disputed.

- 1915: "Ezekiel's Last Sermon," which left an unconfirmed eighteen dead in the rising waters of

Indian Creek, after barricading themselves in Henderson-Golding's lone church. Accounts have them singing as the waters sloshed against the front doors. Ezekiel, the preacher (no last name), had been found gibbering and bloody in the woods years before. Though never confirmed, the assumption was that he was the lone survivor of a lost wagon train, one that left no wheel rims or oxen bones to prove its demise. His eventual congregation would get worked into a frenzy with his sermons, and Ezekiel was said to froth at the mouth himself, using his Bible as a gavel. Fragmentary accounts suggest that many of the murdered bodies supposedly buried on the rocky slope of Caribou-Targhee National Forest across from Proofrock were sanctioned by his edicts—his punishment for ungodly or "heathen" ways was death, which was the divine responsibility of whichever parishioner witnessed or suspected such behavior. Stacey Graves's [see below] Native American mother, being one of those "heathens," was purported to have suffered such judgment at the hands of her husband, Letch Graves, presumably with the tacit approval of Ezekiel. In the years subsequent to Henderson-Golding's drowning, Ezekiel was transformed in local legend to Pleasant Valley's first boogeyman: parents would warn their children not to go out after dark or Ezekiel would grab them with his overlarge hands and take them down to Drown Town, to sing in his cursed choir. The next urban legend, however, would be Stacey Graves's mother, purported to be habitually skulking along the shores of the newly risen Indian Lake, looking for her lost daughter Stacey, but, in her grief and confusion, taking whatever child or early teenager she happened upon.

- 1920: The Lake Witch, Stacey Graves. The story goes that this eight-year-old "daughter of Proofrock"—a euphemism for communally approved neglect—was playing with some boys of the town in the shallows where the pier sits today. The game was "Witch." It involved proving a girl wasn't a witch by heaving her into the water. If she sank, then she wasn't evil. If the water rejected her, however, as running waters do to witches (Indian Lake is still, in "magical" terms, evidently a creek), then she was evil. Stacey Graves was selected for this honor primarily because she was the only girl of the play-group that day, but her Native American descent probably factored in, as did the "victimless" nature of the crime. The story these boys ran back into town with that evening, then, was that, when they slung that dirty Indian girl into the lake, she landed on top of it—it wouldn't let her in! Scared herself of her own surprising nature, Stacey Graves ran on all fours across the water and into legend, either hiding in the unpopulated wilderness or searching for her supposedly murdered mother. Whether supernatural or victim of an accident and then left to sink, she was never seen again. Her story would replace both

Ezekiel's and her mother's in the folkloric cycle of Pleasant Valley, and then, having lucked onto that productive overlap between fact and fiction, proximity and distance, caution and terror, it would persist all the way up to the Independence Day Massacre.

- 1934: Those Who Go after Elk. During the Great Depression and before hunting regulations and wildlife management, the men of Proofrock would paddle across Indian Lake to hunt moose and elk and deer, and then "float" them back across to town—this is according to long-time Proofrock resident Christine Gillette, of Pleasant Valley Assisted Living. According to her, after the first hunter of this six-person party got an "early elk," attempted to ferry it home himself, and ended up snagging the corpse of a young girl in the lake, then the more violent portion of that winter transpired: still needing meat, the other five hunters had to forge deeper into the forest, eventually harvesting two elk. Their return is where the trouble started. One by one over two nights they were picked off, until the lone survivor, their "Indian guide," crashed out onto shore, breathless. Lacking a pack or sledge, he had slabs of raw elk tied to his body—without meat, a family in the Great Depression could starve. The men standing guard in boats along shore paddled toward him… at which point the ethnography in the library cuts off. Did the men rescue him? Did he try to swim the lake? Did he retreat into the forest? If his story had an end, Mr. Armitage, then he quite possibly could have vied with Stacey Graves for status as a local legend.

- 1964: The Great Idaho Fire, originating from an untended campfire and burning unchecked through Caribou-Targhee National Forest for five days, until Pleasant Valley gambled with Glen Dam's structural integrity by raising the level of the lake in order to save Proofrock. Two recreational campers died in the blaze, and one volunteer firefighter. Stories persist of the flames herding the wildlife to the far shore of Indian Lake. The moose waded out and then swam across. You've seen the picture in the library, of the two bull moose walking down Main Street? Though not dated, presumably that photograph is proof of the wildlife's retreat from the fire. The elk and deer, however, not as comfortable in as large a body of water as Indian Lake, attempted to walk the top of the dam. This is *not* documented in photographs but is preserved in terse language in the then-damkeeper's daily log, where he recounts the deer and elk falling off the far side, their legs stiff, their bodies tumbling through open air. The ones that fell the other way, into the lake, perished as well, albeit slower, there being no shore gradual enough in that part of the lake for them to clamber up.
- 1965: Camp Blood, where the legend of Stacey Graves

found new purchase. During this grand opening of Camp Winnemucca, four campers were killed, with the last, Angus Hardy, narrowly escaping a "girl with big hair, a girl in a tattered nightgown." As the campfire stories those first few nights had the campers all on edge about the chance of Stacey Graves being out there with them, she was cast as the culprit. However, once the story was flensed of its fantastic elements, a camper was revealed to be the guilty party: the orphan Amy Brockmeir, niece of Remar Lundy, purported illegitimate son of Tobias Golding and Helen Henderson. Amy Brockmeir was remanded to the asylum in Idaho Falls; she died soon thereafter, after which Remar Lundy took legal action against Camp Winnemucca, effectively shutting it down. His case hinged on the revelation, and associated tragedy, of Amy Brockmeir having been not his niece, but his late-in-life illegitimate offspring. As for Lundy's previous children, only one survived—the mother of our elementary and high school janitor, whose reputation and presumed proclivities involving hidden cameras and illicit recordings I believe you're familiar with, being a member of the faculty. But of course rumor and suspicion have no place in a history.

- 1993: Melanie Hardy, twelve years old, daughter of the new sheriff, drowns in Indian Lake, accompanied by—according to the Idaho Statesman—her classmates Junior "Tab" Daniels, Jr., Kimberley Ledbetter, Clate

Rodgers, Lonnie Chambers, Rexall Bridger, and Misty Christy. No charges were ever pressed, though speculation on par with that on the death of Natalie Wood persists about the events of that day.

- 2015: The Lake Witch Slayings, which, yes, is Jennifer Daniels's preferred term, not the term that circulates in the media accounts. But "Independence Day Massacre" technically only includes the twelve killings on the night of the Fourth, meaning it discounts the two University of Groningen students lost in Indian Lake (the girl yet unrecovered); Deacon Samuels, killed by a grizzly bear on the shore of Camp Blood; Clate Rodgers, killed in a boating accident in Proofrock; the two Terra Nova construction workers as yet missing, presumed dead; and the seven dead on the yacht in Terra Nova—which, yes, is very personal.

As for which of these victims or legendary figures will now be cast as Pleasant Valley's new boogeyman, deserving of a mask on that dollar-store wall you were talking about, only time will tell. While Dark Mill South's visage is currently the most iconic (masks labeled "Danny Trejo," "Nathan Explosion," and "Glenn Danzig"—I trust these names and faces mean something?), his crimes the best documented (not that rumor counts here either, but supposedly a certain illicit recording of him in the high school exists), Stacey Graves has, historically, had more staying power. Are little dead girls scarier for 2020, or hulking serial killers? Or will Letch Graves's murdered wife rise to fill those shadows parents need filled, in order to keep their children scared of the dark? Is it now Ezekiel's time again? Will Tobias Golding come back, seeking justice with a golden pickaxe?

And let's not forget Jennifer Daniels's father, still bearing his patricidal wounds, or that lost Dutch student, still searching for her boyfriend, or Melanie Hardy, lake water seeping from her mouth, or that Depression-era hunter with meat tied all over himself—unrecovered bodies are bodies that can be animated with story. As Karl Marx says, *History repeats itself, first as tragedy, second as farce*, which is to say: all these episodes of violence eventually become cartoons. Time mollifies, multiple tellings codify, and then history repackages.

But perhaps Proofrock should take steps to stay in that mollifi-cation stage a little longer yet, Mr. Armitage. Hardly recovered from the Independence Day Massacre, I submit that we don't need to see Dark Mill South looking out at us from above our bargain shoe-inserts and off-brand bags of chips.

Neither do we need the rest of that gallery of killers and victims, unless representations of them can warn potential transfer students away from Proofrock.

We're already going to have enough empty seats at graduation, I mean.

I think of that passage you photocopied for us from Günter Grass's *Tin Drum*, where post–World War II Germans pioneer "onion bars," so they can gather as a people to cut onions and cry.

Proofrock needs some of those onions.

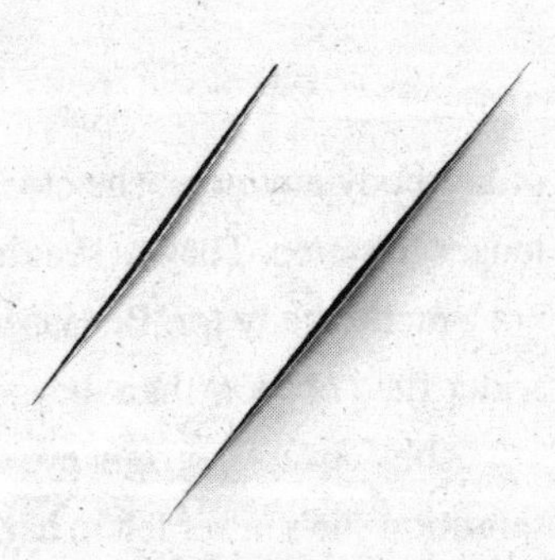

BLACK CHRISTMAS

Abby Grandlin must be in her backyard. In the summer. That's when her dad cooks his venison sausage on their wood-pellet grill, and then cuts that long horseshoe of meat into thick greasy coins on the big white platter and waiters it around to everyone he's invited over, handing them a toothpick to select their own bite, then watching as it bursts tenderly in their mouth.

It's that done-but-not-too-done smell that Abby remembers best.

But he's… he's burning them? Definitely. Her heart thumps, her throat constricts, her ears try to dial in that laugh he does when he's sneaked more beer from the cooler than he's supposed to have.

Where are you, Dad?

She sits up fast, instantly reeling, her forearm shiny with whatever grease the skin exudes as last defense when it's nestled up to a flickering Yankee candle.

Abby hits that hot glass tube of a jar with her elbow and it clatters away, the wax splashing, the flame guttering, guttering… gone.

That burnt deer sausage smell isn't venison, either. But that's the least of Abby's concerns, she's realizing.

She sits up straighter and nearly falls sideways. Not from pain, though there is pain, but—dizziness. And then, like she's not part of her body anymore, she clocks what's going on: her eyes are no longer in stereo. They're sending data into her head that her head's not exactly ready for. Because… because her eyes are taking in a wider field of view than they should be, than they ever have?

Abby covers her right eye with her wet right hand, and the next sensation she's never felt in her life is half the world squishing, and then going red. Her eyeball is hanging out on its stalk and when the heel of her hand presses against where her cheekbone should be, what she's really doing is smushing her right eye into some new cavern in her face.

She throws up but doesn't lean forward to do it, so it just burbles down her chin.

"Dad," she says, or tries to.

She knows she should scream, that that's the right thing to do at a time like this, but, even more than that, she doesn't want to break this soft perfect silence of the gym at night.

It's dim in here, only two candles burning now, maybe three if that sideways one at the free throw line can count, so she can't see where Wynona and Jensen are, but they're not her concern anymore, she knows.

She should be dead, she's pretty sure.

And, also, she almost *is* dead.

Keeping her loose eyeball cupped under her chin, afraid that if it falls out any farther then the stalk it's on is going to turn out to be the first part of a tendril loosely coiled in her head, a ball of enervated muscle wound tight that she's been using for a brain this whole time, and once that starts to uncoil, she'll go with, never come back, she uses her left hand to pull herself forward across the hardwood. Her legs are to the side and tucked back very ladylike, but that's just because that's all she can get them to do: contract.

Somewhere ahead of her is her purse. Her *phone*.

She never should have come here with Wynona, she knows now. But it wasn't exactly "with" Wynona, was it? No, the real reason she came, it was Jensen. Not because she's at all interested in him—*yuck?*—but because she didn't trust Wynona with him. When Jensen had knocked on Wynona's door, Abby and Wynona had been having a perfectly good time without any boys. But then Wynona had held her finger up to tell Jensen to wait just one minute for her to slip into something warm, and she'd stepped into her room and taken her grey sports bra off, arranged herself into the bright yellow one, like she had a couple of Easter eggs to present to him.

Abby didn't want to let her do something she'd regret.

And, for all she knew, Jensen was taking Wynona to some grand and traumatizing prank being staged by Kristen and Cinnamon and Gwen, the bitches three.

Which led to this, whatever this is.

Abby pulls herself to one of the candles, rests for a moment, almost passes out, then makes herself keep going, keep going, the candle riding in front of her now. This one she's careful not to tip over. She needs it.

Two minutes later she's to the sideline, where the team sits when there's a game.

It's also the parking lot for the ball racks. Which are on wheels.

One by one, Abby uses her left hand to push the balls through, out the back side of the rack. Her right hand is still trying to hold her eye in, clap it in darkness so her brain can... not "work," exactly, but fail less, anyway.

And, so, where *is* Jensen? Wynona? Weren't they here when Abby stumbled in, to warn them? Did they see her, turn tail, pull some eject lever, never mind the one who just saved them?

Abby turns her head as much as it will, trying to locate Wynona's bright white t-shirt in the darkness, but no luck.

She got out, then. She got away. Because she *didn't* blunder down the hall to the nurse's office for fucking *hydrogen peroxide*, to save an article of underclothing that shouldn't have even been on display in the first place.

Not that Abby ever made it to the nurse's office.

She pushes the last ball out of the rack and works her armpit up to sort of hang on the third shelf—not really shelves, more like parallel rods for the balls to sit in. Doesn't matter: it takes her weight. It wants to fall over, but she can push back with her feet a little, now.

It's enough. Not quite the wheelchair she needs—what she needs is a stretcher, and three ambulances, maybe a helicopter—but it rolls faster than she can slide.

"Nona!" she manages to yell, hoping.

Nothing.

Her purse is by the door, that's where it is. Half a court away, now, and she forgot the stupid candle, and her arm still smells like crispy venison, and she can't do this.

But then she imagines that the stands are full.

The whole house is watching her.

All the women up there have their hands balled into fists, to give her strength, and all the men are hovering over their seats because it's all they can do not to launch down to the gym floor, help this girl, this daughter, this sister.

This is all on her, though.

No, this is on her mom, isn't it? Her mom the basketball star. Even went to college on it. Taught Abby proper form before… before Abby had to say goodbye to her in that hospital down in Idaho Falls.

After which she quit the team, because she wasn't playing for them anymore.

The game was personal to her, now. It was between her and her mom. And she was out on their driveway draining shots and pulling spin moves every weekend, snatching down rebounds and throwing elbows.

She'd considered taking it easy on Jensen and Wynona in their big HORSE game, but then she decided that that would just make it last longer—that a quick, naked death was much better for Jensen. If she could just get him out of the picture, then maybe Wynona could retain some shred of her dignity.

Just to give it away some other day. But not this one, anyway.

And now, now here's Abby Grandlin, motherless baller, out on the gym floor, playing the game of her life, and every seat has an ass in it, and even the kids are watching, taking a lesson from this, being part of this moment.

Abby pulls with her left knee, pushes with her right foot, blood seeping from her face or her head or she can't tell, but it's soaking her, and she's almost there, she's almost there, she's—

Not even past the scorer's table yet.

Letha shouldn't be on the stoop of the sheriff's office when the phone at Meg's desk rings, but she is.

It's Banner.

She's watching him on the snowcat.

She knows from him calling in on the radio—which isn't as user-friendly as he'd guaranteed—that he's biting the bullet and swinging by Lonnie's to gas up.

From the stoop she can see him at the second of the two pumps. He isn't even wearing his right jacket, the long black trench that looks military, not Wall Street, so he has his bare hands in his armpits, and is coming up onto his toes over and over, either to try to generate some heat or to will the diesel to come faster.

But: not fast enough.

Letha cringes for him when Lonnie ambles out, inspecting his precious snowcat from all sides before sidling up to Banner.

Five minutes later, the tank evidently topped off, Lonnie's squatted by the rear tracks, and moving them up and down like to show the slack to Banner, and probably telling him about what disastrous end that slack could lead to. When Lonnie climbs up behind the wheel and backs the snowcat into the first bay, Banner just stands there like a second-grader, raising his shoulders in apology to Letha.

She nods to him that she can hold things together.

He's right there, after all.

After double-checking every door and just blocking off the women's restroom altogether, since that stupid little window in there won't come down, she's back on the stoop, ready to see Banner churning through the snow to her, the tracks or whatever tightened—*that* disaster averted, thank you, Lonnie.

This time checking on the snowcat's progress, though, or *lack* of progress—nothing against Lonnie, but she'll buy the county a fleet of snow machines if it means he doesn't get to nitpick each one—her heart swells when there's a form trundling through the snow.

Whoever this is, they're not in county khaki, but some giant blue parka, and… waders?

"What?" Letha says through her teeth.

Who would be out in this?

She steps back when the answer rises, unbidden: Dark Mill South, that's who.

Except… except the mug shots of him on the news always show him with his hair down. And whoever this is, they've got the parka's hood pulled up and over, then ratcheted tight against the wind, so there's only one little black tunnel for them to look through.

"Keanu Reeves," Letha hears herself saying. "*The Watcher*, 2000."

It's the one where he wears a hoodie, not a mask. But he's definitely into the whole killing thing—which is to say, after Letha had burned through all the slashers the first time, she cruised through its first and second cousins, taking wider and wider loops so she could be ready for whoever came calling. Mr. Brooks, Henry Lee Lucas, Citizen X, John Doe, Francis Dolarhyde, anybody with a necktie fetish and a British accent, all taxi drivers and single white females. Technically, she knows, Dark Mill South is from that shelf. But really he's Kane from *See No Evil*, he's Frank Zito from *Maniac*, which puts him square in horrorland. And, since he's not a poltergeist or a zombie, a werewolf or a vampire, then, by default, he's a slasher. Or, doing business as one, anyway.

The real proof will be whether bullets can stop him or not, Letha supposes. If they can, then he's a serial killer. If it takes a final girl to put him down, though, then he was a slasher all along.

And, this has to be him out there, doesn't it? He's tall and big, hulking and dangerous.

What if it can all stop here, right? By someone with the right resolve?

And… what's he *doing*?

He's picking things up from the snow. Stiff stuff: ski clothes? He holds them up just like a normal person, trying to make sense of them. It's like… it's like whoever was wearing them just blipped away, to some safer place.

He goes from this jacket to those pants, that ski mask, this glove, balling them under his arm. They're obviously too little for him to wear, but who knows why monsters like him do what they do.

And the phone's still ringing on Meg's desk.

Already, Letha's had to stash Adrienne in Rex Allen's office and unplug the phone in there, just so—*maybe*—Adie can catch a nap. Never mind all the staplers and binders and eyes-only files a toddler can redistribute, but that's later's problem.

Right *now's* problem is that there's this blue-parka'd killer trundling through the snow. Not coming to the sheriff's, not angling over to Lonnie's either, but… is he going to the pier? Does he not know Cinn's at the retirement home, the *other* way?

"It's good that he doesn't," Letha mutters to herself.

But, too, he's going to be looking for her, isn't he? And the logical places are here, where Adie is, and the house, where Donna and Gal are. Neither of which is an option. Not while Letha's around.

Meaning: it's time to see just what kind of monster he is—serial killer or slasher.

Letha steps back into the warmth of the office, doesn't realize her retainer's stiffened in the cold until she tries to adjust her chin like she needs to, but there's no time for that. She pulls up the tangled mass of keys Banner left.

One of them works for the gun case on the wall.

She runs her finger along the rifles and shotgun, finally settles on Rex Allen's goose gun, which she knows he's paranoid someone else is going to fire someday.

"Welcome to today," Letha says to him, hauling the long gun down and thumbing in the first shells she can grub up from the shallow drawer. They're 7½, which she knows from the videos she watches is birdshot, but oh well. No time to find double-aught or a slug.

The phone's still ringing when she sweeps back past.

She nods to it, telling it she hasn't forgotten it, then backs through the first glass door like rolling off the side of a boat into the water. Meaning, standing in the entryway, facing up to the second glass door, she can still elect to *not* do this, and nobody will have to know, nobody will see her backing down from this responsibility.

Standing in this institutional foyer only gives her more resolve, though.

She knees the outside door open, having to really push it against the snow already drifted up against it, and two steps later she's in the muck, the sucking cold. Standing on the stoop again, she racks the first shell in, brings the long gun up, leads that blue parka a couple steps, and, before she can talk herself out of it, and without blinking, she lets go.

Because this A5 is full-choke, it whips her shoulder so hard it spins her around. From the videos she watches, she's memorized the how and where and what to do with all types of firearms, even up to AK's, but the guys doing the mansplaining in those videos all have sixty or eighty pounds on Letha, and also have their feet set for the recoil.

Letha slams back into the front door of the sheriff's office, feels it giving, and her whole body tenses, time slowing down for her: she can see Adrienne down in the office alone, while her mom bleeds out right here. So, she tightens every muscle against the glass shards she knows are coming.

One of those muscles is her trigger finger, and this goose gun's an auto.

It blasts again, even harder this time, driving Letha down *through* the breaking door.

She pulls her left arm over her face to save her eyes, doesn't know what's going on with her back anymore.

Five seconds later, frozen in place by fear, she takes a peek.

The little concrete and steel overhang above the stoop has a big crater in it now, and there's still pieces crumbling down.

More important—Letha sits up, feels slivers of glass all under her—Dark Mill South out there isn't walking anymore.

She hit him.

He's laid out, slapping at himself. Because: *birdshot*. Plus his parka, and whatever layers he's got on under that.

What this means, though?

He wasn't stopped by a gun. He is what he is.

Letha extracts herself gingerly from the door, feels behind for blood, but there isn't any. She leans Rex Allen's prize goose gun into the corner and—

It blasts *again*.

Because she's closer to the business end of it this time, the powdered brick stings the parts of her face it can still get to, a hundred tiny pinpricks of flame that Letha isn't near fast enough to slap away. All she can do is flinch, jerk.

That sends her tumbling off the stoop, out into the snow, which is *deep*-deep. It swallows her whole, her nostrils instantly filling with powder, her eyes packing shut with coldness. But this isn't an avalanche. And just because she can't open her mouth to suck air doesn't mean she's suffocating. She knows her way up. She knows how to blow her nose clear.

Calm, calm, she says inside.

Never mind that Dark Mill South has to know who just lobbed birdshot at him. Never mind that she can't see him at the moment.

Letha clambers up as fast as she can, and, when no giant is about to tackle her, she wipes herself down. Breathes.

More of the little awning is crumbling down now, all around her, and there's a big gouge in the brick, and the narrow window alongside the door is shattered too. And all those stony flecks and glassy slivers are raining down on that pretty shotgun, probably scratching the stock.

There's still two shots in it, though. "A5" means auto-5: five shells, if there's not a plug. Rex Allen, being an officer of the law, probably should have a plug, but Letha's pretty sure he doesn't. That would mar the original design.

Letha steps back up onto the stoop, hauls the shotgun to her again, staying well clear of the open end of the barrel, since this thing has the *definition* of a hair trigger.

She only realizes she's mostly deaf when the muted yells filter through.

She cranks around to Dark Mill South, and Banner and Lonnie are already to him. But Banner's pistol isn't drawn, and Lonnie doesn't have a crowbar or a chain, just that bucket he keeps by the pumps, with the windshield squeegee in it.

"No!" Letha screams, and holds the shotgun at port arms, sets her feet, and fires again, into the sky, the big gun jumping, but not getting away from her this time.

Banner turns to her, holding his hands out to tell her enough, enough, and Lonnie stops advancing, wary of this woman with a shotgun.

"It's him!" Letha calls out, the sound filling her head, her teeth unable to unclench, and as if to prove it, Dark Mill South stands, still slapping at himself, and peels out of the parka—it's smoldering, its synthetic down or whatever evidently flammable when hot lead sears through it.

And, and—

"Shit," Letha says, letting the gun fall away, into the snow.

It's Rexall.

He was… he was probably heading up to Main to trudge down to the high school to take care of a burst pipe, or adjust the boiler, or it doesn't matter.

She *didn't* just shoot Dark Mill South. She shot the town janitor.

"I'm sorry," Letha says, mostly to herself, and that damn phone will *not stop.*

Pissed, she turns, pulls the doorhandle. It comes away in her hand, so she just steps through the remains of the door, trying to avoid the jagged edges.

Aren't all the phones down? How can whoever this is be calling so much?

And, of course: Adrienne's crying down the hall.

It's not her fault, though. There's loud noises. This is a strange place. Crying is how you tell your mother you're scared, that you need her to come get you, pat you safe.

Letha turns that way, to round the reception counter, skirt Meg's desk, beeline Rex Allen's office, but: that *phone*.

She stops, hisses out breath, and yanks it up, says into it as best she can, "*What?*"

On the other end, there's just breathing at first.

Letha switches ears, presses the phone tighter, which is when the inside door, the first, blows open all at once, the storm forcing its way in.

The door slaps the wall hard enough that it shatters just like the other door, the dull aluminum frame swinging back in slowly, now that the cold wind can't keep it propped open.

Great. Wonderful.

Down the hall now too, the women's restroom door is clattering because there's a hard draft pulling under it, trying to dive out the window.

This is too fucking much.

Kid crying, Rexall shot, glass everywhere, snow blowing into the entry.

"Billy?" Letha hisses into the phone, just for her own get-back—he's the sick caller in *Black Christmas*.

"N-n-*no*," the girl on the other end says, and she's either *way* on the other end, or Letha's hearing's still dampened.

"Who is this?" she says, switching the receiver to her left hand now, so she can pull her cell up from her back pocket.

Sure enough: one flickering bar.

The cell tower's been in and out all day.

Meaning: this is one lucky-ass call.

"Fast, fast," Letha says, not sure how long this connection can last.

"It's Abby G-Grandlin," the girl barely on the other end says. "You need—you need to come up here."

"Up where?" Letha says.

"The gym," Abby manages to say. "They're—they're all dead, I think. Including… me."

Letha closes her eyes, makes herself open them, and, holding the phone to her throat, stretches its spiral cord around Meg's desk so she can see Banner through the broken door, out in the storm. He and Lonnie are wrestling with Rexall, and it doesn't look like they're winning.

"We're coming," she tells Abby.

Banner is on his ass again, and he's thinking that he should maybe just stay there.

If he struggles back up, gets Rexall under control, then—then the rest of this day's just going to avalanche down over him: the snowcat, out of service for the moment; a killer in town, targeting Cinnamon Baker, and carving through all her friends to get to her; no backup; this *storm*; his wife, who's just supposed to be covering the phones for Meg, not taking potshots at citizens; that citizen resisting… not "arrest," but he was just peppered with shot out of nowhere, maybe isn't thinking right.

It's Rexall, though. Has he ever been thinking right?

On one of his early patrols, Francie'd told Banner what she knew about when Rexall had gotten the hell out of Proofrock for a year and a half about ten years ago, to find gainful employment down in Idaho Falls. Which turned out to be at a funeral home. It was just a part-time thing, vacuuming and dusting afterhours. But then the snapshots started showing up. They were from Rexall's flip phone, so were grainy, but you could see what he was seeing well enough: dead women. Not completely stripped out of their funeral clothes. But, stripped enough. Rexall was unbuttoning their shirts and propping a pale, bloodless breast out, then arranging a candle on the edge of the coffin as backdrop, and then opening his phone, getting the angle just right.

Because the funeral home didn't want a lawsuit, and because proving the source of these photos would take police involvement, which would end up public, the owner's cousins had come to town, manhandled this afterhours custodian into the bed of their truck, trussed him hand and foot, stuffed his mouth with an oily red rag, glued his lips shut over it with that Zip Lip stuff they use for corpses, then driven him back up to the address of his last reference—Golding Elementary, where he'd swept and mopped in high school.

But Banner and Lonnie aren't those manhandling cousins, obviously. And Rexall is what Banner's dad would call a *hoss*: after pushing Banner back onto his ass again, he slings Lonnie out into the snow like a human Frisbee.

There's dots of blood on one side of Rexall's face, from the goose gun. Banner knows it by sound, but, too, it's the only gun in the rack in the front office that's full-choke—the only one that could have reached out these fifty yards. Letha knows her firearms, he's got to give her that.

She perhaps needs a little guidance yet on target selection, however.

And Rexall might have even come quietly, except then Letha started in firing again, and again.

Because she's protecting Adrienne, Banner tells himself. There's nothing she won't do to keep that little girl safe. Just—all those horror movies she watches, right? They've taught her to shoot first, ask questions never, because there's no on-ramp to danger, there's not any slow and boring escalation. It's always immediately life and death, with Letha Mondragon-Tompkins.

Banner loves her for it. It lets him feel safe out on patrol, when he can't be there. But it is kind of messing with his whole "being a deputy"–thing, he guesses. If he can be completely honest.

And, no, Rex Allen is *not* going to be thrilled about Rexall getting shot. But—it *is* Rexall. What's really going to get Banner's ass in a sling is that goose gun. It's from Belgium, is supposed to be being kept safe, in a position of honor.

That's later, though.

This is now.

Banner fights up from the powder, untangles from the earbud cables that must be from Rexall—is that *rap* coming through them?—and, using the form Coach always told his linebackers they had to use when the idiot with the ball's both bigger than you *and* has momentum, he drives forward, catching Rexall in the side, an illegal spear, and then he pushes not back but *up*, a spleen-ripper.

It's not that he wants to sideline Rexall for the season, so much. It's that he doesn't want to get his *own* ass stomped any more than it already is. And the trick to that when you're out-sized, it's taking the ground away from this tight end, this fullback—this *janitor*—and then letting his own weight slam him down.

It finally works.

All of Rexall's three hundred or however many pounds is on

Banner's right shoulder, and he's rising, rising… and then falling on his back. Banner can tell it takes his wind away.

Except, now Lonnie's wading in not just with the heavy duty long-handled squeegee he keeps in a white five-gallon bucket for cleaning Proofrock's windshields, but with the squeegee *and* the bucket. Not on purpose, but because the blue wiper fluid he keeps in that bucket's frozen around the squeegee head. It must weigh forty pounds, and it confirms what Rex Allen told Banner once: that Lonnie waters that shit down to save money. If he didn't, it wouldn't be frozen right now.

But Banner can't stop to think about that.

Lonnie's already swinging it overhead like a giant hammer, to come down onto Rexall's face. Which is going to do a lot more damage than a goose gun at half a football field away.

Banner rolls to the left, freeing his right side, and draws his snow-packed Glock, racks the slide back, and shoots twice from the ground.

The white bucket of frozen blue explodes into chunks above Lonnie's head and his swing is just the long handle of the squeegee now. It overbalances him, nearly lands him splat in the middle of Rexall, still gasping for breath.

"Stop! Stop! Stop stop *stop*!" Banner screams, trying to stand, his legs numb, the world muted.

Lonnie steps back, his lips trembling the way they always do when he's about to fall into a stuttering hole.

Banner angles the pistol down onto Rexall and Rexall raises his hands too, showing all his fingers.

This fucking day.

To make it worse, there's a distant buzzing worming its way through Banner's deafness.

He shakes his head, conks himself on the side of the head in case his ears are just plugged with snow, and what he sees is a square headlight coming fast.

"Shit," he says, and dives out of the way, which turns out to be right onto Rexall, who gathers Banner to him and rolls hard away, probably saving him.

The snowmobile skids sideways, spraying snow onto Banner and Rexall and Lonnie.

Banner clears his face and stands, leading with his pistol, Rexall and Lonnie forgotten.

At the edge of the floating whiteness, he can see Letha in the doorway to the sheriff's office. She's reaching down for that shotgun again. Meaning this is about to seriously all go to hell if Banner doesn't—

"There's more," Jennifer Daniels says from the snowmobile's seat, cocking some ski goggles up onto her forehead.

"More what?" Banner says.

"More dead kids," Jennifer says back, then sees Rexall. "What's *he* doing here?"

"Getting shot?" Rexall says back, leaning forward to blow splatty snow from his nose. Then, "Hey, Jade. Missed you at your dad's funeral."

"I was there at his *death*," Jennifer hisses back, her hand still on that throttle like she wants to fire her bad machine back up, jam the skids into her dad's best friend, just for old times' sake.

"They should have sent you up," Rexall says, lumbering to his feet and keeping a weather eye on Lonnie, whose lower lip is still spasming with stacked-up words.

"Yeah, well," Jennifer says, stepping down and looking back

to the sheriff's office. "Can't say they didn't try."

"Doesn't matter," Rexall says, then shrugs like this is no big thing. "He's back anyway. And he's bigger than he was. Gonna take more than some puke-ass machete swung by a *girl* to—"

Bam!

Banner nearly falls down, trying to get his pistol around to whatever this was: Letha, walking in, firing the shotgun straight up.

"Will this do?" she says in her close-mouthed way, staring daggers into Rexall that are probably more dangerous than whatever she's thumbed into that A5's tube.

Jennifer doesn't smile, but she sort of does, her lips pursed, and for a little frozen moment, Banner sees her and Letha side by side, the main two survivors from the last round, ready to go again, if that's what it's coming down to.

Except—"Everybody *stop*!" he hears himself insisting, with all the volume he has. "Nobody's shooting anybody, okay? Okay?"

To prove this, he makes a slow show of holding his pistol high and light, and guiding it into the snowcone his holster is, the barrel surely stuffing with slush, but screw it. De-escalation is more important now than proper firearm maintenance.

Letha shrugs about this new rule that nobody's shooting anybody: it'll hold until it doesn't.

"Adie good?" Banner asks her, and she nods a curt nod.

"There's three dead at Pleasant Valley," Jennifer says then.

Banner feels something in his chest falling off a metal shelf, and clattering into pieces in his stomach.

"Who?" he says.

Jennifer squints to remember, then nods, says, "Kristen? Mark?"

"Seniors," Letha fills in. "Cinn? Ginger?"

Jennifer shakes her head no, not them. But she does add, "And—I don't know his name. He worked the front desk?"

"B-b-b-b-b-b," Lonnie says.

Rexall's amused by this.

"B-b-blond *hair*?" he finishes for Lonnie. "That'd be Jocelyn Cates's kid."

"Philip," Banner fills in. "One *L*."

"He was supposed to come here on this," Jennifer says, patting the snowmobile. "But when I went to check on what was taking him so long, he had a—it was a *dry-cleaning* bag, I think. Over his head."

Banner turns away. The cold doesn't even matter anymore.

What's this, *five* high schoolers dead, now? And, what are Letha and Jennifer communicating to each other now, with their eyes?

"What?" he says to them.

Letha shakes her head, as if there's too many ears here.

"But they're all already dead, right?" she says to Jennifer.

Jennifer nods once, and Letha comes back to Banner.

"There's one still alive at the high school," she says. "Abby, um—"

"*Grandlin...*" Rexall plugs in, emphasizing it in some gross way that gets Jennifer stepping forward, like she's going to climb him, reach into his mouth, pull his heart out and then feed it back to him.

Banner stops her, pushes her back harder than he needs to, considering her size.

But these are extraordinary circumstances.

"She's hurt?" he says to Letha.

Letha nods.

"*Fuck!*" Banner can't help but say, almost scream, both his hands to his head now, trying to hold all these emergencies inside so he can maybe make sense of at least one of them.

"We go to the one who needs help," Jennifer says. "The high school. The nursing home can wait."

"How did—she *called* you?" Banner says then, to Letha.

"Signal was back," Letha explains.

He palms his own phone, sees that one thready dot that's the first of his bars.

"He's coming for you, count on that," Rexall says to Jennifer. "Little family reunion," he adds for her, with some approximation of a wink, except about a thousand times more lecherous.

"Can we lock him up?" Jennifer says to Banner, without breaking eye contact with Rexall.

"Seconded," Letha says flatly.

"Thi-thi-thi—" Lonnie says.

"It's unanimous," Jennifer says, saving Lonnie the trouble.

"I'm the *victim* here?" Rexall says, holding his parka out to show all the little fountains of singed white puff.

"For your own safety," Banner tells him, and knows for sure, now, that his contract won't be getting renewed.

But maybe he can still save Abby Grandlin.

Back when, Jennifer had a ring of keys on a pullcord that would get her into any door of Henderson High.

Then, when those were taken away, she threw a trashcan through the front doors, she seems to recall.

It all used to matter so much.

Everything was a statement, a gesture, a challenge.

All of that's sucked into the past, though. It already feels like it maybe happened to somebody else. Like she saw it all through the tracking lines of her old television in her bedroom.

Now her room isn't really even her room anymore, though.

The house she has the title to—she refuses to call it her father's house, doesn't want to have to live like that—it was evidently Proofrock's party pad for a season or two. Meaning her bedroom was probably hookup station number two, number one being the bigger bedroom at the end of the hall.

The two nights she's been there, she's curled up on the caved-in couch. The old console television in the living room's had its screen kicked in, and been home to a few listless fires, it looks like—very 2029, Kyle Reese's Cyberdyne-wrecked future.

It's starting to line up with Jennifer's wrecked present.

The one where her hand goes to the pocket of the coveralls she's not wearing, for the keys she doesn't have, which would open these front doors of Henderson High.

"Deputy?" she says to Banner.

It's him and her and Doc Wilson. When the good doctor wouldn't rouse from their insistent knocks on his door, Banner had finally kicked it in.

Doc Wilson was sitting at the card table in his kitchen, dealing himself some vodka.

"What?" Banner says about the locked door they need to get through. "We should have asked Rexall, shit."

Jennifer shakes her head no about that.

It was bad enough riding three to the snowmobile, Doc Wilson's hands gripping her right under her breasts. Having Rexall as a fourth would have probably meant… sitting in his lap?

Not likely.

"How'd *they* get in?" Banner says just aloud, as if lodging the right objection will get these doors open.

"We have time to figure that out?" Jennifer asks back.

When Banner's just staring, his two brain cells swapping back and forth and coming up with zilch, Jennifer steps over to the trashcan, to take a running start with it, fling it into that pristine wall of glass.

But the trashcan is bolted down.

It wrenches her back, forces painful blood back into her frozen fingers.

"Shit!" she says. Then, to Banner, "Shoot it! Abby's dying!"

Banner looks behind him, like expecting Rex Allen to nod that this is okay, and, when he reaches down for the butt of his pistol—

"No," he says.

His holster's empty.

In a glance, Jennifer can see how it happened: his holster was packed with snow, meaning his pistol wouldn't jam down deep enough to catch. Add bouncing around Proofrock on a snowmobile, and, bam: a pistol that'll only show up when all of this melts. 'Long about May.

That doesn't mean Banner isn't checking the ground all around him now, though. And then backtracking to the snowmobile.

"How is this party injured, did you say?" Doc Wilson asks, already sipping straight from his thermos of coffee that smells like it's flammable.

Jennifer shakes her head, disgusted with this situation.

She turns sharply, not answering Doc Wilson, and steps back to the snowmobile, connects the kill switch without hooking it onto her jacket, and pulls Philip Cates's goggles down over her eyes.

"No, no, don't!" Banner says from the fluff of snow he's now inspecting for firearms.

"For Abby," Jennifer says, firing the snowmobile up, the engine screaming over her voice—screaming *as* her voice.

She twists the throttle back hard, her whole right shoulder going down with it, and the snowmobile fishtails a bit then launches, those glass doors coming *fast*-fast.

Jennifer dives off ten feet shy, slides at an angle away, a girl-shaped snowball, and looks up through the foggy goggles just in time to see the snowmobile crash into Henderson High.

The glass keeps falling for about thirty seconds after the snowmobile's parked itself in the trophy case.

"Go, *go*!" Jennifer says to Banner and Doc Wilson when Banner starts to step over, haul her up.

They do.

Jennifer rolls over on her back, stares up into the swirling whiteness.

Almost instantly, her goggles are coated in powder. The result is she loses her bearing, feels like she's falling—like she's *been* falling for four years, and now she's splatted down right in front of the high school she never graduated from.

She shakes her head no, not wanting this feeling, and tries to roll out of it, slinging the goggles away so she can find herself again.

Another slab of glass falls pendulously down from the very top of that big frame, and, instead of shattering, it stabs into some of the snow that had been packed up against the door, stabs in and stands there at an angle.

Jennifer clambers to her feet, steps well around that glass, and immediately spots the snowmobile's kill switch, hooked onto the top left corner of the display case—Banner's tall, doesn't think not everyone is. It was good he pulled it, though. The air still tastes like exhaust, meaning if he hadn't, they'd all be swimmy in the head in a few minutes.

"Thanks, Deputy," Jennifer mumbles, taking a slow look around.

This is the first time she's been back in this building since that summer, isn't it? Since she carved *The Lake Witch Slayings* into the tender blue metal of a restroom, and Hardy had to fire her.

That is what they turned out to be, though.

Even if that's not what it says in her court transcripts, or in any of the newspapers or books.

Not that Jennifer kept up, once she figured out which way the wind was blowing.

She crunches forward, her purple-leather boots mostly wet by now. They were made for being tucked under a defendant's table in court, not for wading through killing fields. She would have taken Philip Cates's boots like she'd taken his ski gear, but boots had felt more intimate somehow, and she knew she would have felt bad, leaving him barefoot in the snow.

In hindsight, it was a stupid decision, but being smart's not as easy as everybody makes it out to be.

Jennifer looks behind her, just to be sure she's alone, and—shit. Right over there's the Quiet Room, where you go when the world's too much and you just need to sit in a room with zero stimulation for a half hour.

"Can I live there, please?" Jennifer mumbles.

On the way past the display case, she tippy-toes to pull the kill switch down on the sly, pocket it. She doesn't want to hear the snowmobile firing up without her. Banner's trying to take care of them, but he's not even a real deputy yet.

Jennifer walks down the center of the hall, her tightrope the blurry shadow in the middle where the emergency lights don't quite touch.

Behind her, the storm's whistling through the open door.

Come spring semester, there's going to be some serious clean-up for Rexall, and whoever his apprentice is now. Pipes are going to freeze, animals are going to have found their way in, papers are going to be blowing all around.

There's going to be some bloodstains too.

Then in a few months it's going to be one of those graduations where, instead of all the seats filled, some are going to be left ceremonially empty, right? Whoever's principal now will give token diplomas to the dead kids' parents, along with a single red rose, and, if there's any justice, any decency, the media won't be there to document this.

No reason for it to live forever. Just let it be the beautiful terrible thing it is, and then keep moving, keep moving.

That's what Jennifer's doing.

She shuffles past the two chemistry labs, gives English the same leery eye as ever, and then—no, she's not ready.

History.

Her breath catches in her throat, and she's telling herself there's a life on the line down the hall, maybe *lives*, that there's a killer to be figured out, found, and put down, but, all the same… she steps into the doorway of the old classroom, her eyes hot, and now she's reaching for him with her fingertips, and also at the same time pulling her hand back, to hold it to her chest.

Mr. Holmes.

She shakes her head no, that she can't do this, but she's already stepping the rest of the way in.

Just like she knew there'd be, there's still stupid quotes from "historical" people on posters all around the room. There's dates and names and places, half-erased on the chalkboard. There's the desks all in sort-of rows, the same as it had been since kindergarten.

But there's no Mr. Holmes leaned back against his desk, spinning them what feels like another bullshit story about people in Henderson-Golding looking up from their oil lanterns, up into the tall blackness of what would become Caribou-Targhee, and seeing the distant sparks from mining picks chipping into rock.

Jennifer always thought he maybe wanted to go there, to Drown Town before it was Drown Town, that he was one of those who thought he was born too late. And it wasn't that he could have been somebody back then; it was that he could have been nobody.

From her holding cell over five weeks, draft after draft, she'd written his wife—his *widow*—a two-page letter. About how her husband had been a dad to her, sort of, in secret. How he let her write papers about horror instead of history, just because he could tell that's where her heart was. That every time she hears a buzzing in the sky, she looks up, sure it's going to be him, that he really got away that night, that he's still up there in his ultralight.

She tore all those letters up, though.

None of them said it even close to right.

Finally what she sent, which had to go through her lawyer, not the approved way, was a single unsmoked cigarette, with a light little grey heart drawn in pencil on the side of that white paper.

Who even *is* the history teacher now?

Jennifer steps in between the desks, her heart swelling from being here again.

Whoever it is, they can't be doing even half the job Mr. Holmes was. They don't know the real Proofrock, the real Fremont County, the real Idaho. They didn't grow up getting their summer buzzcut down on Main Street. They never stood on shore and watched Hardy sling his airboat around, misting all the kids lined up on the pier. They were never pirates on the high seas of Indian Lake.

They shouldn't even be teaching history here anymore, Jennifer thinks. They should give it a rest for four or five more years, in honor.

And now she's up to what was his desk.

She touches it with her fingertips, knows it's his headstone.

"Sir," she says, trying to keep her breathing normal and failing so fucking hard.

Her tears splat on the papers and she drags her sleeve across her face, can't be doing this.

She turns to face the empty classroom.

Because nobody's watching, she tries to do that slow little heel-spin Mr. Holmes had down, that he used as a part of his lectures, his rambles, and now she's facing the chalkboard.

She nods and it's real now, it's real again, he's really gone.

When she finally walks back out, *Grady Bear Sherlock Holmes* is written in the high corner very small, not with chalk but a black Sharpie. The blackest Sharpie. And if Rexall uses some solvent to remove it, she's officially kicking his ass up one side of Main and down the other. *Twice.*

Not sure where the action is, or was, she drifts down the halls. There should be wet footprints, but it's dark, and she'll get there eventually.

Or, she *is* there: where the main hall goes to either the science wing or the art wing.

Some idiot's mounted a bull elk there, to stare everybody down? Like some gatekeeper making them choose "science" or "art"?

"What bullshit is this?" Jennifer says. About the elk, sure, but, more, about the guy speared over its face.

There are antlers poking up through his chest, and his eyes and mouth are open.

Jennifer watches him for a solid minute, isn't sure what she's waiting for. Just, she knows she doesn't want to let it in. Not yet.

"Shit," she says, aware of how *not* cued into her surroundings she's been, and looks suddenly behind her, because you're never as alone as you think you are.

It's just empty hallway again, still. The memory of backpacks and secrets and hushed laughter.

Not *Slaughter High*, like Jennifer used to always imagine. The teachers from *The Faculty* aren't out to get her. Neither is Mrs. Tingle. She's just, like Brad Pitt, cutting class, doesn't want to end up a student body.

"1981, Alex," she mutters, for *Student Bodies*, just so she won't say "1984," which would be *Silent Night, Deadly Night*, which this kill with the elk most definitely is, no matter how much she doesn't want it to be true.

But no. No no *no*. She doesn't think like that anymore. She's just… she's hiding in the video store, like Letha was saying. She's seeing connections that wouldn't even be there if she didn't know all the shit still swirling around inside her.

Saying it out loud or not, though, this kid is still speared on these antlers, isn't he? And there's still two—no, *three*—dead high schoolers over at Pleasant Valley. Counting the two from the motel parking lot, this makes… six. And that's not counting whatever Banner and Doc Wilson are wading into, down… which direction?

Jennifer looks down the science hall, down the art hall, and ends up making wet tracks for her old bathroom—the Skank Station. Instead of stepping in, though—

"Hello?" she says through the cocked-open doors of the boys' gym.

Doc Wilson has his sleeping bag of a jacket off, has the white girl with the red face wrapped up in it.

She's jerking. Her whole body.

The gym is big and dark, but over in the stands there's a flashlight—Banner.

He's locating the dead, Jennifer knows.

Have they seen the kid on the elk yet, even?

"What can I do?" Jennifer says, taking a knee by Doc Wilson.

"Coffee," he says without looking up. Meaning: he needs steady hands to save this life.

Jennifer finds the thermos, pours the lid full, passes it over. When Doc Wilson takes it from her, she sees—has to see—this girl's bulging, leaky eyeball, and it takes her breath away.

This isn't corn syrup and latex, air bladders and hand pumps.

Jennifer holds it together long enough not to spill the coffee, then stumbles away, is leaning against the slick-brick wall when suddenly Banner's standing beside her.

"How's she doing?" he asks, about this girl.

"Abby," Jennifer dredges up, like saying her actual name can be a lifeline she climbs back up.

"Wynona Fleming's over there," Banner mumbles, his tone

telling Jennifer that it's not pretty. That it's the direct opposite of "pretty."

"Why is he targeting high schoolers this time?" Jennifer says.

"I don't even know if this is all of them," Banner says.

Jennifer, doing finger-antlers, says, "You saw the one on the—?"

Banner nods.

"Maybe she was texting with whoever did that to them?" he says then. "Kids do that, you know, they text all the—"

"I'm not from 1989," Jennifer tells him, and together they find Abby's bloody phone, its screen glowing awake under all that tacky red.

Jennifer takes it to the girls' restroom around the corner, and, when there's no light, she calls Banner in.

He steps in gingerly, like this is a trap.

"I'm not going to turn you in," Jennifer tells him, finding the paper towel roller in the beam of his flashlight. "But I don't guarantee you're not being recorded."

"What?"

"Proofrock's very own Chester the Molester," Jennifer says, tilting her head up and around, to the idea of hidden cameras.

"Oh yeah," Banner says. "Rexall."

"He's not the most upstanding citizen," Jennifer tells him, wiping the phone, having to wet the paper towel, which is zero-bit absorbent. "Unless, of course, he's *watching* one of his recordings..."

"This is the time for jokes, yeah," Banner says, stepping in to burn his bright beam onto the screen, and Jennifer's fingertips. After being so frozen, the light's warm.

"We can cry instead if you want."

"Did you really do it?" Banner asks then.

Jennifer tries not to change the carriage of her shoulders, the tilt of her eyes, the steadiness of her fingers.

But it's not easy.

"My dad, you mean," she says.

"Since we're talking about his best friend."

It tracks, Jennifer knows. You don't think about Rexall without Tab Daniels stepping in from those same shadows.

Still, "The court cleared me," she says.

"That's not what I'm asking."

"Did I swing a machete into him?" Jennifer says, the phone almost done. "You saw Tiff's video, didn't you?"

"She printed all the frames out," Banner says. "She's got, like, a photo album of it, moment by moment."

"A flipbook. And they call me twisted?"

"Did you?"

"I thought he was someone else," Jennifer mutters, presenting the mostly clean phone and staring right into Banner's eyes. Then, "Ask your wife, she might remember something about him that night."

"Letha?"

"Unless you've got another wife."

Instead of dignifying that, Banner's looking around the women's restroom like a fourth-grader.

"Everything you expected?" Jennifer asks. "Over there's where we put lingerie on, have pillow fights."

"'Skank Station,'" Banner reads slowly, from above the last mirror.

"Home sweet home," Jennifer says, and steps over, feels up there for the eyeliner pencil these four-years-later girls probably don't even know about.

It's still there.

"What's that?" Banner asks.

Jennifer presents it for inspection, says, "Mine, I left it here."

She pockets it before he can press her, and then she's trying to swipe into the phone.

"Here," Banner says, trading her the flashlight for the phone, but of course he doesn't know Abby's PIN, either.

There is a stack of texts on the lockscreen that pops back up after each failure, though. All from "Daddy Dearest."

"Shit," Banner says, about them. "I'm going to have to tell him, aren't I?"

"You're going to have to tell a lot of them," Jennifer says. "What next, Deputy?"

"We're not done here," Banner says, and Jennifer doesn't get it, but follows when he sweeps out, back into the gym.

Abby Grandlin isn't convulsing anymore, which probably isn't exactly wonderful, medically speaking.

"You don't know about fingerprints," Banner says to Jennifer.

"I know about fingerpr—" Jennifer starts to say, but he's already pressing Abby's limp thumb to the phone's screen.

When he stands again, the phone's open.

He swipes into messages, but—

"She was only talking with Wynona," he says.

"Was she Milton's little sister?" Jennifer asks, not even sure she could actually pick Milton Fleming from a line-up anymore. He was just another face in second grade, and at graduation.

Banner passes the phone back over, as if Jennifer needs it.

"Rex Allen will be back soon," he says.

"Hardy's here," Jennifer offers.

"He's not sheriff."

"Rex Allen barely is."

Banner steps away.

"Hey!" Jennifer says, holding the phone out to him.

"Being in a bathroom…" he says, meaning it's pee time.

"Need me?" Jennifer says down to Doc Wilson.

He doesn't answer, is doing something intimate and necessary to Abby's face, or breathing passage.

Jennifer steps away, gives them their privacy. Not because she trusts him with an unconscious human with breasts, but because she can tell he's in triage mode, not grope-and-caress mode.

Still, she hangs close, just to be sure.

Right when Abby's phone dims, she wakes it back up, is still in.

Looking around, which is a dead giveaway she's about to try something, she taps into the settings, turns the lockscreen off. It means confirming with Abby's limp thumb again, but Doc Wilson's otherwise occupied.

Jennifer scrolls through Abby's contacts.

Cinnamon Baker.

"Oh yeah," Jennifer says, and, lightly, because she's not sure she should be doing this, she touches that name.

It takes a few seconds for the line to ring—the signal's still thready—but then, on the fourth ring, a voice says, "Abs?"

"Cinnamon Baker?" Jennifer asks.

"Who is this?" she asks back.

"I'm at the high school, where are you?"

"Why?"

"Because there's somebody—you *know* why."

"Jade Daniels? Why do you have Abby's phone? Is she all—?"

"Where are you?"

"Do I need protection? I'm at the—Pleasant Valley. I thought you were here too. Is Abby with you?"

Jennifer switches ears, steps away from Doc Wilson.

"Your friends Mark and Kristen?" she says.

"Don't—I can't—"

"You have to, Cinnamon."

"Cinn. It's just Cinn."

"Is it true what your sister said?"

"Ginger? You *talked* to her? But she doesn't—"

"She did," Jennifer says, pacing.

"What did she tell you?"

"That you and her found some—some…"

"Oh, that," Cinn says. "We told the sheriff. He didn't clean it up? That was three, no, four years—I was in *junior high*."

"What was it?"

"Why does it matter?"

"Because everything does, Cinnamon."

"Cinn. It was just—" She coughs, like about to dry-heave. "It was some leftover from the Independence Day thing."

"The Independence Day *Massacre*."

"Or maybe it was just fish guts, I don't know. It's not like we *touched* it."

"So you left it there?"

"Why would we—yes!" And then, quieter, to some nurse off-phone: "No, no, it's… I'll eat it right after this?"

"Jocelyn Cates's son is dead too," Jennifer says. "I'm sorry. And—and the… the Fleming girl. Milton's little sister."

"*Wynona?*" Cinn shrieks.

"And some boy," Jennifer adds, quieter.

It's not her responsibility to drop all this on this girl, she knows. But, too, if she finds out about it all at the third-reel bodydump, then it might slow her run down, let her catch a blade in the back. This is for her own good. Let her cry and shrivel now, so she won't later.

"What was his… what does he look like?" Cinn asks.

"Sandy hair," Jennifer says, seeing him again, pinned on the elk. "Robert Pattinson eyes, like a vampire?"

"Jensen…" Cinn fills in, sobbing now. *"Why is this happening?"*

Good, good, Jennifer tells herself. That's exactly what the final girl needs to be thinking.

Except, of course, Cinn doesn't need to dial back to some prank she and her evil sister and their evil friends played on some unfortunate in eighth grade—their parents were busy being massacred then. And anyway, Dark Mill South wasn't in town to be wronged back then, or *ever*, meaning…

"It's not about revenge this time," Jennifer says.

"What do you mean, *revenge*? I volunteer, I donate, I never—"

"No, no, of course you do, and don't, and would never," Jennifer says, switching ears again, like the one on the right side's full. "This is… do you watch the news?"

"Dark Mill South," Cinn whispers.

"His beef is with everybody still drawing breath," Jennifer explains. "And—and for some reason he's targeted you and your friends."

"Me?"

"I'm sorry. But—"

"Then I can stop all this if I just... I mean, if I let him—?"

"No," Jennifer says. "That's not what final girls do."

"Final *what*?"

"Your sister knows," Jennifer says. "At least, she knows all the movies."

"She doesn't have to be at cheer practice four hours after school every day. But—can I just leave? Will that work?"

"The storm, no. And that won't stop him."

"What will?"

"You have to kill them with what they like to kill with," Jennifer says, squatted down now to think, because she hasn't had to think like this in... in four years. "Something sharp, or pointy. And then when they're down, you run over them a lot of times, or keep stabbing. Like, cut their Achilles tendons, gouge their eyes out, break their fingers, stab them in the—"

"Fire," Cinn says.

"No, no, not fire," Jennifer says. "Just—use whatever's there, when the time comes."

"So he's coming *here*?" Cinn asks back, such that Jennifer can kind of see her on her hospital bed at Pleasant Valley, drawing her knees up to herself and watching the door, the window.

"If that's where you stay."

"But my *sister's* up here," Cinn whispers. "She won't—I can't let him—"

"Where's the party?" Jennifer asks. "That's where he'll show up!"

"The party?"

"Where are all the kids getting together?"

"Well, I mean, it's usually..." Cinn trails off.

"My house," Jennifer fills in.

"We didn't think you were coming back," Cinn says. "And I never—"

"Doesn't matter. The party's got to be somewhere else, then. His kind can't stay away from—"

At which point the call drops. Not even the sound of air rushing in or some great emptiness. Just: nothing.

Jennifer studies the bars, and that little dot's not holding on very well.

She tries to dial, can't make a connection.

"Anything?" Banner asks her from the baseline of the court.

But what if she's lying? Jennifer asks herself.

What if Cinn and Ginger *did* find some tumorous mass pulsing under the pier? Almost definitely, it's some bullshit concoction Ginger made up in her fevered brain, through a cloud of narcotics and wishful thinking.

But, if not?

What if Dark Mill South just happens to be in town right when whatever Cinn and Ginger fed for all these years is finally grown up, and coming to town to shred a few teenage bodies? What if he's not killing anybody at all, but just trying to find a place to hunker down for the winter?

Worse—no no no, Jennifer tells herself, but she knows this is the drain her thinking's swirling toward: what if that bloody leftover handful of the Independence Day Massacre metastasized into… Stacey Graves?

She and the lake *are* connected in some way.

Maybe she escaped Ezekiel's big hands and bobbed up to the last place she knew when she was a real girl—Proofrock—but couldn't climb any higher than the underside of the pier?

"Then it's not over," Jennifer says. "It was just on pause."

Because slashers never really die. They just go to sleep for a few years.

But they're always counting the days until round two.

No, this time the party won't be on the water, under an inflatable movie screen.

Still, you can't lock high schoolers up too long without them all getting together to cut loose, as Dewey says.

That's not yet, though.

There's still time for Jennifer to… she doesn't want to, but at the same time she knows it's the only way… there's still time for her to prove Ginger's story wrong, by sneaking around to Terra Nova, seeing if some bedroom or basement over there is a hatchery, or an incubator, or a den.

Except?

This time she's not going to have to go the long way around, is she?

"Hey, I tried backing the snowmobile out of the display case," Banner's saying, "but—you didn't take that kill switch, did you?"

The little plastic key the engine won't start without.

"What?" Jennifer asks, trying to squint her whole face.

"The *kill* switch," Banner says.

"That plastic key?" Jennifer asks, so innocent, even trying to wap her Bambi-lashes up and down, never mind that that's more Letha's domain.

"We're stuck here without it," Banner says.

"I thought it was just—" Jennifer says, patting all her pockets, then a-ha'ing it. "I… I used the ladies' before I came here. Maybe it fell out of my pocket?"

"Which one?" Banner asks.

"Down the art hall."

Banner sighs, then points to Doc Wilson and Abby Grandlin, says, "Stay here, for if they need anything?"

"Am I deputized now?"

"Has hell frozen over?" Banner asks back, on his way out.

"Seen outside?" Jennifer comes back with, to the swinging door.

She counts to twenty, which should be enough time for him to have passed the dead-boy elk, and then she's running for that same junction, but—very John Bender—sliding around the corner and trying to accelerate for the front of the school.

Last time she sneaked across to Terra Nova, she had to walk the dam, the chalky bluff behind Camp Blood.

Now, though, now she can go straight across.

WHAT ROUGH BEAST

Lode Star" is a term that comes from compasses, which are magnetic, and so always point generally to the "vein of ore" in the sky: Polaris, Star of the Evening, friend to sailors—geographic north, the pole the magnetite in pigeons' brains homes in on. Another name for the North Star is "Cynosure," which is a person or thing that's the center of attention.

The cynosure for Proofrock in December was Dark Mill South, who prefers to orient his victims such that they face that same magnetic north, when and if there's time to set such a tableau—as there was with both Jensen Jones and Wynona Fleming, among others.

As you requested, here I will propose a hypothesis for that com-pulsion. But before I do, no—this in response to your notes on my previous submission—until my report card comes in June, my mother won't even know I've done this independent study with you, Mr. Armitage. So, corollary with that is that I have no reason to have told her that you showed me a clip of that recording of Dark Mill South as Dugout Dick in Elk Bend, which I know must have been an effort to acquire, and no small expense.

To reset, here, though: why would Dark Mill South arrange his victims such that they face north? To answer that, we first have to delve into the understory of the internet, and attempt to settle on which version of him we're talking about, which, as William Hesseltine says, is *akin to trying to nail jelly to the wall*.

But I'll do my best.

As near as I can tell, the different origin theories for Dark Mill South settle into two categories: his Native American heritage, and his relationship with other legendary figures.

That Dark Mill South is on the tribal rolls of the Red Lake Band of Chippewa—the Ojibwe I was talking about in an earlier paper, who are really the Anishinaabe—is fact. Or, I should say, "DM South" is on those rolls.

And here our troubles begin, Mr. Armitage.

- The Birth Certificate. There's various, and variously manipulated, versions of the birth certificate ascribed to Dark Mill South to be found. None of which actually have either "Dark" or "Mill" in front of "South." However, there apparently was, at one time, a family with that surname on the Red Lake Indian Reservation. It's presumed that surname is a transliteration of a different and more meaningful name held by someone at the turn of the previous century, when former naming conventions were "normalized" by people not familiar with the culture or the language. Of fervent interest online is the date all of these versions of that birth certificate share—"1912"—making Dark Mill South, if he is indeed "DM South," 107 years old at the time of his rampage through Proofrock. It's because of this date that Dark Mill South is often made out to be the Native version of the Wandering Jew, cursed to walk the earth until the Second Coming.

- The Dakota 38, whom Abraham Lincoln ordered hanged en masse—about which we've already spoken. Proponents of this theory cast Dark Mill South as one of those thirty-eight, risen to seek justice for him and his wrongly convicted fellow tribesmen. That accounts of that day stop with the hangings, and don't document what was done with the bodies afterward, only adds credence to this theory for true believers, in that it allows a vast open space from which one lone Dakota can climb up from the mass grave, or the ashes of the bonfire, his chest heaving, his eyes dark, his hands clenching into fists, his murderous gaze roving from sea to shining sea.
- The Boarding School. As is no secret anymore, the policy of stealing Native American children and forcing them into Christian curriculums at residential schools was deplorable, as was the policy to "kill the Indian, save the man" by doling out punishments for speaking Native languages, for wearing their uniforms incorrectly, for practicing forbidden religions—the list goes on. Note that this theory is in dialogue with the previous one, in that it also has Dark Mill South climbing up from the grave he was disposed in—presumably after

having died as a result of neglect, starvation, sexual abuse, and loneliness—and then, in a graft from the Birth Certificate theory, walking the earth until he's gotten adequate revenge on all the "black robes" who killed him, his fellow abductees, and his culture, all in the name of their god. As for how those who would have Dark Mill South be at war with the church explain his seemingly arbitrary, opportunistic killings: a child of the boarding school system, who had never seen white people until the moment of his abduction, would naturally assume that since the clergy abusing him was white, that "white" was then the defining characteristic of the enemy.

Though I of course want to respect Native American tradition and sentiment, Mr. Armitage, common sense dictates that all of these theories have to come down to wishful thinking. I don't say this to demean or reduce, but to posit the likelihood that there's a more rational explanation.

But before we get there, we have to get more irrational for a moment:

- The Golem, which is another graft from Judaism. This is the hulking protector or "revenger" that gets pitted against those who would harm or oppress the Jewish people. Made of clay, supernaturally strong, and animated by magic, the Golem is a fearsome presence, to be sure, but also something of a mindless automaton, in that it's controlled by the wronged and desperate person who raised it—and nearly always, of course, loses control of it, leaving it to, as Dark Mill South does, rampage until forcibly stopped.

- Grendel, the monster of the Old English poem *Beowulf*. Grendel is less a rampager, more a ravager—specifically, of Heorot, a mead hall and occasional dormitory for warriors. Like the Golem, Grendel can only be stopped with force, by someone pure of heart and intention. Dark Mill South being identified with Grendel, then, is of course an indictment of law enforcement, in that, were any of them pure of heart and intention, then Dark Mill South would have been stopped years ago, rather than ducking into state after state, and killing at will.

However, taking Occam's Razor into account, we have to ask not what's the most fantastic explanation, but the simplest? Yes, Sherlock Holmes famously tells us that "Once you eliminate the impossible, whatever remains, no matter how improbable, must be the truth," but I humbly submit that what's left after eliminating the preceding "impossible" explanations for Dark Mill South is, in fact, not all that improbable.

Monsters happen, Mr. Armitage.

I don't need to tell you of all people this.

And so I hang my argument on a single, ill-focused snapshot, only purported to be Dark Mill South:

- The Video Store. In this snapshot's foreground is the intended subject: a brother and sister, probably twins, between eight and ten years old, enacting a tug of war between a clamshell videotape case of *The Fox and the Hound* (1981). That neither of their hands even slightly covers the title is our indication that this is being posed by a parent. But the children are not our subject, Mr. Armitage. Behind them, left of center, standing behind the rental counter, is a hulking Native American man, for this instant happening to be staring directly into the lens, as if challenging it. Though his long hair leaves most of his face in shadow, his eyes are sharp glints of white in there, and his height, assuming the rental counter is standard, is well over six feet.

This snapshot surfaced online during the first year of Dark Mill South's trial. Presumably one of these twins, now adults, recognized him on the news, dug through an old photo album from the attic, snapped a picture of a picture, and put it on social media. Early comments surrounding it and its repostings are mostly about trying to fit this video store job into Dark Mill South's known timeline.

Since that timeline is so difficult to establish, though—he was probably in Minnesota in the nineties, and he was in Utah by 2015, so he must have crossed the vast Midwest at some point, perhaps procuring work in a video store along the way—interest in this snapshot of unknown provenance fizzled, and it became a curiosity, another maybe, and so got relegated to less and less visited pages and sites.

But?

When we take into account the horror movie associations with Dark Mill South's killings in Proofrock, I submit that this snapshot is perhaps revealing, in that it provides a time in his life in which he could have familiarized himself with the films he would eventually emulate.

So, I said we had to first settle on a version of Dark Mill South we could believe in. This last one makes the most sense to me. Or, at least, it doesn't break any rules of nature, or require magical thinking. When video rental stores were common, people did work at them. Even Native Americans.

But how does this version of Dark Mill South inform his compulsion to face his victims north?

Though I prefer novels and reading to film and television, I do nevertheless know that a certain novel has been adapted to film multiple times.

Mary Shelley's *Frankenstein; or, The Modern Prometheus* (1818).

If the adaptations are faithful to the novel—and I assume they are, as why stray from what works?—then Dark Mill South the video store clerk could well have taken one such adaptation home, and been not just enchanted with it, but programmed by it. In the novel's final act, Victor Frankenstein pursues the Creature north through Europe, into Russia, and then beyond, onto the Arctic Ocean, after which the Creature would seem to be heading to the North Pole.

Above which, of course, sits a certain star.

Dark Mill South, perhaps already dimly aware that the world was looking at him as a similar "Creature," could have identified with Dr. Frankenstein's creation, in that both of them had been ill-treated by the world, largely for their imposing size, and presumed violent natures—Native Americans being attractive in the nostalgic sense so long as they pose no threat.

So, arranging his victims such that they would stare north, then, could be Dark Mill South asking them to understand him, Mr. Armitage. To watch him, lonely and alone, leap from ice floe to ice floe, receding into the cold fog, removing himself from human society once and for all.

But, of course, he didn't ask just one or two people to sit there and understand his plight.

He needed a whole theaterful.

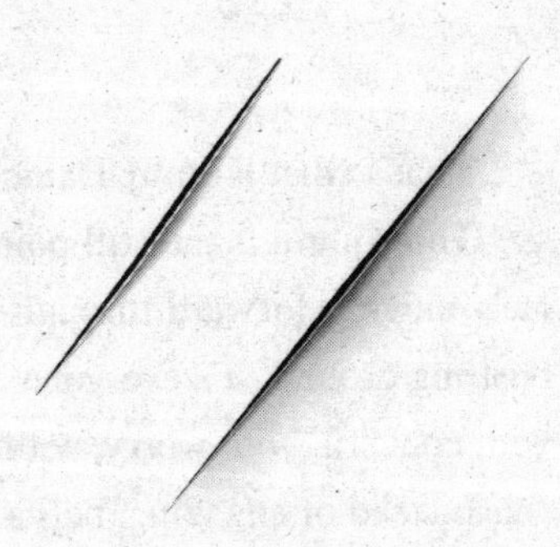

THE BURNING

When the automatic door of the dollar store tries to swing in but stops, the power cylinder frozen, slushy on the inside, Kimmy Daniels only flicks her eyes to this disturbance. But not her face, her head, her shoulders.

Online, which is where she really lives, she's found a forty-four minute video of one of the Queen's Guard standing like a toy soldier in his red wool and bearskin hat, his back ramrod straight, face expressionless.

The recording wasn't made by someone heckling him, trying to force a reaction, but by someone watching this moment unfold, and then keep unfolding. Over those forty-four minutes, tourists arrange themselves around him for photos, which Kimmy supposes makes sense—part of the London experience. Some whisper into his ear, some put cigarette butts into the barrel of his rifle, or flash him, moon him, and others run at him like they're going to jam their shoulders into his midsection, only to veer off at the last moment, the crowd cheering this on.

The Guard never flinches, never reacts.

His post might be ceremonial, his rifle not loaded, but still, he's above all this.

That's what Kimmy Daniels can't stop watching.

This Guard is the still point in the turning world, she knows. He's moving forward through time, but it's everyone else who's bustling around, it's everyone else who's wearing themselves out with concern, with worry, with trying.

Instead of engaging, he's a full step back from all that, is just standing his post.

Kimmy can appreciate that.

But, at the same time, she knows if she asks Philo, her sort of common-law husband, to watch how amazing this Queen's Guard guy is, he'll assure her, and anybody else in their living room, that *he* could get a reaction from that punk. These last six months, since his DNA test came back that he was a quarter Native American, he's been insisting Kimmy call him "Holy Crow."

Holy Crow.

Before too long, he'll probably realize Tab had been Indian as well, and then Kimmy will be the "Indian lover," the "blond squaw," the "red man's delight," who knows.

If she stands still enough, though, it'll all just wash right past, won't it?

After work every day, she sits on the couch, "Holy Crow" sinking into his chair a few feet away, but she's not really sitting with her feet tucked up beside her. In her head, her eyes are locked on a point sixty feet away.

She's pretty sure that's the trick.

As if to confirm she could be in this Queen's Guard—had she been a dude, had she been in the military in Britain, had she not got pregnant in high school—back in September, right before the first snow, the store got an early shipment of unsold Christmas junk from 2018. Instead of setting it up in a Christmas tree display like the diagram in the box, Millicent, the manager, had just dumped all three tubs of it into two shopping baskets and rolled them to the front of the store so customers would have to skirt them on the way in, skirt them and consider them, maybe not be able to leave this candy cane behind, or that plastic sleigh.

It's only a dollar, after all, right? And everybody loves Christmas. Everybody wants some of that holiday cheer.

In the lulls between customers in September, Kimmy went through the baskets, organizing them somewhat: the breakable ornaments all at the front so they won't shatter under heavier stuff, the twinkle lights and tinsel piled in the child's seats, and all the different Santas in the back, their boxes stacked like bricks, all of them looking through the side of the basket, out at the sidewalk.

The one item that had no twin, no lot, that didn't go with any of the others, that felt like fate to Kimmy, was a four-inch little nutcracker that someone in the warehouse had probably found under a shelf and thrown in this box to hide it, not have to inventory it. An upright wooden soldier in glossy red, his shiny black heels forever knocked together, his back board-straight, his mouth just an uninvolved line, neither grim nor judgmental.

Kimmy took him to her register, set him up between the plastic partition and the cash drawer so only she could see him, and when her shifts were over, she hid him up under the conveyor belt.

Now he watches her with his painted eyes through her endless shifts. He never moves, never flinches, never tips his beer slowly over on the coffee table because it's warm, never sleeps through lunch, never yells at the football players on the television like he knows them personally, and can't believe they're doing this to him.

Like Kimmy, too, this little guy doesn't jerk his head over to the automatic door, stuck just a few inches open, but still trying.

And? Kimmy knows full well that, were she not made of stone, had that video not conditioned her, showed her how it can be done, she would have jerked from the shock of that door moving—the rest of the store is dark. Millicent's got some of the clamp lamps tied into the hundred-foot extension cord plugged into the generator out back, which is also keeping the register ready to do business, but otherwise the dollar store's dead. Kimmy wouldn't even be here except Millicent came and got her on a *snowmobile*, telling Kimmy she was the only dependable one, and "thank you for being so reliable."

Kimmy kept her face expressionless.

She walked out to Millicent's youngest son's snowmobile, but she imagined Millicent had brought a handtruck, was dollying this Queen's Guard out the trailer for her shift in the public eye, where she would be tested by hecklers, by kids, by show-offs.

Kimmy didn't know the door at the front of the store is live, though. Millicent made a show of unlocking it—Kimmy has no keys, wants no keys—but Kimmy assumed that any of the customers Millicent guaranteed were going to need nearly-expired loaves of bread or tubes of tennis balls or reading glasses were going to have to shoulder in when the door didn't open.

But it's trying, must be on the same circuit as the register.

Not that that's any of Kimmy's concern.

She just stands, and waits, and doesn't react.

Like the Queen's Guard, she's wearing her thick clothes, her big boots, still has her hat on—the generator isn't big enough to run the heater, or even, Millicent apologized, a space heater.

This is what time-and-a-half feels like, Kimmy tells herself. It's cold, it's quiet, it's dark, but the loyalty the store will earn from this or that customer by having been there when they needed something will pay off in the long run, supposedly.

Millicent's already snowmobiled back to her house, of course. She'll be back at four to lock up early and ferry Kimmy home, where she'll try to get through another evening without saying Philo's new name, since she's pretty sure every time she says it, a little piece of her soul dies.

It should have been dead long ago, she knows, but souls are like livers: they regenerate and regenerate, until you've finally poisoned them enough that the only thing they can do is kill you, take you down with them.

After dinner, and in spite of promising herself not to anymore, Kimmy might just dial up that Queen's Guard video again. She knows she's sort of addicted to it, and that little addictions can lead to big ones, but watching it's got to be healthier than what she was looping before: that recording of Jenny swinging a machete into Tab.

That recording is her divorce papers—it's exactly when she quit being married. What had started at a random party her junior year was finally and really over. Never mind that Tab was supposed to have died already when his Grand Prix rolled, his senior year. That was what the world wanted, what the world had tried to make happen. But he'd squeaked through with a jangly grin like always, and come out the other side shrugging one shoulder, asking who was going to get the beer for the night—not him, he was charmed.

The recording of his last moments is fuzzy and mostly shadows, but it's enough, and it's everywhere, too: as soon as one's reported and taken down, two more pop up to replace it.

But Kimmy doesn't watch that one so much anymore. She stopped because, right after that machete makes contact, that high schooler recording it with her phone shrieks and drags the recording suddenly to the left.

If Kimmy pauses it right there, then what's in that frame, what's in that darkness, it's the old camp halfway around the lake. The one she only went to that night after the football game because she wanted to be part of what everybody was always talking about on Monday morning. The bonfire where Tab asked her if she wanted to see the "Stabbin' Cabin," as he called it.

She thought it referred to those kids killed here back in the sixties. It was a different kind of stabbing, as it turned out.

But she tells herself she doesn't regret that.

If she doesn't let Tab lead her through that broken door, then there's never any Jenny, and without Jenny's small laugh, without her kindergarten art projects, without her trying to hang sheets on the laundry line and trying so hard, but she's too short, and doesn't understand old-style clothespins…

Without Jenny, Kimmy doesn't make it through those first few years of marriage to Tab. Jenny was always the reason, the prize, the little piece of secret magic who made it all worth it. Never mind where Kimmy could have ended up had she gotten her diploma—now Jenny has hers. Kimmy was there for it, to be sure it was real, that at least one of them would have the chance now to get out.

She hadn't clapped when Jenny walked the stage, but that was just because she didn't want faces turning to her, accusing her, asking her where she'd been until now.

Inside, though, her heart had been a balloon, filling up with air.

One that popped on July Fourth. Along with everyone else's.

Now everyone in Proofrock comes into the store dragging their burst balloons, Kimmy can tell.

It's better to have never had one at all, she's pretty sure.

It's better to just stand your post, man your register, and let the hustle and bustle and grief and regret just sweep past—it doesn't even matter. To prove it, Kimmy dials that forty-four minute video up in her head again, watching the blond woman shaking what she's got right in that Queen's Guard's face. His pupils don't even dilate or contract, because he's above all this grubby stuff. Nothing can hurt him, not so long as he doesn't let it.

Instead of trying to imagine the training that must have gone into this, Kimmy assigns different backstories to him: he's working on a diorama for the second-grade science fair when his father storms through, steps over to sweep all those hours of work away, hardly even breaking stride; he's standing at a fence in junior high, watching a hamstrung goat try to get away from three dogs; he's hiding in the bedroom of his first marriage, faking sleep while something unspeakable happens down the hall.

Or maybe he's really asleep.

After a while, you can forget you're pretending, and just burrow down, hide.

But Kimmy doesn't think about that anymore either.

She was a kid herself. She didn't know. She couldn't imagine Tab, a father, could—it's not her fault. She didn't know then about standing guard, and how important that is.

If she'd just had Jenny later, then, then… then she probably doesn't have her at all, right? Because she's already left Tab.

It's binds like this that show her she's doing the right thing, staring at some point sixty feet away. Or, *twenty* feet away: she leans against a different part of her station, to watch whoever this is work the door.

Snow is swirling in ahead of him or her, swirling in and curling high, dissipating like breath, like the storm is a giant Santa Claus lying out there on Main, trying to pry into the dollar store.

Come, Kimmy tells it. *Do it already.*

Mash this whole store flat, please, and me with it.

The door shudders from an impatient shoulder, the ice caked onto its glass calving off, and then it opens a foot more, the power cylinder groaning with effort but not really assisting at all, just dragging the generator down.

A moment later, *Jenny* slides through, Kimmy's breath suddenly clenched in her chest, the fingers of her right hand flinching up as if to lift a hand in greeting. But, Guard that she is, she doesn't wave, or let herself do anything.

It's been, what? Four years? Five?

Last time it was hair dye, $1.99 plus tax.

Kimmy doesn't raise her eyebrows at Jenny, crossing from the frozen-open door to duck into an aisle, and Jenny doesn't cock her chin up to say hey after all this time, all these years.

Her *hair*, though.

It's crusted with ice, but still, this is how it was in her second grade, isn't it? Second, third, fourth, all the way up to—to sixth, yes. Her hair's the one good thing she ever got from Tab.

It takes her twelve steps to disappear into aisle 3, the pharmacy stuff, and then the shadows between the clamp lamps are passing her among themselves and she's just the sound of ski pant legs swishing against each other. Usually, in winter, people's boots will squelch on the tile, but it's cold enough in here that the ice in Jenny's treads probably isn't even melting enough to make that sound.

When the swishing of the pants is a rising sound, is about to crash at Kimmy's register, she turns around to face the customer, "greet them with a smile" as Millicent insists.

Jenny unceremoniously dumps her selections onto the belt: a clatter of steak knives with wooden handles, an oversize novelty lighter, pink mittens with jagged white stripes, a bag of teriyaki beef jerky, a can of WD-40, and bright blue swim goggles, the kind that fit right down against your eyes, like contact lenses with rubber straps.

When Kimmy looks up to Jenny about this, about what it could mean, or say, Jenny's looking purposefully out at the street.

Kimmy tears a plastic bag off, arranges the items inside, then double-bags the first bag, so a knife poking through won't spill everything else. She hands it over without scanning any of it in.

Jenny considers this, looks around, checking the corners for cameras, maybe—is she on probation now?—and then, finally, she takes the bag, is swishing out, no nod thanks, no grunt of approval.

Which is fair.

Like she used to, Kimmy moves through the store, finding the goggles, the kitchenware, the spray lubricant, the winter clothes display, the snacks.

At the register she scans each of them in, slides the $14.48 out of her wallet and into the register, then moves out into the dark aisles, replacing the items, hanging each of them like she would a Christmas ornament and walking fast away.

Your hair, she knows she should have said, after all these years.

Except she didn't.

Except she couldn't.

On the impulse rack are the white, off-brand tic tacs Millicent says must be walking out, as inventory never matches their actual stock.

Kimmy tells herself not to, but she's already doing it—opening the tic tacs' little flap and shaking some out into her hand, then shaking more out, clapping them into her mouth, the mint burning her gums, her throat.

What she read online is that if a Queen's Guard is going to pass out from heat exhaustion or vasovagal fainting, then he needs to maintain the same posture, so that he falls like a toy soldier would, not catching himself, just letting his face slam into the ground.

Kimmy longs for that kind of discipline. For the transformation finally being complete. She imagines her teeth shattering from the impact, her mouth full of white breakage and blood, not generic tic tacs.

She shakes some more out onto her palm, and only realizes she's crying when the tic tacs are trembling, dancing, jumping.

She closes her hand tight around them.

The wind and snow are coming in through the front door that the draggy cylinder couldn't open, and can't quite shut now.

Kimmy tracks up from the powder gathering on the blue mat to the whiteness outside, and for a moment, between gusts, there's a—a tall form, and a high eye watching her through the glass, an eye that doesn't seem human, that seems more like the way a cow or a horse looks at you, turning its long head to the side to see more deeply into your soul.

Because she's not a Queen's Guard at all, not really—she can't keep anything safe, not even herself—Kimmy flinches back from this, her handful of tic tacs falling down and down.

There's annoying shit, there's stupid shit, and then there's *this*.

Letha's on her hands and knees in the snow, in the middle of the worst storm in a century—and in Idaho, that's saying something.

But she's got to find them: her pills.

The blue and tan capsule is easy. It's right there on top. She pinches it up, chocks it between her lips.

The all-red one is tumbling and rolling in the wind, though. Letha skitters forward on hands and knees, traps the pill under her palm like a bug, then lifts that handful of snow, teases the red from the white, parks this one in her lips as well.

Retracing her steps—her *crawl*—she has to dig down. The snow is accumulating that fast, yes.

The two left are both tablets, one big, one the smallest possible dot.

If she can just find *one*, please. And, while she's asking: maybe the one she needs the most? Like, *right*-right now?

Letha's chest is shuddering, she knows. It's not crying, it's… it's hating herself is what it is. Did she think she could pour her noon dose out into her hand like it was just another day? Did she not think the wind cared about pills and tablets that weigh nothing but mean everything? Where is her head?

On all the dead kids, she tells herself back. At the motel. The nursing home. The high school.

But still.

The easy thing to do would be to just stand back up, trudge over to the sheriff's office, pretend this never happened. Which is all good and fine until some two-year-old is digging in the gravel here this summer and finds some "candy," and has to be rushed to the emergency room—Letha *cannot* allow this. Not even the chance of it. She doesn't sleep for the rest of winter if she has to keep thinking about having left a pharmaceutical landmine like that. Justice would be Adrienne finding it anyway, wouldn't it be?

No, this is on Letha. Never mind the cold. Never mind the wind. Never mind that she can't watch behind her. Never mind that, yes, she has backups in her pocket, as close to her skin as they can get, so she can always be sure of them.

She touches a dot of white up, her eyes shaped like wonder—the steroid, the stupid little steroid—but it's just a fleck of ice, a frozen tear, she doesn't know.

She presses it between her fingers until it's gone.

Really? Even if it weren't snowing, that little tablet would be gone, just one speck of thousands in this square foot alone. And, and: if a kid does find it and eat it this summer? If this one single itty-bitty nothing makes it that long, which it won't? It's just a single dose of anti-inflammatory. Months of them can mess with bone density—Letha swigs calcium every morning—but one single one? That's just a heavy shot of ibuprofen, pretty much. Not even that.

Which is good.

Now she just has to find the bigger tablet. The one she *needs*.

And going fast hurts more than it helps. It's not about how much snow you scoop up, it's about how well you sift it, how well you inspect it, blowing off your palm.

It's about how much you *want* it, in which case—

"Ahh," Letha says.

There it is, that perfect circle of white, its edges the only thing signaling that it's really and truly there in her hand again.

Instead of wedging it between her lips with the other two, Letha nudges it under the cuff of her thermals, right against the pulse of her wrist, and stands unsteadily, having to lean against the wind. Feeling the way it buffets her, wants to take her with it, scrape and tumble her down to nothing, lets her feel like she's in a battle, and her only ammunition, really, it's this handful of scavenged pills.

Oh, the stories we tell ourselves, her therapist is always saying, in commiseration.

Except this isn't that. This is real.

Letha sits down hard on the bench, never mind the snow that comes up to her elbows.

She takes one of the pills from her lips, puts it with the tablet in her cuff, and mentally prepares for this next part of the ordeal. Before all the surgeries, she could have dry-swallowed all three of these at once, no problem, bring it on, but before all her surgeries, she wouldn't have *needed* all these pills.

The reason she can't slam them all at once now is that it would involve unhinging her mouthgear and delicately prying her teeth open, terrified with each moment of stretching that the new tendons in her jaw, under her ears on both sides, are going to tear away again, starting this whole process all over for the *third* time. Without the brace, her chin could marionette down against her throat again, the skin of her face tightening from that, never mind her moisturizer regimen.

And she doesn't want to start over, please.

For Banner, for Adrienne, for everyone, she pretends it's nothing, that she's tough, that she's grateful to be alive, that this is just the price for that.

Key word: *pretends*.

Not "shudders inside," not "cringes every moment," not "always a breath away from giving up."

And, she *is* grateful. She wants for nothing. She has a beautiful family. If she ever complains, she knows, then… then that can all be taken away, can't it? Because of a moment of weakness on her part?

"I'm sorry," she says as best she can, she's not sure to who. Herself, maybe. The world. Anybody tuned in to her garbled words.

To get the pills in and down without unhinging her retainer, she wets the tip of her index finger against her top gums, just behind her right canine. Finding moisture in places she never considered usably wet is something she's learned since her tongue got imprisoned behind her teeth. Vegetable bags for produce at the grocery store are the first place it came up. Flipping through Banner's paperwork for him was the second. This—medicine time—isn't the third, but counting all of the day's differences really just means committing them to memory and dwelling on them, so she's stopped at 2.

The dissolvable shell of the blue and tan pill adheres perfectly to this stolen moisture, so now the pill's magically balanced on the tip of her finger, and *not* blowing away, thank you very much. With her other hand, she holds her left cheek out far enough to guide her index finger in, work whichever med this is back around her molars, her mind kicking up textbook images of Bartolomeu Dias rounding the horn of Africa—stupid history class. Her throat wants to gag, *needs* to gag, but throwing up is a choking hazard for her now. All she's got in her is an avocado shake five hours ago, but that can stop her throat up as well as anything, she knows.

Using her tongue, she gets the pill cued up, makes herself swallow hard, and then keeps it swallowed.

After the blue and tan, she repeats the process with the red one—her world is immunosuppressants—and, finally, as dessert, the little round tablet that doesn't want to stick to her finger, making her have to Pez-dispenser her head back, exposing her throat out here in the open.

It's the painkiller, though, so it's worth it. Never mind the taste—bitter, harsh, dangerous. When it finally goes down, scraping the whole way, Letha can feel every hungry thing inside her opening up for it, each part of her wanting just a single grain, please. And maybe another. And maybe the rest of them too, please. And: *now.*

Yes, her phone buzzed, telling her it was time for her pills again, but no, she hadn't exactly needed that reminder. She can't become a junkie, though. For Adrienne's sake. For Banner's. And for herself, she guesses, if she still factors into any of the equations.

But no one could expect her to hurt all the time and not take anything for it.

It hardly even leaves her swimmy in the head anymore. And, so long as she remembers the stool softeners with a glass of water each night at bedtime, there's not even any adverse effects—other than getting shaky and hollow if she's late with the next round.

She's never late, always has extras on her.

And, no, she's not looking back to the taped-over front door of the sheriff's office, doesn't want to see Banner standing there holding Adie, watching his wife get herself doped up again.

Because she prefers to take her meds in private, without an audience, she told him she was just going to pick up all that ski gear Rexall had been collecting when she shot him—it's the least she can do: finish his janitorial duties. A harmless nothing-lie, one she made not a lie by actually picking these clothes up. As she was doing it, though… are they clues to something? Or, is there even really a mystery in the first place?

Some slashers, she knows, are all about that: who's doing it, and why. Figure it out early and you might get to survive.

This one, though, it's more like a fox has gotten into the henhouse, is biting at whoever's flapping and squawking.

A big, dark, scary fox.

That doesn't mean he can't be put down, though. By the right girl.

Cinn?

Letha doesn't want that for her, the girl's gone through enough—her parents, her sister, the rumors at school about her and the new history teacher—but she has to acknowledge that Cinn makes the most sense.

It can't be Letha or Jennifer, anyway. It can't be Letha because, she knows now, she never really was a final girl. It was Jennifer who stopped the Independence Day Massacre from being worse than it already was.

But, Jennifer doing that… doesn't it mean she's already made that transformation? That she's already processed through, come out stronger, more killer?

Now it's Cinn's turn.

That's just the terrible way it works. Sorry, kid.

And, yes, now Letha *is* looking back at the taped-over door, and, no, thankfully, Banner isn't there. After his run back from Henderson High, what he needs is some more water, and a blanket, and maybe some dry clothes, different boots.

He'd been trying to beat Jennifer back to the office, even though she's supposed to be on a stolen snowmobile, would have made it minutes before if that's where she was going.

Letha just passed Adrienne across to him, jacketed up, said she was going to go get those clothes that were trying to blow away.

Only, now, she's put most of them on. They're good ski gear, and fit right—her and Cinn are about the same height, and Cinn is who these are from, right? This is the outfit Gal hand-delivered yesterday?

Doesn't matter. Letha will bury her hands in the pockets and huddle back to the office soon enough.

But not right now.

Sure, she feels bad about the front door. Yeah, Rex Allen's prize shotgun's scratched up. Okay, so she peppered a citizen with birdshot.

None of that's life and death, though. None of it's on par with what Banner told her's happened up at the high school. With what Jennifer said happened at the nursing home. With what's still going *on*.

Letha wraps her hand into a fist because she can't clench her jaw, and that small change in blood pressure finally flushes the Oxy into her bloodstream the right way, the warm-numb way. It's like she just activated her superpowers.

It's not so cold anymore.

Her vision is sharper, her thoughts faster, more pure.

Don't get used to this, she tells herself, but she's not really listening.

If Dark Mill South steps out in front of her right now, then watch out. She won't come at him directly, isn't *that* high, that pure, but she will try to hook her boot into the side of his knee, and then be running, leading him out onto the ice. Because she's dressed for it now. Because he's got to outweigh her by more than double, and there's got to be some thin spot out there.

She'll run all day, all night, until he either collapses from exposure or falls through, down into Ezekiel's Cold Box. For permanent. And every time she starts to falter, her lungs frothing red, her legs numb, she'll think of Adrienne, of Banner, and she'll regather, regroup, she'll touch her fingertips to the ice, push up again, stagger on.

You don't need a good jaw to run. You just need heart. You just have to want it.

Letha wants it.

She nods, promising herself to give Dark Mill South sixty more seconds to appear in the storm before her.

"I'm right here," she says out loud, all around.

Forty-five more seconds, now.

Banner's not watching anymore. Probably he's getting Adrienne settled in somewhere, or seeing to Rexall in holding, or gassing up the generator, or trying again to raise Rex Allen on the radio, or… it doesn't matter.

Just, please, let it be Letha who squares off against this particular fox in the henhouse? Not Banner. All he's got are bullets, and authority, neither of which has currency in the slasher.

Thirty seconds.

At least, whatever Banner's doing in the office, he's doing it in comparative silence. For the few minutes before he was knocking on the back door, his fingers too frozen to make his keys work, the phones had stopped ringing. Meaning either the lines were down again, or the cell towers were. Both, probably.

"Put it on my tab," Letha mumbles. Along with a new shotgun for Rex Allen. And a fleet of snow machines. A wall of cell towers ringing Pleasant Valley would save them all a lot of trouble right about now, wouldn't it?

Not that this will ever happen again.

It shouldn't even be happening now.

In all the slashers Letha's been memorizing, the least believable part isn't Jason or Michael getting back up, or this all being Freddy's dream, or nobody figuring out Ghostface is plural, or that a children's doll can rack up this high a bodycount. It's that—*Cheerleader Camp*, say, or *Sleepaway Camp*: dead kids are showing up, but the administrators never make a big deal about that.

Maybe this is how that happens, right? These seven or eight dead kids in Proofrock definitely matter… but they're on delay, too. Only Letha and Banner and Jennifer even know about them all, and there's no way they can make a town-wide announcement about them, to get everyone to lock their doors, check their windows, load their guns.

The result?

Dead kids are showing up, and nobody in the moment's making a big deal about it. Meaning more and more kids can just *keep* stacking up.

How is Cinn even going to deal with this, in five years? She'll end up like her sister, probably, which is a crappy prize for fighting through the horror.

Well, either that or she'll have a synthetic jaw, and be eighty percent a secret junkie.

Fifteen seconds.

Reprieve almost over.

Time for Letha to climb up out of her own thoughts and try to figure a way to survive, to close the beaches, to keep her husband from having to try to stop a killer he's not equipped *to* stop.

Almost directly behind her, thirty yards behind her, which in this storm might as well be a mile, Lonnie's still coddling his precious snow machine in the first bay of his shop. Almost directly in front of her is where twelve people died, once upon a holiday. Including her dad.

Right where she's sitting is where she first really looked into Jennifer's eyes, when she was Jade.

It was hot that day, she recalls. And it never let up until… until all the funerals were over, she guesses. Until all the victims of the Independence Day Massacre were buried and cried over.

What will Proofrock do after this, though? You can't bury people in ground frozen solid. You don't cry over a grave if your tears are going to freeze. But that doesn't mean you don't have to cry, either.

And, these high school seniors—some of them have only been in Proofrock for a few months, right? Where will their parents even *want* to bury them?

"Put it on my tab," Letha says again, nodding that she'll pay for those transports, those services. For whatever, it doesn't even matter. Just drops in the bucket, or drops *out* of the bucket, but the level in the bucket never goes down, and even if it ever does, there's buckets and buckets lined up behind it, more than Letha can ever spend.

No seconds, now.

Letha stares down into the whiteness at her feet, which she was just digging in… what's the movie where the guy digs in the toilet for a heroin suppository he didn't mean to shit out?

Doesn't matter.

That's not her.

She doesn't even say words like "shit."

She looks away from where she was digging, looks past where she walked, chasing the ski clothes, and… a footprint?

No, it's too narrow, too much a circle, isn't a footprint, but a—a *hoof* print.

Letha takes a knee, moving slow like this is something she can sneak up on, and lets her fingers feel into that already-filling space. At the bottom of it is where the hoof compacted the snow into ice.

Why would a deer or elk or moose or whatever be crossing the ice *today*? And, why come to town at all?

She closes her eyes to better feel this hoof print out, to commit it to memory, and, down like that, communing with whatever this animal is, or trying to commune, she hears a *chainsaw* rev up right beside her.

She doesn't flinch, has been waiting for just this, has been asking for this.

Thank you, she says inside, breathing in deep because she's about to surge forward with everything she has, surge forward and run into the whiteness with perfect form, keep running until she's saved everyone in Proofrock.

But she can't help it, she has to look first. To see.

At first there's just swirling whiteness, the storm gusting, snow swirling, but when it clears—when it clears…

It's Jennifer, sitting on that snowmobile she sort of stole. Her jacket's rimed with snow, her hands are in the most ridiculous knit mittens, her hood is cinched down tight over her face, and she's got swim goggles on her eyes. It makes her look like an Inuit in a black and white photograph from a hundred years ago, with their walrus ivory slit-glasses to keep them from going snowblind.

Letha only knows about those glasses because Mr. Samuels or Mr. Baker, she can't remember which, named his old cigarette boat the Umiak, and that had been a teaching moment—Letha had opened a tab for Cinn and Ginger, explained this other culture to them at the same time she was sort of learning about it herself.

"My dad used to do that too," Jennifer says through the wind, and the snowmobile's puttering engine.

"What?" Letha says, looking down at her hand in the snow, in this hoof print.

"He thought that because he was Indian, that meant he had hunting in the blood."

"Did he?" Letha asks, standing, shaking the snow off.

"He could always find another six-pack, yeah," Jennifer says, twisting the throttle back like to confirm the snowmobile's still running.

When it idles back down, she tracks where Letha's looking: the sheriff's office.

"Need a ride?" Jennifer asks.

The office's taped-over door is foggy, rippling, empty.

"Where you headed?" Letha says.

Jennifer chucks her chin out onto the ice, across Indian Lake, says, "Terra Nova."

"Terra Nova," Letha hears herself repeating, the name trapped in the cave of her teeth, trying to drown her. She looks out into that great whiteness as well.

She should huddle back to the office, she knows.

She should spell Banner, feed Adrienne, apologize again to Rexall, clean the sheriff's family gun up, tape the door better, and maybe close the beaches as well, while she's at it.

Instead, she steps over to Jennifer, settles into that seat behind her, and wraps her arms around Jennifer's waist.

"I don't have goggles," she says in her garbled way, laying her head against Jennifer's back and closing her eyes.

"Just hold on," Jennifer says, and twists the throttle, pulling them ahead, deeper into this, whatever it is, and Letha can feel eyes on her back, but she keeps hers shut tight.

Maybe they wear crime-scene gloves in the big shops where they put paper over the floormats of the cars they service, but Lonnie's never gotten the hang of them. What this means is that when he rubs his lips, watching the rich girl pull away on that snowmobile, he smells grease, probably has half a pitch-black mustache smeared under his nose. Again.

But he should be happy to still even have fingers, he knows. Rex Allen's going to hear *all* about his new hire discharging his weapon at an upstanding citizen of Proofrock. There's the cost of the bucket, there's the lost washer fluid, there's the broke squeegee, but there's been some real and true suffering, too: once Lonnie got back to the shop to finish adjusting the tensioners on the snowcat's tracks, and giving her a good once-over besides—forty-five dollars per hour—the propane heater keeping frost from forming on the wrenches thawed him out some as well.

It drove him to his knees.

He thought his coveralls and barn jacket had protected him from the flying shards his bucket had been turned into, but: nope. Some people never get a break. Those tiny splinters had embedded themselves into his neck and shoulders at the speed of sound, probably, like a fleet of sharp-nosed alien ships dive-bombing him.

Add heat and time, and his special blend of hose water and window washer had melted, and started trickling into his trapezius muscles. The little dabs of blood that he tried to slap away were watery, and splashed onto the backs of his ears. And then the stinging started in. It wasn't like when he'd been a kid climbing a tree and head-butted up into a humming nest that poured bumblebees down his collar, but it wasn't any Sunday drive, either. It was more like… like if sugar ants ever swarmed up and got pissed all at once? For maybe two minutes, he thought he was dying.

What if the washer fluid reached his heart, seized it up?

What if some of those angry little spaceships had hulls of dirty white plastic from the bucket, and were tumbling through his blood vessels to stop up his brain, stroke him out?

And… what if his hearing had been damaged, right? All he'd been doing was trying to get control of Rexall. Is this the treatment Good Samaritans can expect in Proofrock?

Anyway, Rexall for sure and for certain had it coming. How many times over the last twenty-six years has he mocked Lonnie's stutter? Never mind that this damn stutter's his fucking fault anyway, his and Clate's. And Tab's too, Lonnie supposes. Even Kimmy Daniels and Misty Christy—they'd all been there that day.

But not Melanie. It wasn't her fault. All she did was drown, drown screaming that a cold hand had touched the back of her knee. It hadn't been Lonnie, he knew that, it had been one of those other idiots, never mind that they were all spaced out at the moment to pee. Clate would have found a way, and he was her boyfriend anyway, so was the only one who *could* have touched her on the leg without getting his ass kicked.

It didn't matter, though. Melanie had been joking, they all knew.

Or, figured. Getting them back for when Rexall—he was still *Remy*, then, which everyone was sure to spell "Reamie"—had fake-drowned Tab. Who had just been "Junior" then, Lonnie guesses. But Kimmy was already Kimmy, and Lonnie was just Lonnie, wasn't yet, as Rexall liked to say it, sputtering to spit out, "La-La-La-*Lon*nie."

According to Doc Wilson, still wet behind the ears himself in 1993, Lonnie's stutter was just his mind trying to deal with him being part of the circle of kids who watched another kid drown, but his tongue would calm down the further he got from that day on the lake.

Good call, Doc.

Good c-c-c-*call*.

But Lonnie was lodging a complaint against that deputy, no two ways around it. He should have taken that football scholarship, not gotten all puffed up with the law. But he had married well, that was for sure. Never mind that little rich girl's Black. All the checks she writes, they're gold. And when Rex Allen explains to Lonnie how a civil suit about hearing damage and pain and suffering will empty the county coffers, well, then maybe somebody else steps in with a settlement, right? Somebody who doesn't want her preppy-ass husband fired off his first job?

Someone currently speeding across Indian Lake with the town's ex- and future reject—the Red girl and the Black one.

From the window of his first bay, Lonnie sees all: Hardy, creaking around on his walker, waiting to die; the new history teach, dressed up like the opening of a James Bond movie; Rexall, flopping around in the snow like those tiny spaceships had been targeting *him* first; that lost elk, crusted with snow.

He knows some secrets, too: behind the shop because it won't fit in either of the bays is the snowplow that lost it in the motel parking lot, nearly crashed into the creek.

Something is going on there, Lonnie knows. The note Mr. High and Mighty Deputy left in the drop box for keys just said to pull the snowplow out of the trees. The cab had been piled with snow from whatever happened to the windshield, but the real story was all the snow that shook off when Lonnie got it pulled out and fired up: the hood had been coated in what Lonnie at first assumed was hydraulic fluid, from a busted line supposed to be driving the cylinders that lifted and dropped the plow.

Hydraulic fluid doesn't freeze, though. And it doesn't turn red again when you spit on it.

Only blood does that.

Meaning… this snowplow driver had, evidently, been drunk or whatever, and overshot his parking slot, then, when the trees were blocking the doors, he'd kicked through the windshield and crawled through, cutting himself open in the process, that sharp glass somehow burrowing all the way into an artery.

It was the only thing that tracked.

And there would be a story there, Lonnie knew. One it might behoove someone to line his palms with cash for keeping quiet?

It's not like the settlement for the bucket is going to be immediate, right?

Lonnie chuckles, uses the elbow of his jacket to clean the glass, and when he leans forward to peer through it, see something else he can maybe make some money from, the whole bay door shatters, crashes in over him, and he knows that the reject and the rich girl had to have heard him thinking, felt him watching, and came back t-t-to—

He can't quite get it out.

Before finding Jocelyn Cates's son suffocated in the parking bay of Pleasant Valley Retirement Village, his eyes and mouth open behind that thin plastic, his hands still clawing at his throat, Jennifer had never driven anything as stupid and unlikely as a snowmobile. None of her correspondence courses the last four years included snowmobile training. She would apply what she knows from driving cars, but… well.

She did used to have a bicycle in elementary, but that was another time, another girl.

Still, as near as she can tell, this snowmobile's just twist and go, pretty much. Then turn the handlebars this way and that. Doesn't take a rocket scientist.

Jennifer slows to ease down from shore to the frozen surface of the lake, then opens it back up. Behind her, up against her, Letha squeezes her midsection tighter, clamps her legs on Jennifer's hips better.

In town, in the thick powder of Main, the snowmobile sort of chugged, was having to try, it felt like. Out here on the ice, it's flying, is nearly out of control. There's snow just the same, of course, the storm isn't particular, but the lake's different, faster, slicker. Jennifer can turn, but it's less with the skids, more with which way she leans, following that bodyweight *with* the skids, if that can make sense.

It doesn't matter if it makes sense or not. It's working.

When she trudged out to the dam yesterday, it took her nearly two hours of step after cold step. Now, on this bad machine, they're already almost across, have to be, and then, way before she's ready—

"*Shit!*" she screams, standing on the running boards, Letha's hands sliding down to her hips.

The modular dock the Founders had installed on Terra Nova's shore is *right there*, and, with the lake frozen, it's taller.

Jennifer leans over as hard as she can, trying to get the right track—the inside track—to dig in, praying the skids up front can have at least *some* bite, because if they don't, if she and Letha hit this dock like they're about to, then… the snowmobile will fit under those plastic boards, but their heads won't.

Not even deciding to, more a body-level decision, Jennifer lets go of the grips and dives away, has her arms boxer-style around her head because she's going to roll for miles, it feels like.

Instead, she's sliding on her hip at the same speed she was going. Meaning she has a front-seat for what happens: Letha, that dead man's key in her hand, ripped from the zipper pull of Jennifer's jacket, is taking stock of her new situation—the dock coming for her, the lake so slick under her, the snowmobile a runaway.

"*Jump!*" Jennifer screams, pleads, hopes, but—this is Letha Mondragon. And four years hasn't slowed her down even one little bit. Neither has motherhood, or marriage, or having a plastic jaw.

She scooches forward, takes the handlebars like born to them, and turns *into* the skid Jennifer was trying to force, her body hanging far enough over the side that her right knee's kicking up an angry roostertail of powder. That's just half her maneuver, though. Now she's letting the snowmobile's own weight carry the ass end around to the front, so she's going straight backwards—which is when she finally stands, thankfully, that being the first motion of jumping *off*.

That's not what Letha's doing, though. Instead, she's standing to give every last ounce of her weight to the tracks, spinning for all they're worth—oh, it's not the flat of the tracks Letha's trying to get grabbing, it's that sharp turn where they come up to go back around.

With the new distribution of weight, and the new angle, they finally dig in, exactly as they wouldn't for Jennifer.

The tracks slow under this new traction, the engine whines higher, and Letha has that throttle twisted all the way back and around again, probably, but the front edge of that hard little dock is still coming, she's not going to make it, she's about to lose her head, she's about to be crushed against the bars—

As Jennifer slides past, she has a perfect line on how near this miss is. A matter of inches. If Letha still had her shampoo-commercial hair, it would be sighing up onto the top of the dock. And she never even looks back to see if this is it for her. Because she's *insisting.* Because this can only go one way. And it finally does, after that standstill moment when her forward motion stops, the treads dug in enough to surge her forward a foot, then a yard, then enough.

She lets off the throttle and collapses into the seat, and now the ice under Jennifer isn't ice anymore, it's shore, and she's rolling uphill through powder, her world only white and cold, her mouth and eyes and nose and ears packed with it, her stupid swim goggles anywhere, nowhere. How can *they* be what falls off when her head—much looser—is still attached?

She's sitting with her hands around her knees when Letha eases up on the snowmobile, kills the engine with the dead man's key, then hooks it onto the front of her jacket.

"I think I'm running out of lives, here," Jennifer says, letting Letha haul her up.

"'Oh, god, I look twenty years old,'" Letha deadpans back in her best Nancy Thompson.

"I hate you, you know," Jennifer tells her.

"Back at ya," Letha says.

Together, they turn to Terra Nova.

"Shit," Letha says, and Jennifer looks over at her, nods appreciatively: she's getting better at this whole cussing thing. "Why?" Letha says then, the wind ripping her words to tatters. "Why are we here?"

Jennifer hooks her head for Letha to follow, because out in the blasting-cold wind is no place to try to explain complicated shit.

The first house looming over them, only there in snatches through the storm, meaning they have to assemble it in their heads from shadow and memory, was supposed to have been Letha's.

It's crispy black now but still standing, a charred ghost of itself.

Before stepping up onto the porch, Jennifer senses Letha's stopped.

"What?" Jennifer says, but Letha's just looking up and up. She shakes her head no, nothing, then ducks ahead, takes the hand Jennifer's got out. It's not because Letha needs steadying, it's because she might be about to fall through the porch, into some haunted crawlspace. Stories like they're in, they *love* crawlspaces.

The boards hold, though. Jennifer, inside, nods a quick thank you to Shooting Glasses, for nailing the porch together so well. She still can't seem to call him "Grade." Who names their kid that? Who names anybody that?

When she's about to haul on the fancy, blackened doorknob, Letha stops her, steps ahead, does it herself. Like this is a ritual only she can complete.

The door's stuck at first, so Letha shoulders it hard, harder than Jennifer could.

Instead of swinging open, it falls in—*timmmmber*—probably waking every ghost in Terra Nova.

Letha steps in onto that tall fancy door like a welcome mat, and Jennifer follows, her eyes everywhere at once. Since she never knew what it was starting to look like before, she doesn't have anything to match it to, like Letha must, but she'd wager that the beer cans and rubbers weren't part of the original design. The mattress of trash-clothes in the corner, either—including what looks like the most cast-off county coveralls ever. Does Proofrock have a homeless population now?

"Here," Letha says, and steps purposefully ahead, through all of this, ducks into a tall arched doorway and into the house-size kitchen, which gets them away from the wind now blowing in.

The stove's been ripped out, was probably a five-thousand-dollar job, so, worth getting back across the lake in a quiet boat, at night. The refrigerator was more built-in, so just the doors are gone, probably in frustration. Out under the snow between the houses, they're probably still propped up, Jennifer knows. Propped up and ventilated, as target practice. One thing about Idaho: it don't look good if it's not riddled with bullet holes. Dogs pee on what they own. In Proofrock, those lifted legs expose guns.

"Tiara said she used to cook with her mom when she was a kid," Letha says, running her hand over the granite top of the island, ash piling up in front of her fingertips.

Jennifer can still remember Tiara, Letha's blond bombshell of a stepmom, hanging out in the open space past the yacht's tower, her hands and feet pedaling, trying to fight gravity. And, "bombshell" isn't the nice thing to think, since Tiara did definitely explode upon impact.

"What's funny?" Letha asks.

Jennifer shakes her head no, nothing.

Letha takes one last look around then seats herself easily on the counter by the fridge, her grace still intact.

"Here we are," she says. Which is of course a question.

"You didn't leave Adrienne with him, did you?" Jennifer asks, fiddling with a loose cabinet knob, the door either burned open or rusted that way.

"Rexall?" Letha says, with her pinched version of a grin. "Ban was there."

"'Ban,'" Jennifer parrots.

"He's… he's not the same as he used to be," Letha says. "People change. They grow up. Did you know that he sat by my hospital bed the whole time, right after… you know? The movie? And he's told me he feels bad about how he used to—in high school—how he… you know."

"Doesn't matter," Jennifer says, forcing that cabinet door shut, which is suddenly the most important thing. "You're not stupid. You wouldn't be with him if he still was."

"Thank you," Letha says, then: "I think?"

"I was gonna tell you why we're here," Jennifer says. "It's because Ginger told me—"

"Wait, wait. You *talked* to her?"

"Yeah?"

"When?"

"I was over there, at the nursing home?"

"But—"

"I didn't exactly sign the visitor sheet," Jennifer says, leaning over to get a line down into the drain of the sink. It's just open space down there. The kind someone could be looking up from. The kind someone maybe *should* be looking up from.

"But she doesn't talk to anyone except for Cinn—I mean, she used—"

"She talked with me," Jennifer says. "She said her and her sister found… that they found some gross thing growing up under the pier. Like a pack of old hamburger meat–gross. And they fed it, kept it over here."

Letha just stares at Jennifer about this.

"Her *and* Cinn," she finally says, like no way can she believe this.

Jennifer nods.

"Then they're speaking again," Letha says. "Good. They should."

"What do you mean?"

"Ginger's doctors say—"

"Her *doctors* say?"

"Maybe she's talking to other people now, but she—she doesn't talk to me," Letha says. "Evidently I would remind her… never mind. Her doctors say she's harboring a lot of resentment at Cinn, for having left her over here that night."

"So Ginger hates Cinnamon?" Jennifer says.

"Sounds like a children's book when you say it like that," Letha says. "But yeah. Sort of. Or, she used to, I mean. But… you say they found something? *Together?*"

"She was lying, wasn't she?" Jennifer says.

"Not if she believes it," Letha says back, always willing to give someone the benefit of the doubt.

"I knew it was too *Hellraiser*," Jennifer says, opening the cabinet under the sink all at once. It's empty. No evil thing curled up there.

"*Hellraiser*?" Letha says.

"It's where—"

"I know what it is," Letha says. "A woman finds her… what's his name? 'Frank,' yeah. Frank gets torn to shreds by Pinhead and—"

"Chatterbox and Butterball," Jennifer recites.

"The Chatter*er*," Letha gently corrects. "But, yes, his voice box is kind of on display, you're right. Anyway, Frank's, like, adhered under the boards?"

"A tumor."

"More like a zygote," Letha says with a shrug, like meaning no confrontation here. "And he fed on blood. So, wanting him back, needing him back, Julia fed him more and more blood?"

"That's what Ginger said Cinnamon was doing," Jennifer says, disgusted with herself for having believed this particular children's book. "But not people. Roadkill, that kind of stuff."

"When is she supposed to have had time?" Letha says. "Cinn's social calendar is… she's—"

"You, four years ago?" Jennifer completes.

"But, why would they be letting Ginger watch Clive Barker movies?" Letha says.

Jennifer stares through the doorway, out into the living room, the door so open in there. "I don't know anything anymore," she says.

"But you came over here to find this—this *Frank*?" Letha asks.

"I'm trying to figure out why Cinnamon's at the center of all these dead high school seniors," Jennifer says. "You know how this works. That first night, at the motel, he left her alive when he could have killed her. That means—"

"That it's about her." Letha winces like whatever thought she just had hurts.

"Tell me," Jennifer says.

"Unless she's Mandy Lane," Letha says with a halfway shrug, like she doesn't believe this but has to lob it out there anyway. "Or, you know. *Eleanor*," Letha adds, her eyes locked on Jennifer.

"I don't play these games anymore," Jennifer says. "They're… you're right, I was hiding in the video store. Trying to build myself a little fort of clamshell cases. It was stupid."

"You were saving your own life, Ja—Jennifer."

Jennifer looks up to Letha then fast away, can't risk that connection.

"Do you think we get to choose?" Letha asks, then.

"I don't—what do you mean?"

"*Bay of Blood* just happened to be in that bin in that gas station in Idaho Falls?"

Jennifer dials back four years in her head. "You *did* read my history papers," she says.

"Cinn has pictures of them on her phone."

"She snuck into your room on the yacht?"

"The new history teacher found copies Mr. Holmes had saved," Letha says. "He inherited the file cabinet, I guess?"

"Mr. Holmes *saved* them?" Jennifer says, almost ready to actually smile, here.

Letha shrugs, says, "And I *know* you've still got all those slashers in your head somewhere. You know Mandy Lane. You know Eleanor."

"For whatever that's worth."

"So I've wasted these last four years, watching them all myself?"

"It's just… you're watching them to say you're sorry, for not listening to me back then. But you can stop now, okay? Apology accepted. I wouldn't have listened to me either."

Letha's hands are planted on the granite counter to either side of her knees. She leans forward on them, tilts her head over to look directly at Jennifer, say it: "Eleanor. Another final girl who turns out to be the killer."

"I told you, I don't—"

"Yeah, well, don't care. *Eleanor.*"

"This isn't why I'm over here, Letha. I'm not here to play trivia—"

"Eleanor."

"Why do you care so much?"

"Because the girl I used to know is still in there somewhere. And we need her if we're going to survive this. *Eleanor.*"

"I can't. I'm just—once I figure this out, I'll tell Banner, then I'm going back to my place and—"

"Eleanor!"

"I don't even know anymore. Fuck! What are you trying to do!"

Letha slides down, her eyes locked on Jennifer's for her whole walk around the island, like she's balancing books on her head.

"Eleanor," she says, quieter, reaching forward to punctuate it by shoving Jennifer's shoulders.

"So glad you came along."

"Eleanor, Jennifer," Letha says again, walking right into Jennifer so Jennifer has to back into the doorway.

"Fuck you! That's not me anymore, I told you! I was a scared little girl, I thought— I thought if I knew all the rules, then that would mean—that would mean nothing would happen to me!"

And now she's crying, goddamnit.

"Nothing would happen to you *again*," Letha says, right in her face. "Now—*Eleanor.*"

Jennifer hides her face in her hands, hates hates *hates* being seen like this.

"You're still you, I know you are," Letha says right into her ear. "Just tell me, tell me who Eleanor is, tell me—"

"*Night School*, 1981!" Jennifer screams right into Letha's face, driving *her* back now.

"And, and… Angela too."

"Felissa Rose," Letha says, still backing up but smiling too. "*Sleepaway Camp*'s too easy. *Liz*. At boarding school."

"Her name should have given it away," Jennifer says right back. "Lizzie Borden took an axe, gave her mother forty whacks. *The Hole*, 2001. In the bomb shelter, Alex, *without* an axe. Talking axes—"

"*Edge of the Axe*, 1988," Letha cuts in. "Lillian something."

"Nebbs," Jennifer fills in. "*Cry Wolf*, *Triangle*, *Curse of Chucky*—"

"Not really *Curse*," Letha says, like apologetic—sorry to be seeing Jennifer slip.

"*Curse* is *Intruder*, a quarter century later," Jennifer says, whipping her tears away with the sleeve of her jacket. "The final girl didn't *do* it, she's been framed."

Letha grins a sharp, strained grin, is backed up against the fridge, no more ground to give.

Jennifer, instead of adding any more killer final girls to this list, just sputters a laugh out, a harsh little bark she didn't even know she was holding in, and Letha draws her to her, and they stand like that, hugging, shuddering, two girls against the world.

No: two *women*.

"Back to Frank, then," Letha says after maybe a minute, holding Jennifer at arm's length now, like keeping her upright.

"Frank was asking for it," Jennifer says.

"And Cinn's not," Letha says, turning around, taking her place on the counter again, something tall girls can do without having to think about.

"But why her?"

"Maybe they have a sixth sense? Slashers, I mean. They can pick a final girl out of the crowd, like. Predator, the T-800."

Jennifer can almost see those readouts in her visual field again, after all these years.

"But why like this?" she says, finger-drawing nothings in the ash on the island.

"Like what?" Letha asks back.

"Those first two… um, Glenda—"

"Gwen," Letha corrects. "Gwen and Toby."

"She was hung and gutted just like Casey Becker."

"So this is *Scream*?"

"You didn't see those two at the nursing home," Jennifer says. "They were—" She pushes her finger up from her throat, miming Kevin Bacon's death. "*Friday the 13th* all the way."

"Dark Mill South hid under a *bed*?" Letha asks, not believing it.

"I think he knows all the same movies we do, yeah."

"Shit."

"And then, Jocelyn Cates's kid. He was… dry-cleaning bag over his head."

"Black Christmas."

"And at the high school, those others—"

"Wynona and Jensen and Abby."

"The guy, 'Jensen,'" Jennifer says. "He was up on some elk horns."

"Antlers," Letha corrects.

"What?"

"Horns aren't antlers—never mind."

"Mr. Holmes much?" Jennifer says across to her.

"Only every chance I get," Letha says softly, and Jennifer wishes she had a pause button right there, so she could hit it, run away into another room, cry more, until she couldn't breathe, then clean her face up, come back like nothing happened.

"I'm talking Linnea Quigley," she says, though. "*Silent Night, Deadly Night.*"

"That's Christmas too," Letha says, getting it.

"Or that one in the *Friday* remake, where that one girl's so proud of her—"

Jennifer mimes breasts.

"That's a deer, not an elk," Letha says. "But I like that one better."

"A remake more than Killer Claus?"

"I like that it's not Linnea."

Jennifer asks the question with her eyes, and Letha answers: "'Adrienne' is Adie's *middle* name. Her first is—"

"Linnea?"

Letha nods, looking away.

"You're now officially my hero," Jennifer tells her.

"*Get Out*," Letha says back.

"You get out."

"No," Letha says. "The movie, I mean. Jordan Peele."

"Jordan who?"

"*Get Out*, the movie?"

"I've been locked up for four years?"

"Sorry, sorry," Letha says. "Jensen doesn't have to be *Silent Night*, or the *Friday* remake. In *Get Out*, somebody's killed with a mounted deer head too."

"Deer, not elk."

"Antlers are antlers."

"And they're sure not horns," Jennifer says with a smile. "You really named her 'Linnea'?"

"Linnea's a survivor."

"She dies in every movie."

"Her characters do, but *she* goes from movie to movie," Letha says. "She never dies."

"Hunh," Jennifer says. "Never thought of it like that."

"She's not the only one."

"Only what?"

"To go from slasher to slasher. She just has the best name."

"Kane Hodder's a pretty good name," Jennifer says. "He played Jason *and* Freddy. Freddy's arm at least."

"Victor Crowley too," Letha says, grinning to be talking to an equal in slasher Q, it seems. "And, if we're talking showing up in different slashers, then Amy Steel was the final girl in *Friday the 13th Part 2*—"

"And *April Fool's Day*," Jennifer says, sort of insulted. "You know the stunt dude who played Jason the ambulance driver was also Michael in *Return*?"

"Sarah Michelle Gellar was in two marquee slashers in the same year," Letha says right back.

"But she's no Linnea."

"There can be only one," Letha says. "That's what I want for Adie. I mean, I don't want her ever to be Cinn like this, but—"

"You don't get to pick your genre," Jennifer fills in.

"Unless you're you," Letha says.

"If I could go back..." Jennifer says.

"It's not your fault, the Independence Day Massacre. We never should have—"

Letha opens her arm to the grand, ruined house all around them.

Jennifer shrugs, says, "*Flatliners*?"

"Six degrees of Kevin Bacon?"

"I mean—what if… I keep thinking what if I brought something back, right? I got here two days before he did. What if he's here because I am?"

"Dark Mill South."

Jennifer nods.

"You didn't die and come back, though," Letha says.

"Didn't I?"

Letha doesn't answer, probably because she can see Jennifer's already made up her mind, here: this is her fault. Her trial and DMS's going over so close to each other, both in Boise, and then both of them ending up in Proofrock, of all places…

But this is bogging them down.

"We should rename this Forest Green," Jennifer says, trying to bring them back to trivia-land, instead of guilt central.

"Or Hillcrest," Letha says, taking that cue.

"And Buffy wasn't the only one in *Scream 2* and *I Know What You Did Last Summer* that year," Jennifer says. "Chris Durand was Michael Myers and also stunt-doubled for Ghostface."

"You been holding that one in for four years?" Letha asks, drifting out of the kitchen.

Jennifer falls in behind her, says, "Ginger said Cinnamon was keeping it over here somewhere."

"'It,'" Letha repeats. "You think it's her, don't you?"

"Who else could come back like that, from a… a goop of brains or whatever?"

"Stacey Stacey Stacey Graves," Letha says, meaning she must know that jumprope rhyme as well. She's looking all around the living room now. "'The house that Freddy built,'" she cites, shrugging after it.

"Think his name was Grade Paulson, actually," Jennifer says.

Letha sneaks a look over, but doesn't ask.

"Thank you," Jennifer tells her then, after all this time. "For—my dad… you know. That night."

"No idea what you're talking about," Letha says, turning away again, to look down the long hall leading deeper into the house. Then, "So, what? You want to look around for a… a *Frank*?"

Jennifer shrugs, isn't as into it anymore.

"Maybe on the snowmobile?" she says. "My feet are already—"

"She didn't say if Cinn was supposed to have been using a—a basement, an attic? Mr. Singleton's indoor swimming pool?"

"He built a swimming pool when his house was *by* a swimming pool?" Jennifer asks, hooking her head out to the lake.

Letha shrugs, evidently doesn't want to explain the rich to the hopelessly poor.

"No," Jennifer says. "She just said it was over here."

"Maybe Stacey Graves is nice this time," Letha says. "Like Midian."

"Midian?"

"*Nightbreed,*" Letha says. "Clive Barker."

"Him again," Jennifer says. "You're talking… that TV thing?"

"Got a Blu-ray in—right before… you know."

"Hunh," Jennifer says. "And so the student becomes the master."

She grandly offers her imaginary crown across to Letha, only realizes at the last moment that, being invisible, it may as well be a tiara.

"Just so you can pour pig's blood on me?" Letha asks.

"Have I always been this annoying?" Jennifer asks with a smile. "Everything's not a movie reference."

"There's nobody else I can talk about it with."

"*No* idea what that's like..." Jennifer says, settling down on the bottom step of the curving, fairy-tale staircase and pulling her dollar-store haul up from a pocket. "Hungry?"

Digging for the beef jerky, she first has to pull out the WD-40, the novelty lighter that makes Letha wow her eyes out, the five wood-handled steak knives, and...

A *Christmas ornament*?

"Cute," Letha says, picking it up and sitting down beside Jennifer with it: a little red soldier. "You really plan for everything, don't you?"

"Ha," Jennifer says, and uses one of the knives to saw into the top of the beef jerky bag. She offers the first piece to Letha—"*Teriyaki*..."—but Letha shakes her head no. "It's past lunch, y'know?" Jennifer says, shaking the bag to show that there's definitely enough for both of them.

Letha flashes the metal across her teeth.

"Oh, sorry," Jennifer says, tearing a bite off herself. Then, quieter, sort of reluctant, "If I chewed it for you?"

"You would?"

"You would for me," Jennifer says. "I mean, you would for anybody, and I'm part of that crowd."

"I'm not as good as you think."

"A real potty mouth these days, yeah."

Letha elbows Jennifer, but her dimples are showing. She sets the red soldier down between them, holds the WD-40 up like a question.

"In case we need to start a fire," Jennifer tells her, just managing not to add "again" at the end. "My dad always kept a can by the burn pit."

"Finish the job," Letha says, looking all around. "And these?"

The knives.

"You really have to ask?" Jennifer says, swallowing too early, so her eyes water. But it doesn't stop her from tearing off another rubbery hunk.

"You do know that's not real meat?" Letha says.

"Real calories," Jennifer says through the spicy bite. Then, "When John Carpenter shot extra scenes for the version of *Halloween* that played on TV, since the theatrical wasn't long enough, the reshoots for Laurie's bedroom were in the house that was 1428 Elm Street."

"We're not asking the real question, are we?" Letha the philosopher says, then.

"What do you mean?" Jennifer asks. "Craven or Carpenter? Jason or Freddy? *Psycho* or *Peeping Tom*? Bava or Argento?"

"No, not—" Letha says, shrugging. "In that bathroom in Woodsboro High. Who is that stepping down, taking a slash at Sidney?"

"You first," Jennifer says, chewing the plastic meat.

Letha nods that that's fair, that's fair.

"We're supposed to think it's another random prankster, aren't we?" she says, squinting like trying to scry into this.

"One of the ones Himbry expels."

"But… it is the women's room, right? Did this person walk in in costume, or walk in and then dress up in the stall?"

"And how to know Sidney's coming to *this* bathroom at *this* time, right?"

"Yeah, that too," Letha says. "How long was this Ghostface there?"

"It was just Father Death, then," Jennifer says, tearing off some more jerky. "He doesn't become Ghostface until Tatum names him in the garage at Stu's party."

"Billy or Stu, then?" Letha says. "They go in in costume, they wait, they wait, and… they're not really trying to kill Sidney, just terrorize her."

"Because they want her to come to the big party, later," Jennifer says. "That's where the real fun's gonna go down. And Billy can't kill her until he has sex with her—he follows the rules. Virgins can't die. Their hymens are like armor."

"But it can't be Billy anyway," Letha says. "He was just with Sidney in the hall—awkward moment."

"Speaking of," Jennifer says around this bite of meat that seems to be growing.

"What?" Letha says.

"In *Scream 2*, when it's that Wilson guy and Tori whoever—how did the *Stab* people know about that scene? Billy's dead, and Sid wouldn't be talking to Hollywood. Sure, somebody passing by might have seen the two of them there, but they don't hear the whole conversation."

"Are you saying *Stab*'s fake?" Letha asks with a grin.

"It's real for *Scream 2*," Jennifer says. "But it does kind of make *Scream 2* fake, yeah."

"Speaking of *sequels*," Letha says. "It could have been Roman in that bathroom, standing on that toilet. Sidney's brother—half-brother. He wears those kinds of boots in *3*, doesn't he?"

"But the sheriff's wearing them in the first," Jennifer says right back. "So, who, then, Ms. Stalls-a-Lot? Who is it for you?"

"Stu," Letha pronounces, all holy and reverential. "When he catches up with Sidney and Tatum on the sidewalk, he's out of breath and sweaty, and just a little too happy."

"He's Stu."

"Even for him, I mean."

"Quick shoe change?"

"I already said he's out of breath. But he would have known Billy and Sidney were having their big *Stab* scene, so he sneaked into the closest women's room, the one Sid's probably going to duck into when she's all broken up and confused."

Jennifer considers this from all angles, says, though, finally, "But really, the only person we're sure it's *not* is Sidney herself."

"Paranoid much?"

"Only when I'm breathing."

"You, then?" Letha asks.

"Me what?"

"You think it's Stu?"

"Sure, why not."

"Thanks for playing," Letha says. "Really giving it your all here, aren't you."

"There's out in the weeds, with Eleanor and Angela, and then there's in the lake."

"Sink or swim, slasher girl."

"We're not supposed to know, that's my answer," Jennifer says. "It's *Scream*'s peculiar magic. Same way we're not absolutely sure who Casey Becker recognizes when she pulls that mask off. Stu, because he's her ex, or Billy, because he's all movie-crazy."

"'It could be anybody,' how original," Letha says, taking the jerky from Jennifer not to bite, or even rub along her gums, but to smell.

It makes her close her eyes in pleasure.

"I'm not saying that scene isn't… that I haven't lived with it," Jennifer says, trying to match Letha's thinking-through efforts with sincerity, at least.

Letha turns to her, holds the jerky under Jennifer's mouth like a mic.

"Tell us more," Letha says with her reporter voice.

"You do remember Gale Weathers gets punched, right?" Jennifer says, and bites into the jerky mic, taking the whole stick back.

"What?" Letha says then. "You 'lived' with that scene?"

"Never mind, nothing."

"We're just talking about a slasher."

"They were never just that for me," Jennifer says. "I don't think they are for you, either. Now."

Letha holds Jennifer's eyes in that way she has.

"I used to—" Jennifer says, trying to get the words right and not stupid, "it used to be my dad standing on top of that toilet, on top of every toilet, okay? He was always there, waiting for me. When he, when someone like that—you bring them everywhere. You can't outrun them, I don't know. Father Death indeed, yeah."

Letha puts her hand over Jennifer's, holds it to Jennifer's knee.

"Listen," she says. "Something *I* never told anyone, okay?"

"Quid pro quo."

"Yeah, you're the Latin expert, Clarice. But—okay, I'll just do it. Anyway, the trial's over, right?"

Jennifer narrows her eyes, has absolutely zero clue where this might be going.

"When I dug you out from all those dead elk?" Letha asks, as warm-up into whatever this is going to be.

"I never thanked you, did I?" Jennifer says, trying to keep it light. Even though she guesses she's the one who geared it down, too.

Footshooters Anonymous: member and president, right here.

"When I was—" Letha says, swallowing hard, "I saw, mixed in with all the elk... I thought it was a human hand. Well, I mean, a glove. I didn't look closer."

"Mismatched Gloves..." Jennifer says, with awe.

"What? I don't know, I never found the other. But—elk will eat a leather glove if they find it, won't they? Like, the salt from the sweat?"

Jennifer squinches her whole face, trying to make herself calm, calm. But in her head it's Shooting Glasses that first night, and Cowboy Boots. And Mismatched Gloves.

"And I'm... I'm glad we came here," Letha's saying now, from what feels like far, far away.

"To Terra Nova?" Jennifer hears herself ask back.

"To Proofrock," Letha says, quieter. "I never would have met you, otherwise."

"Or had Linnea Adrienne Banner-Mondragon."

Letha's whole body shudders with laughter. She shakes her head no, says, "*Tompkins*-Mondragon. You did that on purpose, didn't you?"

Jennifer puts her hand on top of Letha's, that's already on top of her other hand, and it's so stupid, so Hallmark, but—is this what it's supposed to feel like? After twenty-two years?

"But no, I don't mean—" Letha starts, patting Jennifer's knee with the flat of her hand like to make her point, not be misunderstood on this even a little, "we shouldn't have come over *here*, we're the ones who woke Stacey—"

"I know, I get it."

"And we shouldn't have come here this time either," Letha adds, kind of sadder. "You and me. There's supposed to be sinkholes over in the meadow now. When you—when the lake rose, a lot of the caves over here collapsed."

"Maybe that's what she used?"

"Excuse me?"

"*Cinnamon*," Jennifer says, "'Cinn,' whatever—the Spice Girl. Maybe she used a sinkhole for that Frank-thing she found."

"That Ginger *says* they found."

"But if she *did*. Maybe she used a caved-in cave, right?"

"Because she didn't know what it was going to be," Letha says, nodding, narrowing her eyes like trying to see this. "So… so lock it up, in case it grows up to be mean. Meaning… it's still down there?"

Jennifer shrugs maybe. Why not?

"Nancy Thompson's bedroom was really Laurie Strode's bedroom?" Letha says then, still digesting this impossible but perfect-amazing fact.

"I can show you," Jennifer says. "I mean, I could have, before all my tapes… you know."

"I probably own it," Letha says, no big.

Jennifer considers this. Wonders at this. Finally has to ask, "How does it feel, to own *Halloween*?"

"'There's a reason we're supposed to be afraid of this night,'" Letha says back.

Jennifer considers this, rolls it around her head, finally has to say, "What's that from?"

"What you were saying," Letha says, shrugging one shoulder. *"Halloween."*

"No, it's not. Not 1978, and not Zombie's."

"Oh yeah," Letha says. "You wouldn't—there's a new sequel. With the same name, no number."

"Seriously? How long have I been checked out?"

Letha shrugs one shoulder and Jennifer doesn't push it, is trying to roll one of the steak knives across the backs of her knuckles. When she starts to lose it, she flips her hand around, which sends the knife spinning down.

It sticks perfectly in the scorched hardwood.

"Shit, sorry," she says.

"Here," Letha says, and takes one of the other knives, carves a rough J into the wood. Jennifer uses one of the other knives to carve an L just beside it, to the left.

"Perfect," Jennifer says, and grips the knife in her fist, drives it down as punctuation, but it's a dollar-store job: there's not rivets drawing the two pieces of wood into a handle, there's… glue? a prayer?

The handle breaks away and Jennifer's right hand keeps sliding down.

When she jerks it back, the little sawteeth have chewed into the heel of her hand, and the blood's already welling up like this is *The Thing*, and it's trying to get away.

She squeezes her wrist with her left hand and Letha's right there on this, ready to make it better. But there's no gauze. Neither of them even has a scarf on.

When Jennifer realizes the vertical scar on her left wrist is facing up, practically flashing neon, she turns her arm over fast, but Letha's already seen. Already *been* seeing.

"Fucking cold over here," Jennifer says, her lips grim and thin.

"I'll turn the heater up," Letha says, trying to lighten the mood, even going so far as to look down the hall where the thermostat must be, or was maybe going to have been.

When she stops moving, Jennifer leans forward, looks down her eyeline, and—

"*No*," she says, pushing back.

It doesn't turn the hulking shape of Dark Mill South in the hall to smoke.

He launches his hook hand off his forehead in mocking salute.

Jennifer falls back, her chest so cold, no breath coming into it at all, and the way she can tell Letha's twice the final girl she ever was is that she stands, placing herself between Jennifer on the floor and Dark Mill South in the hallway.

"You," Letha says.

He chuckles, steps forward, and, because she's on her ass, Jennifer's face isn't even two feet from Letha's left hand: between each finger of her fist is a steak knife, handle-in, blade-out.

Freddy, Jennifer says inside, in celebration.

And then Letha's right hand is drawing one of those knives out, the blade pinched between the thumb and forefinger.

As fluid and beautiful as anything, not ever even considering that this won't work, she spins that steak knife at high speed down the hall at Dark Mill South.

It flashes in the light of the open door, is moving so fast, is such an elegant weapon, really. How can it miss when it's so purely lethal?

It doesn't.

It sticks in Dark Mill South's chest, and for the first time, Jennifer drinks him in, almost gags on it: the way Jason gets larger and deadlier as the franchise goes on, until he's a full-on six and a half feet tall in the remake? Dark Mill South is what Jason would be in, about, *Friday the 13th Part 18*—he's a fucking *giant*. And, that way the Kane Hodder version would heave air in and out, showing frustration? Dark Mill South has that down.

He doesn't need a mask, either, is already a combination of Freddy's burnt face and Michael's dead eyes. And, while Jennifer's at it, Victor Crowley's hair, why not: it's a shroud, hasn't been brushed since his big escape, probably.

He reaches up with his left hand, to remove this slight annoyance from his chest.

Before he can, though, or, while he is, another knife flashes across, stabs through the *back* of that hand.

He thins his lips about this, actually annoyed, now.

"Get the fuck out of my house," Letha tells him.

In response, he bites down on that chintzy wooden handle, pulls the knife from his hand slow, just to show how little this is getting to him.

"Leeth, Leeth!" Jennifer says, trying to scramble up, escape, run back to their cave of dead elk, who cares, but Letha's got the last two knives in her right hand now, is stepping out to the middle of the living room.

"Run," Letha hisses back to Jennifer, and then she's slinging those last two knives down the hall.

Jennifer can't see, but she hears them both hit—the sound is distinct, and sort of wet—and then she hears the most beautiful sound: some seriously massive body, crashing down onto the hardwood from a great height.

She stands, only realizes once she's standing that Letha's hauled her up again.

"Go, go!" Letha says, pushing Jennifer ahead of her. "That won't—"

"No, no, while he's down," Jennifer says. "Nobody ever carves on them when they're down but not dead, we need to—"

She doesn't get to finish: a bloody steak knife spins between her face and Letha's, hits handle-first into the doorframe they're standing beside. The knife handle flies apart, leaving just that thrumming blade.

Next, Letha's pushing Jennifer through that doorway, taking her place just as another knife comes in at high speed.

It's thrown hard enough when it hits Letha's shoulder that it splashes out at her collarbone.

"No, no!" Jennifer says, reaching back to hold Letha up. "You've—you've got a daughter! A husband! A life! It should be *me*!"

She pushes Letha back into the kitchen, steps into the doorway to… she has no fucking idea: to stall Dark Mill South for two seconds?

Letha pulls Jennifer back, though.

A second later, a third knife sticks into the doorframe, the two sides of its handle calving off as well, tapping into the hardwood floor one by one, like they tried to hold on, they really did, but… they're just from the dollar store, come on, this is all they could manage.

Jennifer turns with Letha to, she doesn't know—*run*?

But now Letha's stuffing her under the sink, closing her in. And then she's… she's bashing the back door open. Before Jennifer can panic, a heavy foot steps into the kitchen.

Jennifer breathes in, holds it.

Even when the counter above her creaks.

She looks up through the drain, can see Dark Mill South up close and way too personal, now.

He's growling in his chest.

His blood is dripping down into the sink, and… and it's only natural to look down, see what kind of puddle you're leaving, isn't it?

What happens when he sees a lone, terrified eye watching him?

But, what's he even doing?

Looking out the window, Jennifer tells herself.

At which point she gets it: Letha is… this is that paper Jennifer wrote for Mr. Holmes a lifetime ago, about how the final girl is like that mother bird who flops and flaps away from the predator, pretending her wing is broken, tempting the hungry whatever away from her nest, away from her chicks.

Except, Letha's left shoulder and arm really *are* out of commission.

"Hunh," Dark Mill South says, pure frustration, and pushes away from the sink all at once, the whole cabinet shaking with it. The whole house, maybe.

Jennifer counts to one hundred after he's gone, then unfolds delicately onto the kitchen floor, the ash coating her. She stays like that for another hundred count, and when nothing creaks or breathes, she finally comes up to a hunched stance, not quite taller than the island.

The back door is still open. Jennifer steps into it to follow Letha and Dark Mill South, but… she comes back in. Because: how many times has she watched someone in a slasher walk blithely through a doorway, only to catch a pickaxe or machete to the face?

Instead, she backs slowly to the door with the window in it, that delivers her down to the cavernous garage.

For maybe twenty seconds she stands there taking stock, letting her eyes adjust, running through why Theo Mondragon would need three—no, four—slots to park cars when Terra Nova is Lake Access Only.

Forget it, she tells herself.

What's important is that it's another way out of the house. Only hopefully not guarded by some hulking killer.

She steps forward gingerly, and what's supposed to be slick concrete is ash and snow, because the side door to the garage is hanging on its hinges, has been kicked in.

Worse—shit shit shit—there's ginormous footsteps moving through that ash and snow. Meaning Dark Mill South didn't duck out the back door Letha used, probably for the same reason Jennifer didn't: it could be a trap.

"He's seen all the same movies you have," Jennifer hisses to herself, hoping the sound of her own voice will calm her.

Wrong.

What's good about this, though, is that he wouldn't have set up outside that broken door just on the distant chance that the short girl was going to try sneaking out it. Unless he really studied Letha's footprints, he might even think both girls ran away together.

Jennifer, banking on that, follows his footsteps across to the big tool bench, which he veered toward before stepping out.

Just like she's doing now, he must have stood here, studied this pegboard above the tool bench.

All the tools are scorched in place. Except the one he ripped away, leaving a silhouette behind it.

The hedge clippers.

Jennifer shakes her head no, please, but says it anyway: "*The Burning*, 1981."

Just, it looks like: this year too.

HELL NIGHT

The tinsel was my idea, Mr. Armitage.

If you ask Cinnamon, she'll say I wasn't involved at all, but you know her—if a bulldozer loses control at the top of a hill, is coming down the hill for me, taking out trees and fences and cars along the way, then Cinnamon will step in between me and it, and she won't give an inch. She won't even look away. That's just how she's made. You would think she gets that from her dad, Mars Baker, from the big stands he used to make in the courtroom and the press, but you probably never knew her and Ginger's mom, Macy Todd. Or, you only know the public Macy Todd. Not the one we knew.

Cinnamon is a clone of her, like sometimes happens. The good parts, I mean. Illustration: this one time we're all flying into Boise. This is the early days, before ground even got broke for Terra Nova, when Deacon Samuels was still trying to sell us on Proofrock and Indian Lake and Pleasant Valley—on Idaho. I'd flown commercial with Dad, and it was my first time traveling like that. I was entranced by the flight attendants, by all the other passengers sitting around us. This was another world.

Yes, I check my privilege now. But I didn't even know that word back then. When the flight was over, I smuggled two packages of peanuts off in my backpack, certain the flight attendants were coordinating to steal them back.

Because Dad had to handle some business on the phone and the rest of our party was on later flights, he left me with Macy Todd, which really meant I was getting to hang with the big girls, with Cinnamon and Ginger. This trip was just getting better and better.

Usually girls four years older will only grudgingly tolerate a kid like me, but, to Cinnamon and Ginger, I was a doll they could dress up—the little sister they never had. Macy Todd took me under her wing and we staked out some chairs in front of a restaurant, out in the walkway. While Macy Todd read her book (she despised smartphones, and thought listening to music in public was an embarrassment to everyone involved), Cinnamon and Ginger taught me how the springy chairs we were sitting in would leave waffle prints on the backs of our legs—it was winter, but we were all wearing shorts. As the game progressed, two of us would sit in the lap of the third for twenty seconds, then thirty seconds, then a minute, to see how deep we could press that waffle print into the backs of our legs.

Macy Todd would look up to us from time to time, consider our game, then smile her sharp smile, shake her head in amusement, and go back to reading. My mom had of course sat me down by then, told me that Cinnamon and Ginger's mother had done something very bad to a man years and years ago, and that I was never to mention it, so of course I didn't. But it did always make me watch her in a different way.

And I know this isn't about the Independence Day Massacre yet like you asked, but I'm getting there, don't worry.

When the rest of this Idaho Expedition's party was still late—that was Mr. Singleton's name for it—my father came over from whatever private corner he'd found to apologize to Macy Todd for this. She brushed it off, told him we were fine, obviously, and then asked him to guard us for a moment while she got us some salads. Given the choice, we would have asked for chicken fingers, but Macy Todd's severity didn't stop at music in public: we would each get side salads, appropriate to our sizes, and they would each have balsamic vinaigrette on them, not anything so crude and "NASCAR" as Ranch.

While she was at the bar of the restaurant we were parked by, coordinating these salads, which for her involved a deep interrogation about ingredients, their sources, and preparation methods, my father—and I don't blame him; he never was the attentive type—drifted off, lost in the meeting he was sort of in. Technically he could have still seen us, but, listening as closely as he was, I don't think he was seeing anything, really: the people sleeping across the seats, having to thread their legs and arms through the armrests; the woman rushing through from gate to gate, never realizing her peach-colored rollerbag was turned around wheels-up; the boy who dropped his pretzel on the ground, considered it, then picked it up, continued eating.

My father also didn't see the high schooler who walked by us one time, a second time, and then—Ginger was the first to notice—a *third* time.

Cinnamon and Ginger were twelve going on seventeen here.

I had no awareness what was going on.

By the time Macy Todd returned with our three salads and three bottled waters—always bottled, with her—this high schooler was sitting in a booth across the walkway with Ginger, his hand on her bare thigh.

Macy Todd's eyes didn't change in the least, but she did incline her head over to the right a few degrees.

"Girls," she said to Cinnamon and me. "Your food."

Our hearts were beating so hard we couldn't have eaten, though.

"Pardon me," Macy Todd said down to us, then walked neatly over to this high schooler. He had a guitar leaned against his knee. It's cliche, I know, but he really did, Mr. Armitage. Later, Ginger, thrilled nearly beyond words and head over heels in some kind of love, would tell us he was coming back from a church trip to Mexico, that this service was his senior project.

On the way across the walkway to him, Macy Todd—not to speak ill of the dead; really, to show the power she had—was unbuttoning the top two buttons of her black blouse. At the booth Ginger and this boy were in, she leaned over, probably giving him a view that stopped his breath. Ginger never forgave her for this as far as I know, but over the next two minutes, her mother—who never announced herself as such—quieting Ginger with a glare, lured this boy from that booth, past the shoe-shine station, and into the family bath-room.

Ginger drifted back to us, the three of us watching that shut door so intently.

Three minutes later Macy Todd stepped out, looked left and right, and then settled back into her book beside us, her blouse buttoned all the way up again.

As long as we watched that family bathroom door, it never opened, and then we were being hustled up the mountain to Terra Nova, Ginger's heart forever broken, Cinnamon watching her mother so closely. Not because she hated her, but because she was understanding what had just happened, I think. What had almost happened, if someone hadn't stepped in to stop it.

That's why I say Cinnamon is like her, Mr. Armitage. She might be a mirror image of her sister, but she's cut from the same cloth her mother was.

If you ask Ginger about the tinsel, she'll just stare at the wall, for which I feel partly responsible. We should have forced her to come with us that night. I know that now. But, the same as we'd let her leave our table in the Boise Airport, go with that boy, I guess we also let her stay in the yacht by herself, until we could come back.

But, the tinsel. Cinnamon would probably tell you it was just her and Ginger, but I was there too. And it was my idea. Before they let me come with them onto shore after dark—sneaking off the yacht was nothing—Cinnamon and Ginger had just been leaving random batteries and earrings they didn't want on shore for the little girl they showed me grainy recordings of.

My contribution was the tinsel.

If we gave her enough of it, she was supposed to thread it through her hair, tie it around her wrists, and then we could watch her from the deck, our feet hanging through the railing. She would be flashing in the moonlight, limned in silver.

It worked… sort of.

From the back of the yacht, we did see that clutch of silver racing away across the lake, but it was falling behind like sparks from a meteor. We imagined we could hear each strand sizzling against the water before it sank.

But it did confirm for us what the footprints suggested: she could walk on water. Meaning she was probably a ghost.

It made her the best secret ever.

We watched the trail cam recordings of her over and over all the time, even passing Cinnamon's phone back and forth during Letha's graduation. Cinnamon and Ginger cut their fingers with a stolen razorblade, making up an oath about how they would never reveal her. They didn't pressure me into cutting myself and making the same promise, but I wanted to.

They let me.

And you know about the yacht we woke up to the night of the third, of course—everyone knows—and I already wrote about us leaving Ginger in the closet, since her anxiety wouldn't let her swim across the lake with that construction worker.

What you probably don't know from all your reconstructions and from everyone else's reports and from whatever video and audio recordings you've been able to gather is that neither Cinnamon nor myself had ever seen *Jaws* before that night. When we paddled into all the dressed-up boats floating against each other, my teeth weren't even chattering anymore, and I couldn't swim, was just holding onto that nail in the construction worker's back, but I looked up to the movie that was somehow still happening, even though everyone behind us was dead, dying, or trying not to.

It was the part with the yellow barrel, and then that old sheriff's face was huge and concerned on-screen, and that's what I remember best: it felt like he was looking across the lake to what had just happened, and he was trying to communicate that to all these people in the water—trying to warn them to get out, to clear the beaches.

I've read about *Jaws* since then—1975, Steven Spielberg, based on the Peter Benchley novel of the same name—and my mind knows that this old sheriff is afraid of the water, afraid of the shark, but my heart remembers it differently.

Then the construction worker and Cinnamon are pushing me up onto the pier; the sheriff's airboat is misting water everywhere; a gun is being fired; people are screaming—I wish I could moment-by-moment it for you, Mr. Armitage, but it was sensory overload piled onto emotional bereftness, and I couldn't process.

My next memory is… it's not silence, it's wailing, I guess you would call it. The living crying for the dead and the dying. I'm still on the pier, and Cinnamon is hugging me to her and crying, and it's making me cry too, I don't even know why.

Some minutes or an hour later, a police officer or a medic bundles us up into a blanket, but the blanket's wet. She walks us up the pier, and since the parking lot is just more wailing and dying, she opens the door of the sheriff's big white truck, tells us to stay warm in there, that we'll be fine, that everything will be okay.

We wait in the truck until dawn, forgotten, watching stretchers of dead people carried past, the whole world flashing red and blue.

Across the lake, Terra Nova is burning.

"There it goes," I remember Cinnamon saying, and taking my hand in hers.

Because I'm still shivering, she plunders the sheriff's truck for another blanket, anything dry, and, from the very back, the cargo area, she hauls up a trash bag of clothes, pours them out between us.

We put on as many of them as we can—they smell like cigarette smoke—and what we find among them are videocassette tapes. Horror movies.

Because I keep crying and not being able to breathe, Cinnamon tries to keep me occupied by reading the sensationalistic descriptions off the backs of those cases to me, and that's my main memory of the Independence Day Massacre: her reading to me about movies I would never see but can never forget: *Slaughter High* and *Graduation Day* and *The Initiation* and *Happy Birthday to Me* and the rest of Jennifer Daniels's tapes—including the one with the title I'm using for this submission.

The only video missing, Cinnamon would tell me later, was *A Bay of Blood*.

But it wasn't really missing. It was right there through the wind-shield. It was lapping up on the shore, staining the gravel red.

Cinnamon hugged me to her, and in her hair, from what we'd just waded through, there was a single strand of silver tinsel threaded through the blond.

She never knew.

I pulled it down, crumpled it, dropped it between the seat and the console.

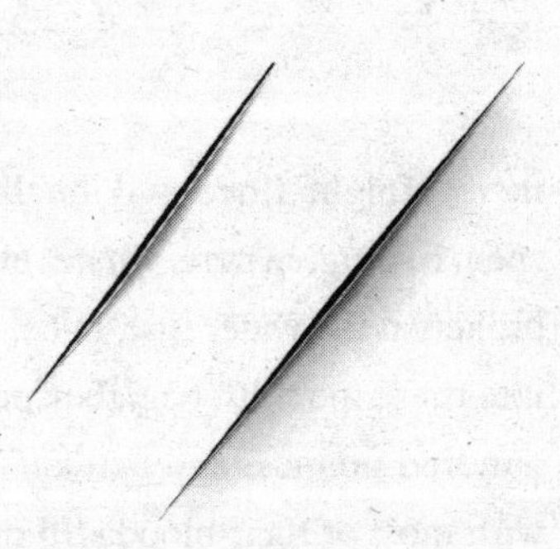

IT FOLLOWS

Standing out in the blowing snow, his frozen-stiff hair rattling like an empty wasp nest, his chest seeping blood from that girl with the knives, Dark Mill South looks down at the hedge clippers he figures will do the job.

He hadn't had any plans for those two girls specifically, but then they knocked the front door of that house down, startling him awake. If they followed him over here, then they're making the decision for him, aren't they? The fox will run, yes, but the fox also has teeth.

Dark Mill South bares his, glares into the blowing snow, and jerks the clippers apart as easy as a wishbone, letting the silver side fall away, only keeping the black blade. It's higher quality steel.

He slashes it back and forth in front of him, testing its weight, its reach. It's nothing like a machete, it won't throw for crap, and it's probably sharpened more for chopping than for pulling across necks and leaving that necessary red line, but, up close, in tight enough quarters, it'll still plunge into a chest, a gut, and splash out the other side.

That's all he really needs, isn't it?

He'll have to remember to angle the handle down so as to get the blade going in where he wants, and it won't come out the back in a straight line, will be like standing in the shallows and spearfishing, where whatever you thrust down at a fish looks broken at the water line, but… it's just a couple of girls. Pieced up into the same trash bag, they probably don't go much over a couple hundred pounds, and that's *if* he can even get them into that bag with most of their blood still on the inside.

But that's never how it works, is it?

And not like he has a bag, either.

He threads his hair from his eyes with his iced-over hook, carves another X in the air like trying to make a hole in the wind to walk through. If he'd been thinking, he'd have snatched the framing hammer out of the garage, not these, but going back would be cheating.

If you start a job with tool X, then tool X is the only thing you can allow yourself to make use of.

Dark Mill South learned the rules young, a long time ago.

Another one is that, since now people know about this place, he can't stay here anymore. And it had been so perfect: dark, out of the way, abandoned. The kind of place you can spend a whole winter, if need be. There's probably even bullshit stories about it being haunted.

After these two girls, though, he tells himself he's going back for that framing hammer. Never mind that it's probably got one of those bullshit shock-reducing handles, the kind that mute the feel of skull crunching. Scavengers can't be choosers. And, never mind the handle, it's that checkered head he's thinking of now, and the way hair and blood mat into it when you really get going—he has to rub himself with the inside of his right wrist.

He spins the clipper blade he's kept and catches it perfect against his left palm, learning the balance already. He's always had a facility with weapons. And this one, it's kind of like a broken-off spear-head, might be good to haft to a pole, for hunting actual animals this winter.

If he can just make this side of the lake his.

Maybe he hangs these two girls up on trees, to warn the people from that town off, right? Same way ranchers put coyotes on fences and let them rot.

Except, if the girls are meant to be seen, then he'll have to hang them low on some of the trees close to shore, won't he? And if he does that, then the bears that haven't gone to sleep will come in to feed, undo his warning.

You can't hang them high, though. Deer and people, they always case the woods at their own height and lower, hardly ever think to look up.

Doesn't matter, Dark Mill South tells himself, trudging along the girls' trail in the snow.

There's not going to be enough of them to hang on a tree anyway.

And—yep: the blood's starting. That one he caught in the shoulder with the knife, she's spattering red into the snow. If she were a real fighter, she'd push her friend ahead and stand in the trail, wait for what's coming.

But there aren't any real fighters anymore. Just killers and the killed.

Dark Mill South grins a little, keeps moving. He's breathing deep now, because it won't be long.

To the right is the large dim shape of another house, but the tracks don't veer that way. Meaning these girls are just asking for it. If they were smart, they'd split up, make him choose which is first, maybe giving the other one time to slip back out onto the ice, slipside across to that town they're from.

But—Dark Mill South stops, studies the open space over the frozen lake.

They didn't just *walk* across, did they?

And they're not wearing snowshoes, and they didn't have skates across their shoulders.

They *rode* across, he knows with a grunt.

Either a snowcat or a snowmobile—something with treads.

He nods, cycles through each in his head. The cat'll take a key, and, being alone so far as they know, the key would still be in the ignition. A snowmobile has a dead man's key, though, and unless you wrap that bright cord around and around the plastic head of that key, then it's easier to just do like you're supposed to and clip it to your jacket.

Meaning one of them's probably wearing it.

Something to remember.

With a snowmobile, this part of the mountain opens up, doesn't it? Cut back through that sleepy town, ride the ditch uphill to the next one, or just go under the highway and up the other side of the mountain, to some cabin with a couple cords of wood already stacked alongside.

That could work.

But first, these girls who can ring the alarm, give him away.

He's thinking they're going to have to pay in skin, too.

A few years ago, way up in the Black Hills, he'd hunkered behind a rise and watched some hunters. They'd just popped a big mule deer, and now one of them was talking to the others while he made a series of precise cuts around this doe's shanks, and her neck, and along her underside. He wasn't gutting her, though, wasn't getting meat at all yet.

Dark Mill South had just watched, waiting. Curious.

It paid off when one of the other hunters backed their pickup up to the deer, and that hunter with the knife looped rope from the deer to the trailer ball, and then, unaccountably, from the deer to a tree stump.

To stretch her? Get her tight between that stump and the truck? Would that make the guts plop out with just a flick of the blade, maybe? Or was this a new way to squeeze the blood out?

Neither.

When the truck jerked forward, the rope it was pulling was only tied to that doe's skin, evidently. It peeled it right off the same way a magician pulls a tablecloth out from under all the candlesticks. Because that other hunter had cut it in just the right places.

Left behind, tied to the stump, was that big deer, just muscle and fat now, her legs contracting back in.

The hunters cheered.

Up on the rise, Dark Mill South did too, inside.

This is the same way he got the idea for the stools and the electricity: from watching a white man in his backyard use a car battery to punish a goat over and over, the goat's screams ragged and human at first, like trying to call in the rest of the goats, but then weaker, once it figured out no one was coming.

This could be even better, though.

And maybe now's the time to try it out.

If he can find that snowmobile, fashion a rope of some kind, and make the cuts just right, then, if he's lucky, he might be able to rip the skin right off these girls, leave them flopping and jumping in the snow.

Because that was the improvement he saw immediately, watching those hunters: leave the animal *alive* when you do it.

Would it even snatch the eyelids away?

He stops in the trail, chocks the blade under his right arm, and feels his own eyelids with his mostly numb index finger.

They are connected. If the face skin peels, then the eyelids go with it.

Now the question is just where to cut. Around the ankles and wrists, definitely. Just lightly, skin-deep. And up either the frontside or the back.

Which would be better?

The front, he decides.

That way, they're looking up at the moment the rope tightens on their wrists and ankles. And maybe they fall on their backs, can look up, see him standing there to their north—because of course he'd have pulled them west to east.

When he steps to the side, though, if he's waited until they're absolutely locked on him as their one chance in hell, maybe their eyes will stay where he was for a moment, and they can get a glimpse of that magnificent curtain of light way, way out there, way *up* there, and—

And, with their last breath, they'll thank him. Because part of them's being allowed to step *through* that curtain, and because, if they're lucky, then they'll be like him that night when he was twelve, running away through the yellow grass, his legs sheeted with blood, his face wet with tears, and that same shimmering light undulated into existence directly ahead of him, splashing a pink shadow out behind him, leaving only his darker self running ahead, across the years, faster and faster, until they all collapsed together around him and he was standing by a trashcan in the dirty snow, the fingers of his missing right hand twined in the hair of a man's sawed off head.

Or was that in summer, and he was standing in a river?

Doesn't matter.

What does, now that he considers it, is the complication of him having to be standing there to enjoy a skinless girl flopping at his feet and *also* the snowmobile's throttle needing to be twisted back to make that happen, but… he'll figure it out. He always does. How he knows he will? This place is charmed. Walking across the frozen lake, the wind hitting hard enough that it was hard to stay standing, he'd sensed another form out there with him, and so stilled himself, waited.

One minute, two minutes, ice forming on the right side of his face, then, finally, it took shape in the swirling snow: a bull elk, ventured out onto the ice for . . . elk reasons.

Judging by how white he was, meaning how long he had been out here in the suck, Dark Mill South knew that he still had a mile or two to go, probably.

Until the elk drew closer, to sniff him, and he saw that big bull's coat wasn't frozen. It was *white*.

Dark Mill South's heart beat once, struggling to come up into his throat.

The elk sniffed him again to be sure, then ripped his massive walnut antlers away, their sharp pale points slashing a finger's width from Dark Mill South's eyes.

His heart beat again, finally.

The elk folded back into the storm, continuing his long walk across, and Dark Mill South grinned in the cold, knew two things for sure: he was supposed to be here, and he was on the right side of this. Luck was going to keep falling his way.

Like this: two girls announcing themselves with the clap of a door, falling.

But people are always doing some version of that, aren't they? Asking for it over and over, until Dark Mill South steps in, gives it to them?

He chuckles, spits.

That white elk might be long gone, but he's still watching over Dark Mill South, he knows.

Which doesn't mean everything's going to just be handed to him, of course.

He'd have it no other way.

He nods, wipes the accumulated snow from his blade, and steps into the girls' moose trail—that's what it is. A deer will leave peg holes in the snow, but watch a moose in four feet of snow. It just barrels through like a train, leaving more of a gouge than footsteps.

It's smart of them, though, isn't it? Walking single file like this? Either smart or lucky. Could be they're not even considering the trail they're leaving. Just, one of them's stronger, is the snowbreaker of them, and the other, not weighing as much, is taking advantage of a path already made, but… doesn't matter either.

Neither does whatever sad resistance they think's going to be enough. All they're going to have when he catches up with them, he knows, all they *can* have, is whatever they can scrounge up from these broken-down houses. They already threw all their knives at him.

And they're probably just running away, aren't looking for the right length of rebar, aren't diving for the snowmobile, which has to be back at the lake, since he didn't hear it pull up to the house.

Sometimes it's good when it's easy, right?

He deserves easy.

And now he's rubbing himself again, but there's no time for that.

He runs his hair out of his eyes with his hook, and then—fuck it—just winds it around enough to pull it tight, saws it off with the black blade, carving himself a square window to look out of.

And no, he doesn't expect to get this skinning right the first time. A girl isn't a deer, after all.

But there's two of them out there. Even if he messes up with the first, he's got a spare, doesn't he? When it works, though. Will the skinless girl run off into the snow, just a dab of muscular red, or will she lie there shaking, afraid of what she's become, her eyes begging him to step down into the delicate bones of her face?

The first, he hopes.

That's a thing he'd pay to see.

This is Mr. Pangborne's house, Letha is pretty sure. The one she found Jennifer in, forever ago.

Gal's house, then.

Meaning her bedroom must be upstairs. What was going to have been her bedroom, before.

Everything in Letha's life is divided with that word, *before*. On one side of it she has a father, and on the other side she has a jaw molded from plastic.

But, her therapist gently insists, that's not the right way to think about it, is it?

Rather, on one side she has an idyllic childhood stacked with picture-perfect memories, and on this side, now, she has a husband, a beautiful little daughter, and together they're making memories that no one will ever be able to take away.

It's all about perspective. It's all about what you choose to build your psychological and emotional house on. It's all about what light you choose to shine on the past, and the present.

Which is all well and fine for an hour every Monday and Wednesday.

For running from a maniac killer through the ruins of your old life, in a snowstorm trying to swallow you, your shoulder on fire, your undershirt heavy with blood, your jaw humming, Letha thinks it's probably better to dwell, for once, on how she survived the ugly parts.

There hasn't been a single time on the recumbent bike in the basement that, pedaling herself numb, she hasn't told herself that there's a movie screen across the lake from her, and it's playing *Jaws*, and if she can just get there fast enough, she can stop all this from happening.

Her thighs are iron, and Banner knows better than to come down while she's riding, ask her where the ketchup is.

It's in me, she says inside—the ketchup—and the guy looking to scoop it out is better than six and a half feet tall, and doesn't care about knives to the chest, or through his hand, and the cold probably isn't slowing him down either. Her only wish is that she would have *thought* instead of just running—if she were out on the lake, leading him in circles, she might could still save Jennifer, and Proofrock. But, like Sidney says, slashers are all about some big-breasted girl running up the stairs when she should be running out the front door.

A truth bomb she drops right before Kevin Williamson runs her upstairs.

And it goes all the way back to Laurie Strode, dropping that icky butcher knife—it's hard to do the right thing in the moment, with a real live killer in your face. *After* that moment, though? When you're hiding under the windowsill of a burnt house, a steak knife still poking through your shoulder, its surprisingly grabby teeth scraping the collarbone each time you breathe, and probably nicking deeper into whatever important vessel it's nicking into? Then it's obvious what you should have done, and how you should have done it.

Given another takeback, Letha would have used the cover of the storm to make a sharp left, run thirty or forty yards through the snow, then do the Danny Torrance shuffle: walk backwards through her own footprints, finally getting to where she turned and continuing on with her original line, to Mr. Pangborne's never lived-in living room, which it would now look like she'd run *from*, instead of to.

But, if she'd just taken Rex Allen's goose gun out to Melanie's bench so she could truck it across to Terra Nova, then she could have blown a hole through Dark Mill South in her own once-upon-a-time house.

He might be able to shake off knives from the dollar store, but, at fifteen feet, full-choke birdshot would still be tight enough to have knocked him down for a little bit, at least.

And, if not the first shot, then the second, and the third, and however many shells she would have had in her pocket.

Evil isn't armor, after all.

All she can do, finally, is pray that Jennifer held her breath under the sink, and that Dark Mill South cued into the open back door, and that maybe those knives had at least been enough of an annoyance to tunnel his vision down to the girl who'd thrown them.

After that, it's all about how fast the storm is erasing her footprints.

Maybe the Danny Torrance shuffle would have been all for nothing, anyway, the holes in the snow rounding off any prints fast enough that their direction would make no difference.

And? What's she going to do once Dark Mill South fills the empty doorway?

She could lure his great and solid weight out to a collapse-y part, she guesses, send him through the floor Jason-style. But he'd probably just come back on fire.

No, the only thing to do when he shows up, it's run, and then run some more. And, now that she's thinking straight, lure him out onto the ice, maybe out to the dam, past the cones, where the ice is supposed to be thin enough from the turbine intakes to collapse under the weight of a body.

The only other option is to scurry from house to house, and hope the cold gets to him before it gets to her.

Fat chance, though, she knows. He probably has a fire roiling in his chest that provides all the heat he needs.

"Sorry, baby," Letha says to the idea of Adrienne.

Mommy's going to be late for dinner, and will probably just be a picture on the wall for the first day of kindergarten, and for science fair in fourth grade, and for that first kiss freshman year, and for prom, when her dad is going to have to be the one to help her with her hair, her gown, her corsage.

And now Letha's crying. Can't control her lips.

She wipes the tears away with the sleeve of this ski jacket, wipes harder when there's more—*You're being stupid, you're already giving up!*—and then actually falls back onto her butt when the phone in her bra buzzes.

Sidney would love this, that Letha's got her phone holstered in her left cup.

Sitting on the back of the snowmobile, though, she was afraid it would work its way out of her rear pocket, skitter away across the ice, drift down to Drown Town with spring melt.

And?

She has *signal* over here? For an accidental moment, her heart surges, because if there's signal, then that means her dad's turned the jammer off. Either that or she's close enough to the yacht to pick up its Wi-Fi.

But, it's 2019, not 2015: no dad, no yacht.

She unzips, delicately removes the phone, careful not to move the steak knife in her shoulder *too* much, and—of course. This isn't a call or text. There's still no signal on this side of Indian Lake. The buzzing is a reminder. Pill time, "PT" by name, or code, because if anybody she's having coffee with sees it, it can be "physical therapy," and who would be impolite enough to ask about that?

Related: who in Proofrock would have coffee with her?

Evil isn't armor, but money sort of is. In high school, it was her dad who was rich. She was only rich by association. So, people could still talk to her as a person. Now that she's writing the checks, though… she's an outcast, is too high on her Scrooge McDuck pile of golden coins for anyone to ever even consider asking her to coffee at Dot's.

Banner tells her it's more about nobody knowing what she can and can't eat and drink, with her jaw situation, but Letha can tell. She can see it in the eyes of everyone she's asking for a library book, or for which aisle the staples are on: the least kindness from this daughter of Terra Nova can change this other person's life so, so completely.

Or, not.

And, when *not*, then… resentment. She's an uppity Black girl risen beyond her station, and using that to look down her nose at all the unfortunates, working in some version of the coal mines to pad her bank account.

She knows she shouldn't make it about race, that that probably doesn't speak well to her, but, over the years, being the second plus-one for her dad at function after function, she's learned to tell between those who are intimidated by money and those who have to tell themselves to smile nice to the Black family who made it.

And it's not necessarily either/or. People's eyes are Legion.

To top it off? She kind of hates herself for having what she has, too, because it's blood money: if her dad doesn't die, then she's just an entitled princess *to* the media empire, not the one at the reins of a golden chariot crossing the sky every day, so far above the grubby world.

Anyway: pill time.

Letha angles her body to reach her little tube of opiates and steroids and anti-inflammatories and immunosuppressants. Dark Mill South may very well remove her head from her body in the next five minutes, but Letha Mondragon *isn't* dying from an infection that results from her body rejecting the foreign materials she needs to live.

And, really? She's got the dose after this one with her, too, doesn't she?

If there was ever a good reason to double up on the Oxy, then a steak knife through the shoulder might qualify.

But no.

She doesn't know for sure what's coming. Better to hold a dose back.

Letha shakes a *single* dose of pills into her left palm, passes the bigger white tablet to her right hand—her left arm isn't coming up to her mouth anytime soon—grabs some moisture from her gums, and gets the Oxy down. Then it's wash-rinse-repeat, laboriously getting the other three down her throat as well.

Because she's in the backwash of her big adrenaline rush, her insides hollowed out and hungry, the Oxy flushes up and down her body in the most wonderful way. It coats her thinking in what she always thinks of as cold Vaseline.

"Come and get me," she hisses into the living room wall most of her face is pressed against.

She's just a pair of eyes peeking through a broken window in one of eight houses.

Well, one of eight houses, but the only one with rounded-off footprints leading up onto its porch. And… as weak as she must be, that single Oxy tablet is feeling more like a whole bottle. When was the last time she ate anything? Or, rather, *drank* anything.

Avocado shake, seven this morning, right before warming up the truck to go get Jennifer? Eight hours ago?

Still, thankfully, her shoulder is only a dull and distant pain now, and she hasn't thought about the wrongness of her jaw for probably five minutes, which is something like a record.

She grins with the hopelessness of her situation, her eyes still leaking, but who cares, and all the shit circulating through her blood must be leaving her sentimental: instead of sliding her phone back into her bra, she opens the camera, swipes over to video, and, after four deliberate breaths to center herself, she makes another one of her just-in-case recordings for Adrienne, trying to tell her what's important, and trying not to cry too much, but then, only thirty seconds in, a large form coalesces for a moment some twenty feet out, through the blowing snow.

"More later," Letha whispers into her phone, and slides it into its place in her left cup, her hand numb from the Oxy. Or from fear. From pre-death.

But, *pre-death*?

"That's just life, girl," she mumbles in the cage of her teeth.

She zips up, the back of her dead index finger snagging the leading point of the steak knife, which evidently still *can* hurt. Her back straightens then sways in, her breath catching even though inflated lungs make her shoulder scream even more.

No, Mommy can't lead a merry chase out on the ice, she knows now, and is apologizing for. All she can do is play invisible, and hope that when she's found, Banner thinks to look into her camera roll, play that recording.

But at least she led this killer away from Jennifer.

Maybe Jennifer can stop him, somehow.

"*I'm sorry, I'm sorry, I'm sorry,*" Letha can't seem to stop muttering, her head filling with it, and then he's there on the porch, the boards actually dipping down from his weight, which Letha wouldn't have expected. This house is deeper in, though. It must have burned longer.

If only she had that big novelty lighter and the WD-40.

Or even that toy soldier. He's small enough that the bayonet on his rifle could take an eye out, and his shoulders are narrow enough to fit all the way through that orbit, into the mushy brains Dark Mill South has to have.

Like a machete through the head ever stopped Jason.

But Letha knows one thing: she's not dying on her knees.

Instead of waiting for her end to find her, she stands up all at once, the broken window framing her, giving her hiding place away.

Dark Mill South looks over to her.

"You don't belong here," she says through her teeth.

He grins. His lips are knotted and scarred and twisted, but still, Letha can tell that he likes this—someone not scrambling away.

Then you'll love this, she says inside, and reaches behind her head with her right hand and pulls that little knife back through, and out, its grabby teeth carving into flesh and muscle it missed, going in. Letha clenches hard enough from this lightning rush of surging pain that the stupid contraption in her mouth starts to creak and give.

She holds the bloody knife in front of her, is at least going to leave him with one more scar, one last memory of the girl who wouldn't give up, one last reminder that not everyone goes down easy.

Dark Mill South nods about this.

Instead of coming for her right through the window like she expects, he steps ahead, into the doorless doorway, and Letha pivots around to meet him head-on, because some things you can't run from, and because this is it, because it's been too long, because she can't help it, she *screams,* her teeth parting for the first time in so long, all her anger pouring out louder and louder, her whole upper body leaning forward, her chin tapping the puffy chest of her jacket she's pretty sure, an off-putting enough thing that even Dark Mill South stops in his tracks, his eyes widening to take this, whatever it is, in.

It's me, Letha says inside, almost falling over frontward now from this effort, from this wash of pain, from the tearing sound so close to her ears, from—from all the moments she's about to miss with Adrienne, with Ban, but if she's falling, then she's falling into him, she's digging with this puny little knife, never mind that black one he's got, she's going in through the belly for the spine, and she's not stopping until—

But he's just standing there?

Letha falls forward onto one knee, onto the hand holding that knife.

She tries to make another sound, anything, but doesn't have anything left, can't even hold herself up like this anymore, can't even—

Slowly, then, so slowly, Dark Mill South timbers forward, his hook coming fast at Letha, her sucking backward in what feels like slow motion, giving his hook time to rip the front of her jacket open, take some of it with him.

And then, not even catching himself with his other arm, he's falling flat onto his face before her, the living room floorboards under him creaking and cracking, then giving, sending him down to Mr. Pangborne's basement.

Standing in the doorway behind him, a long blue hammer held in both hands at the end of its high swing, blood and long black hair matted on its head, is Jennifer.

Letha wants to smile with her heart, because she can't with her face.

She reaches her right hand up for Jennifer, the steak knife

clattering away, down with Dark Mill South, her chin loose, the hinges of her jaws screaming muted pain into her ears.

Jennifer steps forward, looking everywhere at once, not even close to dropping that big hammer, her breath coming in gasps.

A board falls from the ceiling, into the new hole in the living room floor. Into the *growing* hole.

Letha looks up the same way you do when you feel the sky falling.

She can feel the wood of the porch she's on starting to tilt, to take her with, and she looks up to Jennifer.

Another board up there hangs down by a single nail, pendulums back and forth, finally tumbles into the darkness.

"*Jennifer!*" Letha somehow gets out through her broken mouth, her broken face, even though it's already too late, she's already falling, but if she's only got one last thing to drink in... she looks out across the frozen lake, to the taped-over door she can no longer see, with her husband and daughter standing behind it, waiting for Mommy.

"It's Jade, actually," Letha hears Jennifer say right before all the sound and fury, the snow and ash of a whole house collapsing, and the last thing this princess of Terra Nova feels is a hand hot on her wrist.

When Jade pulls, it nearly tears that princess in half.

Banner sets Adrienne down in Meg's spinny chair—it's her favorite thing—kneels in front of her to be sure she understands how important it is that good girls stay right here, and then he's running down the hall to whatever the hell's going on in the holding cells.

Like this day isn't already full of enough shit?

Was this what it was like for Hardy, back in 2015?

No way, Banner knows.

All Hardy was juggling was complaints about the Terra Nova staging area, probably. And the bear, don't forget that bear. And all the dead people on the yacht, and all the dead people on the Fourth.

Makes sense Hardy wants the high-up silence of the dam, Banner tells himself.

He could do a few shifts up there now himself.

And? For the ninety seconds the phones had been live again—when they all started in ringing at once, he'd come around with his pistol out—he'd tried Letha first, and, when the towers were evidently still down, he'd dialed the only place he thought might get an answer: Pleasant Valley Assisted Living.

It's a minute and a half he wishes he had back.

In those ninety seconds, he'd had to learn in detail he didn't want how Mark and Kristen and Philip died. Cinn still wasn't one of them, which was great, wonderful, finally something good, but he also knows that every good development has an equal and shittier *further* development—that's something Francie impressed on him Day One, regarding domestic calls.

The equal and shittier fallout of Cinn not being dead like her three friends is that she's also missing, unaccounted for, *gone*.

She doesn't have her warm clothes, either. Banner's pretty sure that ski outfit Letha was chasing after out there, that Rexall had been collecting as well, was the one Donna Pangborne's kid had delivered up to the station on their fancy snowmobile.

Per Rex Allen's orders, Banner hadn't answered any of the questions Gal—on her delivery run—had more or less been asking with her eyes. Or maybe what she'd really been saying was that Banner was only five years older than Cinn, and that her giving official statements in just her bra and panties and boots wasn't quite proper, wasn't helping Cinn any in the reputation department, her already having had some difficulties along those lines at the high school.

But Cinnamon Baker would never hook up with a teacher. And a teacher would never hook up with a student.

Still, Rex Allen had sent Francie down in October to make sure. Discreetly.

So, Banner just took the shopping bag of ski clothes Gal was handing across, tried to make zero eye contact, and didn't even tell little Gal to be careful going back up the hill, because that might count as an official comment.

What Banner suspected was that Cinn had had to shimmy *out* of that ski outfit in order to fit through the window of the ladies' room. She'd pushed it out ahead of her, to slip back into, but it'd blown away before she could pull it on again. Case closed, thank you very much.

And now she's out there in the mix again, probably trying to lead Dark Mill South away from where any other potential victims might be. Because she's like Letha—Letha's even said that to him before, when making the case for Cinn to watch Adrienne: that girl will fight tooth and nail, she'll put herself between danger and her charge without thinking twice.

Unlike Ginger, who would sit on the other side of the room and watch a kid cry in the corner for hours, just to see how long their little throat might or might not last.

According to one of the orderlies Banner had to deliver home after a rowdy night, the last time that orderly saw someone carry themselves like Ginger was when that construction worker Greyson

Brust was locked way down in the east wing like "the man in the iron mask," whatever the hell that meant. But, apparently this construction worker had had the same insect-y fascination with human behavior as Ginger does.

When Ginger's finally released, starts showing up for holidays, then Thanksgiving's gonna be a riot, yeah.

There's not enough beer in the world.

But, first, Banner has to even get back around *to* another November. First he has to somehow wade through the rising sewage this day is.

Case in point: Rexall must be standing with his back to the bars and running full-tilt for the cinderblock wall on the other side, ramming into it with all of his three-hundred-whatever pounds.

Or maybe he's hanging onto the bars, trying to pull them back in?

Either way, if he hurts himself *or* the cell, it's on Banner. And if it's himself he's hurting then… who's to say those injuries weren't sustained as a result of police brutality? Was the probationary deputy not fighting out in the snow with the litigant, defendant—whatever Rexall would be, Banner doesn't know. It was hard enough passing the three tests it took to come on the force. Leave the lawyering to someone else.

As for how he's going to make Rexall stop whatever he's doing… it'll be a feet-on-the-ground decision. And, of course, when he's halfway down the long hall to holding is when the phones in the front office light up again. But he can't turn around, has to see about Rexall—the prisoner is the arresting officer's responsibility, at least until officially handed over to another officer.

If only.

Banner crashes through the first door at the end of the hall, then the door to holding, and immediately to the right, Rexall is cringing back *against* the bars?

Banner slides to a stop, hanging onto the bars himself.

The cinderblock back wall is leaking dust.

"Did a truck hit it?" Banner says down to Rexall.

"It's her, it's her," Rexall's saying breathlessly.

Banner narrows his eyes, considering this, then shakes his head no: Rexall can only be talking about Stacey Graves, can't he? From Letha, Banner knows that she might have been really real, that *some*one with too much strength ripped half Leeth's face off then tossed her across the top of the water like a ragdoll that night, but… would a dead little girl have enough strength to try to come through a cinderblock wall?

More importantly: *why?*

Banner stealthily reaches back for the grip of his pistol, then looks down when it's not in its holster—of fucking *course*.

And Rexall is still repeating, "It's her, it's her."

"Shut it!" Banner tells him, but now Rexall is sputtering on, about… Misty Christy, the dead realtor? And Lonnie?

Lonnie nearly just brained him, though. Maybe this can make sense. Maybe it's Lonnie in the cat, coming to finish the job.

But, "Tab, Clate, Kimmy," Rexall goes on—more people than would even fit *into* the cat. And some of them are dead.

"*Shut up!*" Banner tells him again, and works his pepper spray up from his belt.

There's something going on at the metal door at the end of the walkway between the cells, now.

Banner's twitchy finger *nearly* fills the whole holding area with pepper spray.

"Sheriff Allen?" he says, weakly. "Francie?"

Who else but law would come to the back door, right? *Right?*

"Thank you, thank you," he says, trying to reholster the pepper spray and of course missing. The little canister tumbles and rolls against the bars of the cell.

An instant later, it's snatched away: Rexall, reaching through.

Banner falls back, hands up, but… Rexall's rushing the back wall?

He smashes the pepper spray through the high-up wire glass and sprays it, yelling behind it like to give it aim, give it reach.

When the canister's spent, he is too.

He turns his back to the wall, slides down it, and the pepper spray rolls and clatters across the cell, away from him. It stops at the bars.

Gingerly, trying not to breathe in case of blowback, Banner two-fingers it up and through, reholsters it, because Rex Allen doesn't necessarily have to know about this, does he?

"Don't open it," Rexall says, about the door.

Banner opens it.

All that's there is an aluminum walker with one tennis ball foot. One walker and a lot of snow swirling in.

"What the—?" he says, and steps out, ready for anything. Anything but Hardy, collapsed beside the door, snow already coating him white, his breath coming in frosted spurts, his eyes rimmed red from pepper spray.

"Not how we did it in my day," he says.

"I—I—" Banner says, but has nothing, really. "It was Rexall. He—he—"

"Had your Mace?" Hardy growls right back, seemingly

impressed with the ignorance on display, here.

"Not anymore," Banner says as quietly as possible, and steps out past Hardy, takes a look down along the back side of the jail.

Because Hardy came this way on his walker, there's no tracks to say what happened.

"Hunh," Banner says, and wedges Hardy's walker in under the old sheriff, holds the door.

"You haven't asked me why I'm here, Deputy," Hardy says, still squinting.

"Do I even want to know?" Banner asks.

"There's a bunch of kids down on Main," Hardy says between coughs.

"And?" Banner asks.

"And nothing good can come from that," Hardy finishes.

Banner can't disagree.

"Your little girl came to the door to let me in," Hardy says, then, meaning the front door, the taped-over door—Adrienne didn't stay in the spinny chair like she was supposed to. Surprise.

"It doesn't open anymore," Banner says, pretty sure he's nailing the lid on his own coffin. "Letha used this door when she left."

"To go where?" Hardy asks, probably because he saw the truck still parked out front, across the handicapped slots.

"With Jennifer Daniels, I guess," Banner says, chucking his chin out behind Hardy.

Hardy turns, peers into the swirling whiteness hiding the lake, then shakes his head about this, says, "Don't guess anything good can come of that either."

He stabs his walker into the doorway, pulls himself in.

Banner stands there holding the door, telling himself that

Letha's right about to materialize through the snow. And then right about to again.

When she doesn't, he stands there a moment longer, waiting.

"He wishes he could stop himself, but there's no easy way."

It's the opening line from one of his dad's stupid country music songs, that are forever imprinted on his soul, his psyche, his heart.

Given the choice, he'd of course rather mentally cue up Phil Collins's "In the Air Tonight." When he closes his eyes just right, he's standing on that dock like Pamela Voorhees in the flashback from *Freddy vs. Jason*, watching Jason drown in Crystal Lake. And for some reason not rushing out into the waters to save him.

Does she just stand there because this is the counselors' responsibility? Which is to say: their blame, their fault.

Or… evil thought, evil thought… has her son been holding her back? Will him drowning be escape for her, from the burdens of a motherhood Elias left her alone with? Or can she, in her son's final thrashings, already see the delicious revenge she'll now get to enact? Has part of her *always* been lying under that narrow bunk bed in that cabin at Camp Blood, holding an arrow across her chest, the raspy razor edge of that broadhead hungry to push through that thin mattress?

Claude Armitage thinks maybe, yeah.

He understands lying there in that tight darkness, just waiting for a reason to present itself. His lungs swelling with possibility when the bed frame creaks, taking the weight of two people who have no idea what's about to happen, and how beautiful it's going to be.

He wishes he could stop himself, yes, but there's no easy way—you can't control what you think, what you want, what you need.

You can, though, at sixteen, while your dad's at work, bend all of his golf clubs over your knee—it's so satisfying when that metal crimps over. You can, after he comes at your mannequin collection with that broken driver, hold a lighter under the sleeve of each of his prize country records, going up and down with that hungry-hungry flame, just enough to lightly scorch the sleeve, but who cares about the stupid sleeve? It's the vinyl in there that needs to get tacky, melt flat.

Johnny Paycheck, Tammy Wynette, Tompall Glaser, Billy Joe Shaver—it took until sunup, almost, and partway through he had to refill the lighter, but it was worth it.

He didn't wish he could stop himself then.

In response, while he was at school the next week, his dad unspooled all of his slasher videotapes, left them coiled and iridescent and forever crinkled in front of the television, like, with their dying gasps, they'd tried to slither to the one home they truly knew.

There was no easy way out, but Claude found one anyway: good enough grades to get out of high school early, blast off into college, make all kinds of money, never look back, take nothing with him but that last name.

Of all the masks staring back at him on two of the walls of his study, the one he puts on in his darkest moods is the only one he took with him when he left Columbus, Ohio, behind: his dad's cowboy hat, the one he always said was the actual one Johnny Lee wore in *Urban Cowboy*, the movie that was a bible to him. It's crimped and burnished and the brim is curled and it's seen some times, has a sweat ring you could probably pull DNA from to prove or disprove its authenticity, and you can't wear it low and evil on your forehead or else you can't see out from under it to do any of the necessary dirty work, but its feather hatband with the fantail crest up front is as perfect as anything's ever been.

Even better, his dad doesn't have it anymore.

But that hat, and the welding goggles that go with it, only comes out for the most special of special occasions.

For right now, because who else is going to be out here on the ice, it's a pull-over rubber job: Bicycle Girl from *The Walking Dead*. Not that zombies are even slasher-adjacent—well, not unless you count *Friday the 13th Part VI*, where Jason either *Lives* or keeps stalking around anyway—but this Bicycle Girl's face… it's stupid, Claude knows, it's stupid and maybe even kind of embarrassing, but…

What if *Curtains* had gotten a sequel?

It would be easy to duck into the hag mask for that iconic ice-skating scene that scarred a whole generation, but a true fan doesn't take the easy way. No, a realtrue *believer* ports in what they know about the Captain Kirk mask that replaced the Emmett Kelly clown face for *Halloween*. Specifically, how, when they hauled it out for the sequel after it had been watching the world from under Debra Hill's bed for a couple of years, it was stained yellow from all the cigarettes she smoked.

It was the most beautiful thing, was something no one could have ever guessed: that the mask could evolve right along with the story. Sure, Jason's hockey mask shows axe and machete scars, but, allowing for different make-up crews, Freddy pretty much looks the same from beginning to end, and of course Ghostface is the same from installment to installment, at least on the outside. Chucky shows damage like Jason, but his mask is his whole little body. Leatherface is always drying a new peel on the line, maybe according to the day of the week or his mood, but, like Jade says in her papers: dude's not a slasher. He just looks like one.

That hag in *Curtains*, though…

Had she gone into a sequel, or a stack of sequels, then the same mask would have lost its power to scare, wouldn't it? It would probably never quite lose its "Wicked Queen in the Disney mirror"–offputtingness, and it could still startle, sure, like that pig mask *Saw* uses to such good effect, but… what if it started to break down by the second movie? The third?

It would start to look like Bicycle Girl from *The Walking Dead*, Claude knows.

She even has hair that's a few shades paler than *Curtains*' "red," making her feel washed out.

And, what would that bring to the story? That's the thrilling part to consider. The hag mask could be—it could be like that cursed wooden mask in *You Might Be the Killer*, couldn't it? A supernatural parasite that controls the wearer, compels them to kill and kill again, just, not with martial arts like the 1981 movie of that name, but machetes and axes and worse and better. *Curtains II: Season of the Hag* could give its trodden-upon wearer "freedom" to get revenge on her victims one by one, while also cowering in corners right along with them, just trying to survive this night.

Also, a pull-over rubber mask is pretty good at keeping the cold out.

Given his druthers, of course, the Proofrock he prefers would have embraced its hallowed spot in history, and let him arrange a formation of mannequins out here right after the lake iced up, so they would be frozen in place now. Cruising through them on his skis, with this mask, and this shorty scythe… it makes his heart swell nearly to bursting.

Just, his dad cracked in the ribs of all his mannequins years ago, and then peed into their hollow interiors.

And, anyway, if the ice was just freezing, Claude knows, he would have had to lean on Sara, the history teacher from the elementary, for children. Because no way would the newly frozen lake support an adult's weight. So he'd have to conscript some third-graders to slide out here on their bellies, pushing pieces of mannequins in front of them, to assemble when Claude yelled at them from shore that that was far enough. Then they would pull the little green cooler across to them, with the ski rope he'd already tied to it—nobody would miss the cooler from the town canoe.

Inside it would be warm wet towels, to drape over these standing mannequins' feet. Wet towels that would freeze hard after dark, because no way would these third-graders' parents let their sons and daughters bundle up enough to lie out there holding these mannequins in place.

Be realistic, Mr. Armitage.

It's what Gal says to him sometimes, when he's pushing her to up her vocab game, to go ahead and assume the audience *is* sophisticated enough for that syntax. It's what Cinnamon used to say to him, before she got too old.

Speaking of those two: do they talk, and is that going to be trouble?

More important: Who even cares? It's winter break, the semester's over, and here he is letting his thoughts clot up in his head again. And that only leads to stroking out.

Better to save the stroking for tonight, with all his masks watching him, the candle flickering, and a certain Goblin score playing.

It's not like there's papers to grade or tests to make.

There's just this: hissing over the ice, through the misting frost, an actually sharp scythe held low and angry by his right thigh, the wind only burning his eyes, not his cheeks or chin or forehead.

Faster, faster, he tells himself, slaloming through imaginary mannequins. Through a whole stationary *pool* of victims.

After the next coffee break and pee, and provided there's no former sheriffs to be ferrying around town by the elbow, he'll be coming back with a different mask, he knows. A different game. A different Golden Age slasher to swish through. Earlier today, it was a recurve bow. Now it's this scythe. Next?

He's not sure. Whatever it is, though, it'll be the "good exercise" he's planning to tell anyone who stumbles upon him out here, the scythe or paper-cutter blade or whatever handily dropped twenty feet back, to be collected later, the mask harmless, just a thing he wears against the wind, what?

Exercise for the body *and* for the mind.

And each time he carves his two momentary lines up by the pier, it'll be like he's a ghost cruising through the Independence Day Massacre, or a time-traveler coming back to document, to capture that scent in the air of just-opened bodies, the sounds of rending and tearing, groaning and crying and thrashing, and he'll want to watch the movie playing up on the screen, but that'll only expose his throat, he knows.

You don't make it long in a slasher, looking up, daydreaming.

Behind, sure, that's where the information is, and ahead, of course, that's where the danger's coming from, but never up, for some *Fire in the Sky* action.

To either side, like always, he's seeing hollow plastic bodies, the reek of urine rising from the holes shattered into their sides, but that's good; you *need* them.

They make you go faster, harder. They focus your eyes ahead better.

He doesn't wish he could stop himself, no, and there might not be an easy way out, but there probably is a bloody one.

Or two, or three.

However many it takes.

Behind the mask he grins a sharp grin, a knowing grin, and then—it doesn't always happen, but today's a good day—the beat of his heart trips from its usual systole-diastole counterpunch into the distant, gated reverb Phil Collins makes last for the best fifty-two seconds in all of musicdom, and, like every time this happens, Claude Armitage looks out across the water again for Jason, drowning.

What he sees through the blowing snow, just for a flicker of a moment, is... a *light* in a window, in Terra Nova?

He hockey stops, his whole body tuned for that brief, tantalizing orange speck to glimmer in again.

Something *is* in the air tonight.

Oh lord.

He might need his dad's cowboy hat after all.

He was a good soldier, Jade tells herself.

Before she doused the little wooden guy in WD-40 and lit him up with the lighter that was so big it took both her hands, she'd kissed him on the tiny face.

Never mind that fire never kills the killer.

Never mind the snow coating the fallen-down house, that's going to douse the fire.

Never mind Letha on her knees in some of that same snow, her strong fingers hooked into the pocket of Jade's snow pants, which may or may not have been peeled off a dead Proofrock kid in the darkness of a parking garage. Along with his jacket, the goggles she hadn't even been able to hold onto.

He didn't need them, though.

And you do? Jade's still asking herself. It's not on her to take Dark Mill South down, after all. That's for Cinn, if she's still alive.

Jade can sure as hell slow him down, though. And *not* being a human Popsicle can help with that.

As could this fire she's trying to start.

All Jade can see of it is the tiny candle the soldier is. If she'd thrown him into a pile of rotting elk, then all of Idaho would burn, of course. But throwing an actual flame into dry wood, *with* accelerant… it's guttering out. Because that's how the world is.

It doesn't have to be like that, though.

Jade scrapes the WD-40's head into the heel of her left hand until the little white spigot cracks off. Before all that aerosoled oil can spurt out, she hurls the whole can at that dab of flame, and it's hissing and spitting the whole way through its arc, and right when this is looking like one more Hail Mary thrown into the uncaring void, that flammable oil ghosts across that little red soldier, and—it's a flaming line of pee leading back to the can. It explodes, lighting everything in its blast radius.

And no, Jade insists, that flaming line of pee is *not* the same one that dog pisses in the fourth *Nightmare*, to crack the ground above Freddy open, let him come back into the world. This can hopefully be more like the fuel truck that kills that prettyboy in the next *Nightmare*.

Not that she has the luxury of waiting around for that ball of flame.

"C'mon," she says to Letha, hauling her up, getting under one of her arms enough to take her weight, hitch-walk her against the freezing wind.

"Last time we were over here like this, it was you helping me," Jade says, grunting with effort. "Consider us even, now."

Because Jade's under Letha's right arm, and her left is useless, that means she doesn't have a hand free to hold her jaw shut.

"Don't worry," Jade says to Letha. "It'll take him a few minutes to climb out of that."

"B-b-b—" Letha says, or tries to—you need lips actually *touching* each other to make a B-sound.

Not that Letha's making any words for the foreseeable future. When you scream your death-scream like she was doing, if you go on to live after that, then you don't get a voice for a month or two, Jade knows.

But *goddamn*, this girl.

She wasn't even running from Dark Mill South, was she? She was about to do what no one had ever done: stand up to him, and try to take him down with her. And with nothing but a dollar-store knife she'd pulled from her own shoulder.

And? Jade saw this in Letha Mondragon nearly five years ago, in that restroom down by the boys' gym, when Letha strode up out of her stall, stationed herself at the sink.

Awe isn't even the right word.

"Listen," Jade tells her, readjusting herself under Letha's arm, which is trying to pull Jade's hair out by the roots, "and I think you of all people will appreciate this. I didn't come here to die, right?"

In response, Letha's eyes spill all her tears down her face.

Jade wipes them away as best she can with the cuff of her sleeve, and keeps them moving.

"*I Didn't Come Here to Die*, Alex," she mutters, teeth clenched from the effort of walking for two. "2010."

Two steps later, they spill forward into the snow.

Two *minutes* later, they're still the slowest three-legged race, angling for Letha's old house, her never-was house.

"Alice—Alice Cooper," she says to Letha.

Letha directs her woozy eyes over to Jade. Her eyes are all she has left to speak with.

"He did the song for Jason six," Jade says. "And he was in *Nightmare* six."

Letha looks ahead, maybe waiting for the shape of her house to sift into place through the storm.

"But you knew that," Jade adds. "Kid stuff, right?"

She wipes tears from Letha's right cheek. The rest of her face is already frosted white—frozen tears Jade didn't think to catch.

"Fucking *December*," she says, about all of this. "Couldn't he wait for July, like a respectable slasher?"

Three minutes later they're to the back door of the Mondragon house.

Instead of allowing them the seductive warmth of its kitchen, Jade walks them around the side of the house, to the snowmobile.

She situates Letha on the back, holding her steady the whole while, then eases in in front of her, guiding Letha's arms around.

Only—

"Shit," Jade says.

She turns delicately, to unhook the kill switch from Letha's jacket, only… it's not there?

Letha looks down her front as well, and sags even smaller. A line of blood seeps from the left corner of her open-wide mouth. Jade's impulse is to wipe it away, but Letha would see the red on Jade's hand, for sure.

Leave it, then.

Let it dry.

Jade checks Letha's pockets, checks her own pockets, but she knows it's hopeless: when she jerked Letha from the house coming down all around them, she'd been dragging her through boards and ceiling falling all around them—one of them had to have snagged that spiral cable, making sure it got buried along with Dark Mill South.

Either that or Dark Mill South's hook hand snagged it on his way down.

"*Shit*," Jade says again, harsher.

What? Letha asks with her eyes.

"We gotta go," Jade says back, and stands off of the snowmobile's long seat, being careful not to catch her heel on Letha's chin.

Letha does her best to stand as well.

Jade props her against the house, steps back to the snowmobile, and unholsters the long blue hammer from her belt. It's still matted with hair and blood.

She draws it back like an axe, brings it down onto the snowmobile over and over.

By the time she's done, all the fairing's shattered off, and the handlebars are bent down, and she's torn the seat with the rip claw, for whatever that's worth.

Letha clamps her hand on Jade's shoulder, shakes her head no once, which means *enough*.

She's right.

All she's doing is slowing Dark Mill South down, here. Not stopping him. Not denying him Proofrock.

Like a torn-up seat is going to be insult enough to keep him from getting this snowmobile going again somehow? Like walking across the lake is enough trouble that he'll just retire to some bedroom or basement over here, wait the storm out? Or, no—he'd find some cave or sinkhole, more like. Caves and sinkholes are better slasher lairs than old houses, for sure.

In one of them over in the meadow, probably, are the brittle bones of Cody and Mismatched Gloves and a whole herd of elk, Jade imagines.

Dark Mill South should feel right at home.

Like Brad Pitt says in *Se7en*, it's all about sitting around reading *Guns & Ammo*, masturbating in your own feces—or is it "with"?

"Either way," Jade says, and slides her heavy hammer back through the little tightener strap on these snow pants, which starts a rip that continues down the hip.

Figures.

She yanks the hammer up, slams it into the strap on the other side, but that just tears the already-happening rip more.

When she looks up to Letha for commiseration, or just for someone to witness what she's being asked to tolerate, here, Letha lifts her good hand, points back into the house.

"No, we've got to—" Jade says, looking behind them for the tall, dark, and pissed-off form about to be taking shape through the swirling snow.

Letha keeps pointing.

"Okay, okay," Jade says, and, holding her pants up, she steps into the house again, onto that fallen front door.

Ninety seconds later she steps out in those county coveralls.

As old and trashed out as they are, though, they look more like a mechanic's, like—she can't help but think it, with a thrill—like *Michael's*. She spins the hammer around her hand, catches it perfect, and drives the handle down through the loop now at her thigh.

Fuck yeah.

She holds her hand up to Letha, unzips enough to dig in the pocket of the snow outfit she's still got on—it's padding now, under the coveralls—comes up with her eyeliner.

There's no time for it, but it's armor.

She breathes it smeary in the cup of her hand then opens her eyes wide, lays that blackness on thick, and just having this back makes her feel like Tina from *Friday the 13th Part VII: The New Blood*, full-on ready to wage some bad-ass war. Just, Tina's secret weapon wasn't telekinesis like everybody always says, it was the series coming full-circle: the original hit so hard in the summer of 1980 specifically because of that *Carrie*-ending Savini tagged on as a fun afterthought, and now, six sequels later, Carrie *herself* is rising to put a certain boy back into the lake.

If that's not beauty, then Jade Daniels doesn't know what is.

Her finding some coveralls to wear is just the same. The warmth they provide doesn't have anything to do with heat, but with *story*.

You can do this, she tells herself, and ducks under Letha's arm again, stands with her, and together they stagger down the steep slope, step out onto the lake.

Out on the ice, the temperature's got to be ten degrees colder, the wind a wall of tiny daggers.

Jade pulls Letha closer, tries to take all those icy daggers herself, and for the thousandth time she wonders how the old-time Blackfeet did it. Them and all the other Indians back then. Before Gore-Tex, before car heaters, before bags of beef jerky. On a day like this?

Every day, wouldn't have it just been easier to die?

Except—they didn't.

They pushed through. They insisted. They fought.

Fifty thousand ancestors, going back and back, each of them a final girl.

But, that's just it, isn't it? They were plural, not singular, that's where horror movies have it all wrong, that's where the slasher lies: it's not about a lone girl carving her way to daylight, is it?

It's about two girls making it across the ice *together.*

It's not fifty thousand ancestors in a single-file line, it's clumps of survivors fighting off saber tooth cats and dire wolves and other clumps of people.

It's about putting the children and the old people in the middle and then making a circle around them, pointing out with every spear and shaking your head no, saying not this day.

Not this day.

By the time Jade and Letha are what she's pretty sure should be the halfway point across the lake, that mantra's the only thing keeping her feet moving. That and the thought of Linnea Adrienne Tompkins-Mondragon, waiting for her mommy.

And then, of course, the sun slips behind the mountains.

The temperature takes another nosedive.

Jade's teeth are chattering. What she tells herself is that she's lucky that they can still even do that.

Letha, instead of being the dead weight she should be, is walking nearly as well as Jade is. Only stumbling every twenty or thirty yards, which has to take a force of will Jade can't even really conceive, especially taking her blood loss into account.

Maybe ten feet past what Jade thinks is the middle of this walk across Indian Lake on the coldest night in memory, her feet and face and hands and mind numb, a buzzing works its way through the shell frozen around her. It drains down her back, touches her spine with icy fingers, and she knows without having to think it that, out here where nobody can see, where nobody will call foul, Leatherface can finally step out of the darkness for her, his chainsaw sputtering blue smoke, its sharp teeth already whirring, hungry for Jade's back.

Just because he's not a slasher doesn't mean he doesn't make you pee your pants a little.

Jade turns, ready to be chewed in half, turned into a red smear on the ice, and then falls away instead, taking Letha with her, their arms finding each other, pulling close so their snowmobile can buzz past.

It doesn't have a headlight anymore, because Jade's hammer took it out, and it sounds wrong somehow, and, worse, with someone as large as Dark Mill South on it, it looks like a kid's toy, but it's working.

And there's that guilty kill switch, plugged in, its bright spiral cable looped around the bent bars instead of hooked to Dark Mill South.

Slashers don't follow the safety guidelines, so much.

Jade hugs Letha smaller and keeps them that way until the

blowing snow's starting to drift behind them, bury them in a mound.

Any moment, she knows, that chainsaw Dark Mill South's sitting across can strike back in out of nowhere.

But it doesn't, and then it doesn't some more.

When it's finally down to freezing here or freezing somewhere farther on, Jade stands her and Letha up, shuffles on into the whiteness, and only looks back when she realizes the hammer isn't in her loop anymore. Meaning it's ice-welded to the surface of the lake back wherever it was they were hiding.

Letha makes some vocalization that Jade thinks must end with a question mark.

"Nothing, nothing," Jade tells her, and walks them on, and when she falls back, leaving Letha standing there, it's not on purpose.

It's because one of her old dreams is coming true: slow-motion skating towards them across the ice is the hag from *Curtains*.

How Jade knows she's only even been a pretend final girl is that her first impulse is to scramble away, to leave Letha standing there for that dangerous little scythe.

And that she screams from fear, not rage.

This *Curtains* hag slides to a fancy stop, though, isn't on skates at all, but… skis?

She peels her face up, is a guy maybe forty, forty-five.

He's looking back and forth from Letha to Jade, Jade to Letha.

The corners of his mouth twitch up into a boyish grin.

"What are you—what are you—?" he says, hooking the scythe back around into the top of his backpack then rushing forward to catch Letha when she starts to slump over.

Jade doesn't want to, but she pushes herself back farther, away from this.

This non-hag holds his hand out to her, shaking his head no, no.

"It's—it's… I teach history here," he says, then his face goes slack with wonder, and Jade thinks he might be going to cry from his eyes and his mouth and his nose all at once. "*Jennifer Daniels?*" he whispers reverentially, blinking fast, Letha cradled in his arms.

"Jade," Jade says, not even close to loud enough. Then, "*History?*"

"I have so many questions," he says back, kind of giggling in his throat now, and Jade nods, knows the feeling.

Thirty frozen minutes later, the pier is a shadow through the blowing snow for the three of them.

Jade locks her eyes on it, tries to visually pull herself ahead, ahead. *Step, step,* is all she can say to herself.

Beside her, *right* beside her, Letha's weight evidently not enough to get him winded, this new history teacher—"Armitage"—is somehow still unloading slasher stuff on her, or in her general area. It's like, for his whole life he's been a barrel filling with facts and theories and trivia, and all it took was seeing Jade out here that finally cracked him open. Meaning, it's all shooting out, and Jade's caught in that spray.

At first he was trying to convince her that nudity in slashers wasn't exploitational, it was just feeding the audience's need for the real, since they can tell at some level that all these kills are fake, but the nudity, there's no faking that—"except for that exploding breast in *Return to Horror High*, right?"

Jade just grunted, wasn't playing along.

It didn't stop him in the least.

He flipped channels, went off for long minutes about how the final girl in a slasher was a perfect reversal or inversion of the damsel in distress, see? Wasn't she, isn't she? Jade shrugged, kept walking, lips pursed, eyes grim. Next he was wondering what if Adrienne King hadn't had a stalker between the first and second *Fridays*—could she, along with Jamie Lee Curtis's Laurie Strode, have made it to where the default setting for a final girl was "recurring" instead of one-and-done? And how would that have changed *everything*, right? If Nancy's in the second *Nightmare*?

Jade doesn't say "Ripley" under her breath, because she wants this to be over, please.

Except now he's turned sideways to her, is holding Letha out as proof of what he's calling the "*Breakfast Club*–ification" of the slasher—how the Golden Age was actually super progressive, in that all creeds and races and nationalities and classes and genders and sexualities made up the slasher crew, they were all brought together by… not by survival so much as by running away from a common threat.

To punctuate it, really send his point home, he steps forward and raises his fist into the sky for a silhouette moment, a celebration, a victory, diversity and unification over fragmentation and othering—*Don't you, forget about me*—but all Jade can think in her current flatlined state is, Was *she* ever this annoying? How did anybody even tolerate being around her?

Good grief, Charlie Brown.

Give it a rest already.

"Hey," she says then, pointing ahead with her lips.

There's something by the pier. A shape, a form, a shadow.

Armitage stops, considers this as well.

Jade's first impulse is "roadkill." By rough shape, it looks like a deer that's been slapped by a cowcatcher up on the highway, then bloated and stiffened in the sun, and run over about fifty more times.

Except this isn't the highway, and that's not a deer.

It's Lonnie. From the gas station. His eyes are frozen open. Well, *eye*—the one he has left.

Jade falls to her knees, steeples her hands over her mouth.

He isn't just dead, either. He's been rearranged. His limbs are all bent and wrong, pieces of him torn but not all the way through, meaning his joints go farther than they should. And other parts as well. Large chunks of his meat have been ripped half off, left flapping, the blood only congealed because of the cold.

"*It Follows*," Armitage says, with unadulterated wonder, and Jade looks to him, wants to ask him, "It follows *what*?" but then her face flushes when she gets it: the indie slasher one-upping *Final Destination*, from the year before the Lake Witch Slayings. Specifically, five minutes into the opening, where there's a dead girl twisted and crumpled just like Lonnie is here—a blood sacrifice, to get things going.

Up from the wreckage that's Lonnie, jammed onto the bank under Melanie's memorial bench, is the snowmobile, quiet now.

Already disappearing in the snow, leading up into town, are the same dragging footprints Jade followed through Terra Nova.

She had a long blue hammer then, though.

Now—

She looks down to her hands, so small, she looks over to Letha, barely conscious, and then she looks to this Armitage history teacher, his lips trying to form his next question but failing to find the words.

Jade understands.

TRIGGER POINT

As we all know now, Dark Mill South's escape wasn't as daring and Houdini as America thought, and wanted. Not that a whole mountainside of snow crashing downslope at a hundred miles per hour is in any sense boring. But there was nothing intentional or strategic about it. Researchers can identify the conditions that precipitate an avalanche, authorities can issue warnings, but, until an avalanche actually starts, until that seismograph jumps or the whistle blows or all the phones on the mountain screech their AVW screech, an avalanche is always potential, never actual.

It got actual on December 12th, 2019, eight miles south of Proofrock on Highway 20.

And, though true believers would have the mountain shaking its snow off specifically to facilitate Dark Mill South's escape—the timing and the result are their main evidence—the facts are that human factors play the larger part.

I'm not talking about the federal agents, either, Mr. Armitage.

Yes, they've been excoriated in all the armchair

reconstructions, both on the national news and over coffee, and, yes, with hindsight, they probably shouldn't have attempted 20 in a whiteout. But, given the alternatives, I imagine many a federal agent would make the same decision.

And neither does it make sense that Dark Mill South, being Native American, could somehow "whistle" the snow down to take out his transport. Yes, serial killers in America often achieve mythic status, are subject to and benefit from the same folklore dynamic that props up Paul Bunyan and Daniel Boone, George Washington and Thomas Jefferson, but that's all after the fact.

In the moment? With nature's eraser barreling downhill, shaving trees off at ground level and tossing boulders like so much flotsam? I have to imagine that Dark Mill South flinched just the same as the agents transporting him. Or, if not flinched, then at least grimaced, knowing that this is how it ends.

The avalanche was demonstrating once again that nature is an Etch A Sketch, and sometimes it must get shaken in order to start things over. It's a natural, albeit violent, process, Mr. Armitage. And before it, highways crumble, are swept away. Prisoner convoys are blotted out as if they never were. Fourteen federal agents are lost.

But serial killers, of course, serial killers are forever, aren't they?

There couldn't have been time for last missives through the radios or cellphones. No last prayers. One moment they're trudging along, and the next, a swirling white darkness is solidifying to their right, a wall of destruction rushing at them, already enveloping them.

The proof of this is that that supposed agent stationed directly behind Dark Mill South evidently didn't have time to pull their trigger. Most likely, their SUV was both airborne and buried by the time their lizard brain alerted them of danger.

Never mind their sworn duty, the one that would have saved Proofrock another cycle of violence.

But, of course, the question of what started this ill-timed avalanche persists even today, all these months later, and probably isn't getting definitively answered anytime soon, as none of the agents or snowplow drivers present at the time are alive to give testimony.

As with Dark Mill South's origins, though, theories abound.

The one I subscribe to, for purposes of this argument paper, is that the avalanche that swept the convoy down the scree slope on the east side of the highway and finally deposited it in a holding basin of sorts, before the long drop down to Indian Creek at the bottom of the drainage, was triggered either by vibration or by sound—and of course those are really one and the same.

By all accounts, when the thundering snow finally settled, no vehicle was visible, nor glowing headlights, nor chimneys shaped around engine exhaust. But that powdery surface was, supposedly, broken open in wone and only one place, as if a vehicle door had been kicked open to serve as a hatch.

This is the birth—the rebirth—of America's serial killer of the moment: Dark Mill South.

According to the first responders to the scene, his footsteps weren't in the least bit hesitant, nor drunken-seeming, from being tossed about in the avalanche.

Where they lead, with no hesitation, is back up to the highway.

This is where Dark Mill South takes his first victim in four years, Mr. Armitage—and, though the vehicle associated with this is fitted with a dashboard camera as state policy requires, neither Dark Mill South nor this first victim is in that camera's field of view, sorry. I know how perfect this would have been for your video collection.

And no, out of respect I won't name this snowplow driver. If that means a point-reduction for this assignment, then, like Sir Gawain, in the tradition of Sydney Carton, I lower my head to take that necessary blow.

But of course the lightest search online returns invectives using this driver's name as well as deifications using his name—he's both villain and hero, here: hero to those who would worship Dark Mill South, villain to those who suffered as a result of his escape.

I'm of the second camp, obviously.

Which doesn't mean I think this snowplow driver intentionally sabotaged the convoy that night. His intentions were, I believe, as he saw them, pure. As were the intentions of his two fellow snowplow drivers who volunteered to escort the convoy over the pass in their tandem-axle dumptrucks with snowplows mounted on front.

But those other two drivers were swept away with the convoy, while this driver, the point in their phalanx, saw the avalanche sweep past in his rearview mirror.

Of extreme interest here as pertains to my position on the trigger point for this avalanche is that neither his snowplow, nor the snowplows of his fellow drivers, now entombed in ice down the mountain, were rated for use on Highway 20.

They were too heavy, Mr. Armitage.

If a gunshot or a branch bursting open from cold can start a mountain-side sliding, or if a single pinecone snowballing down from the treeline can become that wall of obliteration, then… what about 250 combined tons of rolling, grumbling steel, scraping its giant blades against the rough surface of the blacktop at a high—and heedless—rate of speed?

Yes, this is my argument paper, Mr. Armitage, but I hardly feel argumentation is needed for this, it's so obvious.

Perhaps it's then best to close not with a conclusion reiterating my premises, but with a dramatic re-creation: that snowplow driver, the lone survivor of this disaster, standing by his truck in amazement, possibly laughing and crying both, just to be, against all odds, still alive. He's in awe of this majestic destruction, at the vast scale of it all, and the nearness of it. The matter of feet that probably saved him.

As for why he's standing there, I think it's because he's watching a lone figure climb the scree slope, sometimes having to go to all fours to continue upward.

Perhaps his plan is to hug this survivor, to dance on the road with him or her.

Instead—and this is fact, not conjecture—he would end up dead and broken on the road, his truck stolen, his right hand pierced through, as if from a large hook. Meaning he must have extended his hand to help this lone survivor make that last scramble over the edge.

At which point he was forcibly pulled into the maw of this grand catastrophe his enthusiasm for justice had carelessly engineered.

So it goes on the road to Proofrock, Idaho, Mr. Armitage.

Better known, perhaps, as Dark Mill South's playground.

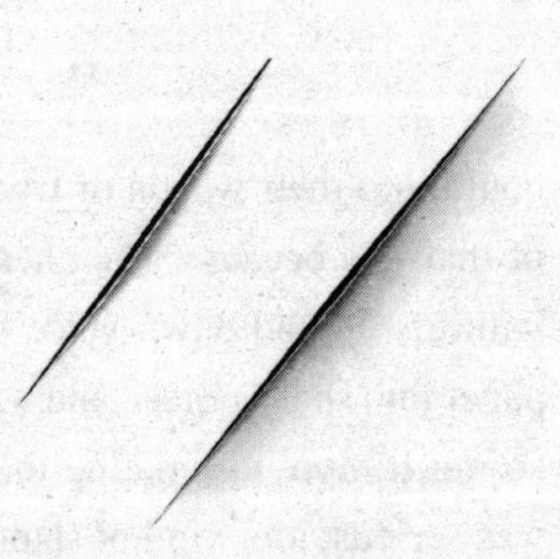

HAPPY DEATH DAY

For a long time, she was in the lake.

Before, she'd only ever been able to see under the water about as far as her hand in front of her face, but then... then that didn't matter.

It was cold, but "cold" was just a word she'd once heard, already slipping away.

When the sun glimmered down through the surface, she would drift among those shards of light, not closing her eyes but her mind, until she could pretend to be feeling that brightness up there.

What she remembered was summer, inexactly: a feeling of being released from time, of days melting into days, until a whole series of them behind her could just be "then," "before," with more to come, and a grinning impulse to rush into them with her arms and her eyes and her heart wide open.

When she had arms, and eyes, a heart.

She wasn't lonely, though.

There were friends all through Indian Lake, from the dam and all the way back to the other side.

For the first few years, she lived with Silas.

His was a story she had held onto. He was the boy from Henderson-Golding, whose family was packing everything they could into their wagon or truck or trailer, she's forever uncertain of that. It's because when her father was telling this story to her with his up and down voice he had also been folding a piece of paper into sharp points, and what he was doing with his hands was so much more fascinating than wagons and trucks. But his tone was serious, too, kind of slanted down at the same angle his face took when he was looking over the tops of his glasses, meaning this was a warning of some kind. So she nodded, soaking it in.

This boy was playing in the waters of the creek that was pooling into a lake, right up to their doorstep. His family had waited until too late to leave, so they were all rushing around and blaming each other, everybody grabbing this and that, and making pleading cases for it. The boy hid from it all with his boat shaped from catalog pages, floating it not exactly *in* the water, since it would swamp, but on the foamy scum that was frothing near shore. He would splash out after it and then start over, until, the next time he looked up, his house was empty. The truck or wagon was gone. His family had left without him. Not on purpose, but because the wooden stool he was supposed to be sitting on, that he'd been told not to leave for any reason, had been walled in by furniture and supplies, making a chamber he would be safe in.

His family was even taking the doors from their house, to walk through again a few hundred feet up the mountain, in whatever this new town was going to get named.

The boy looked around at all the nothing, and then his boat was bobbing away, and fingers of water were soaking into its steep sides. He splashed out after it, to save it—it was his best one so far—and by the time his family came back to collect him, sure he was going to be at the edge of the lapping water, he wasn't.

He was just gone.

"He'd followed his little paper boat," her father told her, handing her the one he'd folded, and it was a lesson, a serious lesson she had to listen to, but it also came with a new toy.

And the boy wasn't just a story, it turned out.

She found him bobbing a few feet off the lake floor, suspended in silt, that white boat still in his hand.

She named him "Silas" because that was an old-fashioned name, and she held his hand and together they would look up each year when the people from the nursing home, who remember the old stories, would get wheeled to shore to push their paper boats out onto the water, in memory.

Without Silas to hold her hand those first few years, she might have forgotten everything, dissipated into the murk, become one with the lake. But when you've got a friend, you can see yourself in their face, and stay separate.

What Silas told her was that he'd gone out into the deeper water because he wanted to see town one last time.

She promised to see it for him, and tell him all about it, but when she moved that way, it was… different. Over the years she would figure this out more, but this was the first time: when she stayed in one place for too long, the silt and debris suspended in the water would slow around her, congeal into gossamer tendrils like the finest, most delicate hair, but mushy like moss, like the lake was trying to gift her a body, a form, a shape, but all it had was what was within reach of where she was right then, however long that "then" lasted.

She could still, with effort, extract herself from those cocoon shapes, though, those moss dummies. Extract herself and then watch these body memories loosen, relax, eventually drifting up to the surface to decay, becoming blots of darkness that soaked the sunlight up.

Silas watched with her, in wonder, and she assured him that would never happen to him, that she would keep him safe.

It was a lie, but she meant it, too, and that had to matter, didn't it?

She drifted downslope, along the lake bed that used to be a hill, because that's where Silas said his town used to be.

It was easy to find, the most obvious gathering of shapes down there.

She drifted down the main street, hiding on the sidewalk to let that giant fish float past, making its rounds. She didn't know its name, but she could tell it was old, it was ancient, that it fed on the small crumbles that sifted down from above, and that those crumbles added up.

There was the mercantile. The saloon with its roof fallen in, its whole self leaning into the store, both their wall boards soft enough that they were bending in. There was a firetruck parked by another building, a rock building that didn't care about the constant water. The rock building was rock-colored like it should have been, but the firetruck wasn't red anymore. Its two headlights watched her like eyes, and when she looked back to it after passing it, she wasn't sure why, not until that giant fish floated over the truck, up from its alley. Its eyes were as wide as the truck's headlights, its body maybe longer, but crusted and mottled. She didn't know fish like her dad did, but she knew if she were to describe this one to him, from mouth to tail, he would smile, nod, and tell her what it had to be, and that those kind weren't even supposed to be in this part of the world, that this one must have been sleeping in the ground for ages when the water of the creek became a lake over it, and seeped tendrils of wet down through the dirt.

To her, for now, it was the god of these low waters, feeding on the particles of rot that made their way down from the sunlight.

It swished its great tail once, languorously, massively, and then rode that down this main street.

She kept moving the other way.

At the end of the street was the church, with its doors closed.

She could still hear the raised voices coming from it in what felt like a dirge, like a plea, like a last chorus that was the only thing keeping their stone walls from collapsing in on them.

Ezekiel can't still be alive, Silas told her, after her report.

She shrugged, didn't know about any Ezekiel. Just that there was something about the song that made her want to listen, and keep listening. She might have listened for a year or two, even, the silt and debris slowing in her thoughts, taking on a form she had to pull herself from, and then push away, so it could go be a mat of rotting yuck on the surface.

Higher up the slope of the lake bed was a jumble of rusting, silt-coated appliances and Christmas trees, and even one boat. She couldn't stop watching this boat. From under the water, she only ever saw the smooth fast bottoms of them. But here was a whole one.

She made up story after story for its journey down here to her.

Deeper but not all the way at the bottom were the other people, all of their eyes and mouths open, their arms raised as if they were still falling, not suspended forever.

But she avoided them. Not because of their stares, but because one of them remembered her. He was older now, his face all messed up, but he was still the same boy she remembered, and she could tell in his eyes that he knew her, that he would say her name if she drew too close, and that he might laugh in his way after he said it, and she didn't know what she would do then.

Higher up, well above them, were the animals.

She petted their shoulders and necks, and rubbed the tight skin between their eyes, telling them she was sorry this had happened to them. It wasn't fair. They couldn't breathe water. They needed the sunlight, and their families. There were dogs, mostly. She didn't understand how or why, but here they were. There were eleven deer, two moose, and three elk, one of them with antlers that looked the same underwater as they had above: wooden roots branching up and up in worship of the moon, to hug that pale light.

They were wondrous.

Highest up the slope were the trees she knew weren't trees, but posts that *had* been trees—no, "pillars." "Posts"? Two lines of them walked up to shore, and a dark and fetching rectangle of shadow hung between them, that she would sometimes come up to and then go fast away from, as fast as she could, almost to the dam but not quite all the way—she knew to avoid those waters. They were all the way off limits to her. But they also pulled at her the most of anything, gave her that "summer" feeling. She knew it was a memory, a trap, but it was hard to stay away from.

Silas couldn't explain it, the elk with the branching antlers couldn't explain it, the fish that was a god knew but wouldn't say, and there were no actual words in the song coming from the church, just a murmur, a feeling, a prayer.

Still, the thrill of flashing from high up the slope by the walking pillars to those dangerous waters by the dam was a game she played over and over, sometimes even flashing closer than she should to the people hanging in the water under the animals, their mouths open as if calling out to someone.

It was during one of those runs that the Thing occurred. It was like when the silt and debris tried to congeal around her, but it was faster, worse, better.

She was hiding in the shadows between the walking pillars, about to slip away into the dark, wriggle and race for the dangerous waters of the dam, when a circular blade *whirred* ahead of her, ensconcing itself in a halo of bubbles.

Boats were no threat, she'd figured that out long ago, but she liked those spinning white halos, would watch them every time they happened.

Only, this time, that halo, for the first time ever, changed color, from frantic white to deep red.

And the red, when it bloomed her way, was *warm*, and slowed her thoughts.

It was a sensation she hadn't felt in… in ever.

Was that what summer actually felt like?

There was solid matter in the redness, too, not ice but softer, meatier, and when it touched her, there was a thrill so intense it made her surge up, away from this intense pleasure, this impossibly hot *Thing*, and for the first time in she didn't know how many years, she was above the water, out of the lake.

She opened her heart, grabbed onto the first thing she could, that rectangular black shadow with the, as it turned out, rough splintery underside, and then she hung on, clung on, hunching into herself tighter and tighter, only sad she hadn't gotten to tell Silas goodbye.

But he would understand.

If you can leave, you leave.

This is impossible, and stupid, so they pretty much have to do it.

Forget the class of '18, who raised enough money to install heating elements on the roof of the nursing home, to keep sheets of ice from crashing down onto old people in wheelchairs who just want some fresh air, never specifically *asked* to be cut in half from above. That community service was just about selling brownies and popcorn, which doesn't take any more effort than sitting at a table and taking donations. And everybody knows that Letha Mondragon had slipped a certain check into the lockbox anyway. Or, had it slipped, since she was busy squeezing a baby out.

Yeah, it's good that no oldster's going to get bisected by a plummeting razorblade of ice, sure, who doesn't want senior citizens in one piece instead of two, but the class of '18 didn't have to *sweat* to raise that money.

The class of 2021 is different, is going to leave a different mark.

Case in point: when whoever runs the town snowplow didn't get out and do their job, that meant Main Street was going to be impassable for the duration of this storm, impacting all the businesses that depended on traffic, and this, to the class of 2021, was basically unacceptable.

Since cell service was gone, Penny Wayne—and then Penny Wayne *and* Bobo Richardson—went door to door collecting volunteers.

Counting Penny and Bobo, eight seniors were willing, nearly that many weren't home, their panicked parents asking Penny if *she* knew where they might be, and the rest were recent arrivals to Henderson High, so Penny and Bobo hadn't been sure where they lived.

As for the eight who were willing to suit up, lean out into the wind for the good of Proofrock, it was less about community service and, really, more about there being no internet. That meant no games, no shows to stream, no social media. They could have watched whatever DVDs their dads had left over from before marriage, except the power was spotty as well, and siphoning television juice out of the generator would take some convincing. So, it was stay home and deal with their parents' idle interrogations about future plans and current dating situations, or trundle out into the bitter cold to shovel snow while even more snow was still coming down.

The great outdoors won.

The idea was to rack up nearly half of their mandatory community service hours in a single day, the scam being that braving the elements meant each hour spent scooping counted as three, at least when they factored in their actual physical endangerment: hypothermia, frostbite, overexertion, back strain, blisters under the gloves, the mental strain of no cell or Wi-Fi, and whatever jeopardy was involved with getting gored by the "big deer" Bobo's mom said she'd seen out the window.

The *unspoken* portion of this community service effort, of course, was the self-serving aspect. Yes, clearing the sidewalks for foot traffic would allow anyone in dire need of their medications to shuffle to the drugstore, and anyone with desperate cash transactions to complete could foreseeably get those done at the bank, if it elected to open its doors, and… the quilt store? Couldn't there be a run on quilts on a day like today? And who doesn't need coffee and cupcakes at Dot's?

But their collective shoveling effort didn't start at the front door of the drugstore, or any of the other retail storefronts. It started at their own: Proofrock Video.

All funds raised over the course of the school year, minus operating expenses, were to be funneled into the prom budget.

Never mind that if the power was too thready to watch DVDs, then probably no one would be renting them. Their senior business project was going to be open all the same, perhaps earning the undying loyalty of that one person who decided to come in, walk the candlelit aisles.

The candlesticks were all four feet high, supplied by Jace Rodriguez's mom, and there were tasteful random-shaped candles flickering throughout the store at strategic locations, and they'd saved the nine wicks of the one stray menorah for the register, where transactions were to be of the IOU variety, since the cash drawer wouldn't open without electricity.

All of which Penny had documented on her phone, for the video essay that was to be their final project, for which they would receive a group grade not dependent on net gains or customer ratings but on the business model itself, and the conclusions they could draw for this retail endeavor.

So, starting out, Penny had taken pains to be sure to record each volunteer up close and personal, partially as a way to call out those *not* in attendance, but also to be sure to capture the bitter cold apparent on each face—for which she had to ask these volunteers to peel their ski masks and goggles. After a snot check, she would record each volunteer saying how "It takes a village!" or "Proofrock pride!" or "Henderson Hawks forever!" and then move on to the next.

To a person, each of the shovelers she directed her phone's camera at was either plugged into earbuds or wearing over-the-head headphones under their windproof hoods. And they might as well: with the shovels scraping and the wind blowing, talking to each other, even at high volume, was pretty much impossible. Even the snot check had to be done by sign language and mime.

When they started out, the snow against the building was drifting nearly up to their hips. Two hours later, it's down to their knees for three storefronts in each direction, and, for brief flashes between gusts, there's even concrete at their feet sometimes.

There's always six people on shovel duty, one thawing out at the register, and one walking the line, being sure no one's pushing too hard, that no one needs a rest inside, that no one's lost.

It's an adventure. They're small-business owners. Only the strong survive, and they're open for business, at least—ready to thrive, there for their customers, making the sacrifices needed to provide continuity of operation, or services, or… whatever a video rental outfit has to offer in the age of streaming.

"*Nostalgia*," was what Cinnamon said it could offer, when the class was pitching ideas for what business they could run for the senior year.

Cinnamon who, of course, wasn't at her house when Penny knocked. Just Gal and her mother sipping hot chocolate at the door, wearing scarves and sweatshirts and mittens, their generator humming from the other side of the fence, a cat threading itself back and forth between their shins as if showing off how toasty warm it was inside the house.

And neither Mrs. Pangborne nor Gal had been able to say where Cinnamon was, sorry. Same with Abby Grandlin's dad, Mark Costins's little brother, Wynona Fleming's mom, Gwen Stapleton's sister, and Mrs. Cates—though at least Mrs. Cates had been crying, which suggested that Philip wasn't flush to the wall just out of sight, listening.

So, the eight die-hards shovel and scoop and bulldoze, their com-munity service hours multiplying over their heads like hit points they're earning.

There's zero point zero chance of them actually clearing the whole sidewalk, they can all tell this now, but there will at least be footage of them working to keep the video store open for business, and they all saw Dorothy trundling into her coffee shop, meaning surely some pity mugs of something hot and a tray of something warm are on the way.

Penny's back to shoveling, about to graduate to line-check duty, which is the last step before her fourth time at the register, when a shape coalesces through the snow. It's standing by the bank, about even with the ATM, and her first instinct, conditioned into her by all the cop dramas her mom watches, is that the camera over that little money dispenser is going to capture whoever this is, for later.

And that's a relief.

Never mind the snow gusting through, obliterating all sight lines.

Never mind that the lens on the camera is almost definitely frozen over—the blurriest, crustiest peephole.

Never mind that she's not even sure if ATMs still work when the power's mostly out.

"H-hello?" Penny says, and scoops a load of snow into the street behind her.

The shape is just standing there.

Penny looks up the line for if anyone else is seeing this, but the closest shoveler is fifteen feet ahead. Penny cocks her goggles up on her head to see better, but now this figure is gone again. If it was ever even there.

It's probably Toby, she thinks. He plays center, has that kind of height, and, dressed up for the elements, might look that bulky.

But what's he doing just standing out there like a scarecrow?

"Come in, help!" Penny calls, waving her arm as wide as she can because her voice can't be making it through the wind.

The snow swirls again, as if delivering this shape specifically into her view.

It's just watching her. Watching all of them.

"Toby?" she says, weaker, not near loud enough.

Or… Jensen? But how would he have heard? Probably he hound-dogged it to Wynona's or Gwen's, heard about this impromptu street party from whoever answered the door, and—he's Jensen. He goes where the girls are.

But he's not that tall.

It's not Philip either. Philip Cates would never walk anywhere in the snow, not when he can show his new snowmobile off.

Penny bares her teeth, thinking about him. If he slides up over the curb, sprays snow onto the square or two of concrete she's cleared, then… one ass-kicking, coming up.

But now the shape's gone again, swirled away.

Right before it faded, though, Penny got the sense of dark hair rising around its head, off its shoulders.

She also got a sense that she was being x-rayed.

"Fuck it," she says, and pulls her goggles back on. She's not freezing her lashes for Toby and his stupid dramatics—always wanting to make a grand entrance, always expecting the home crowd to stand when he jogs out onto whatever he's using for a court today.

Still, she does like to watch him jog in those shorts…

Penny turns her back purposefully on him, so she can startle around when he's closer, maybe fall into his arms, his big hands having to catch her. There's been worse things happen in the history of the world, hasn't there?

Penny chuckles to herself, runs her yellow shovel into the white snow again, thinks there has to be an easier way, and then—yep—a hand is to her upper left arm, her shoulder, sort of.

She spins around, yelping as any half-decent meet-cute requires, and—

"*Cinnamon?*" she says, their faces maybe two inches apart.

"We've got to get inside!" Cinnamon says, all worked up about… what? The cold? This is Idaho, girl. C'mon.

Penny steps back grinning, looks down the line, and… it's just her and Cinnamon, now.

"I already got them in!" Cinnamon says, shaking Penny to make her point.

"Were you—" Penny says, looking down Main, where she was sure Toby was creeping up on her all in good fun.

It couldn't have been her, though.

She looks the other way, and, parked at an angle just shy of Proofrock Video is… the truck Cinnamon came in? Except, that's Deputy Tompkins's truck, isn't it? Its parking lights are on, and its wipers are fighting the snow as best they can.

"What—wh—" Penny starts, but now Cinnamon's practically dragging her.

"Leave it!" Cinnamon says about the shovel Penny's holding to, so Penny does.

She's a ragdoll bouncing along behind Cinnamon, now.

"Where were you?" Penny manages to ask. "We came by your—"

"Busy surviving," Cinnamon says, and opens the video store's front door, shoves Penny in ahead of her.

"What do you mean?" Penny asks.

The other seven small-business owners are thawing out at the end of the first aisle, the new releases one that's supposed to be like an impulse rack, with the Blu-rays up at eye-level, the individually wrapped candy down at kid-level.

"What's happening?" Penny says, appointing herself voice of the group.

"There's a killer out there," Cinnamon says, standing in the open door, her perfect blond hair cascading down out of her hood like a ski resort commercial.

"Killer?" Penny says, checking the glass front window as if it's possible to see through it anymore.

"I saw—Toby, and Gwen," Cinnamon says. "And..." She's starting to cry, has to reel that in, it looks like. "And Mark and Kristen."

"They're *dead*?" Jace says, his voice going shriekier than he'd like, probably.

Cinnamon nods fast, seems to prefer nodding to having to give these facts voice anymore.

"Just stay inside," she says to all of them. "Promise me, all of you?"

One by one, everyone shrugs sure, some of them nodding, all of them squinting because this doesn't really make sense.

"Is it another massacre?" Bobo asks weakly.

Cinnamon doesn't want to answer, but her eyes say *yes*.

"What about you?" Penny says.

Cinnamon sneaks a look to all the open space behind her, then cases all the frozen faces waiting for her to explain all this.

"I can't stay here," she finally says. "He's—it's me he wants, I'm putting you in danger even… even being here."

"Why does he want you?" TJ asks. It's the obvious question.

"Because I got away from him?" Cinnamon says, holding her gloved hands up, hopeless fashion. "I guess I'm unfinished business?"

"Where are you going to go?" Penny asks, stepping forward to hold Cinnamon's gloved fingers in her hands.

"I don't—I don't… just stay *here*," she says, and is already backing out, the door blowing shut hard behind her, the cowbell above it clattering.

Penny steps forward, locks the deadbolt.

Just when you thought it was safe to go back in the water, Claude Armitage is telling himself with a secret grin. Or, *In space, no one can hear you scream.*

The night He came home?

According to Jade, this time the killer isn't a little dead girl, but a big alive man.

Be afraid, then. *Be very afraid.*

No, no: *Sometimes dead is better*, yeah. And of course, got to mix some *Chain Saw* action in: *Who will survive, and what will be left of them?*

It's finally really actually happening, and he's right here at ground zero!

It's *not* only a movie, it's *not* only a movie.

But he can't let Jade see him trying not to grin.

Letha Mondragon probably could cue in to the joy he's trying to suppress, since he's been carrying her since they stepped up onto shore, but she's in and out, and she keeps spasming or convulsing or something in his arms. It's the weirdest feeling. *Man* is *the warmest place*, he tells himself, imagining the Thing in her, about to take hold of her chest from the inside, spread her ribcage open, xenomorph up and periscope around for a first meal.

This is so much more than he ever dared hope.

Lonnie, back on the ice?

How is it even possible to twist someone up that much? Lonnie'd gone from tongue-tied to… to being a human Gordian knot. Claude's first instinct had been to snap a picture for his collection, and then a backup photo as well from a different angle, and maybe even a selfie with Lonnie, one *with* the Bicycle Girl mask on, holding the little scythe up as if this is his handiwork, then one without, but… decorum, decency. He's supposed to be mournful, apprehensive, his lips quivering with regret for the lives lost, his eyes blinking too fast from unadulterated terror.

Oh, but the questions he has for Jade.

All the taglines swirling through his head, threatening with each step to leak out his mouth, through his grin? She would know each one, and their different-market alternates as well. And she could finally reveal, once and for all, if it was her or Letha Mondragon who faced down Stacey Graves at the Independence Day Massacre.

And, if it was Jade, then… why did Stacey Graves's little body never float back up with the rest of them? Over the summer, after a scuba certification class down in Boise, Claude had discreetly slipped into an insulated wet suit and then ducked under the waters around the pier, sifting through the lake bed for clues, letting the muck and silt run through the beam of his scuba flashlight, but… there were phones, there were beer bottles, there were tangles of fishing poles and the rotting remains of generations of three-ring binders, there was the rusted wheel of some long-gone truck he decided was Cross Bull Joe's, but there was no great black hook. Worse, there were no bones of any kind. Not Jade's missing dad, not a little girl's who should have been dead a century ago. Not even any of the jaws that had been ripped off that night, which he was sure *had* to be there.

Still, now that rusted wheel has a place of pride in his study, along with the beer bottles. He's even drank from two of them, without washing them out first.

And, from a documentary he stumbled upon, he now knows about magnet fishing. It's usually done off bridges, but there's no reason he can't do it at night in a quiet boat alongside the pier, ranging out in gentle, GPS-directed arcs. A magnet won't get him any bones, but it's going to find him something, he knows. He's already ordered the kit. It's just a big heavy magnet with a neodymium rope, and a climbing-grade carabiner to connect them, but simple's good, isn't it?

All the best slashers are simple.

This one, for example: Rob Zombie–ish killer escapes, turns up in town, carves through as many kids as he can until some plucky girl finally puts him down. All in twenty-four, thirty-six hours, under cover of a storm, with the sheriff out of town, cellphones down, power unreliable.

Claude couldn't have designed it any better himself.

And he's getting to walk through it with Jade freaking *Daniels*.

And, going by her terms, Lonnie's probably even the prelude to the third-reel bodydump, isn't he? Meaning either the big party's already going on, or they're headed there now.

Claude's plan is to be Gale Weathers, sneaking Kenny's hidden camera in among the action. Except that camera's going to be in the chest pocket of his jacket, its lens just peeking out. All he has to do is find a couple of moments alone, to delete everything else on his phone, so as to make room for all the footage he's about to capture.

Except, where Jade's taking them… the post office, the library? No: the sheriff's office. Hunh. That's not where the party's going down. No kids equals no party, and Jade knows her slasher math better than that.

When Claude slows, Jade looks back, her eyes flat and humorless, and she must think Letha's slowing this slasher fan down. Her solution: take the skis he's dragging behind him on the parachute cord he had in his pack.

She lumberjacks them over her shoulder and trudges ahead, breaking the snow with her soaked, frozen boots. Claude wants to pull ahead, break that path for her with his cross-country boots—they're not the best for walking, but they're not bad—except Letha *is* weighing him down just a little.

He looks down to her shattered face, his eyes not even starting to linger on the pant-pant rise-and-fall of her chest. He doesn't not sneak a peek because she's Black, of course—he's equal opportunity—it's that she's older than any girl in a slasher should be.

Junior year, beginning of senior year, that's the sweet spot, isn't it?

Cinnamon, Jade said, when he asked who this was all about this time.

Technically she's aged out, but she's not a bad choice, all in all. It does complicate things for him, but… current killers surely outweigh old enmities, don't they?

As for what Cinnamon did to draw this kind of attention from someone like Dark Mill South… there's no way an interstate serial killer—now graduated to slasher—could have seen Cinnamon in Claude's study, randomly pulling a certain cowboy hat down over her eyes like Jessica Alba from *Sin City* and then firing imaginary sixguns into his wall of masks, but maybe that disrespect smeared an aura of some sort on her, right? Her thoughtless action, in the absence of a real prank or crime, maybe that made her the kind of radioactive that slashers key on?

Granted, final girls are usually wearing more than a bra and a cowboy hat when they kickstart a cycle of justice that ends in a sea of blood, but… it's the millennium, right? And, when will it *stop* being the millennium? Will that be the evergreen motivation for eighty-one more years?

Claude hopes so.

And then—then second star to the right, straight on 'til morning, on 'til 2455, the year of *Jason X*.

For sure.

And Claude's footage of *this* slasher cycle will be part of that, now. And all because he was out on the ice playing *Curtains*. All because he took a flyer, pretended to care about Idaho history for a school board.

He knows the sheriff thinks he's writing a book on the Independence Day Massacre, but it's nothing so base as that. All the accounts he's collecting are for his *private* collection, which is probably going to be curated into a museum some fine day, one mocked up like a video rental store for the first room, but then you walk through a thick, dark curtain and you're in the land of memorabilia and props, lobby cards and film cells under glass, meaning now you're in a proper movie palace. The logical next room, then, is the Real Thing that informs those movies: stills from Claude Armitage's soon-to-be-recorded video of this bitter cold dusk in Proofrock, the *new* center of slasherdom, as Haddonfield had once been, as Crystal Lake used to be, as Springwood forever is.

No, Sheriff Allen, this is bigger than a *book*, thank you. Have you ever seen the TV spot for *Popcorn*, sir? "Before the horror of *Halloween*. Before the fear of *Friday the 13th*. Before the evil of *A Nightmare on Elm Street*."

Under all of them is your high little mountain town.

For proof, there's actual blood on Claude's jacket now.

And more blood to come.

And, because he's just an observer, a slasher raconteur, a devotee, a fly on the wall with the biggest most hungry eyes, he's functionally immune to beheadings, eviscerations, to… to whatever happened to Lonnie back there.

It's glorious.

"You good?" Jade asks, because he's flagging again.

"Good," Claude says, and of course doesn't tell her that it's not fatigue slowing him down. He's just lost in his head again. Walking through that someday museum. Trying to savor every footstep of this impossible journey he's lucking his way into.

All he's missing, really, is some footage of Dark Mill South from before today. After the trial but before this almost-here showdown. Because, as Carpenter taught in 1978, you've got to have the looming presence before the carving begins, don't you? Work the threat and dread into the muscle *before* that muscle contracts in terror.

But something'll turn up. It always does. Especially when you're this charmed.

"Almost there," Jade calls out, fumbling the skis away and finally just jabbing them into the snow in a tall X-marks-the-spot. That spot being a few yards in front of the sheriff's office.

When she goes to haul the door open for him, though… there's no door?

It's just frozen-stiff plastic, taped into place.

"*Ding dong, you're dead*," Claude says in what he thinks is an under-his-breath tag, but that's right where Letha is—under his breath: she moans, writhes, tries to wriggle out of his arms.

Claude repositions, gets his legs under him better, hitching her higher on his chest, and now the deputy is on the other side of that foggy plastic, directing them around the side of the building. He's waiting at the door when they round that corner, and he runs out, takes Letha from him. He's trying to form words, but can't seem to.

"She'll be okay," Claude says.

"You don't—you're the *history* teacher, not a doctor!" the deputy snaps back.

"I know the genre," Claude says back with an easy shrug, and then holds the door himself, for the deputy to maneuver his tall wife in. Jade's next, and Claude follows, unable not to register the long glare she maintains with Rexall the school janitor, sitting on a narrow bunk in the cell on the right.

"He's ba-ack," Rexall singsongs across to Jade like a taunt.

"He's never even been here before," Jade tells him, not breaking her stride.

"You know who I mean," Rexall says with a satisfied smirk, then flicks his eyes to the door they just walked through in a way that Claude has to look back, to see if there's a large shape filling that doorway now—there *is*.

Claude stumbles a step, bumping into Jade. It makes him feel for all the world like Shaggy, jerking ahead into Velma.

Jade looks back, irritated, not *not* Velma, and says it for all of them: "Cinnamon."

"Just Cinn, thanks," Cinnamon says, stepping all the way in and pulling the heavy door shut behind her, her breathing deep from whatever wade through the snow got her here.

She levels her laser glare on "Mr. Armitage" but doesn't say anything.

"What are you doing here?" Jade's already asking—*demanding*, because there's not an ounce of hesitation in this one.

"I think I can explain some shit," Cinnamon says, cocking her head over about Rexall, as if either he doesn't belong, or, in this context, she's not recognizing him. He lifts his chin to her like *hey*, but she doesn't give anything back.

Translation: he's beneath her.

Claude steps to the side to let her pass, giving her all the room she wants, and she takes it, doesn't even let her puffy jacket scrape his in passing, which takes some doing, since they're practically the Stay-Puft Marshmallow kaiju and the Michelin Man, here.

Rexall chuckles about this.

"What?" Jade says to him.

"You've been gone a long time, girlie," Rexall says to her.

She studies him a moment, then falls in behind Cinnamon.

Maybe this *is* the party, Claude allows. And they haven't even been into the front part of the building, yet. It could be the big dance at the end of *Prom Night*, or—no, no: that disco ballroom in *Jason Takes Manhattan*, except, instead of it being empty enough for a slow murder, Jamie Lee Curtis is pulling some *Staying Alive* moves out on the packed dance floor.

When it was her staying-alive moves that launched the whole Golden Age itself.

Some days just keep on unfolding and unfolding, don't they?

"Mr. Bridger," Claude says to Rexall in passing.

"Teach," Rexall says back, their eyes holding for a moment too long, Claude knows. But he's bringing up the rear—nobody to clock this.

They're he-ere... Claude Armitage says to himself about the five of them walking forward, into this, only, he's a few steps behind already—his music and camera roll aren't going to delete themselves, after all.

Melanie's bench isn't a lost cause by now—it'll never be that, not as long as he can shuffle out to it—but the shit's coming down thick enough now that Hardy would need to conscript Deputy Fife to sweep *him* off while he was keeping the bench clean, so... tomorrow, then. Maybe the eye of this snow hurricane will be hovering over Proofrock by then, providing a column of light for an old man to go out, tend to what needs tending.

It does feel good to be back in the offices again, though. Like he always told Trudy, home was wherever she was. But this feels pretty good too. No Meggie, so the place is kind of a sty, the front door even down to plastic sheeting, but to each sheriff his own. Or, for today: to each *deputy* his own.

Not that he's not going to have words with Rex Allen, next week.

In Hardy's day, if Don Chambers, his shirts still showing pinholes from wearing the badge, were to come in, announce that some fool kids were playing out in the snow on Main, then Hardy would have hustled out there his *own* damn self, chased their narrow asses home. This Tompkins kid, though… it's shameful. Because he couldn't leave his daughter, who would be perfectly safe here, he surrendered his truck keys to that blond Baker twin, more or less deputizing her to go save her classmates.

Never mind that when she doesn't come back, then Tompkins will have to be going out into it anyway. Just, now, minus a set of wheels.

As for Hardy, he's here for the night, he imagines. Well, maybe Lonnie will get the tracks back together on the snowcat, he supposes, ferry everyone to their front doors. But this former sheriff isn't holding his breath.

And, staying here, it won't be so bad.

Right now he's got a little girl on his knee, and she's pulling on his wondrous Russian hat, that dense, soft fur between her fingers making her smile, and—while her dad's gone back to the holding cells—Hardy's telling her the story of the sable, and making it up as he goes, like he used to for Melanie: sables are really house cats that got left behind when their human family moved into the city, so they had to learn to live out in the woods, in the deep snow, but their legs weren't long enough, their fur not thick enough, so they grew better fur, and, instead of taller legs, they made their body long like a weasel's, so they could move like snakes on top of the snow, and tunnel down through it, and dart through the water like muskrats, but they still like to race up into the trees higher and higher every day, always looking for their family to be coming back, because it's going to be such a good surprise, how much they've changed, it's going to be the best joke ever, look at me, look at me.

And now she's got the hat. It's nearly as big as her.

Hardy has to blink fast to keep the tears away.

Melanie was sitting on his knee just the same when he folded her first paper boat for her.

Tomorrow, he tells her.

He'll sweep her bench clean tomorrow.

Maybe this summer he'll even take this one out to it, hike her up on it so she can see out across the lake, and she'll point to the other shore like this old man, living here his whole life, can't have seen it yet.

And?

Through her eyes, he hasn't. Over her shoulder, he hasn't.

Hardy shakes his head no, that he *won't* be talking to Rex Allen next week, about his new deputy.

Let him stay on.

What the hell.

He wouldn't have left this little one here either, he imagines.

"You keep it," he tells her about his retirement hat, but she probably already was going to keep it.

And—the way she flinches into his chest when the door from the holding cells slaps open, the way she clings to him so he can keep her safe.

Hardy wraps his thick arm around her and angles them away so she's less in the line of whatever this is going to be, but—

It's the kid, the deputy. And he's carrying his wife. And there's blood.

Because this is Proofrock, Hardy tells himself.

He keeps Adrienne from seeing her mom like this, and then there's Jennifer, and, behind her, the Baker girl, actually *back* from herding her classmates to safety, and… that history teacher from the high school?

"*What?*" Hardy barks across to any of them, to all of them.

"Where's the first-aid kit?" Tompkins asks back.

Hardy makes eyes to Jennifer to take the girl, then he's on his walker, pulling across the room to the water cooler. The kit's on the wall right by it, always has been. Instead of opening its plastic door, he rips it off the wall altogether, tosses it across the room to the history teacher, who snatches it, passes it down behind the counter to Tompkins.

He's got his wife laid down on Meg's desk, all the shit slid off it, and Letha's trying to push his hands away but she's moving through a fog, she's not really there anymore.

"*Who did this to her?*" Tompkins says then, without looking up to Jade and the teacher, and Hardy can tell from his tone of voice that this is the moment right here when the kid's grown up into the man. A man of the law.

"Jennifer?" Hardy says across the room, when she's just standing there.

She slashes her eyes up to him, says, "It's Jade, Sheriff."

"Jade," the Baker girl repeats, like tasting it.

The history teacher doesn't say anything, just slides his phone into the shallow chest pocket of his jacket, which is an idiot move, as, peeking out like that, he's going to lose it.

"You know who did it," Jade says to Deputy Tompkins.

"Dark Mill South?" the Baker girl says, her eyes flitting from face to face.

Jade says, "We were over in Terra Nova. He was too."

"Did you—?" Deputy Tompkins asks.

"We dropped a house on him," Jade says.

"A *house*?" the history teacher says.

"Doesn't matter," Jennifer says. "He's already here. We saw… Lonnie."

"By the pier," the history teacher adds in, with a distinct note of… excitement? "He was all—" He mimes… what? Being twisted up? Dead?

"Everybody calm down," Hardy grumbles. "First, her"—Letha Mondragon.

"Here," the teacher says, going to her, waiting for permission from Deputy Tompkins.

"You can—?" Jade asks.

"My mother's a nurse," he says.

"That doesn't mean you are," the Baker girl tells him.

"Anybody else qualified?" the teacher asks all around, getting no takers.

"Do it," Deputy Tompkins says, giving the teacher room.

With the Baker girl staring daggers into his back, he doctors Letha Mondragon's shoulder with the first-aid kit. Then he's on to trying to stabilize her jaw with gauze. Just, every time that wrapping touches her skin, she whimpers, moans, writhes. Jade delivers the kid back to Hardy then leans over Letha, threads her short hair out of the way as best she can without coming into contact with her face. Deputy Tompkins holds his wife's hands in his, trying, Hardy knows, to siphon her pain away, take it on himself.

It's a maneuver widowers know well.

Hardy hikes the kid onto his knee.

"Does she have any medicine?" this Armitage asks, enunciating over-clearly instead of raising his voice, and Deputy Tompkins digs a rattling pill fob up from one of Letha's pockets.

"How do we give it to her, though?" Deputy Tompkins asks.

It's a good question: her jaw is cinched tight with the gauze, now.

"Here," Jade says, taking the stainless little tube and upending it on the table almost in a single move. "She takes them at the same time?" she asks, and Deputy Tompkins nods. "Well then," Jade says, and uses the rounded bottom of the fob to crush the two tablets into powder, cracks the two capsules over them like tiny oblong eggs, then casts around for… a Sharpie lid.

She scoops this concoction off the table onto a Post-it note, then folds the note into a funnel, drains the grains down into the Sharpie lid—*after* blowing it out.

"But aren't those capsules time-release?" Armitage asks weakly.

"Yeah, well, it's time," Jade tells him.

With that, she pulls Letha's bloody lips apart slightly, pours this medicine in, saying, "Swallow, swallow."

Letha does in what looks like a single painful gulp. Deputy Tompkins nods a solemn thank you to Jade, and then steps in to be the closest one to his wife.

"Let her come over," he says to Hardy then, and Hardy hesitates, but he gets it, too: if this little girl's mom is on the way out, then this could be goodbye.

Adrienne keeps one hand latched onto his walker all the way across the office, and she can tell her mom is hurt. It makes her feet shuffle, her footsteps small. Her dad lifts her up onto the table and Adrienne lays her head on her mom's chest as gently as any feather's ever drifted down, and Hardy has to tighten his lips, look over to the foggy, plastic door.

"So what now?" Armitage says, looking from Jade to Deputy Tompkins.

"I'm here too," the Baker girl says.

"Which one are you, anyway?" Hardy asks.

"Cinnamon," Jade says.

"Cinn," Armitage corrects, his eyes already skating away.

"I got them inside the store," Cinn announces.

"Them?" Jade asks.

"A bunch of the seniors were—doesn't matter," Cinn says.

Then, "*Store?*" Jade says.

"Doesn't matter either," Cinn says, seating herself on the high counter that's the first thing you walk into—Meg's idea some ten years ago, to form a kind of wall the public has to stop at, until she can get to them.

Hardy walks his walker around behind him so he can lean back on it like a stool. One of the few advantages of the thing.

"The question stands," Armitage says. "We can't just wait here."

"You're right," Deputy Tompkins says, kind of reluctantly, it seems. "I have to... Doc Wilson, he's probably still over at the high school, isn't he?"

"You need him for her," Jade says about Letha, seeing where he's going.

"The truck's good enough?" he says to Cinn, who kind of squinches her lips up in pre-apology. "*What?*" Deputy Tompkins asks, already not liking the answer they can all sense coming.

"It kind of mired down," Cinn says. "Sorry?"

"Should have chained up," Hardy tells them all.

Deputy Tompkins nods, knows that.

Chaining up in the deep stuff is no easy thing, though.

"I can walk it," Deputy Tompkins says.

"I'll go," Jade tells him. "You should—her."

"I'm going with you," Armitage tells her.

"I'm still here?" Cinn says, insulted.

"You're the one he's *after*," Jade says. "We should put you in the other cell back there. It's the only safe place."

"Not so safe," Deputy Tompkins says. "Somebody was already trying to get to Rexall. You didn't see who, Mr. Hardy?"

"*Sheriff* Hardy," Jade corrects.

"No, he's right," Hardy says, then, "Did I see what, son?"

"Whoever was hitting the side of the building with their truck."

"There was no truck," Hardy says. "I would have—truck tracks wouldn't go away that fast."

"It'd get stuck anyway," Cinn adds.

She's right. It's just a long grass slope on that side of the building, no asphalt or concrete for tires to dig down to.

"Snowcat?" Jade asks.

"It's taken apart," Hardy tells her.

"So he's really after her?" Deputy Tompkins asks Jade then, about Cinn.

"*I* can go," Cinn says, hopping down easily.

"Bullshit," Hardy says. "There's guns here, not out there."

"Guns never work," Jade mumbles.

"She's right," Armitage says with a shrug.

"What the hell?" Deputy Tompkins says to both of them.

"Really, if I can just keep *moving*," Cinn offers, "then nobody else will… be in the way."

"She's not wrong," Jade says to all. "That's—has that ever been tried?"

"What?" Armitage asks.

"Keeping the final girl in motion," Jade says. "Usually she gets put in some version of a silo, but that only makes it easier for him. She's a damsel in the tower, then."

"'Damsel,'" Armitage says with a knowing grin.

"'Him?'" though, Hardy asks.

"The dragon, the slasher," Armitage says, not wanting to slow this down, it feels like. "*Cherry Falls* tried—"

"And how did that work out?" Jade says right back to him. Then, "But… you know what happens, if we try to pass her"—Cinn—"around town like a baton? Then he starts killing everyone else, so that the only way she can stop the killing is to come in out of the cold." To Cinn, now: "You would, wouldn't you? Come in, I mean."

Cinn nods yes, she would.

"So would she," Jade says, about Letha.

"So would you," Deputy Tompkins says to Jade.

She shrugs that off like she doesn't factor in, here.

Adrienne's sitting up now, looking from speaker to speaker as if waiting for a word she knows.

Cinn steps in, scoops her up, rests her on her hip just like a mom.

"So, what, then?" Deputy Tompkins says.

"Doc Wilson," Jade says. "There is no greater plan, no survival strategy. Nothing that'll work, I mean. He'll catch her somewhere"—Cinn again—"and… I don't know. Maybe we're there to help, maybe we're not. Sorry, Cinnamon."

"Just Cinn."

Adrienne's playing with the drawstrings on Cinnamon's hood, now.

"But if she's *here*," Hardy says, obviously, "then we *are* around to help, aren't we?"

"Not if we're off getting the doc," Jade says. "This is always how it works, isn't it?"

"Splitting up," Armitage says, on her same wavelength.

"We know we shouldn't," Jade says, "but it seems like the most rational course of action in the moment."

"How long, there and back?" Hardy asks.

"Walking through this?" Deputy Tompkins says back. "Forty-five minutes. An hour. And that's *if* Doc Wilson's still there. I'll probably have to pull him on a sled or something, I don't know. He's…"

Deputy Tompkins doesn't finish it.

"*Old*," Hardy completes for him. "You can say it. I know what I am, Deputy. But I can still pull a trigger. Set me up in the corner, I'll stand guard."

"*Sit* guard," Armitage corrects.

"She'll be safe," Hardy tells him back, nodding to Letha. And Adrienne.

"Thank you," Jade says.

Hardy nods to her, still holding Deputy Tompkins's eyes, waiting.

Finally, Deputy Tompkins nods once, hating it.

But Jade's right: this is the only course that makes sense.

"It wasn't even supposed to go like this," Cinn says then, rubbing a fleck from the corner of Adrienne's mouth.

When Cinn looks up, all eyes are on her.

She cringes slightly from the attention, as if regretting having said this out loud.

"What do you mean?" Jade says, having to work to control her voice, it sounds like.

"I was just—" Cinn says, but Jade's glare stops her. "Okay, *okay*," she says, shifting Adrienne to her other hip, Adrienne's grip on the drawstring threatening to close her hood. She gently extracts that pushbutton ball from Adrienne's small fingers, shrugs like this is nothing, says, "You can't blame her, okay? I mean, legally. Because none of it ever, like, *happened*. It was just… she was just telling me, it was all fantasy, nothing real."

"Your sister," Jade fills in.

"Ginger," Deputy Tompkins says.

Now Cinn's eyes are shiny wet.

"I shouldn't even—"

"But you will," Jade tells her.

"I remember you, you know?" she says to Jade. "From the yacht, that night? When you were coming out of the bathroom?"

"*What?*" Deputy Tompkins says.

"Doesn't matter," Jade says, still holding Cinn's eyes.

"No, it does," Cinn says, snuffling a bit but not letting it slow her down. "Nearly all our parents died that night. Except Mrs. Pangborne, and Lana."

"Lana Singleton," Hardy fills in.

He was in surgery, but he read the report about Rex Allen digging her and her son out of some scuba-gear closet on the yacht, and how when he opened the door, all the tanks were rigged to roll out at him, and the next thing coming out, screaming behind a speargun, was little Lana Singleton, defending Lemmy.

Where are they now, even?

Gone, hopefully. Far from Idaho.

Rex Allen's still got the scar on his shoulder, probably, but if the only scars you get doing the job are on your skin, then count yourself lucky.

"But, what I mean," Cinn goes on. "Ginger, she—she..."

"She talks to you?" Jade asks.

This stops Cinn a bit. "She's my *sister*," she says, and that hint of insult under her voice seems to make Jade grin a bit, like she likes that Cinn has some fight in her.

"Go on," Armitage tells her.

"I'll go on when I'm *ready*," Cinn tells him right back. And he's one of her teachers, right?

Hardy logs this. Maybe it'll make sense later.

"And, really, you have to understand," Cinn says, getting her drawstring back from Adrienne again, "she's not wrong. Ginge, I mean. Our mom and dad did get killed that night. And most of the rest of our moms and dads as well." She nods fast down to Letha, as if Hardy or Jade or Deputy Tompkins could ever forget the toll.

"So, what?" Jade says. "She wanted payback? Revenge?"

"She thinks it was... unbalanced," Cinn says. "Ninety, ninety-five percent of Terra Nova died that night. And not even one percent of Proofrock." She shrugs like there's no arguing with numbers.

"Then it's not Proofrock she wants justice from," Jade says. "It's me, isn't it? I'm the one who could have stopped it."

"You *did* stop it," Deputy Tompkins tells her.

"Not soon enough," Jade says, still holding Cinn's eyes. "Right?"

Cinn doesn't like it, but she has to nod, has to agree.

"Me too, then," Hardy says. "It was my watch. And Jen—*Jade* here told me in every way she could, but I was... I didn't believe her."

"You're already paying, according to Ginge," Cinn says, nodding to Hardy's walker. To his guts, spilling into the lake.

"So what was the plan?" Jade asks.

"Doesn't matter," Deputy Tompkins says. "We need to—"

"She wouldn't be wedging this in if it didn't matter," Jade tells him. Then, back to Cinn, "So? She going to invade my dreams, or… or menace me from out by the laundry line? Can I expect to wake up with my head in a complicated bear trap, what?"

"What?" Cinn says, not following. "She didn't get to—to *do* any of it."

"Because she's locked up," Deputy Tompkins says, shrugging it true.

"She can… she comes and has dinner with us sometimes? She can get out whenever she wants."

"Figured as much," Jade says.

"What do you mean with that?" Hardy asks her.

"I talked to her too," Jade says. "She… she knows a lot about horror movies, you could say."

"That's just because she wants to be like Letha," Cinn says, defending her sister. "Letha's her hero."

"And I'm the villain," Jade says. "Cool, fine, great. Fair, even. I am the bad guy."

"She knew not to come for you," Cinn says. "Letha would… she wouldn't like that, right? So, her plan—God, I can't believe I'm saying this."

"Frank," Jade says, and it just hangs there.

"*Cenobites* Frank?" Armitage finally steps forward to ask. "Lament Configuration Frank?"

Jade nods for Cinn, says, "*Hellraiser* Frank."

"You're losing me," Hardy says to them.

"Just let her finish," Jade says, holding her hand up for Hardy not to interrupt, please. That these are delicate negotiations, no blunderers allowed.

Hardy holds his hands up, tapping out.

"It wasn't like she probably told you, though," Cinn says. "We did find… it was gross, I don't know what it was. And, this is my fault. I told Ginge I had it over at the old house in Terra Nova, that I was—that I was *feeding* it. And that it was growing. Ginger wanted it to turn into an… into a *monster* or something. She called it anthro—anthro—"

"An*tro*pophagus," Jade fills in.

"*Humongous*, pretty much," Armitage sneaks in.

"You watch these movies too?" Hardy says to him.

Armitage doesn't acknowledge, is laser focused on what Jade says next: "Rawhead Rex, Pumpkinhead, Gunther…"

"That alien from *TerrorVision*," Armitage says right back.

"Enough!" Deputy Tompkins tells both of them, stopping whatever game this is trying to be.

"But it—it was just, I don't know," Cinn says, at the end of some emotional rope, it sounds like. "I made that up about it growing, so she would have something to believe in?"

"Feeding delusions to the delusional," Jade says. "Great job, sis."

"You don't know what it's like," Cinn says back to her. "We used to be so close, and now, now…"

"So, what?" Jade asks. "This Frank was going to chew through Proofrock?"

"Just the senior class," Cinn says, quiet-like.

"Second-remove slashing," Armitage fills in, like identifying a bug on a tray.

"How do you know about that?" Jade asks him.

"He found all your old papers," Cinn says, kind of spitting it, it seems. "They're at his house, in his personal collection."

"How do *you* know this?" Deputy Tompkins asks.

Cinn shrugs one shoulder, gets that drawstring from Adrienne again, says, "I didn't really try to feed it or anything, though. It was probably a kitten a fish spit up or something. I did take it across the lake, but just to throw it in one of those sinkholes. End of story."

"And this was going to involve me how?" Jade asks.

"It was supposed to look like you were doing it," Cinn says, holding Jade's eyes for a moment. "Ginger wanted to let this... whatever it was going to be, let it go right when you got back to town. But, like I said, she never, it was all just..."

"Fantasy," Hardy says, wading back in.

Cinn nods, says, "But then—"

"*He* came home," Armitage finishes.

"Except it's not home?" Jade fires back. "It's just random, Dark Mill South showing up here."

"Random like *Slumber Party Massacre*," Armitage says. "A mad dog killer, not a revenge killer."

"Which is still pretty damn random?" Jade says. "So, thank you, Cinnamon, Cinn, whatever. I guess, I don't know. When you left the nursing home, though, she was still there?"

"Yeah?" Cinn says, then, quieter: "I don't know?"

"Doesn't matter," Jade says, standing to get this expedition started at last. "I saw him, Dark Mill South. It's not your sister in football pads and a mask."

"I saw him too," Cinn says, quieter. "At the motel."

"Then you know," Jade tells her. "So, you stay here. If Letha needs anything—"

"Of course," Cinn says, stepping closer to Meg's desk.

"And you," Jade says to Hardy, and finishes it by walking over to the already-unlocked gun rack, pulling down the longest gun.

She tosses it across to Hardy, trusting him to catch it. As if this is some action movie.

"That's Sheriff Allen's favorite," Deputy Tompkins warns.

"Any wild geese show up here, they'll wish they hadn't," Hardy says, checking the shotgun out, though he already knows it.

"This is stupid," Jade says, shaking her head.

"Got a better idea?" Armitage asks.

Jade doesn't.

"Gimme your coat," she says to Cinn, snapping for it, and Cinn works Adrienne back and forth to slip out of the big parka she's wearing. She holds it across.

"Letha's always talking about you," she says.

"Yeah, well," Jade says. "Small town, not much going on, right?"

"So I'll just—" Cinn says, setting Adrienne down on the desk across from Meg's, and Hardy doesn't see it at first. Or, he only sees it in Jade's reaction. In her slack face, and how she's reeling back just fractionally. But it's huge, too.

He tracks to where she's looking, and… it doesn't make sense at first. His head tries to organize what his eyes are telling him, and all he comes up with is that Cinn's playing toreador with Adrienne, head-butting her just to get that little-kid giggle.

It makes sense, sort of, except for the unavoidable fact that Cinn's standing up by the desk.

Hardy tracks up her, following her right hand up past her face, to, to—

To her bare scalp.

Meaning… meaning Adrienne is still holding the blond wig this twin was wearing.

"*Ginger*," Jade says, aghast, and the corners of this other Baker girl's mouth twitch up into a sort of grin, and then she's charging right at Jade. Jade falls back, trying to lessen this coming impact, but now Ginger's juking the other way, planting one foot up onto Meg's desk right by Letha and *vaulting* across to the next desk.

All this before Hardy can even raise the shotgun five degrees up from resting.

All this before Deputy Tompkins can even find his feet under him.

When he does, he's diving for Meg's desk, to cover his wife.

Meaning this Ginger Baker, she's already in the hall, papers and wire-cage inboxes and desk calendars fluttering and clattering be-hind her.

Hardy finally gets Rex Allen's long goose gun up, but Jade guides it on to the ceiling, shakes her head no, it's too late.

"They're identical except for the hair," she says, "I should have seen this coming," and follows Ginger Baker as best she can, but Jade's not tall enough to vault desks, isn't fast enough to leave papers hanging in her wake. When she finally gets to the hall, she edges around the corner in case Ginger Baker's armed herself with a stapler or a dirty mop.

A few steps later, Hardy hears Jade opening the metal door into holding, hears her interrogating Rexall, and can about imagine how that goes.

By the time he walkers into the hall after her, she's coming back, is a livewire of pissed-off.

She shakes her head no, then stops, turns to the ladies' room, remembering it. There's a chair cocked in front of it. Or, halfway in front of it, now.

"Oh, bull*shit*," she says, and kicks the door open.

The wind pulls at her hair and she turns away, leaving Hardy to chock the door open with his walker, stare down the bathroom window, still rusted open after all these years.

Deputy Tompkins gets there a step late, holding another shotgun from the rack, his other hand spilling shells.

"That's how she got out last time too," he says.

"Last time?" Jade says, incredulous.

"When she was her sister, I mean."

"That's how we *all* get out," Jade tells him in disgust, going the other way now, back to the front office.

Hardy follows as best he can, is just in time to see this high school teacher unlimber a little hand-held *scythe* from his backpack, slice the plastic door open diagonally, like cutting open a hole in the world.

"Coming?" he says back to Jade, his eyes most definitely grinning, which Hardy doesn't feel particularly good about.

"You've got her?" Jade says back to Deputy Tompkins, about Letha.

"Both of them," Deputy Tompkins says back, already holding his crying daughter, that pretty blond wig still trailing from her fingers like a scalp she's taken.

This is Indian Lake, after all.

"*Go*," Hardy tells Jade, shooing her out with the butt of the goose gun, trusting her to find a way to stop all this from happening, and Jade holds his eyes a moment, long enough to shake her head no about all this. That she can't believe it's happening again either.

And then she's gone.

Three customers over six hours. And, technically, since Kimmy paid the register out of her own pocket, she was one of those three customers.

It hasn't even been worth however much gas the generator chugged down and smoked back out. But, too, time-and-a-half's time-and-a-half.

Kimmy hits the head, because she knows that riding on the back of Millicent's buzzsaw of a snowmobile is going to make her have to pee. She has to bring a candle in with her, set it in the soap tray.

The water still runs, of course. This might be the biggest snow since forever, but going double digits below zero's nothing new for Proofrock—its pipes are always insulated.

Instead of taking the bathroom candle with her, Kimmy blows it out, leaves a folding book of matches beside it for whoever gets scammed into coming in tomorrow.

Probably her again.

Then it's making the rounds through the store. By the second candle she learns what she should have learned from the costume dramas she used to be a junkie for: candles blow out easier if you cup your hand behind the flame.

Because this isn't the first time she's been alone in the store with the lights out, she's sure to leave one candle flickering, to carry with her like a torch back to the alley, to turn the generator off. Philo—Holy *Crow*—tells her that with chainsaws and snowblowers, Weedwackers and generators, you always want to run them *dry*, but… it's not Kimmy's generator. She pulls the choke out all at once, the exhaust coughing down, and then, once she's in silence, she pushes the choke back in, because, really, she doesn't know what's the recommended way to turn one of these off, and doesn't want to catch hell for having messed it up.

Walking back through the store, her steps deliberate and slow so as not to snuff her flame, she doesn't let herself look side to side any. Because of course the shadows are going to be playing tricks. Of course all the displays and endcaps are going to look different, now.

It's just the store, though, she tells herself.

It's the same one she's known for going on ten years, now. The only difference is that it's empty and dark.

Making herself think rational thoughts and rational thoughts only should work, she knows, but still, her back's straighter than she's telling it to be. Her steps are deliberate and slow, yes, but they're also shorter than usual. The better to turn and run with.

Will she keep the candle, then, or fling it behind her so she's running into blackness, into endless shadow?

And? What would a real Queen's Guard do, right? Besides not getting stranded in the same town he grew up in, of course. Besides not working in the dollar store for a whole decade. Besides not shacking up with someone who's decided his name is Holy Crow, and that his spirit animal is, of course, a wolf. Thus all his t-shirt and belt buckle choices lately.

But this isn't about Philo.

If a Queen's Guard is standing his post and—and a surprise solar eclipse comes, say. Never mind that eclipses run more on a schedule. Kimmy's not stupid. But still. What if the sun darkens all the same, the shadows pooling around this Guard's feet then spreading like ink across the sidewalk, climbing the opposite building?

That Guard doesn't panic, give in to fear, run away.

It doesn't matter that no one's watching. It doesn't matter that it's too dark for anyone to see if he does or doesn't keep standing guard.

He doesn't move a muscle. He doesn't lick his lips. He doesn't scratch that itch.

He just waits for the darkness to pass.

Kimmy closes her eyes, imagining a shadow that deep, that quiet, that alone. One where who she is or what she's done or where she is doesn't matter. All that does is who she is inside. Who she always meant to be.

The calmness coats her like a second skin, like a single drop touching her forehead and then spreading cool over her whole body, cool because now her body heat's trapped in with her, and that's enough, that's all she needs.

"Jennifer," she says in that perfect moment.

All day she's been playing it back, her daughter walking purposefully through the store for this, for that. Her resolve, the certainty of her steps, it doesn't come from Kimmy, and it sure as hell isn't from Tab.

It's all hers, all Jenny's.

Under it is a roiling sea of anger, Kimmy knows, and understands, and that anger's swirling with betrayal and pain and resentment, but... there were good times too. There was hanging the sheets out on the line in the first days of summer, Jenny in first grade, a big girl now, but not too big to run to her momma's leg when unaccountable snowflakes start drifting down out of the sky, like happens at altitude throughout the year.

Kimmy will never forget reaching down with her hand to run her fingers through her daughter's hair, that contact telling her she was safe, that they both were, that this is magic, it's nothing to be scared of.

Kimmy opens her eyes a different person. It's temporary, she knows, finding her center like that, tethering her heart to a memory again, but it's good that it doesn't last, it's good that moments like that can be a refuge she retreats to only when she really needs it.

If she were always hanging the sheets out that day? Then it wouldn't be special anymore.

Does Jenny remember, even?

Kimmy nods yes, she does, she has to. Even if she can't articulate it, that feeling of those great white flakes drifting out of a cloudless sky, the sun shining down after them, that's not something you ever lose.

Open your eyes, she tells herself.

From denying her pupils light, she can see better in the darkened store now.

And, no, she's not going to start running.

Once you start, you never stop until you *are* stopped. This lesson courtesy Tab Daniels, from one of his stupid westerns, probably.

Forget it.

Kimmy balls her hands into fists and stifflegs it down the baking aisle, holding her weak flame before her like the light it casts is a shield. She only stops to fix what the other customer dislodged: the line of candy sprinkle shakers.

Your sugar jones is pretty bad if you brave the storm just for cake mix, muffin liners, evaporated milk, a nonstick cupcake pan, and a shaker of candy sprinkles.

The high school girl who bought them wasn't giving any explanations, though.

"Egg?" Kimmy had asked, even though she's been warned about commenting on customer purchases.

In reply, the girl had O'd her mouth out, showing this curious checkout girl that she already had an egg, and was carrying it in her mouth, pretty much exactly like a freak.

Kimmy swallowed, scanned, made change but no more eye contact, and then, wiping her station down afterward just out of habit, her blue paper towel picked up one of the girl's long blond hairs.

She sprayed its whole length down like drowning it, captured it under her paper towel, and deposited it in the trash.

Then she shaped her own mouth into an O, imagining carrying an unbroken egg like that.

Seahorses do that, sort of? And alligators?

Not people, though.

Unless they're crazy bakers. Unless their sweet tooth is so uncontrollable that they'll brave any storm to satisfy this next craving. Or—or unless their whole insides are nothing but eggs, so that if you touch them, they shatter on the inside. It's what Kimmy used to think about the geese and swans that would touch down in Indian Lake, on their way back and forth: they had to be packed with eggs, beak to tailfeathers, that that was why they came here. The water was soft, would keep shards from pushing up between their feathers, yolk from crying out around their eyeballs.

But Kimmy Daniels isn't a girl anymore, so, she doesn't think like that. Even if a customer's trying to make her.

This was just another useless shift, she tells herself, and every shift there's one more weird thing, isn't there? Cataloging them would be a hopeless enterprise.

At the register again, Kimmy breathes softly to extinguish her last flame, and, with dusk coming on, the front windows show her own reflection instead of the street.

Her heart spikes for a jolt when she remembers that the door was running on the generator, and that the generator's off, the matches so far away in the bathroom, but… she pulls harder than a Queen's Guard probably would—it's undignified—and the door groans from the cold, opens just enough.

Kimmy pulls it shut behind her, before the snow can spill in.

She can't lock it—No Keys Kimmy—but this is a post she can stand until Millicent buzzes up, anyway.

Even though it's nearly a half hour after four already.

But a good store manager knows there's an employee up here. A good manager knows the store needs locking up.

Kimmy steels herself, pulls her hood on and draws it tight over her face, thrusts her hands in her pockets, and, through a gust, she sees the first truck she's seen all day. It's two or three stores down, parked right in the street—no, probably *high-centered* in the snow right in the street.

Not her problem.

She turns away from the wind, casts an eye back into the store, and feels herself become unmoored in time for a moment, as if *she's* that one eye that was peering in at her earlier.

Except that's stupid.

She bounces on the balls of her feet for warmth, trying to will the sound of Millicent's snowmobile into hearing, and when she finally exhales, letting the last of her heat go, her breath is frosted white, a cloud she can't see through, and what it feels like more than anything is that she's just stepped out of a canoe, onto the banks of the old camp halfway around the lake, and is blowing smoke from her first cigarette out before her, and when it clears, one Tab Daniels is going to be watching her over the fire, a longneck tangled in his fingers by his leg.

And?

She would still smile back at him, she knows.

Just for that one perfect day in the future, of hanging bedsheets out on the line.

For a perfect little girl, clinging to her leg.

It would be physically impossible for Jace Rodriguez to care any bit less about whether the stupid video store is open for business or not.

His concerns are more... *Bobo Richardson* related.

He likes to imagine saying "Bobo" into the soft skin just under Bobo's right ear, his lips not quite making contact with the first syllable, then only lightly brushing with the second, both of their eyes closing at the same time even though they can't see each other's faces. Fingertips roving, hip bones alive, clothes suddenly very bothersome.

For the bake sale they did in September, to raise money to stock the shelves with DVDs, Bobo had been stationed beside him for the early Saturday shift and then, on Sunday, they'd both been in their hard plastic chairs again for the after-church crowd. Bobo was the self-assigned brownie pusher, and Jace, deathly allergic to yellow dye #5 and most of the red dye family, ran the lockbox, just to be sure he didn't get any icing on his fingers, accidentally lick it off.

Jace had always been aware of Bobo for the usual reasons, the shallow reasons he tries to rise above, that make him feel forever a victim of biology, but what got his mind and his heart looking Bobo's way during the sale was how, with each brownie he "pushed," he would always confirm that the person buying it didn't have any nut allergies, and wasn't going to share this walnut-laden square of chocolate goodness with any nut-allergic friends or family members.

Should the starting tight end for the varsity football team really be that compassionate?

Jace was wary at first, half-suspicious as you have to be that this was bait being left in his peripheral vision—that Bobo was playing up how dreamy he was, so as to lure Jace into the locker room across the gym, where… the prank would happen, whatever.

If you don't have your radar cranked all the way up, your paranoia ratcheted around twice, then… bad things, worse things. And Jace isn't going to be a statistic, isn't going to be the posterchild of a cause.

By Sunday he knew, though.

The brownies were all gone, replaced with Wynona's mom's red velvet cake—nothing like a brightly colored sin, ten minutes after church.

Because Jace had to decline a sliver of it, though, Bobo pushed his away as well, claiming he wasn't hungry, that he was running forties that afternoon, didn't need anything in his stomach to slow him down.

Jace had to look away to hide his almost-grin.

Bobo's the real deal.

In the shoveling line, they were numbers three and four, front to back, Jace's skin crawling from the idea that Bobo was watching his technique. And when Cinn came through, nearly crying with the effort of getting everyone inside, it wasn't her who put her hand on his shoulder, to turn him around, pull him out of his music, save his life or whatever. It was Bobo.

"Hey, we gotta—" he said to Jace, *for* Jace, hooking his chin back to the front door, his eyes drilling the importance of this across.

"Oh, oh," Jace said, because his stupid mouth is the biggest traitor in the history of traitors.

Moments later, of course, he came up with all the right things he should have said, he could have said, that would have lodged his wit and smile in Bobo, which would have been something at least, but… next time, he told himself.

So far that's pretty much all high school's been: a series of "next times." A higher and higher stack of maybes. But that tower's got to crash down into a perfect moment eventually, doesn't it?

Maybe that day's today.

No lights, the cold making everyone huddle close, some vague supposed "threat" out in the storm? If that's not a recipe for possibility, Jace can't imagine what would be.

"Seen this one?" he asks Bobo, since they're standing so close, the whole group watching the front door.

"This… ?" Bobo asks back, not quite looking over to the new release Blu-ray Jace is holding ever so casually, almost dismissively, completely ready to shrug the movie into oblivion if Bobo isn't into it, even though it's *Ready or Not*, one of his new favorites: the goddess Samara Weaving on the cover in that grimy wedding dress and yellow Chucks, a bandolier sash'd across her chest, not even the *hint* of a grin to her expression or her carriage, because… because her wedding sucked, and her husband turned out to be an asshole *and* a killer.

Once the power's back, Jace can take Bobo through this one, be the in-person commentary track. The laughs, the carnage, the bodies bursting, the righteous goddamn anger that makes you want to stand up on the couch and pump your fist at the ceiling.

He can already see the two of them doing just that in the basement, Jace's dad upstairs "giving them their privacy," as he would say it, but really standing guard, Jace knows. Because this is Proofrock, after all. This is Idaho. The West. America.

"Oh yeah, she's hot," Bobo says, finally stealing a fast look, then, just as an afterthought, kissing the tips of his index and middle fingers lightly, and then reaching over with his hand to tap that kiss onto Samara Weaving, never mind how she's glaring at him.

Jace swallows, the sound loud in his ears, but his lips don't give anything away.

In football terms, in Bobo's terms, this is… it's whatever the opposite of *He shoots! He scores!* would be.

Jace sets the case back on the top shelf just as it was.

"Hey, yo! Dot's!" someone calls up from the register, then.

Jace feels his classmates smearing past him, to whatever this next thing is going to be, but he just moves with the contact of their fluffy coats, his feet planted, the rest of him a wind puppet, his grin painted on, his head rocking back and forth.

Come one, come all, he's saying inside, way behind his eyes.

Who he's talking to is whoever Cinn said is out there. Frosty the killer snowman, maybe. That evil German Santa Claus. Sven from *Frozen*, maybe. That was the goofy reindeer's name, right?

"Sven," Jace says mostly to himself, just trying it out to see if it fits, but the shape that wavers in on the other side of the glass door isn't any cartoon reindeer.

Instead of retaping the stupid front door shut, Banner takes some initiative, makes his *own* decision—thanks for all the help, Sheriff Allen—and drags the conference table in, stands it up, then stacks stools and chairs behind it to keep it from falling back onto Adrienne. She's got instructions to stay on the other side of the counter, and Hardy's stationed at the walkaround to keep her there, kind of making Letha's triage space a playpen, but… kids are wiggly, they're squirmy, and this one might find a way.

The table isn't a door, doesn't stop all the wind from blowing through, but it's not the cold Banner's necessarily worried about. It's someone with a bad brain and worse ideas, crashing through.

Ginger Baker? Dark Mill South? Whoever was ramming Rexall's cell with their… snowmobile? But who would ever ram anything with a snowmobile? That's just asking to shatter your skids, your windscreen.

That snowcat, though. More and more, this is what it had to be: Lonnie, insulted, still pissed, out for blood, not dead yet, firing the cat up, trying to drive it into Rexall's cell.

And those wide tracks he'd just spent so long tightening might have messed the snow up enough out there that it looked like that's just the way it was, from sliding off the roof.

Good job, Banner tells himself, more in private now. He's doing what he always does: solving the mysteries he thinks he can, instead of the ones—like this whole day—that he'll never be able to crack. Big difference of course being that it doesn't matter whether it was Lonnie or not out there, does it?

Banner slides the little two-drawer file cabinet up against the table and calls that good enough. He hipslides over the counter, picks Adrienne up—she's the one good thing in the world right now—and kneels down by Meg's desk, to be close to Letha, who's doped up enough now to only be writhing around every three or four minutes, when her body sends her a reminder of what's happening to it all over again.

"She's tough," Hardy tells Banner, and it's like he's talking about a dog that got slapped by a car, has gone under the porch to live or die.

"She is," Banner says back all the same. Because it's true.

But, how much can one woman take? And, why *twice*, now? And: this isn't a porch, even if Letha has been hit by some version of a car.

"Doc'll know what to do," Hardy says, still in assure-the-kid mode, it feels like.

Banner stands, pacing with Adrienne now.

This morning, Doc Wilson was steady and sure, yeah, his head full of triage, his fingers going to their assigned tasks without hesitation, like born to the job. He might have even saved Abby Grandlin, and she was nine-tenths of the way gone.

Without a drink, though, without a whole *string* of drinks, Doc Wilson… he probably won't even be able to raise a cigarette to his lips, his hand'll be shaking so bad. Meaning the live version of *Operation* he needs to play on Letha might be a reach.

"You used to keep a bottle here?" Banner says to Hardy, using his hand to shield Adrienne from what he's proposing. Not because she can make sense of what he's proposing—getting the good doctor lit—but because she still keys on the word "bottle."

"Of what?" Hardy asks.

"Of whatever. Something strong."

"Good idea," Hardy says. "Gonna be a long night."

"Not for *us*," Banner tells him. "Doc's gonna... you know. Need it."

Hardy holds Banner's eyes a moment, then nods, is following this logic. But, "Rex Allen never approved," he sort of grumbles.

"Where?" Banner asks all the same.

"Lower right drawer."

Bouncing Adrienne, Banner slides past Hardy into the cold hall—that damn bathroom window—and into the sheriff's office.

It feels weird and wrong being here without a bossman sitting at the desk. Special circumstances, though. Life or death.

Banner checks the drawer, holding Adrienne high, and... shit. Of course. Banner's seen Sheriff Allen dip into this drawer, even. Not for a bottle and tumblers, though, but for the straight lemon juice he likes to take shots of, followed by tomato juice. He says they balance each other out inside, that Banner should try it, it centers you right out.

Not today, Sheriff.

Banner knees the drawer shut harder than he has to, less than his impatience wants to, and then Adrienne's doing her cooing thing she does for puppies on television. Puppies and baby donkeys and dragons just out of the egg—anything cute, she's immediately in love. Which is something Banner never would have guessed must be programmed in, but this isn't the time.

"Yeah, pretty, pretty," Banner says, drawing her close to the mounted hawk Sheriff Allen has on the table by the leather loveseat under the window. Taxidermy is the hole he's fallen into since his and Lindy's big split.

Adrienne's reaching for the window itself, though.

"Snow, snow, yeah," Banner says, leaning forward so she can

maybe touch that cold glass with her fingertips, get a safe little jolt of the storm, but then he's jerking back, nearly falling from it.

There *was* something out there, just for a moment.

Lonnie, back from the dead, coming for Rexall again?

Except... no running lights.

And, the sensation Banner's cobbling together in his head from what he only partway saw... he hates it, he'd never admit it, but his first thought, the one he can't help, is that, in a whiteout like this, it can only be that kangaroo-ram thing Luke Skywalker rides in *The Empire Strikes Back*. The one filled with those slimy-shiny guts.

But this isn't far, far away.

This is here, now.

A white-grey horse, then, busted out of its pen.

"What the hell?" Banner mumbles, forgetting he's trying not to cuss around Adrienne.

But: special circumstances.

Life or death.

And then he sees it again for a swirling instant—an elk, a fucking *elk*—and if it wanted to, it could rise up, vault right through that glass.

Adrienne would think the elk was pretty-pretty, but being in a tight space with a young bull with a rack like that, and shoulders full of panic, hooves not used to this institutional carpet... no thank you.

It's just the storm, though. The storm's got all the animals moving down the mountain. There's probably moose walking down Main, again, bears padding past the motel, all of them angling for that long drainage that'll deliver them down where it's warmer, where it's less harsh.

Still, it feels exposed, with only that big window between inside and outside.

Banner ducks out, closes the door gently behind him, and by the end of the hall, he knows where the closest bottle is: Lonnie's. In junior high, Banner's dad had him scraping gaskets at the station for six and a half dollars an hour, and Lonnie was always moseying over to the tool chest, reaching up behind the gear oil, and sneaking a fast nip.

The first hard liquor Banner ever tried, it was from that bottle Lonnie kept back there. At first Banner thought it was a joke, that he'd just swallowed gasoline gone sour, but then at school the next day Lee Scanlon told him that that's how it's *supposed* to feel: like fire in your chest, smoking up your head, clouding your thoughts.

Fucking Lee, man. Banner can still picture him in his Lake Witch get-up, pole-vaulting into the water, *Jaws* blurry behind him. But this is no time to be dwelling on the dead. Not where there's the living to attend to. Not when Letha needs him to get Doc Wilson loaded, so he can save her life.

So: Lonnie's.

And now, passing Adrienne off to Hardy, he's remembering the pegboard with the hooks Lonnie hangs all the keys from. And that one of those keys has to start that big Idaho Falls snowplow now parked behind the gas station.

He was wondering how Doc Wilson was going to wade through the snow, but now he won't have to.

Banner's going to collect that bottle, get those keys, and save the day.

Deputy Tompkins, reporting for duty.

On the one hand, going back to the scene of the crime—of *one* of the batch of killings, anyway—is asking for it, Jade knows, even *if* it's for a good reason like getting medical help. On the other hand… why would *Dark Mill South* go back to the high school?

Does Jason ever come back to the tree he's already left a body in? Does Michael return to the house he just killed everybody in, or does he move on to the next babysitter? Freddy, though, Freddy's different. He comes back to the dream over and over. And maybe that's what all this is to Dark Mill South, right? A waking dream?

That doesn't explain what he was doing over in Terra Nova, though.

If his path is supposed to start at the motel, loop around to the nursing home and the high school… what do all those places have in common? That there's *people* there. Unlike Terra Nova. Terra Nova's where you go when you want to pull a snow cocoon over you, hibernate for the winter, away from prying eyes. And, even if Dark Mill South followed Jade and Letha across the lake—aren't they out of his age-range? Isn't he after Proofrock's graduating class, not the hangers-on just waiting for the ten-year reunion?

Maybe it's that, in this situation, since Jade and Letha are the ones who are sort of the authority figures—they know the genre, anyway—maybe that means that, like the cops guarding the final girl, they *have* to be taken out?

Passing the library, Jade slows, trying to think this all through.

"Doesn't track," she says to herself, trying to cap her thoughts off. And, because she got rid of that imposter of a history teacher, she can speak out loud, not have to worry about him soaking every word in through his very-open pores.

Was she ever that annoying, only able to see the world through slasher goggles?

He was easy to lose, anyway. Being the only one of them with skis, he's now going cross-country to Pleasant Valley Assisted Living, to inquire after Cinnamon Baker. Because—speaking of slasher goggles—chances are Ginger conked her on the head, stuffed her in a closet like Neil Prescott, to take the fall for all these killings.

Jade didn't run through all that with Armitage, though. Instead, she just said that the big showdown can't get started without the final girl, can it?

No washed-in-the-blood slasher fanatic could argue with that.

Really, though, a final showdown is the opposite of what Jade wants, this time. Just because she knows, from last time, what kind of bodycount that leaves.

Be careful what you wish for. It's something you learn the hard way.

No, keeping the final girl in motion won't work. But if Armitage can get Cinnamon back to the station, and Jade can get Doc Wilson back there to work on Letha, then… maybe they can wait this out. It's not brave, it's not cinematic, but the fact of the matter is that, between Banner and Hardy and all those guns on the wall… *something* good can happen, right?

Haven't they earned that, finally? At what point does something have to go their way?

Related, Jade wonders: how many toes will she be losing? She stopped feeling her feet somewhere on the scraping walk across the lake. And there's dead spots on her face, too. They don't hurt, they just push around like hard discs of callus, but she knows that's probably not great. She tells herself her face doesn't matter, though—she was never some great beauty, never the bouncy warrior princess wielding the machete against the masked killer.

Her toes, though. She imagines she's going to need her toes.

Letha's more important right now, though. And, really? You're worrying about toes, when a mother and wife and best friend's *life* is in jeopardy?

No, Jade isn't an upright, good-thinking final girl. Leave that to the Cinnamon Bakers of the world, the Letha Mondragons, who would sacrifice their whole *foot* to save a kitten, probably.

The Jade Danielses of the world, though, they can't stop thinking about their frozen toes.

Trudging numbly across the rise by the post office, pretty sure she's not on the road or the sidewalk, Jade remembers spearing litter here afternoon after dull afternoon—something about the wind or the buildings or her bad karma would always deposit wrappers and lids and worse on this specific patch of grass. She tries not to look over by the wall, for fear she might see a version of herself hiding there, the collar of her custodial coveralls pulled up high around her face. She doesn't look to the skeletal line of hedges, either. They were never tall enough to Michael behind, but they did serve to stash a litter stick, once upon a time. Back when a lot more people in Proofrock were still alive. Proofrock *and* Terra Nova.

But she can't get mired down in the past. Turn your head behind long enough, it'll get lopped by what's rising up in front of you. And then Doc Wilson doesn't get delivered to Letha, and Adrienne grows up without a mom to hold onto, and Jade wouldn't wish that on anyone, will be thrilled to lose some toes if it means Letha gets to live.

She's no final girl, no; she just got lucky once. But she knows the game, can fake it for a few more minutes.

The quickest way to the high school is straight up Main, then right just before the motel, so she can angle across the empty lot that, when there's no snow, has a game trail the deer still use, when the students aren't.

How she's going to hike little Doc Wilson all the way to the station… no idea. But, one problem at a time.

Or, first he has to even still *be* there.

Second, he has to *not* cop a feel if he's riding piggyback on her, because that decision matrix will be a completely different thing: slough him off to freeze or cash her last shreds of dignity in to get him back to Letha?

Maybe there's a third option, though. Take that abuse, let him fix Letha up, then lock him in a cell without a drink, watch his DT's go through all the stages of despair. The kind where Jade's lined bottles up on the other side of the bars, just out of reach.

Banner'll owe her, so he won't interfere.

And, the one bottle Doc Wilson finally pulls to him? It won't be vodka, just warm fizzy water, which is the worst kind of fizzy water.

Dreaming up worse and crueler punishments keeps Jade's legs pumping, and the shit's deep enough that, under Cinnamon Baker's nice jacket—no, no: Ginger's nice jacket—she's coated in sweat, meaning she also doesn't *smell* like a final girl.

She steps onto the bottom of Main Street and it's high-noon empty, a swirling white wasteland, and something dull but massive surges at the base of Jade's consciousness, even though it's just her, here.

She cases all the storefronts she can see, studies the snow for tracks, and can't lock onto any *obvious* reasons she's suddenly breathing deep.

Is this that final girl radar she's seen a thousand times through tracking lines?

And now she's breathing faster, having to blink faster too, because her eyes are being stupid. Her hand stealthily drops to the loop at her right leg, that still doesn't have that wonderful-perfect long-handled blue hammer.

In lieu, she dials back to slow-motion swinging it into the back of Dark Mill South's head, the hammer's weight bringing her up onto her toes, even, because she wasn't just swinging for the fences, she was swinging for Idaho Falls.

And? Just like Laurie Strode dropping that big handy knife now that the horror's definitely and for sure over… couldn't Jade have taken *Silent Night, Deadly Night*'s lead and used the *clawed* end of her hammer, and maybe got lucky, scooped a tablespoon or two of Dark Mill South's dream machinery out into the snow?

Could have would have should have, yeah. None of which count in slasherland.

It's not for her to put him down, though. She's final girl *support* right now.

And… hunh.

For a moment through the swirling skirling snow, like it's painted on canvas that's only tied in two places at the top, she's pretty sure she just saw the truck Letha picked her up in this morning, now stationed right in Jade's path like she can step up into it, and…

What was that poem from high school, that Jade had memorized because it was surprisingly metal? "The horses' heads were turned to eternity"? This truck is the carriage from that goth girl's poem, she knows. It's Death, stopping for her because she couldn't stop for it.

"No thank you," Jade says as politely as she can, but firmly, too. And, to herself: *This isn't what you think it is, girl.* This is just the truck that Ginger, when she was Cinnamon, said she'd mired down.

Just… she'd said it was mired down back at the post office, hadn't she?

Why lie? What's to gain, with that? So the truck got stuck on Main instead of back there. Does that matter even one little bit?

If it does, then… then the only reason it could even *start* to matter was that if Banner went to get his truck, Ginger wanted him going to the post office, not this deep up Main.

It doesn't make the truck any less stuck, though. It just keeps Banner from standing where Jade is right now.

The driver's-side door is open, too, which doesn't track. In a storm like this, stuck or not, you don't want to step back in only to sit down in snow, do you? Sure, when Ginger was Cinnamon just now, detailing her institutionalized twin's motivations, she was really monologuing about her own convoluted reasons—that's how the Reveal works—but, convoluted or not, nobody wants a wet ass.

Still, that door is most definitely open, isn't it?

Jade rolls her shoulders, makes her hands into fists, and tells her legs to robot her down Main Street one more time.

A few steps back from the truck, she can tell that the truck's still *idling*, too. Its taillights are coated in snow, but they're definitely glowing red, and trembling just slightly with the engine, and the wiper blades are still sweeping back and forth, back and forth.

Jade gives the truck a wide berth, draws alongside the cab, peers in through the open door.

The snow is mounded on the seat, has the gauges all covered, the steering wheel white. More important, it's empty.

"Hello!" Jade calls into it all the same, because Ginger could be lying on the backseat, a tire iron held close to her chest, which… shit. Shit shit *shit*. Jade's shaking her head no, but not because what she's thinking isn't true, but because she doesn't want it to be: she'd been working on the assumption that Ginger Baker was just slaloming through some private slasher fantasy, playing "psycho killer," as Tatum would have it, her big revenge plan too complicated to actually work, but—it's thinking of her lying on the backseat of this truck with a crowbar clutched across her chest that's making Jade have to see her also lying under that Mark kid's bed at the nursing home, an *arrow* held across her chest, to push up through his throat.

Then standing after that with an ax, for Kristen. Then walking downstairs for Philip Cates, and collecting a plastic bag on the way, because this killing has to be an homage as well. As someone who knows the slasher shelf front to back *would*. Especially if she's using those kills to speak to someone.

"To me," Jade says, the base of her jaw tingling.

Cinnamon—Ginger speaking *as* Cinnamon—had said Jade was the real target all along, hadn't she? And… and then it must have been Ginger at the high school as well, right? In her blond wig, she could prance right up to Abby and those other two. Except—Jade almost has to close her eyes in relief. Except Cinnamon, the real Cinnamon, told Banner that it had been *Dark Mill South* at the motel.

Unless she was covering for her damaged sister?

Would Cinnamon do that?

Jade closes her eyes in pain, then opens them back fast, because, in a slasher, you watch your six, your twelve, your ten and two—if you don't keep the whole goddamn *clock* in view at all times, then someone'll pull the pointer hands up from that clock, jam them through your skull.

And you'll deserve it.

So, either it's been Ginger all along, and it's just bad luck that Dark Mill South is in town, or… Jade's thinking too deep into this, has her slasher goggles from high school on too tight. Nothing new, right?

To prove herself wrong, she steps in, knocks on the back window of the truck. When nobody sits up, caught, "you got me," Jade reaches timidly forward for the front door switches, unlocks the doors.

She hauls the back door open all at once, already backing up fast from it, wishing again she still had that blue hammer, or any-color hammer, please.

There's just the base for Adrienne's car seat.

What the hell?

Jade reaches in, twists the key, the engine going down, plunging her into a silence she didn't realize she'd been walking through.

"Hello!" she calls out, all around. "Anybody!"

Distant, maybe just a sound she's hoping for, there's a buzzing. The minor-key, maybe imaginary version of the snowmobile she was riding around earlier?

Except, that snowmobile's *dead*-dead, back by Lonnie, back by Melanie's bench.

And this is from the other direction anyway.

Jade steps farther away from the truck.

Why park it *here*, Ginger? What had she, when she was Cinnamon, told Banner? That… that she'd gotten all the kids to safety, something like that?

Ginger Baker, *saving* people instead of killing them?

Jade studies Main for these supposedly saved kids. The bank's behind her, the dollar store ahead of her on the left. Closer in is Dot's, and next to that, the quilting and scrapbook place?

Was Ginger parked here so she could ransack photo album supplies, to memorialize her slashery escapades?

But… what's this storefront right behind the truck, *by* the quilting place?

Jade tries to dial back to unsnowy times, place this, and… was it ever even anything? Has it always just been an empty slot in a dying town?

Oh, oh, that's right: the barber shop, yeah. She's heard of it, but it's never been open in her lifetime, she doesn't think. Since she's been gone, it's turned into something else, hasn't it?

"What are you?" Jade says, stepping forward, rounding the bed of the truck, her hand on the tailgate just because she needs something to hold onto, which is when her numb right shin conks into something.

At first it doesn't register, or, is maybe just the curb, higher than it should be, and in the absolutely wrong place.

Slowly, though, Jade looks down.

"No," she says, dropping to her knee then looking around all at once, because maybe this is precisely what an overlarge somebody *wants* her to be doing.

She can't see far into the swirling whiteness, but… nobody's slashed out for her yet, anyway. She bites her right glove off, lowers her bare, frozen hand to the shape obvious in the snow now.

Sweep, sweep, and—

"No, no," she has to say.

Jade rolls the body over, which isn't easy, and she's already clocking the bare skull, this Cinnamon-Ginger face. Those frozen-open eyes. The screwdriver jammed into the left ear, and, by the angle of the head, used as a handle to crank the neck over, break it.

Ginger never knew what was happening to her, here.

Or: "Ginger?"

Jade sweeps snow from this shaved scalp, and sees what she doesn't want to have to see: new nicks in the skin.

Meaning… meaning Ginger shaved her sister's head after killing her, peeled her out of her big jacket—the one Jade's wearing now—then left her here?

This isn't just about getting revenge on the town, on Jade. It's also about stepping into Cinnamon's *life*. The one she thinks should have been hers, if Cinnamon hadn't left her in the yacht that night.

And now Jade understands the open door on the truck: it really *was* Cinnamon who told Banner she was going to go attend to the kids here on Main. Cinnamon was walking around the back of the truck to do just that when she heard the loudest, most intimate sound she ever would: a screwdriver, driving down her ear canal. And then, with her feet still on the ground, she was staring up into the grey sky.

And Ginger trudged back up to the sheriff's office *as* Cinnamon, and spun her big story about how evil and devious "Ginger" was, which could have worked… except Adrienne unmasked her halfway through.

"I'm sorry, I'm sorry," Jade says down to Cinnamon, touching Cinnamon's cheek lightly, as if the little warmth she has to offer can fairy-tale kiss this final girl back alive.

She's just a dead kid, though. Another dead young woman, all her promise leaking into the snow, all her plans pooling in the skin of her back.

Jade grubs at her knees for the glove she just took off.

At least it was fast for Cinnamon, right?

But this isn't over yet, either—it can be fast for Jade, too: Ginger's still out there somewhere, cold without a jacket, her scalp bare to the wind, all manner of screwdrivers in her hand, and Dark Mill South is still skulking around as well. And the only one who could have stopped him, the only one empowered by the genre *to* stop him, the final girl to his slasher, is lying dead in the snow.

And Letha, the next nearest final girl, is out of commission.

"Leaving who?" Jade says. She wants to laugh about the hopelessness of this, but can't seem to muster it.

Maybe Armitage, the unlikeliest hero, is skiing here now, right? Maybe he's naive enough, hopeful enough, that he can do… *some*thing?

Jade pulls Ginger's hood back on and stands.

Doc Wilson, she reminds herself. *Letha*. Spitballing slasher theories doesn't mean Jade doesn't still have a mission.

Instead of keeping on down the middle of Main like a walking bullseye, she steps up onto the sidewalk, where the snow's not as deep. It's not easier to trudge through because of any awning, this stretch doesn't have that, it's because… it's been *shoveled*?

"Hunh," Jade says, stepping down onto almost-concrete, almost-sidewalk.

Which is when she sees the shattered glass door.

Behind it, there's candles flickering here and there, and—

"Oh, no *way*," Jade says, gulping regret down. "I'm calling bullshit."

Halfway up the aisle of this whatever-the-hell-it-is store, there's another body, like it was running for the front door.

Jade backs away, reminding herself again about her mission but not looking away from this *body*, either.

But then she stops, can't just leave it there.

Can she?

She should, she knows. You don't investigate mysterious sounds, you don't go skinnydipping, and you for sure don't traipse into a place where it's obvious people are already dying.

Too, though—she wasn't supposed to see this, was she? She's not even supposed to be here.

What if it's a trap for Banner? One his stupid ass'll walk right into, like a badge is shield enough. Then this long cold walk Jade's making to keep Adrienne's parents alive is for nothing.

"Don't do it, don't do it," she tells herself, stepping in through the still technically shut door, and—no no no no.

Her mouth opens, her eyes trying to warm with tears whether she wants them to or not.

Is this what Letha was talking about yesterday? Proofrock has a *video* store?

Not videotapes, just thin little DVD cases with no heart made of iridescent tape, but still. As Ellen Ripley says right before the world ends, *We work with what we have.*

"Shit," Jade says, stepping forward, touching the top new release, a movie she doesn't know, some war-torn blonde in a wedding dress, ready for round two, it looks like—what Cinnamon Baker was supposed to have been.

Jade pulls her hand back when, somewhere in the darkness, another plastic case clatters to the floor.

Jade stops breathing, doesn't move, is even trying to will the blood in her veins to be quiet. Her whole body is listening.

Who? she knows not to say. Because she doesn't want to put a bullseye on her face.

Instead, she melts closer to the floor, eyes wide open, and fingertips her way to the body laid out in the aisle, its boots and gloves scattered around it like flower petals at a wedding.

It's a kid, a girl.

Her eyes are open wide as well, but they're dry. She's dead, has bright pink puke splashed up from her mouth, like she died eating cotton candy. But her parka is pink too, meaning her puke is erasing her jaw, almost—

Jade falls back onto her butt, her right arm stabbing out, pulling movies down onto her in clatter, her heart a rabbit in her chest, trying to kick its way free.

It can't be her, it can't be Stacey Graves.

When Jade stands, desperate like she's underwater, fighting for the surface—it's just DVDs, it's just DVDs—she kicks the girl's puffy pink arm, and the hand flops over, showing the blood sheeted down over it like a slick red glove.

From… some stab or slice up under the jacket, which somehow didn't cut the jacket itself, release all its foamy batting?

Well, either that or she had the jacket put back on her *after* being killed.

Because yeah, that tracks.

Shaking her head no, that she doesn't really want to know, and trying to keep an eye on every part of the dark store at once, Jade lowers herself to a knee, feels down for this girl's hand, half certain that the whole arm's been torn off, and stuffed back up the sleeve.

"I'm sorry, I'm sorry," she's saying to the girl, risking a fast glance down, running that pink sleeve up high enough to see that… the blood *starts* at the wrist?

Suicide?

Jade's chest goes cold, her thoughts dial down, and what she's thinking is impossible: if all these dead kids, their deaths modeled on slashers, have been messages to someone who can *unpack* those messages—Jade—then… then a wrist being open like this, this just confirms it, doesn't it?

Jade has a matching line on her wrist.

She can feel it writhing.

"No, no," she mumbles, dropping the hand like if she pushes it away fast enough, she doesn't *have* to know, this doesn't *get* to be about her, for her, it won't have anything to *do* with her, only… what?

This girl's wrist isn't only cut on the underside, where the veins are close to the skin.

It's also cut on the back side?

Jade scans 360 again, absolutely certain she's maxed out on this kneel-by-the-dead-girl gambit—hang around dead bodies long enough in a slasher, you become one—and then studies this hand closer, holding it as delicately as she can.

It's been cut all around, like… like trying to *remove* the hand? If—if this is Dark Mill South, is he carving up his kills so that they all look like they've lost the same hand he has?

Except: Jade eases forward, over this dead girl, and the other hand's got the same red ring around the wrist. And, having to brace herself on her fingertips so as to not faceplant in the girl's body, have to feel that last breath whoosh up past the voice box, which might even turn into a groan, a word, Jade doesn't know… her fingertips slip the littlest bit.

In *more* blood.

This puddle is forming from the girl's feet. No: her ankles. She has the same red bracelets there, flashing Jade back to a diagram she'd see on the hall down by Ag Sciences in high school—the dotted lines on a cow, showing all the cuts of meat.

Is *that* what she's interrupted here?

Jade guesses she did want to know, about thirty seconds ago. Call it morbid fascination, or, really, just call it what it is: compulsion, or genre awareness. In slashers, you die because you don't know stuff. Therefore, the more knowledge you can collect and piece together, the better your survival rate.

But now, now she wants this *out* of her head, please.

Stacey Graves, she could understand: people were making noise on her lake, and she wanted to quiet them, in the only way she knew.

This, though, this is something completely different. In this kind of work, Jade can see the mind behind it, sort of. The way it's reducing this dead girl to a—to a *thing*, an object, a toy.

One Dark Mill South probably isn't finished playing with.

Jade backs up more, feeling behind her with her fingers, and when the wind rattles the front door in its frame—the door she was hoping to fall *out of*—she flinches, retreating sideways into the store now, even though this store is the last place she wants to be.

Because it's right there, now, she takes the aisle closest to the wall on her left, the Comedy aisle it looks like—ha—and… oh, shit.

This time it's a boy, maybe seventeen, eighteen. Another plaything, lodged up against some pegs or shelf supports in the wall, his arms out to either side, most of the weight off his legs.

This one's skin has been mostly pulled off, but imperfectly. Or, partially. Thanks to those cuts around the ankles and wrists, the hands and feet still have their bandaid-colored skin—"flesh-colored" for white people, anyway—but the rest of this kid's skin… god.

It's not all the way gone, but it's pulled back from a slit made up his frontside. The effect is like he's been caught undressing, just, he was on too much meth, so got seriously carried away, kept going after the shirt and pants were off, and started unbuttoning the skin from his muscle.

Just, not "unbutton," but unzip.

The skin on his face isn't off, either, but it's definitely not where it should be. The eyes don't line up anymore, quite, and the mouth, that bright blue vomit running down from it… something's wrong with the mouth, too. Jade doesn't look long enough to be sure, can't—she's gagging, is suddenly aware of her own skin's connection to her muscle in a way she's never had to be.

Does she have the same marbling in her meat, though?

It looks like he's laced with tapeworms, almost.

It makes Jade's soul crawl. It makes her never want to eat meat again. It makes her consider Leatherface in a whole new way.

And, again, it makes her retreat, feeling behind her, sure with every step that her blind fingers are going to stub into a thigh like a tree trunk.

"You shouldn't be here, you shouldn't be here," she hears herself muttering, like she *wants* to be snatched up, be squeezed hard enough that her pink and blue insides erupt out, and her boots slide off, and her skin gets loose, ready to be whipped away.

She backs up again, is to that glorious front door now, only—no, no, please.

It's locked.

Jade rattles it once, makes herself stop.

She's crying with her whole body. Every part of her except her eyes. A whimper escapes, a whimper she hates, but one she can't help.

But you can't collapse, you don't give up.

You keep moving, keep moving.

To the aisle on the right, now. Because Dark Mill South can't be in all three aisles at once, can he?

Jade makes herself small, as small as she feels, she hugs the shelves as close as she can without knocking cases off, and, and—

There's a kid crouched there in front of her, his face powdered white. Not from donuts, but… it's frozen tears.

And—is this a dream, what?

"You're the same color I am," Jade says in wonder, not even whispering, and what this feels like more than anything is that she *has* burrowed back into her safe place, the video store in her heart, and she's found a brother in there. One with the same skin as her.

He pulls her to him, hugs her hard and close, his whole body shuddering, his breath so fast he can't be getting anything from it.

"They're, they're… they're all dead," he whispers.

Jade slowly, hesitantly—this is new territory—pats his back, gives him all the safety and reassurance she has.

Which isn't much.

And, if he's whispering? Then there's a *reason* to whisper. Not just the dead, but the one that made them that way.

"What happened?" she asks.

"Bobo, he plays football," the kid sputters. "He can take anybody down, he's strong, he's good, but—but…"

Jade shakes her head no, doesn't need it said out loud to see it.

Jason Takes Manhattan, where that boxer guy tries his skills on Jason, and gets his head punched off.

"But, but, everyone was already, they were..." the kid says, not able to pull his words together.

"I'm Jade," Jade says, touching the hollow of her throat to indicate herself.

"Jace," the kid says back, making him even more her brother, making this even more some dream she's having, after she got conked on the head.

She's probably laid out cold on the sidewalk, she knows. What she's walking through is the haunted house in her head: all her terrors, come to life for her to traipse through.

When you live and breathe horror, then your dreams, they can kind of match up with that, can't they? It's not called nightmare fuel for nothing.

"What do you mean, they were already... ?" Jade leads off, still holding onto Jace's shoulders to give him an anchor, be the adult.

Which is another thing Jade never thought she would be. Not in this town.

"They were already dead, they were already *dying*," Jace says. "I don't—I don't..." and he crouches ahead, deeper up the aisle, his hand tugging on Jade's.

She follows, not standing all the way up either, but then has no choice but to stop, transfixed.

The wall beside her—this place does have videotapes.

Her old ones.

Don't Go in the Woods, *Don't Go in the House*, *The Initiation*, *Graduation Day*, *StageFright*, *Final Exam*.

Even *Just Before Dawn*, which she left on the yacht, and *A Bay of Blood*, which Hardy never confiscated.

And, above them, neatly lettered, the category: JADE'S PICKS.

Jade gasps, her hand covering her mouth, her face starred with pinpricks of… of wonder. She's reaching out to touch the red spine of *Visiting Hours*, which should wake her from this nightmare, when Jace tugs her ahead.

To another dead kid.

This one's not been skinned yet, but has been stripped *for* skinning. This time the cut goes up along the back, from crack to nape, instead of up the front.

"Because doing it the other way didn't work…" Jade realizes out loud, the skin on her back now the most sensitive part of her body.

"*Happy Death Day*," Jace grandly announces about this dead, prepped kid—*quietly* grandly announces—which Jade doesn't follow. A joke? Is he trying to be clever? She looks from him to the dead kid, trying to track what "Happy Death Day" is supposed to mean, but… is this about that frothy red splattered out from the dead kid's mouth? That's way too bright to be blood, unless this is a Herschell Gordon Lewis flick?

Jade's only seeing the dead's kid face, though. And, when you get killed, you probably *do* throw up whatever you were just eating. She tells herself there's probably a screwdriver or railroad spike jammed into the back of his skull—*The Toolbox Murders* for $500, she tells the Alex always waiting at the podium in her head, tapping his fingers index to pinky, index to pinky.

Jade rolls the dead kid over, his dry muscles creaking against each other in a way she can feel in her bones, and… no screwdriver?

"So what is this on his lips?" she asks, dabbing it onto the pad of her middle finger.

Jace grabs her wrist hard, probably because he's seen too many movies, has some idea Jade is about to taste this.

"I can't eat cupcakes," he says, not looking at the dead kid but leaning back to get a better angle on the long aisle they're so obvious in.

"Hunh," Jade says. "So he—you're telling me he choked on a *cupcake*?"

"*Happy Death Day*," Jace says with more emphasis. "I told you. It's a movie. Don't you—I thought you watched horror?"

"I do, I did, but I've been—"

Jace shushes her, scuttles them into the middle aisle, where, instead of a body, there's a body's *wrapper*: someone's skin, removed.

It makes Jade one hundred percent expect a high school senior, all his or her or their muscle exposed, to come screaming up the aisle for them.

"This can't be—it can't be..." she says.

Beside her, though, landed perfectly upright, is a bright red cupcake with just one bite taken from it.

"He came in right after Cinnamon left," Jace says, doing his eyes like this is the important part of all of this.

"*Cinnamon* was here?" Jade asks.

"She told us he was coming," Jace says, pulling them into the far aisle, which butts right up against the register, where six candles of a menorah are flickering.

"He who?" Jade asks.

"Can't you tell?" Jace says, not completely checked in, Jade can tell now. "The one who comes to collect the dead."

"The grim *reaper*?" Jade whispers.

In reply, Jace licks his fingers, reaches up to pinch each wick of the menorah out one by one, only his arm above the level of the counter.

It's enough.

A great hand reaches down, the fingers long enough to grab his head like an orange, and plucks him up as easy as lifting a cat. A *small* cat.

Jade falls back, her whole body flushing.

Dark Mill South is perched on the counter by the register, just behind the smoking menorah.

"Y-y-*you*," she says up to him.

He grins a broken grin down to her, his lips pulled this way and that from scar tissue, his hair lank and dark around his face, his eyes twin wells, glittering with grim joy.

The forearm past his hook hand is bloody nearly up to the elbow.

Busy times.

"He like you?" he asks, his voice practically a subwoofer, and Jade realizes that he might have never seen her, over in Terra Nova. Just Letha. Meaning he doesn't know who hammered the back of his skull in, and dropped him through the floor of a living room, then left him buried under a house, and lit it on fire.

"Alive, you mean?" she asks.

In reply, Dark Mill South uses his hook to run some of his black hair out to the side. Somehow it means "Indian."

With his other hand, he rotates Jace this way and that, inspect-ing him.

"No, he's not," Jade says. "He's not like *us*, not like you and me."

Dark Mill South fixes Jade in his glare, considers her.

"I think I need to starve them down first," he says, his voice so bass. "It'll make the skin come off better."

Jade knows she shouldn't, she hates herself for it already, this isn't her job, this is Letha's, this is Cinnamon's.

But, once again, it's all down to her, isn't it?

Goddamnit.

Fuck this place, this world, this life.

Still, "*I* haven't eaten for two days," she says, running her sleeve up so she can pinch her skin up, show how loose it is.

Dark Mill South considers this, then looks right into her eyes. Her soul.

"I've been, you know, too *busy*," she adds, reaching up slowly, to tap the back of her own head, right where she hammered him.

Dark Mill South's nostrils flare when he connects those dots.

He flings Jace away, into a spinner rack of DVDs.

Jade stands, knows she's dead already, that she's just spent her life to save some kid she doesn't even know, who could have been her brother in another life, but this isn't a thing you can do halfway, either.

Sure to keep all Dark Mill South's attention on her, she takes one long step back. And then another.

He comes down from the counter, is so light on his feet for someone his size, his bulk, and is grinning about Jade's retreat, grinning like this is how he likes it, it's good when they run, when—

A screaming comes from the darkness behind him.

He's only turned around halfway when some tall boy—not as tall as Dark Mill South, but tall for a normal human—rams him in the chest with a shiny chrome coat tree with a wide base.

It knocks Dark Mill South back a step, his rear foot taking his weight, and then… it's a UFO invasion? Bare DVDs are slinging in from the blackness, just silver lines of light, pretty much.

"No, no—" Jade hears herself say: Just *run*, get away.

These last two kids are trying to make a stand, though, bless them.

One of the DVDs catches Jade above the right eye, opens her brow up. She X's her arms up, rolls back into the aisle, still enough of a sight line on Dark Mill South to see the no-effect these desperate little discs from the future are having on him.

An annoyance at best.

He takes the coat tree base with both hands and yanks it hard to himself.

It pulls the tall boy off balance, stumbles him ahead, which is all Dark Mill South needs.

His hook hand gouges into the left side of the boy's head and his left clamps onto the kid's right wrist, and then Dark Mill South pulls, the kid tearing open where the neck meets the shoulder. Not all the way down through the chest, but enough.

Dark Mill South tosses him aside and steps ahead, the base of the coat tree weighted enough that when he dropped it, it fell standing.

He lifts it by the top, draws it back, and swings that heavy base into the darkness.

A girl goes flopping into the light, the left side of her head caved in, the fragile bones around her sinuses spilling from her mouth in a fast little river of blood—*not* bright pink or icing-blue.

"Go, go, run!" Jade stands up to scream to Jace, and any other idiots back there, lined up to sacrifice themselves.

Dark Mill South turns back to her.

"Everybody's a hero," he says, and his voice is so deep, so

bass, and the inflection, the accent, whatever, it's *Fargo*, pretty much. Which Jade only watched because she'd heard about the woodchipper bit—very *Tucker & Dale*. Or, the other way around.

And: *You're doing it again*, she tells herself.

Hiding in stupid movie shit.

When she should already be running.

Dark Mill South shrugs like letting Jade make the first move here, and Jade takes it, running for all she's worth, and—

She falls immediately. Like every girl who's ever run from a slasher.

Only, this slip, it's on one of those stupid cupcakes—what are the chances?

Just when Jade's up again, that dead kid on the wall's left arm stabs out, smears across her neck, his muscle warm, the skin of his hand cold.

Jade falls the other way, into the shelves, dislodging all of the cases that haven't fallen off already, and when she fights up from that—

He's gone. The dead kid who wasn't as dead as she thought.

"What?" she says, then flinches, sure Dark Mill South is already going to be there.

He's just watching this, though. Isn't very concerned about Jade's big getaway, it doesn't seem. More just amused by it.

"Don't look at me like that!" Jade screams to him, and turns to seriously motorvate out of here, only—so *that's* what happened to the dead kid: reaching his arm out to ride Jade away from this hellhole, he dislodged himself from the pegs or shelf supports, collapsed into the grossest tripping hazard.

Jade's hands, trying to stop her fall, squinch into his insides, and he's still warm and slimy, and something in there's even still pulsing, maybe?

All this in the sliver of a moment before Jade's face slams into his.

She rolls away, spits automatically, and what she spits, she's pretty sure, is a tooth. Not one of her own, either.

She starts to gag but there's no time for that, so, still dry-heaving, she fights halfway up again, her hand planting on this dead boy's raw shoulder, and then she plants one foot on his pelvis hard enough to feel it crack under her boot, which, with her foot functionally frozen, delivers this sensation to her in a way she knows is going to last as long as she does.

Still—she gives herself maybe five more seconds, here, before it's lights out for good.

She vaults all the DVDs that want to land her flat on her back, comes down in some stupid way that locks her knee, making her next running falling step into a hip-jamming pole vault, meaning she's off balance, falling again—

Which is the only thing that saves her.

The coat tree comes spearing through the air close enough to where her head just was that it tugs at her, sends her sprawling.

Unimpeded, the heavy base shatters the frozen front window, which is the whole front wall of the store, pretty much.

The glass hangs for a moment with a ragged hole punched through it, and then it falls and falls, Jade's spread fingers scraping through it on her continued skid. She tucks into her best approximation of a roll, so hopefully her jacket can take these shards, and what finally stops her is the ten-inch little wall under that gone window.

Giving her a perfect view on Dark Mill South, stalking down the COMEDY aisle for her.

From this low, he looms even larger.

"*No!*" Jade screams, holding her hands up because what else can she do, but then… Dark Mill South is slowing?

Jade crabs back, toward the center of the front of the store, where the door was, and she chances a look up into where the window was, which is where Dark Mill South is looking now.

Standing there, her blond hair lifting in the wind, her eyes twin points of fury, is… *Cinnamon Baker*?

"*You killed my sister*," she says into the store, to Dark Mill South, and lets the tip of the machete she's holding stand out from her leg like the worst, best promise.

No, no, you're dead, Jade tells her inside. Except she's obviously not, right? She's standing right there, larger than life, as killer as Letha Mondragon ever was. Meaning… meaning that *is* Ginger out there? Which can only mean that, that—that Ginger was impersonating her sister at the sheriff's office, after which she ran back to the truck, maybe for some big escape, for the next step in her master plan, only—

Dark Mill South.

Before walking *into* this video store, he had to be *outside* this video store, didn't he?

As for the new nicks in Ginger's scalp… at the sheriff's office, when Ginger was blasting off, maybe they'd already been there? Maybe she'd shaved her head one more time before slipping out of the nursing home? Maybe it was damage from Dark Mill South?

Maybe there's no time to *think* about it anymore?

Cinnamon Baker, the real final girl, is here now, probably delivered on the back of a history teacher's snowmobile.

It's time for the big showdown.

Between a hundred-and-twenty-pound girl and a monster of a man.

"No, no, run, *run*!" Jade screams up to Cinnamon, with her whole body. "You can't! He's too—" but Cinnamon Baker is only tuned into Dark Mill South, her eyes practically shooting cat-eyes of flame out from the side.

Because she just saw her sister dead in the snow.

This slasher is about revenge, like all of them, but it's the final girl getting it, this time. Clash of some bad-ass titans, indeed. The kind that grinds peons underfoot.

Sensing this—the inevitability of this fight—Jade falls out the broken door, lands in the snow, her nose and eyes packed with coldness.

Cinnamon Baker looks over to the comical loser Jade has to be, sliding on her ass now, the snow all the way up her sleeve, in her waistband, but who cares, this is almost over.

"*Kill the fuck out of him!*" she screams all the same, having to lean forward, her whole soul behind this.

"Who—who *are* you?" Cinnamon says down to Jade, then does a little grin, steps through the broken window and into the video store.

Who am I? Jade asks herself, not getting it.

No: Who *am* I?

Something was different about it this time, though. Something was distinctly wrong with the way Cinnamon said it. Oh, oh: the emphasis, right? She should have said, "Who—who are *you*?" like she, or Ginger, did on the yacht.

Except—she shouldn't have said anything at *all*, right?

Maybe "I've got this." Or "This is where it ends." Or even—*Predator*—"If it bleeds, we can kill it."

Except it's *Ginger* who knew movie shit, not Cinnamon. And it's *Ginger* who led off the same way in room 308W, replaying the last time they'd seen each other. And it's *Jade* who's getting lost in her head, which is asking to lose it.

She pushes away from the video store, is almost to the curb now, breathing hard.

Any moment now, Cinnamon's getting tossed out through that open window, Jade knows.

How else can it even go?

All there is left to do, really, is put some distance—

Jade stops, listens.

Behind her, up the street. It's the… the buzzing of a snowmobile, isn't it? Armitage turning around, probably.

They can—they can go get Doc Wilson now, can't they?

This can all still work out. It is, it *is* working out.

Jade stumbles out into the road to flag Armitage down, only… who the hell is it?

"Mom?" Jade says, shaking her head no.

But it is. Kimmy Daniels is riding on the back of some woman's snowmobile. A daughter knows her mother's gaunt, angular features anywhere, even in a snowstorm.

Jade looks left, like for an answer to this, which is when she's thumped forward, her mouth packing with snow again.

It's Cinnamon, flung into her. Because, of course, she only weighs as much as a cheerleader.

Jade rolls around fast, desperate, and—Dark Mill South is stepping out the gone window now, an angry red slash seeping across his chest but not slowing him down. Probably making him *faster*, even—that's how it is with slashers.

Jade turns to Cinnamon, trying to rise from the snow. Jade reaches out to give her something to hold onto, and—she hates herself for it, but she has to be sure—she unaccidentally loops her index finger around a blond tress, such that when Cinnamon's standing and Jade's backing away, she's also pulling Cinnamon's hair.

It yanks Cinnamon's head over slightly, but the hair doesn't come away.

Cinnamon doesn't even clock this, has more immediate concerns.

Her mouth is bloody now, her teeth red, and the front of her sweatshirt hoodie is cut open on the diagonal.

Behind it—Jade has to grin in appreciation.

Under that hoodie is some sort of plastic armor. BMX, motocross, hockey, she's not sure, but Cinnamon didn't come here to die, she came here to *kill*.

"You got it, you got it," Jade hisses to her, backing off herself.

Cinnamon looks over to her, her eyes narrowing in late recognition, it feels like.

"The bathroom's not even steamy," she says sort of like a question, completely in her little-girl voice, and then grins a sharp grin after, like flashing that this is a joke.

It makes Jade's scalp prickle. Probably because it had been that night, feeling the fibers of the towel it was wrapped in for the first time.

"Get them out of here?" Cinnamon says, tilting her head to Kimmy Daniels and whoever, just idling on that snowmobile now, rubbernecking whatever this is.

Jade flounders through the snow one way and Cinnamon steps ahead the other way, slipping immediately on the ice that must have formed from whoever shoveled, smushing snow into slush. In this kind of cold, though, that immediately freezes into a skating rink.

Cinnamon goes down hard on her back, and now Jade's looking between her and Kimmy Daniels, standing on the back of that snowmobile, and—

And Dark Mill South.

Who's stepping in over *Jade*, not Cinnamon, stepping over and drawing his hook hand back for the slight effort this is going to take.

Before he can do it, though, a—a brown leather purse explodes against his chest, floats receipts and gum wrappers and tissues all up around his face.

Jade looks over to her mom in wonder, her mom, who's come off the snowmobile, is rushing across the street to trade herself for her daughter, to stand between this bad man and her little girl, damn the consequences—only one consequence matters, and that's Jade.

"*Mom!*" Jade screams, holding her hand up to stop her, which is exactly when the world stops turning for an instant, for all of them.

Jade's back on one elbow, is reaching her open hand across, Dark Mill South is standing there, his hook hand still half-cocked, a yellow credit card receipt adhered to the blood on his chest, and where they're both looking is to Kimmy Daniels, and the ghostly form coalescing behind her. The wooden spikes splashing up through her chest and her throat, and out her mouth.

The perfectly white elk that just impaled her bunches his great neck muscles, lifting Kimmy Daniels off her feet.

He shakes his head, lowers his antlers, lets her slide off, then turns to the side to watch the snowmobile spinning away, folding itself and its rider into the storm.

". . . Mom?" Jade hears herself ask.

The white elk steps gingerly forward, sniffs Jade's mom's mouth then huffs that scent back out, as if insulted, or satisfied, and Jade doesn't want to, but she can't help falling back into how her mom would keep the kitchen door open in the mornings, when she was humming around the house, doing this or that. How she would scrunch her hand into the top of Jade's head and Jade would hold tight onto her leg. How she let Jade skate out the dollar store with hair dye kit after hair dye kit all through high school, until it felt like she was working there just so Jade could steal back everything she was owed.

"Mom..." Jade says again, and now this stupid white elk is studying *her*, and smelling her, or trying to, his great head raised to a certain tendril of air.

Jade pushes back, the snow plowing up behind her, and what stops her is Dark Mill South's solid, solid knee—exactly what she knew was going to happen two minutes earlier, in the video store.

She looks up and up to him, tracks where he's looking: the elk, still. He's casting his blue eyes back up Main, toward the lake, hearing something only he can hear, and then he trots off that direction, the storm taking him back into itself.

And now—Jade can feel it—Dark Mill South is looking down at her, as if the vision that elk was, that *killing* was, has somehow opened a door for him, too.

"Who even are you?" Jade says up to him.

Before Dark Mill South can answer with a hook moving at however fast his chest muscles can swing it, there's a scream like Jade's only heard once, when Letha did it over in Terra Nova—a death cry. The kind that tears your mouth open, so your spirit can claw up, take this fight.

It's Cinnamon Baker.

She's pulled a shovel up from somewhere, the bed of Banner's truck maybe, who cares where it's from, and she's holding it before her like a *pike*, is running hell for leather at Dark Mill South, and she's screaming the whole way.

Jade scrabbles sideways as best she can, out of this, and… and Dark Mill South is clocking this attack with eyes that have seen it all before.

"No," Jade says.

That Dark Mill South doesn't raise a hand to stop this is a bad sign, the worst sign.

He lets Cinnamon give that shovel all her cheerleader weight, all her high school senior momentum.

The blade stops at Dark Mill South's hard upper stomach, right under the sternum, and it does make him take a half-step back, but it doesn't open him up, it doesn't carve him back to the spine like Cinnamon was counting on.

When he takes the shovel by the head, Jade sees why: it's one of those flat ones, for gravel.

And, the other end, now…

Dark Mill South gives the shovel a sharp flick to free it of Cinnamon's hands, then jabs a quick thrust with the rounded handle, catching Cinnamon right in the hollow of the throat.

Jade surges forward, but… what is there to do?

Cinnamon's falling, fallen, is clutching at her throat, can't breathe, maybe ever again.

Dark Mill South steps in, but stops at—something.

His eyes on Cinnamon, he kneels, digs his hand in the snow, and Jade is one *thousand* percent certain he's about to come up with the machete.

It's Ginger Baker.

"Hmph," Jade's pretty sure she hears Dark Mill South grunt. Like a question.

He latches onto Ginger's shoulder and lifts her up to a sitting position, so she's facing east up Main, to the highway.

What Dark Mill South seems to be looking at is her face. He turns it left and right, and stops when the screwdriver rolls into view. He considers it for maybe three seconds and then turns her again, so she's looking with her dead eyes at Cinnamon, spasming, still trying to stand, trying to fight.

Dark Mill South grins, nods.

The next thing is one Jade's seen, but it was only ever movie stupidity, was only ever slashers feeding the fanbase the ridiculousness it craves: Dark Mill South drops Ginger back into the snow as if done with her, but then his left hand comes up holding both her ankles as one.

He jerks her forward, to him, and slings her around once like the hammer throw, then twice, really getting this inertia going, and on the third time around he slams Ginger into Cinnamon, like swinging for the highway.

They both crash into the tailgate of the truck, Banner's aftermarket bumper catching Ginger hard in the back, so she folds the wrong way around, the *crack* wet and somehow mealy.

Cinnamon's face shatters the taillight, exposing its reflective innards, the tight shards holding her up by the jaw and chin for a moment, until the plastic gives, and she slumps down on top of her sister.

She doesn't rise.

The tailgate the rest of her body hit, jarred just right, falls open over her with a heavy clank, like it can keep the snow off.

As if that matters anymore.

Dark Mill South chuckles in appreciation, seems to have gotten what he needed from that little stunt. He steps forward to finish it, to *really* mash them together maybe, crush them back into a single egg, but now that buzzing the white elk evidently heard is whirring in fast.

Dark Mill South looks up just in time to step away from the snowmobile coming for him, but not fast enough to avoid the line of red that driver opens across his torso, this cut crossing the one Cinnamon made, like now he's had coup counted on him *twice*.

"*Armitage!*" Jade screams, falling to her knees again.

Dark Mill South falls back, his left hand clutching this pain he's been dealt, his eyes never leaving this receding snowmobiler.

Forty yards down, Armitage carves the snowmobile around and stands on the footboards, the engine puttering evenly, healthily, that wicked little scythe curving up from his right hand like the worst, best erection.

He holds it up in victory, his right knee coming up with his arm a bit, and it makes Jade flash on the end of *Breakfast Club* again, John Bender's fist raised in victory—that movie imprinted on him deep, she guesses.

Armitage settles back down onto the long seat and throttles up, and Jade doesn't care what movie's playing in his head, does she? So long as he can keep cutting.

The snowmobile surges forward, throwing a roostertail of snow, and now Armitage is a jouster, a knight, his buzzing steed raring up.

Enough cuts like that little scythe can deal, and even Dark Mill South has to fall.

Doesn't he?

"Go, go," Jade's pretty much chanting, Dark Mill South still on his knees, trying to hold himself together.

Armitage speeds up at the end, half-standing, the scythe held high and back, and manages to just slither out of the hook Dark Mill South tries to snag him with.

Another line of deep red opens on Dark Mill South, this time on his side, and deep enough that his left hand automatically tries to hold it shut.

He's on one knee now, and when he stands, he slips, probably on the ice Banner's truck pressed, or that got left from when Jade and Banner came this way earlier, to collect Doc Wilson. Dark Mill South's bloody left hand stabs down into the deep snow to keep his face from planting, and more of that beautiful red slips down his side.

Yes, Jade says about that.

This can be like how *Jason Goes to Hell* starts: with Jason Voorhees in the spotlights at last, being cut to ribbons by that SWAT team.

Only, when Dark Mill South rocks back, getting his balance, no longer needing his left arm to hold him up, what his left *hand* comes up with is, is…

"Can't be," Jade says.

There's no denying it, though: it's the pistol Banner lost.

And never mind that Dark Mill South only has one hand, and that that one hand is his left—he expertly checks the mag, slaps it back in on his thigh, then uses the flat of his hook to cock the slide back, is one hundred percent ready for an action movie.

"*But you're a slasher!*" Jade yells across to him, like she's talking up to the screen in a movie theater.

It's loud enough to get his attention.

He looks through his hair at her and she shrinks back, trying to make herself a smaller shooting dummy. But definitely *some* kind of dummy: before, with his hook, and the snow, it would take him a few bad seconds to get to her. Banner's pistol changes that for the worse. Now he can reach her at hundreds of feet per second.

Does he not know the rules, though? Slashers aren't into guns. One of the papers she wrote for Mr. Holmes, even, back in the days of extra credit, was how the reason bullets never can take the slasher down is that they're not in the gun economy at all, are far outside it, like there's some unspoken deal in place: I won't use you, you can't hurt me.

Dark Mill South should know this at an instinctual level. He's got a hook hand, after all! He might as well be lurking around down at lovers' lane, where you don't shoot people Zodiac-style, Son of Sam–style, you eviscerate them, you hang them up above cars.

Freddy never uses a gun, does he? Ghostface? Michael? Jade can't even imagine Michael Myers using a gun. They're so impersonal, so "all at once" instead of "one at a time." Jason Voorhees? C'mon. He'll use a *spear*gun, sure, but that's just for a 3-D gag. No, any self-respecting slasher finding a pistol in his hand, what he's supposed to do is look down at it like it's a strange bug, then shake his hand until this bitey, attention-drawing thing is gone again.

Not Dark Mill South.

Instead of stabbing a line of flame across into Jade's forehead, he turns back to this snowmobile diving back at him.

If Armitage realizes his target's armed, then he's braver than Jade thought, because he just keeps buzzing in, that short little scythe raised behind him for another dramatic slash—he's the one slaloming through a slasher fantasy, isn't he?

Dark Mill South waits until he's about two storefronts down to unload—*Bam! Bam! Bam!*

Main Street is volley after volley of ear-splitting thunder, loud enough that a lot of the snow that's found a way to hold onto the windows calves off, so it's like the whole street is melting around them. Which only makes Dark Mill South seem taller.

By the time Jade's able to focus in on the zigging and zagging Armitage, the right shoulder of his puffy white jacket is spurting its whiteness up in a little plume that must be feathers.

It spurts red a moment later, and Armitage, either collapsing or avoiding, yanks the front skids over hard enough that they catch in the deep snow, vault him up into the sky in what feels to Jade like the slowest slow motion—slow enough that Dark Mill South is still firing, trying to bring this unlikely bird down to earth.

One of the shots catches Armitage in his right arm, it looks like, and spins him around mid-air so that when he lands, it's on his chin.

The snow swallows him so completely it's as if he never was.

Jade can see Dark Mill South still pulling that trigger, but since she's not hearing anything, that must mean he's empty, that all of Banner's rounds have been fired.

Instead of tossing the pistol to the side like the bad guys usually do, though, Dark Mill South reaches behind him, tucks it into his waistband, then remembers Jade.

He lowers the mangled plane of his face as if tipping his head to her, telling her that this next dance, it's hers, how about that?

Jade feels it in the base of her jaw, the pit of her stomach.

And she's already running, running *away*, running downhill, which is towards the lake.

When the ground seems to shake behind her, all around her, she knows that Dark Mill South is on her heels, is *running*, which is also fucking undignified for a slasher. He's not following *any* of the rules, is he?

Jade hates the whole "falling while running away"–thing, too, especially since she's already done it once or three times in the video store, but she can't help it. The snow's deep, she's in some state of panic two steps past anything she thought she could be, she can pretty much already feel a hook reaching into her throat to pull her windpipe forward, share its glistening whiteness with the open air, and then, then—

The ground really *is* shaking.

Looking behind her, because Dark Mill South has to be right on her, Jade falls one more time, tangling up with what's left of Armitage, but in the last moment before the snow powders up around her again, she sees, she sees… it's not Dark Mill South making Main Street tremble.

It's that rusty huge trash truck of a snowplow he came to town in, bearing down on *him*, throwing probably tons of snow to the side all at once, that snow blowing out every window on the north side of the street.

Behind the wheel is Deputy Banner fucking Tompkins, a grimy bottle of something hopping on the dashboard in front of him, which he has to fling out of the way, exactly like the T-800 swiping a windshield to the side in a truck the same size as this one.

Banner shifts up, a great gout of black exhaust coughing up

from the pipes, and his monstrous huge blade catches Kimmy Daniels, flings her out to the side along with all this snow, her back breaking on a lamppost, which thankfully Jade doesn't have to hear forever in her sleep, since the scrape and thunder of the snowplow is filling her head and her chest.

She grabs onto Armitage and rolls to the side with him as much as she can, hopefully out of the way, then prairie-dogs up just in time to see that it's too *late* for Dark Mill South to dive out of the way—Banner's blade has to be two cars wide, at least, and coming fast. And? Blades are the only thing that can ever put a slasher down, aren't they?

This is all working out.

Until Dark Mill South jumps up, snags his hook onto the *top* of that tall blade.

His tree-trunk legs instantly fly to the side with all the snow shooting out that way, and Jade's hypnotized enough by this that she forgets which side of the street she's on.

She's reminded an instant later, when the truck blasts Armitage into her. Along with what must be thousands of pounds of snow, moving at the speed of some serious-ass bullshit.

It pastes her to the wall of a storefront, and when she falls down, blind, deaf, stinging, snow sliding down all around, it's onto something soft, something groaning and convulsing: Armitage.

Jade wants to tell him they made it, they made it, they shouldn't have, but they *did*, but, first, she can't breathe yet, second, her mouth is packed tight with snow, and third, her eyes are too full of crying for her to even be able to form words anyway.

Banner Tompkins, former linebacker, one hundred percent idiot, husband of the woman Jade secretly considers her best friend, he did it, he did the impossible.

And, somewhere down Main, he's… still doing it?

Jade stands, unsteady on her feet, and stumbles out into the street just in time to see the big snowplow crashing through the parking lot, surely blind from the snow it's throwing, and then—then…

It's too heavy for the pier, can't drive down it like Cross Bull Joe did so many years ago, so that great blade plows *into* the pier, the posts and planks arcing up over the truck and hanging in the grey-white sky. Jade watches that ejecta for a body, for a killer, for a slasher, but it's too fast, there's too much. And the snowplow isn't stopping, *can't* stop, is through the pier now, the frozen lake sending walloping thunderous *cracks* out every which direction, like it's in a panic itself.

Maybe a second after that, the truck finds the dark water under the ice.

It keeps going, its weight making it ride the slope down, ride the lake bed, until only the very back corner of the dump-bed is cocked up out of the water, the front tires probably hanging over what used to be a cliff, back before Proofrock.

Jade starts to run to the lake but stops: Armitage. She bounces on her toes with indecision, but finally goes back to him, situates him against the wall as well as she can, so maybe somebody can find him—there's frothy blood drooling from his mouth—and then she's running, falling every few steps, calling Banner's name ahead of her, a thing she would never in a hundred years have thought she might be doing.

Halfway across the parking lot, she finds him on his knees in the snow, one side of his face scraped raw, his left hand shattered in his glove.

She hugs him around the neck so hard they both fall, and she keeps hugging him, doesn't ever want to let go, never-ever.

Finally, the world quiet again, he sits them up, holding his left hand at that height you hold throbbing pieces of yourself.

"You did it, you did it," she's telling him.

The same as the last one, Stacey Graves, got buried in the lake, so does this next one share that same grave, now. Ezekiel's probably already got Dark Mill South by the ankle, to pull him down and down, because that holy choir down in Drown Town, it needs a baritone after all these years.

"Doc Wilson wasn't there," Banner's saying. "Just that… Abby Grandlin. And she's…"

He doesn't need to finish, Jade can hear it: she's *dead*. Left behind on the gym floor.

"Letha's tough, she'll make it," Jade says, about Doc Wilson being missing in action.

"Her shoulder won't stop bleeding…" Banner says, then his whole body stiffens, and he's guiding Jade behind him. But it's just Hardy, struggling through the snow toward them, that long shotgun strapped across his chest. Jade guesses what just happened to the pier must have been *loud*, probably has all of Proofrock opening their front doors.

"What do you think they'll call this one?" Banner asks with a sick chuckle.

It's better than crying, sort of. It's putting it off, anyway.

"The Tribute Killer," Jade says matter-of-factly.

"Like a tribute *band*?" Banner says, peeling out of his long black jacket and wrapping Jade's shivering self with it, one-handed.

"Except for movies," Jade says, accepting this unasked-for warmth for once in her life. "Letha will tell you when she… when she can. And it wasn't really him, either." She chins out in the direction of the lake. To Dark Mill South.

"But he was—"

"It wasn't *all* him," Jade corrects. "He was just, back there"—the video store—"I don't think he killed them. I mean, not all of them."

"Then who?" Banner asks, then answers himself, hesitantly, "*Ginger*, you mean?"

Jade shrugs a reluctant yes, says, "Sometimes it is who you think it is."

"Why does this keep happening?" Banner asks.

"I used to pray for it to," Jade says, her tears sputtering out again, goddamnit.

"It was high school," Banner says, taking the top of her hand in his unbroken one. "We were all stupid, right? We didn't know what we wanted, we just knew… that this"—Proofrock—"wasn't it."

Jade nods, keeps nodding. It's one way to keep your crying down.

Hardy's maybe ten yards closer. The shotgun is awkward, evidently heavy.

"I should help him," she says, hauling herself around for Hardy. Banner stands, pulls her up.

"I need to—" he says, tilting his head to the station: Letha, Adrienne.

"Get the coffee machine in there going?" Jade says.

"You wish," Banner says, already a step away.

Jade flips him off, which is as close as they can come to anything real, and then: "Sheriff!" she's saying, trying to wade across to Hardy all at once, because the strap of the shotgun's gotten itself cinched on the right handle of his walker somehow, and he's about to fall forward.

But… it's not because of the shotgun.

It's because he's got his right hand lifted, is pointing to the lake.

Jade and Banner both look, they can't *not* look, and—

No.

Dark Mill South is walking across the ice, his hair frozen to his face, his chest rising and falling with anger. He just tilted against a dumptruck, and *won*.

"Shit, shit," Banner says.

"Go, go now," Hardy says to him, waving Banner back, behind him. Behind him and the shotgun he's working up, the long barrel plowing through the deep snow.

Except Jade's to him, is trying to turn him around.

Which he's not having one little bit of.

"You go too," he tells her. "I'll never make it in time. Look at me."

He's right, Jade knows he's right.

But still.

"Sheriff, you can't, I—I *need* you," she says, her arms around him. "My mom, she's—I already lost— I can't lose you too, you're the only one left who… who—"

"*It's just birdshot in there!*" Banner calls out, already wading away, to his wife, his child, his life.

Hardy looks down to the shotgun, shakes his head like oh well.

"I already told you," he says to Jade, "*go*," his eyes never moving from Dark Mill South, and Jade can read it on her old sheriff's face. The Lake Witch Slayings were on *his* watch.

This is his chance to make up for that.

"You *can't*," Jade tells him, pulling, but he's solid on that walker.

"Come on, come on, for *Letha*," Banner says, standing a few yards away, holding his good hand out.

Jade tells herself to let Hardy go, but her fingers aren't listening, are still clutching the woolly lapels of his old man jacket.

"Sheriff…" she's still saying, pleading, crying.

"*Go!*" Hardy tells her again, his voice harder now, gruffer, in charge again, and she finally does, and it's less like walking, more like collapsing. Banner meets her halfway and they're stumbling to the station, Banner holding her up each time she tries to fall from looking back to Hardy.

She doesn't want to see what's going to happen to him. He's going to have to let Dark Mill South get so close if the birdshot's going to do anything.

Jade shakes her head no, she can't let him do this, and—

She rips away from Banner, falls hard in the snow, is already running, back *into* Proofrock, right up Main, the heavy black coat dragging in the snow but never quite tangling her legs all the way up.

"*Jade!*" Banner booms behind her, using every bit of his cop voice.

It doesn't work any better than Hardy's ever did.

Jade just shakes her head no, is a snowplow herself now, fighting through, pushing her numb legs, reaching back into the past, for, for—

She falls into the line of hedges a few feet out from the post office and digs, digs, digs.

She comes up with her old litter stick.

The one with that sharp, grabby point on the end.

"*I'm coming, sir!*" she screams across the parking lot to Hardy, loud enough that he actually looks back.

Because she's running the path the real snowplow carved, it's faster now, and downhill. She commits to it, completely out of control, no chance to stop even if there *was* traction, but she's not going to stop, she's not going to stop until Dark Mill South is, is—

She's holding the litter stick clamped tight to her side like a lance, the dull butt forward, and, maybe ten steps out, Dark Mill South clocks this, and grins one side of his mouth wide enough that Jade can see how perfect his new teeth still are.

He's leaning on Melanie's bench, but, special for Jade, he pushes away to take this blunt impact the same as he took the unsharp leading edge of Cinnamon's shovel, even going so far as to hold his great arms out to the side.

Only, at the last moment, with her last step, Jade flips this handle around, twirling the litter stick at her hip so the *sharp* end plunges not just into Dark Mill South, but *through* him.

It's exactly what she tried to do to her father once upon a July Fourth massacre, but couldn't.

It draws her face inches from Dark Mill South's, so that when she screams and can't stop screaming, it's right into his open mouth. Her scream comes back at her, along with his hot, oddly clean breath.

And his big left hand, wrapping around her throat.

Jade's vision constricts along with her breathing, but instead of trying to claw his vise-grip of a hand down, she wrenches hard on the litter stick, trying to nudge it into some part of him he actually needs, the *human* part of him that has to be in there somewhere.

Behind her, she thinks she can hear Hardy, booming something—his voice, not the shotgun—but that world, it's already falling away, it's already slipping back into the blackness seeping in all around.

Jade can't even scream, doesn't have the air to.

Killing a slasher, it comes at a price, doesn't it?

In the movies, you get to walk out into dawn breaking over this reclaimed serenity, some Gale Weathers packaging the night's horror into a proper lead-in, but in real life… in real life, you don't just push the slasher over the edge, into death. In real life, he stabs a hand back up, takes you with him.

Jade's chest jerks, her lungs clawing for air that isn't there, and she puts all the weight she has into that litter stick, angling it up and up until—

It's over.

Blip.

Nothing.

Just a velvet, sort of thrushing softness, either like she's really-really small, is just some hopeful maggot wriggling across the deep, soft face of some giant flock-velvet painting, or else the painting itself is vast, and on this side of things you don't need arms or legs anymore, you just have to keep wriggling ahead.

Maybe somewhere in these soft black stalks there will be another maggot, too. They'll nudge blindly into each other, and for a moment neither will be alone, both will be part of something bigger, and a warmth will suffuse up and down the two of them, and—

Yes, that, please, Jade says inside, already wriggling the body she still has in anticipation, and that side-to-side action makes the litter stick finally find the off switch deep inside Dark Mill South.

He falls back and back, his slowing-down mouth and last breath shaping what sounds like *Pater noster, qui es in caelis* in a rhythm Jade can almost clock, and he keeps on saying it, but the words are hardly making it past his lips now. All Jade can tell of them, it's that it's an apology. The kind you make when you're… afraid?

Of dying?

His massive hand lets her windpipe go, and she gasps the air that's probably his dying breath.

Jade breathes in deep, and it's cold enough to burn her lungs but that doesn't matter, she can't quit pulling more and more in. It's the best thing ever and also the worst.

She rolls to the side, into the snow, is nestled up to Dark Mill South now, her hands up under her face, her eyes only open so she doesn't lose herself. Slowly, like a thing alive, having to bulge and try before soaking into each next cell, each next hollow, Dark Mill South's blood stains the snow around them into a spilled cherry slurpee, the same bright icing-red as in the video store, and Jade can feel her chest heaving with something between relief and hilarity, but a distinct regret, too, that she never got to see the design painted on that velvet painting she had been caught in with her mother.

But she knows, too: it was a map of Indian Lake, wasn't it? Proofrock on one side, Terra Nova on the other. Camp Blood halfway around, Drown Town out there in the middle.

This is her life.

She closes her mouth because her teeth are freezing, sucks air in through her nose now. It chills her sinuses, but she's thankful to be able to do it.

Minutes or hours later, the creak and smush Jade's been distantly aware of turns into Hardy on his walker, coming in as fast as he can.

Jade sits up, her arms hooking around her knees.

Hardy studies Dark Mill South, nudges him with the barrel of the shotgun, his finger on the trigger the whole while.

"He's gone," Jade says.

Hardy has to agree. "Wish Bear were here to see this," he says, looking out across the ice.

Jade bites her lips, has to blink fast, and sneaks a look up into the sky. Because she might see Mr. Holmes up there, buzzing around in his sky go-cart.

Hardy lifts his walker, plants it alongside Jade, for her to climb, and falls back onto his daughter's memorial bench.

By the time Jade's up, Hardy's cleared a place for her to sit.

She collapses beside him.

"Your neck's bruising," he says across to her.

"And I don't guess you're getting any younger," Jade says back to him.

He plants his left hand on her knee, shakes her whole leg.

"We're Brody and Hooper," she tells him.

"We're sure as hell something," Hardy says, and works his pack up from his chest pocket, shakes a smoke out for Jade, then takes one himself.

When his old fingers can't get his match going, Jade takes over, lights hers, then lights his off of hers.

"Jennifer goddamn Daniels," Hardy finally says.

"It's Jade, sir," Jade says back, and breathes all the corruption in her lungs out.

Well, not the blackness, she supposes.

Not the horror.

Never that.

SLASHER 102

Hope you don't mind me calling this penultimate paper that, Mr. Armitage. As Edmund Leach says, history tends to sacrifice totality in the interest of continuity, and of course you get the continuity I'm reaching for with a title like that. Who wouldn't want to stand alongside the girl finally able to take Dark Mill South down?

And, yes, I mourn with you that your cellphone was lost on that fateful day, all its irreplaceable footage going with it, but I would be remiss if I didn't tell you that a custodian of Henderson High and Golding Elementary is rumored to have a certain recording from December—I phrase it vaguely because slander is a concern, here. While nothing can replace your recordings, of course, still, the tangible is to be trusted more than our collective memory, is it not? While history is never certain, is always narrative, artifacts can and do make their arbitrary way into the future, don't they?

Supposedly, this particular artifact is going for seventy-five dollars.

But, the topic of the day: theories surrounding Dark Mill South's demise.

Preview, Mr. Armitage: they've all adapted to include Jennifer Daniels.

First and perhaps most obvious, was she able to succeed where the federal government and state authorities and a long line of victims before her had failed because, of them all, she was the only one to have previously encountered such a killer? Did her participation in the Independence Day Massacre imbue her with a special insight, or aptitude?

To this I say… not likely. Granted, it takes determination and grit and no small amount of luck to survive one killer, much less two, but, if we allow this dynamic (previous encounters not counting as "experience," but something more magical), then wouldn't the military have already discovered and harnessed it? There would be snipers who are incapable of missing, wouldn't there be? Granted, extending this possibility borders on the ridiculous, but, as you've told us, it's at the extreme where theories show their true colors.

Second, and less obvious: remember Sally Chalumbert, the Sho-shone woman who took Dark Mill South down for the first time? The common assumption about how she was able to do that is that her Native American status granted her dueling privileges with Dark Mill South, himself Native American. Jennifer Daniels, then, also being of Native American extraction, would be similarly privileged—according to this theory.

However, to extend this, wouldn't each task force assigned to track and apprehend killers need to then be as varied in ethnicity as a children's cartoon? One rabbit, one aardvark, one turtle, and so on, just because the killer could be a rabbit, an aardvark, a turtle. As history has taught us, of course, this is never the case. Police forces are by and large as Caucasian as you or I, and they have been for decades now, if not centuries. And none of them have had any problems with their lynchings, their burnings, or the consequences of those acts.

Yes, there is a certain elegance to both Jennifer Daniels and Dark Mill South being Native American, but, if anything, this should be celebrated, not reduced to an explanation—celebrated because the Native American population has evidently recovered enough that, in a remote hideaway like Proofrock, Idaho, there can be two Native Americans, not just one.

The third theory I find, Mr. Armitage, I hesitate to even commit to email. That "DM South" birth certificate from my earlier submission? The one that never actually says "Dark" or "Mill," those names coming instead from a memory extracted from a Leech Lake tribal member over the course of an interview of questionable integrity? I never mentioned where it was found, as it wasn't pertinent, then.

It matters now, Mr. Armitage. At least on the internet.

That birth certificate was recovered from the Morris Industrial School for Indians, in—you guessed it—Minnesota. Though most of the students enrolled in this residential school (current sentiment, which I subscribe to, would prefer "abducted to") were from the Turtle

Mountain band, there were of course children from many of the other surrounding reservations and communities—including Leech Lake.

The Morris Industrial School for Indians was, like many such boarding schools, run by religious concerns. In this case, the Sisters of Mercy (Catholic). Conditions were, as was common then, regrettable, and often punitive. Hardly America's proudest moment. But such is an attempted genocide.

So, if Dark Mill South actually is the "DM South" from Morris's records, then corollary to that is the distinct possibility that he was repeatedly disciplined by those nuns, thereby programming him, in a sense, to "submit" to their authority, the idea on the internet being that inside every (male) serial killer is a scared little boy, ready to repeat the prayer he's been forced to memorize, on threat of more and more extreme punishments, up to and including privation, starvation, and various forms of sexual abuse.

While fine as far as internet theories go, where the threshold for acceptance has more to do with entertainment and unlikeliness than with anything verifiable or even possible, the problem here is that Dark Mill South was never heard to utter anything even vaguely religious. Neither did Jennifer Daniels don a nun's habit and black robes in order to dial him back to being a scared little boy—how would she know to?

This theory is as unlikely as the one that posits that the reason she was able to take Dark Mill South down had everything to do with the composition of the staff she impaled him with: evidently Native Americans, being pre-modern, are supposed to be susceptible to implements composed of materials they don't know to ward themselves against. In this case, fiberglass.

We can take none of these seriously, Mr. Armitage.

If anything empowered Jennifer Daniels to dispatch him, I submit that it was neither magic nor fate nor shared genetics, it was simply that, in the absence of a father, she had come to claim former sheriff Angus Hardy as that for her, and so would do whatever necessary to protect him, up to and including taking on a mountain of a man, and winning.

I say this as someone who lost her own father, Mr. Armitage. I know personal appeals in formal work are the definition of unscholarly, but neither can I deny that, given the chance, I think all of us fatherless daughters would hope to have even a tenth of Jennifer Daniels's resolve, sir. Just a flicker of the fire raging in her.

But, of course, as you now know, that doesn't mean that it all worked out for her.

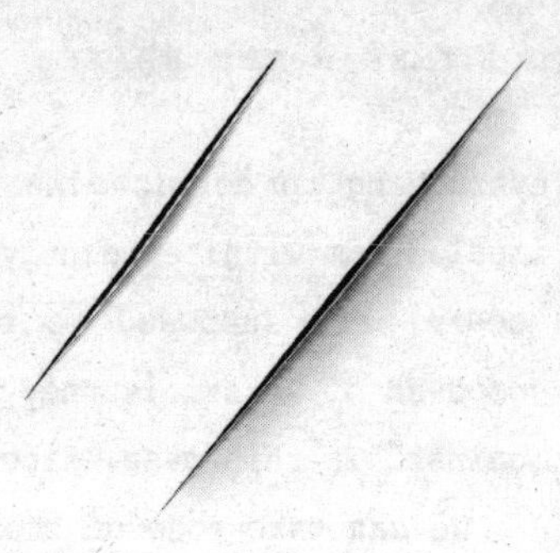

JUST BEFORE DAWN

Galatea Pangborne can't stop thinking about Toby Manx, dead yesterday.

First his father, the principal, and now *him*?

Gal can still see him jogging around the gym twice with the team before each basketball game, his stride so easy, his embarrassed grin so natural. His big sister, Bethany, is down at college, Gal's heard, trying to get far away enough from Proofrock that she won't have to think about it anymore. Her little brother being dead probably won't help with that.

As for the other one who died, Gwen… *Stapleton*, yeah, Gal thinks she must be new to Henderson High. Probably just showed up this year.

At least Cinn lucked through whatever happened at the motel, right? But of course Cinn would find a way through. She's the one who found Gal and Gin in the closet on the yacht that night, and told them to come with her if they wanted to live, her eyes so hot they were practically steaming.

Before that moment, Letha had always been Gal's hero, her model.

That changed when Cinn curled her lip at her sister, too scared to move, and then pulled Gal up and away, into the massacre proper, where that construction worker was for some reason waiting.

There are fighters in the world and there are floaters, right?

Cinn's a fighter, a doer, a survivor.

Hell yes she was able to make it through whatever meatgrinder was chewing seniors up down at Trail's End.

Which doesn't mean Gal hasn't touched Cinn's face on her phone eighty times since lunch, trying to bring her voice through, to reassure her that everything's going to be okay. That the meatgrinder hasn't caught up with her yet. That Gal brought her the best and warmest—and most stylish—ski outfit.

And no way is Cinn still giving her statement thirty hours after the motel, no statement is that detailed, but… it's not like Gal can go drag her home from the sheriff's, either—not like Cinn would *let* herself be dragged away. What did Abraham Lincoln say? Something like—yeah, yeah: "The chords of memory will swell when touched again by the better angels of our nature." Cinnamon Baker *is* that better angel, and she probably won't sleep until she's faced down whoever did that to Toby, her latest crush.

The real reason Gal can't go collect Cinn, though, is Donna Pangborne—Mom. Not only is there some bad actor out there carving through the student body, well, through *two* student bodies anyway, but there's also the ghost of Stacey Graves, who's *more* than real to Donna Pangborne. On top of all that, since Cinn's… "misjudgment," there's *another* predator out there, Gal knows. One who likes to, say, have his office hours late in the day, when the school's empty.

One who has a taste for the young stuff, which Gal supposes she must, technically, be.

But making those office hours one too many times didn't permanently chink Cinn's armor, did it? It didn't tarnish it at all, as far as Gal's concerned. She's still her larger-than-life self, always ready to smile and lend a hand, overcommitting herself to this cause, that effort. Prom committee? Sure. Yearbook staff? Of course. Cheerleading and volleyball? Why not.

Cinnamon Baker can do it all.

Unlike her sister.

But the less said about Ginger Baker, the better.

Still, Cinn's there twice a week to spend time with her, keep her head shaved like she likes it, keep an hour or two of memories burbling, about the way it used to be, before... before that night on the yacht.

The one time Gal went to see Ginger in her room, to see if a familiar, *non*-sisterly face would prompt the response re-creating their big swim across the lake was supposed to have—nope—what she left with was the feeling that there was a wildness in Ginger Baker now. That she'd gone into the woods, but she hadn't come all the way out yet, and maybe never would.

But Cinn, god. First, like Gin, she's the spitting image of her mom, Macy Todd, even has her height, those cheekbones, that forever spill of golden-blond hair, but inside she's all Mars Baker, like her eyes are X-rays, her mind a steel trap. When she looks at you, it's always for about a tenth of a second too long, like she's caught something inside you that you're not even aware of yet. And she's not sure this is the right time to tell you about it.

Gal worships her.

Letha's fine, Letha's great, Black Wonder Woman is alive and well in Proofrock, Idaho, but Cinn, at seventeen—not married, not a mom—is someone a freshman can *aspire* to.

On top of all that, on top of all she does and is, Cinn even finds it in herself to be casually kind, compassionate, caring, as if her happiness is dependent on the happiness of those around her.

Which is why Gal, when she stands for the kitchen, picks her mom's saucer and mug up, says, "More?"

"I couldn't, thanks," Donna Pangborne says, not looking away from the television screen.

They probably shouldn't be running it, but this generator is strong enough for two houses, and they're only really using one room's worth of electricity. And, this isn't some stupid singing competition they're watching over broadcast. It's the ongoing story about that killer who was being transported up the mountain to Montana, and what might have happened to his convoy.

It's all speculation at the moment, as no reports are coming in from the highway—none the journalists have access to anyway—but Gal can tell from the way her mom keeps drawing her breath in that there's reason for concern.

That's why Gal's going to the kitchen in the first place: to try to dial Cinn up.

When she gets there, though, the leftover hot chocolates deposited in the sink, there's no signal, of course. Just like the living room.

Gal looks back to the idea of the couch, her mom perched on the very front of it, not exactly holding a stopwatch over Gal's return. Taking advantage of this inattention, Gal slips out of her house boots, tiptoes upstairs.

Their house is already high for Proofrock, so if there's signal they should be getting it, but… higher's better, right? If only one tower's still functional, then maybe one high corner of the house will be better than another corner.

Like she can logic signal into her phone, yeah.

That doesn't mean she isn't going to try, though.

She stops on her floor, stands outside her door waiting for just a single bar to appear. When it doesn't, she keeps climbing, goes past her mom's level—the house is tall but narrow, almost spindly, kind of has a Victorian feel even though it's completely modern—and finally ends up in what her mom calls the attic, where the "madwoman" lives: Cinn.

The reason her mom funs Cinn about being that madwoman is that she never says no to a commitment. Though, Gal's noted, since the Incident That Didn't Matter, that nobody should have even known about, or talked about, or believed, her mom's backed off the "madwoman" stuff somewhat. Maybe next week it'll be some other Charlotte Brontë joke.

Gal stands in the tight hall between Cinn's bedroom and her custom bathroom, and... it's not that she hasn't been up here before, but, with the lights off like this, she can feel it more than ever: she *knows* this tightness.

It's the yacht all over, isn't it?

It straightens Gal's back, almost elicits a shiver, even though that night is four years behind them already.

Still, though. Her last good memory from before is of Cinn and Gin waking her that night, one of their hands already cupped over Gal's mouth, so she wouldn't Alert the Parents.

That was always Prime Objective One.

Prime Objective *Two* that night had been significantly gigglier: Cinn and Gin led Gal down to their floor, down the long hall past their parents' bedroom, past Letha's bedroom, past the scuba closet, as they called it, to… the bathroom? Seriously?

"What?" Gal said.

"Look," either Cinn or Gin said, pushing the door open.

It was probably going to be something gross, Gal knew. A used rubber again. Something bloody—please, no.

It was hair.

"Who?" Gal had asked in wonder, stepping into this darkness.

Either Cinn or Gin, thrilled beyond words, just shrugged.

If they didn't talk, Gal could never tell them apart, which brought them endless satisfaction.

Whoever had cut their hair in this bathroom, *all* of their hair it looked like, had tried to clean it up, Gal could tell. But they'd cleaned it up like you would in second grade, which was pretty much not at all—it just made it more obvious.

Behind the single faucet of the sink, there was even a hank of…

"*Blue?*" Gal whispered, just as thrilled as the twins now.

They were practically hovering with excitement: nobody on the yacht had *blue* hair!

There was black too, though. Gal rolled it between her thumb and index finger and it was dry enough to rasp, but greasy too.

"Here," either Cinn or Gin said, offering, of all things, an actual magnifying glass.

Gal, hesitant, inspected the hair she was holding, and the split ends had split ends.

Not only did nobody on the yacht have blue hair, but everybody had access to the best conditioners. Even Cinn and Gin's dad, whose incipient baldness nobody ever-ever talked about.

"Who is it?" Gal asked.

"Let's see!" one of them said, and that was how the investigation began. The one that had them on separate search missions on the lowest deck when the screams and thumps and gun blasts started. Had they not been on The Case of the Blue-Haired Intruder that night?

Then they're in their beds on the upper decks.

And then they're torn out of them.

Gal, standing in the madwoman's attic, makes herself squeeze her eyes shut for a long ten count, to prove to herself she's safe, that nothing's going to get her, pull her back into the darkness again.

When it doesn't, when she's paid her dues, she opens her eyes, expecting the trade to be complete, for there to now be at least *two* bars on her phone.

None.

She sags.

"Gal?" she can hear her mom calling from way downstairs.

"Just one minute!" Gal calls back, leaning back to use the stairway as a funnel for her voice.

Since the blackout, they've each been using the bathroom with the door left open, because that feels somehow safer. So, she tries to cant her voice up like she's sitting primly on a toilet.

Speaking of…

Gal leans back to look into Cinn's bathroom. Which is why Cinn chose this small bedroom at the top of the house: the master-size bathroom, duh. Which—Gal imagines Cinn pirouetting across the floor en pointe, like a princess in a Disney movie.

Moving through it to the high window over the shower, which faces the highway?

That is the highest point of the house Gal can possibly hold her phone, isn't it?

She nods, steps easily into that shower, promising herself to have eyes only for the clouded-glass stall with the LED-lit rainfall—it would be very uncool to invade Cinn's privacy when she's off saving the town, after all, wouldn't it? What if Cinn has Toby's yearbook photo taped to the mirror? What if there's something unmentionable plugged in on the counter? A girl's bathroom is really the inside of her head, Gal knows full well, and if this space is a mess, if it shows how many outfits Cinn goes through to get just the right one, then… what will that say about Gal's hero, her idol, her savior, her role model?

What it would say is that that Vicious Rumor from October hit Cinn a lot harder than she let on. That it fractured her sense of self-worth, her confidence.

And, even were that true, it would be none of Gal's business. She's a trespasser, here. Anything she finds out, it's fruit of the poisonous tree: nothing she can ever ask Cinn about. Not if Cinn doesn't bring it up herself.

Anyway, Cinn has enough to deal with, doesn't she? Not just her parents being gone, but Gin still being… just there. And graduation looming, and unfair rumors circulating, and college applications, and and and—

Gal shakes her head, squints her way to the shower because she doesn't trust herself not to peek. When she steps in on the tile, though, to hold her phone up to the window, she can't help but *feel*.

Again, she's right back on the yacht: there's hair crunching under bare feet.

Gal steps back, into the wall, and directs her phone down, taps the flashlight on.

"No, Cinn," she says.

But, yes: Cinn's cut *all* her blond hair off.

So... so now her and Gin, they're indistinguishable again, aren't they? Is this the ultimate kindness, some aspect of sisterly affection Gal doesn't have access to? Is it supposed to show Gin that her and Cinn are still the same, under it all?

Gal's breathing deep now. Too deep. It's making the blood rush in her head. It's making her eyes heat up.

Maybe it's all of that, sure.

But what if it's nothing like that at all? Some girls are cutters, Gal knows, and... could this be another expression of that? Did What Happened in October never stop happening, for Cinn?

Or—or is cutting her beautiful hair off not about her at all, but Him? Does making herself bald punish *Him*?

Gal has to nod, slowly, this new awareness taking hold for her. He is the one who put the scissors in Cinn's hands, isn't he? *Isn't* he?

But, "No, no, no," Gal insists, shaking her head to resist.

Still, her IQ is what it is: she doesn't want to, but she's looking back to these last thirty hours since Toby and Gwen, and trying to remember if it was one of them who started What Should Never Be Said about Cinn and "her hunky history teacher," as the writing on the bathroom walls would have it. And then Gal's looking far, far ahead to Cinn, the returning hero, stepping back into the halls of Henderson High in March or so, her hair bob-short and cute as hell, probably prompting all the other girls to chop their hair as well. It'll be the style. It'll be what all the survivors are wearing this post-massacre season.

And all because... all because of What Happened to Her in October. All because somebody put scissors in her hand. Which is just a set of blades. Is just violence, which shares an important *v* with revenge.

But this isn't really Cinn, Gal tells herself. It can't be. She's been turned *into* this. By Him. Whatever she's doing out there right now, whatever she's done, whatever she needed to become someone else to do, it's not her fault. She's just responding the only way that feels rational. The only way that makes sense. If you wind a toy up and it crashes into a vase, then *you're* responsible for breaking that vase, not the toy, the toy is innocent, the toy is the victim, here—another *v*—never mind the breakage all around it.

Gal balls her right hand into a fist, her lips thinning down to a grim line.

"Just this once," she tells Cinn, nodding.

She can okay Cinn doing this just once, if it's only once. And if they deserved it.

She'll even cover for her if she has to. Probably by working her way into the confidence of the One Who Wound Her Up Like This, and then Tearing His Ass *Down*. Because, now, from knowing all this, from figuring it out, Gal is a toy careening across the floor too, just like Cinn.

"Okay then," she says, still nodding.

Which is when the tile beneath her bare feet trembles.

The sound hits the house an instant later, a series of deep thumping *pops*. From… the lake? The pier?

What?

"*Galatea!*" Donna Pangborne screams from downstairs, the horror starting for her all over again, Gal can tell—the walls of the yacht closing in on her, tunneling her vision, dialing her momma-bear instincts up and up.

"Coming!" Gal yells back, already moving.

Except, this time, not even meaning to, she *does* look over to the counter, where her phone's flashlight is angled, and the first thing she sees, just like taking a picture, is herself in the reflection, in motion, all color drained from her face.

The second thing is a serene white mannequin head, its eyes painted in.

Its scalp is plastic smooth.

Meaning the wig it was wearing is gone.

Gal stops, has to look closer, and when she goes to run her hand along that smooth scalp, just to confirm it's real, her fingers bump into what she thought was a reflection: a second mannequin head, right behind the first, facing away.

Two wigs?

And loose on the counter between them is an empty blister pack, the colors on the cardboard backing dollar-store garish, the exclamation points not exactly helping class it up.

"*Spirit glue*," Gal reads, considering this, many gears turning in her head, opening more and more doors and possibilities.

When she sets the tube back down, it's about fifteen degrees off from where Cinn left it.

She swallows, nods to herself, and straightens it back, as it should be.

Jade is ashing into the chest pocket of her coveralls and staring out across the ice when she finally has to admit she can't deny the crunching coming in behind her and Hardy.

"At least it's not gonna be him, right?" she says, nodding down to the mound of dead Dark Mill South is.

She sort of already knows who it's going to be, too: Cinnamon Baker. Partly because of that rule in slashers, of it always being the last person you'd think, but more because the main thing keeping Jade, or anyone, from thinking it could be Cinnamon is… *she shaved her head for this masquerade*? She sacrificed all that beautiful hair just for revenge? To kill all the Proofrockers who should have died four years ago, balance that scale with pounds and pounds of flesh?

Probably, yeah.

Five minutes ago, Jade has to suppose, Cinnamon sat up from the hips back on Main, sat up Michael-style, all at once, shards of taillight plastic embedded in her face, her body armor still intact. At the sheriff's office, with her conveniently slipping-off wig, she'd been impersonating her sister impersonating *her*, and all to frame her sister, dead in the snow behind the truck, the demented killer of half the graduating class, and—now—no longer a ball and chain on the ankle of the sister about to escape this town.

Macy Todd's daughter indeed.

Jade's guess is that was Cinnamon in the Hannibal Lecter mask at the nursing home too, racing ahead of Jade. And that had been Cinnamon as well, lying under Mark whoever's bed, holding that arrow—her cold-walking to the nursing home was her turning in her tracks to go *back* to the nursing home—and that had to have been her at the high school as well, and at the motel before, and running through the storm between all the buildings the whole time, playing the waifish victim, the Calvin Klein final girl, here to save the day.

But, according to Letha, Cinnamon read all Jade's old extra credit papers, meaning she has to know Jade would figure this out.

Meaning Jade's a loose end, now. She wasn't framed like Cinnamon-as-Ginger said the initial plan was, but she can still be dead.

So of course those crunching footsteps *have* to be Cinnamon, right?

But they're not running yet, either, which means she's still carrying some damage, from Dark Mill South. Well, she's either still carrying some damage, or she's carrying some serious *beast* of an axe, or a chainsaw she's waiting until the last moment to fire up, run into Jade's back so it can *Alien* out her chest.

Jade takes a deep drag, stares across the lake.

The proof that it was all—or mostly—Cinnamon was that Dark Mill South didn't know that screwdriver was in Ginger's head, right? Or, even before that, if he had killed Ginger, then wouldn't Cinnamon, Ginger's spitting image, stepping in with that machete have given him pause, at least? He would have no reason to know the girl he killed had a twin.

Yeah, it was Cinnamon.

The only part Jade can't figure is what that Jace kid in the video store was saying, about the killer cupcake. Killer Klowns Jade can understand, *Killer Klowns from Outer Space* makes perfect sense. But what horror movie would use a *cupcake* as a murder weapon?

At the same time, why would Jace lie?

Assuming he wasn't, then… then that cupcake must be from some movie that came out while Jade was locked up down in Boise. A recent one.

Meaning? Dark Mill South couldn't have seen it, either. When all the crime-scene techs and true-crime bloggers show up to sift through Proofrock's bloody laundry one more time, they'll be lining up these copycat kills with the years those movies came out, and they'll all overlap with Dark Mill South.

Except this cupcake one.

But, because Dark Mill South tore through the video store like he did, will anybody even bother with the poison cupcakes smushing underfoot? The bright red icing of that one mostly whole cupcake will make a nice foreground for some blood spatter, Jade imagines, but nobody will see Cinnamon Baker way in the background of any of those snapshots, wearing an apron and humming her way through a recipe.

There's even *less* chance of any of those cops or bloggers buying the town reject's out-there theory, Jade knows. First she accuses the unassailable Theo Mondragon, the payer of a hundred college tuitions, a *thousand* tuitions, and, when that accusation doesn't stick, she points the finger at one of the daughters of Terra Nova, who barely survived not just one, but *two* massacres?

Cinnamon Baker couldn't have planned on Dark Mill South, no, that's pie-in-the-sky, but she could use him when he showed up, couldn't she? What's that old black and white... *The Leopard Man*, yeah. Some killer in a small town doing his dirty work and foisting it off on an escaped leopard. Or, even better—what was that term Mr. Holmes used to quiz them on? "Stalking horse"?

Jade had failed the quiz on that every time, because what a stalking horse *should* have been was the painted-up horse you let meander into some covered-wagon camp in 1881. What those would-be settlers don't see until too late is that you're walking right behind that horse, your legs in its legs' shadows, your body behind its body. As far as they know, this is just some Indian pony wandered away from its people—a gift, like the rest of this empty-

empty land, so free for the taking.

Until you stand still, let that horse keep walking past where you're now standing.

And you're painted up too, all the colors of night, so that the only flash of white they see is your teeth when you smile.

And then it's *on*.

Jade had explained this to Mr. Holmes, and he'd actually even listened until the end, by which time Jade had been bouncing on the balls of her feet, practically vibrating with the thrill of tearing through this camp with a tomahawk, a knife, her teeth.

"There's stalking horses, there's dark horses, and there's Trojan horses," Mr. Holmes had enumerated on his craggy fingers, his chair leaned back to maximum depth. "And then there's... guerrilla tactics, right?"

"I mean, I could wear a gorilla *costume*, if you think that would make it better," Jade had told him, only sorta-kinda playing, and the way he'd had to hold his lips together to keep from smiling at this—god.

Jade's lower lip quivers and she stabs her cigarette past it, to still it.

"And she knew about that rusted-open window," Jade adds out loud, in conversation with herself.

"In the women's?" Hardy asks, all the same.

Jade nods: in the ladies' room at his old office.

Ginger Baker wouldn't have known ducking in there was the way out. Only Cinnamon would have, because she'd already gone that way, to kill Mark and Kristen at the nursing home, and then double back in her own tracks.

"Who knew about that window?" Hardy says, ratcheting his

head to the side to blow smoke, and Jade says it while turning around: "*Her.*"

Hardy pivots in his seat, leading with his shotgun, and Jade's already squinting from the blood about to mist onto her frozen face, but then she remembers that chest armor Cinnamon's wearing, knows birdshot won't be enough to—

"Shit," Hardy says, disappointed.

The snow gusts into Jade's face, and when she can, she sneaks a quick peek, and… "shit" is right.

Rexall.

"See a girl back there?" Jade asks him. "Blond, bloody, kind of killer?"

Rexall sneers, evidently isn't here to be interrogated.

"Deputy wanted me to tell the two of you to come in out of the cold," he says back, not liking this cold task.

"What girl?" Hardy asks Jade.

"You'll see," she says. "She's the one who's really been—"

What stops her is what's materializing in the swirling white behind Rexall: not unkillable Cinnamon Baker, but…

"Oh," Hardy says, his face slack.

It's the spirit elk.

And, this close, his eyes… they're blue? And, not just blue, Jade tells herself, but—somehow *girlie*, in spite of the massive rack branching up from his head.

Rexall senses this, starts to turn, but it's too late, this elk already has his head down, is surging ahead to gore through him.

Except—Rexall's wearing insulated Carhartt coveralls, and layers under that it looks like. The brow tines the elk's aiming with, they don't penetrate. Instead, Rexall lifts, lifts, and launches ahead, into Hardy and Jade on the bench, Hardy's aluminum walker crunching like a beer can, Jade catching a custodial boot heel to the cheek.

For a flash she sees stars, but the snow her face plants into keeps her all the way awake.

Then, "Sheriff, Sheriff!" she's already screaming, trying to swim through the cold to him, because if this hurt her, then… ?

All she can see is Rexall, though.

He's already up, with Hardy's long shotgun.

The spirit elk is just standing there, twin gouts of steam leaking from his nostrils, his skin jumping in folds, the muscles under there quivering.

He snorts, he paws at the snow, and, when he steps around the bench, his legs too long and regal, he stops for some reason, sniffs at the backrest.

But his hot blue eyes never leave Rexall.

"Las Vegas," Rexall says for strength, it sounds like, and Jade turns from the elk to Rexall to try to make sense of this.

Which is when Rexall fires.

The storm's loud and all around, but this mutes it, mutes everything.

Jade jerks back, sure the shotgun's exploded, but Rexall's still holding it just the same, the recoil nothing to him.

"You think I don't know it's Friday the 13th?" he says now, lower, his eyes shining with tears. Then, "*I* need a hospital? You're the one shot in the head."

And he fires again.

Jade finally looks to the white elk.

His head is ground meat, *dripping* meat. No eyes anymore,

hardly a nose.

His right-side antlers creak over, fall away, taking a large chunk of skull with them, and Rexall shoots again, wading through the snow to be even closer, snub that barrel right up to what's left.

The next shot blasts the head completely off, and the next and the next gouts chunks from the neck stump, opening it up.

He keeps firing after the shotgun's empty, just clicking.

Jade climbs up, over to him, guides the hot barrel of the shotgun down.

And Rexall's… *crying*? Not just crying, blubbering, nearly hyperventilating with… with what? Joy? Pain?

"What the hell?" Jade says to him, for the first time in her life feeling sorry for him.

He looks over to her like surprised he's not alone. Like surprised this isn't… *Las Vegas*? Has he ever even been outside Idaho?

"You know *Friday the 13th*?" Jade asks, timidly.

"The day He died," Rexall says, and drops the shotgun into the snow, his chest heaving, tears rolling down his face, and from the reverent way he intones that, Jade can hear him drunk in her living room, muttering about that rapper Tab was always giving him grief about.

The only real fight Jade knows the two of them ever had was the time Rexall woke on the couch to her father with a bandanna do-rag'd on his head, tied in front.

"It's okay, it's okay," Jade almost says to Rexall.

Except: he's still Rexall, isn't he?

And he's already walking away anyway, the snow nothing to someone of his size.

Behind him, in front of Jade and Hardy, the elk wavers, wavers, finally falls over on his side, puffing the lightest particles of snow into Jade's lungs.

"Oh, oh," Hardy says, when Jade's still watching Rexall trudging away.

Instead of following where Hardy's looking, Jade steps over to hold him up. His lips are bloody, but the look on his face, it's… it's wonder?

"*No*," he says, bringing his right hand up to point.

Jade does, and, and…

The spirit elk?

"It's dead, yeah," Jade says, obviously.

Hardy tries to stagger ahead to the elk all the same, and falls to one knee heavily, in spite of Jade. She manages to get him to the bench, his thick index finger still pointing, pointing.

Jade finally looks to the dead elk again, for whatever he means, and… the elk's trashed, yeah, he took five shotgun blasts to the head, there's nothing left. Big whoop.

Except… what *is* that?

Some weird roundness in the gore?

Like a—like this elk's neck had been attached to a giant ball-joint, that's only now exposed.

But that's not how elk are put together, Jade knows. That's not how anything with a spine is put together.

She shakes her head no, no, that this is too much, this can't be, this doesn't happen, but Hardy doesn't care. He's already trying to walk over there again, and falling almost instantly, trying to climb back up.

"Here, here," Jade says, helping him to the elk.

They both fall on their knees before him.

Blood's still seeping from the neck stump. Hardy reaches in for that roundness that shouldn't be there, his old hands to either side of it, cupping it, and Jade can see now, she can see how wrong this is.

It's a head. A human *head.*

Hardy holds onto it, pulls delicately but with force, and Jade reaches into the gore with him, pulls too, and the insides of this elk, they're not… it's not real meat, somehow. It's already falling apart, like it's just made from dreams and lake water.

Hardy grunts to pull harder and then, when it finally gives, he falls back, pulling what Jade knows has to be this elk's lungs and heart and liver up onto him.

He cradles it like a child, though, his whole body shuddering.

Jade's mouth is opening and closing, because there aren't any words.

"You came back, you came back," she can just hear Hardy saying, and the way he's saying it, the tenderness in his voice…

"*Melanie?*" Jade whispers, her face going warm in all this cold.

And she can see it now, can see that this is a little girl curled up on her father's chest, this is a little girl who drowned nearly thirty years ago in the lake, come back for her daddy.

That's why she stabbed her antlers through Jade's mom: because Kimmy was there, that day. Lonnie too, twisted up out on the ice. And… and Rexall.

Jade looks up to the idea of him, but he's already gone.

When she comes back to Hardy, he's sitting up, his large hand cupping the back of Melanie's head, and her face is right to the hollow of his throat, and she's weak like the just-born, but it's more.

At the edges, she's coming apart, is made of the same gossamer nothing the elk was—just memory and lake trash, as fine as hair, but already falling apart.

"We've got to get her back in the—back in the lake," Jade says, and Hardy looks down to his daughter, to what's happening.

He says, "No, no, she's *already* back, this isn't, it's not—"

It's not fair, no. But it is happening.

"Here, let me," Jade says, holding her arms out, and it takes Hardy about three lifetimes to finally pass his only daughter over.

Jade takes her, the weight nothing, less than nothing. Melanie nuzzles into her collarbone and Jade whispers down to her, "It's okay, it's all right, your dad's here," and she stands, the snow calving off her.

Because Hardy has no walker anymore, and because the shotgun's buried, can't be a crutch, Jade lowers a shoulder for him.

He latches on, pulls himself up, and her legs nearly buckle from it.

But she once climbed the bluff behind Camp Blood in her underwear, she reminds herself.

She once stopped a forest fire from burning her home down.

"Ready?" she says, and then takes one step through the snow, Hardy heavy on her, Melanie shivering in her arms, and then Jade takes another shuffling step, and another, and after what has to be twenty minutes she feels the lake's ice finally under her feet, and she walks them out onto it, farther and farther, the swirling white swallowing them, and she knows the only place there's still going to be open water is over by the dam, where the turbine draws, and that's too far away to possibly get to like this, in this cold, after this day, but Hardy is clamped tight to her shoulder, and a little dead girl is coming apart in her arms, is only holding herself together with memory, it feels like, so Jade steels herself like she always has, like the final girl she is, and she keeps walking.

THE FINAL TERROR

On December 15th, a Sunday, the highway was finally opened, and the authorities streamed into blacked-out, snow-blanketed, cell signal–deprived Proofrock to warn us that there was a fraction of a sliver of a chance that a potentially dangerous prisoner being transported up the mountain might find his way to town.

The person they met, stationed in a tall brown pickup truck at the top of Main Street, was Rexall Bridger. At that time, I believe you and our school custodian were on a nodding recognition basis, Mr. Armitage—both worked in the education mines, in different capacities—but you weren't yet speaking. Correct me if I'm wrong, please, so I can emend, resend.

Rexall Bridger climbed into the federal and state authorities' snow coach and directed them down to Indian Lake, where many of the rest of us were gathered—minus you, of course, in triage at the sheriff's office, along with Letha Mondragon and Cinnamon Baker, the three of you under the care of Dr. Lionel Wilson, retired but conscripted back into active duty by Deputy Banner Tompkins, supposedly at gunpoint. But, as you say, time is the great exaggerator.

A generation or three between an incident and its latest retelling is enough time for legends to be born, and the communal game of Telephone will often introduce enough noise into the transmission that the story can become more a product of supposition and wishful thinking.

My suspicion is that Deputy Tompkins either strongly encouraged Dr. Wilson or otherwise enticed him, perhaps with assurances of his heroic status, should he manage to save all three of you.

As for what transpired once Rexall delivered those officials and authorities down to the shore of Indian Lake, however, I was there, Mr. Armitage. As the ruins of the pier had become a sort of pilgrimage destination for Proofrock, my feet were on that ground. And I use "ruins" in the loosest sense, here, as any actual remains of what had been the pier were obscured under the frozen lake. Or perhaps, in situations like this, "ruins" can be taken to be the ghostly images our memory insists should still be there. For example, were the Statue of Liberty to be removed in toto for maintenance, I can well imagine those habituated to its presence to still, in a manner, "see it" on the horizon, or at least have a pungent sense of its absence distinct from those who had never seen it.

So the pier, for those of us venturing down to the lake, was both there and not there. I can only imagine what its wavering absence felt like for long-time residents, who had taken for granted not only that the pier would always be there, but that it always had been, perhaps even accepting the dim notion that when Glen

Henderson and Tobias Golding had forged into this unnamed valley, they found these posts and planks high up the slope, and assumed it to be a viewing platform built and maintained by the Indigenous inhabitants, for purposes they would leave it to others to scry into.

It had been shaved off, though, and now the empty shore was something you had to see to believe. It was as if Indian Lake had been dialed back to its more pristine state.

Jutting up through the ice out past where the pier used to end was the high back corner of the rampaging snowplow that rumor—since verified—told us had done this. It was as much a wonder to imagine that giant truck submerged out there as it was to see the pier missing.

My mother kept her hand on my shoulder as we stood there, even though I had no impulse to prove the pier's absence by attempting to run out onto it. In the weeks following the pier's destruction, however, Proofrockers young and old would venture out onto the ice singly and in pairs, either in ice skates or snow boots, to move back and forth across where the pier had been, as if this could all be an optical illusion. As if their shins would, at some point in the investigation, bump into the weather-worn butt-ends of those wooden planks.

Many of us were there when Rexall Bridger delivered the authorities down to this section of the shore.

Jennifer Daniels was sitting on the bench that faces the lake. She was smoking a cigarette, as she had been since using the radio in the control booth of the dam to call Deputy Tompkins to come get her in the snowcat. What she had been doing that far out she wouldn't say, though Deputy Tompkins has remarked that it's a good thing Melanie's Ladder had been there for her when she needed it.

Jade looked only briefly to the federal agents and state troopers stepping down from the snow coach, after which she inhaled another chestful of smoke.

Standing up from the hump of snow just past her feet was a tall fiberglass handle, as if Jade, Proofrock's erstwhile custodian, had stopped mopping before the storm settled in, and her mop had frozen in its bucket.

Perched on that wooden handle was a small bird that chirped its displeasure when it had to fly away, due to the approaching officials and authorities.

Jennifer Daniels nodded for them down to the hump of snow she had apparently been guarding, and the less senior of these officials and authorities swept carefully around that handle, and then got on their knees and dug, uncovering the frozen corpse of one Dark Mill South.

Jennifer Daniels turned her head to let her smoke out.

Though we couldn't hear what she might be saying in response to the questions being asked of her, we could nevertheless track her shrugging and facial expressions as she took these officials and authorities through her version of events, surely documenting the high school seniors lost over the last thirty-six hours, even if she didn't know them all by name: Toby Manx and Gwen Stapleton in the motel parking the night of the 12th, followed the next day at the assisted living facility by Mark Costins, Kristen Ames, and Philip Cates, then, at the high school,

Abby Grandlin, Wynona Fleming, and Jensen Jones, all leading to the video store massacre on Main, which claimed Bo Richardson, L'Saul Frederickson, Penny Wayne, Meg Goldberg, Tristan Thomas, and Geoff Sulkes—six of the eight volunteers. The way Jennifer Daniels chucked her chin out to where the pier used to be suggested she didn't forget to count Lonnie Chambers in. The way her eyes dialed back to "emotionless" at the end of this sad tally strongly suggested that she also included her mother, Kimmy Daniels. Sheriff Hardy, Jade had cryptically told Deputy Tompkins, was "together in eternity" with his daughter, whatever that means—my searches just turn up song lyrics.

Hardy's body, as of this writing, and not counting Sheriff Rex Allen and Deputy Francie Mullins, whose bodies have been recovered (along with the county Bronco), is the only one still missing.

So, as it turned out, yes, there had been "a fraction of a sliver of a chance" that Dark Mill South would find his way to Proofrock.

The officials and authorities taped Dark Mill South off, stepping timidly out onto the ice to do the same to the snowplow, and Pleasant Valley Assisted Living, Henderson High, and Proofrock Video all had fluttering cordons as well.

When the officials and authorities came back to Jennifer Daniels on her smoking bench, their follow-up questions had to do with how the injuries to her mother and Lonnie Chambers weren't consistent with the injuries sustained by all of the seniors—save Jensen Jones.

Jade just shrugged their questions off.

Though the pilgrims gathered on shore weren't as many as before, still, with the power not back yet, the goings-on at what had been the pier functioned more or less as our news programming for the day. We were rubberneckers, yes, and not too proud to say so.

I should note too that the holdouts, the Proofrockers reluctant to leave the area of the erstwhile pier, were probably two-thirds comprised of grieving parents standing a sort of vigil, perhaps thinking that if they punished themselves with the elements and with deprivation, then a mistake could still be righted, their children returned to them.

And, though I can't attest Jennifer Daniels was parked on that bench for the whole day—what of food? warmth? facilities?—I can attest that she was there both times my mother and I ventured down. For our second sojourn we had blankets, lawn chairs, and thermoses of soup and coffee. On the walk down my mother proposed the possibility that the parents of the children who were killed could be finding that the continual sight of the pier being gone "fit" with their current circumstances, that it was a visual reminder that, yes indeed, this was a new world they were now marooned in.

My mother's use of nautical terminology of course stemming from the yacht whose presence, before it was scuttled, had been a constant reminder of what had happened the night before the Independence Day Massacre.

"If only someone had thought to bring *us* hot coffee

in our time of need, right?" she added, waggling a neighborly thermos.

So, we were there distributing warmth when the helicopter landed. It was a state copter. Deputy Tompkins clamped his hat on tighter and ran out to meet these passengers. And if you're feeling any tension reading that, then understand that this is four months ago already, nearly to the day. Had these passengers flown in to investigate certain Abelard and Heloise allegations between a history teacher and his formerly favorite student, then you yourself would have probably come to handcuffed to a hospital bed railing.

If you're worried that that helicopter may yet be hovering, too… it isn't.

Instead, let's pretend that a different student, one, say, working on an independent study with you this semester very much without the approval of her mother, that she sifted through auction sites until she found your profile. And, though users' purchases are of course private, the feedback you leave isn't—such is the nature of feedback: it's meant to be perused. So, had I printed all this out, there would now be physical records of your slasher collection taking shape, item by item.

In and of itself, this is innocent, is just an enthusiast accruing what he loves.

However—you recall my eighth submission towards this project you thought you were in charge of, Mr. Armitage? "Slasher 102," from three weeks ago. I elliptically mentioned in there someone we both know, whom I surmised might, if rumor were accurate, have footage of Dark Mill South before he surfaced on Main Street.

Rexall Bridger, school custodian.

I don't believe you knew him then except to nod to, and your lingering injuries are keeping you from school grounds, but I would imagine you made his acquaintance shortly thereafter, your collector's mania unable to leave footage that priceless unclaimed. But of course the two of you *found* a price, did you not?

While Rexall doesn't operate in the world of cash receipts, I warrant that, if pressed by the authorities, he would trade confirmation of any transaction with you for leniency. Meaning, you could hide or delete or throw away that footage, and the story of it will yet remain. And that story won't be of a history teacher hoarding collectibles, it will be of an upright, never-accused-of-"dalliances" citizen withholding what could be crucial evidence associated not just with a murder case, but with *seventeen* murder cases.

The products of this independent study could, in retrospect, be used in court as a series of stepping stones, could they not?

Provided, of course, that history teacher were still in town. No, no—provided that history teacher were still in *Idaho*, or still teaching or otherwise having contact with minors, or, as he sees them, the nubile, bouncy, unthinking victims in a slasher movie, there solely to be exploited.

But this is all hypothetical, of course. Cinnamon,

when she comes back to town, would never want the rumors about her and you made public through a court of law.

For the moment, only she and I and you are aware of any factual basis of those rumors, and the only reason I even know is that I found her in the town canoe crying about it over Thanksgiving break, saying how she was going to paddle out there and kill herself. I don't know if she meant "Indian Lake" or "Terra Nova" or "Camp Blood" or "Drown Town," but, whatever the intended final resting place, she didn't have a paddle, so was just bobbing there at what used to be the pier, scolding herself for not even having been able to do this right.

Just so you can understand where I'm coming from.

And, no, she has not been proofing these papers, is more concerned at the moment with graduating from her hospital bed down the mountain, so she can in turn graduate from high school. However, were she and I in communication, I propose that she might clue me in about the "price" you proposed for access to Jennifer Daniels's high school papers, and how knowledge of them, simply put, costs too much, even for a daughter of Terra Nova.

So, unless you wish it otherwise, only you and I are aware of the content of this independent study. And, since world health organizations have raised certain alarms and put in place certain protocols, leaving us no option but to communicate solely by email, all of this is locked forever in email, should it be needed.

Unless I hear that you wish to pursue this further, I will consider our independent study done, and there will be no need to petition any administrators or higher legal authorities about a grade change, which would probably require further investigation.

But, I wouldn't have you grade me without finishing the project, Mr. Armitage.

I believe I had walked those officials and authorities back to Jennifer Daniels in late afternoon, Sunday the 15th of December? She's sitting on that memorial bench between the parking lot and the shore, and, while there should be cigarette butts all around her, they're instead carefully collected in a Styrofoam coffee cup.

Deputy Tompkins is moving among us. Or, I should say, he's using us as a pretext for keeping an eye on Jennifer Daniels and these helicopter passengers.

I'm stationed partway between, as I was just "chasing" a blow-away Christmas napkin that was *much* too quick for me to catch, at least before it delivered me right where I needed to be in order to eavesdrop.

What the state officials from the helicopter are pressing Jennifer Daniels on is that police tape fluttering on the ice out there. Evidently her story doesn't match what Deputy Tompkins has told them. Deputy Tompkins's version has him careening the snowplow down Main Street, and then, unable to stop it, barreling it into the lake.

Jennifer Daniels's story has Dark Mill South driving it into town the night of the 12th, and abandoning it to the lake, perhaps as a way to hide his presence in Proofrock.

"Why's it matter?" Jennifer Daniels asks these two state officials, looking back and forth between them.

"We just need the facts, ma'am," the woman says.

"'Ma'am'?" Jennifer Daniels says back with a smirk, her eyes cutting past me, to—I have to think—Deputy Tompkins.

"It's going to be there until thaw," the man says. He has no hood or beanie, is still trying to get his combover combed back over from the windstorm of the helicopter rotors.

"Bet so, bet so," Jennifer Daniels says, inhaling deep and meaning-fully on her cigarette.

"We just need to know who's responsible," the woman says.

"For him?" Jennifer Daniels says, pointing with her ember down to Dark Mill South.

"For *that*," the man says, tilting his head out onto the ice. "Reports from the townspeople have the sound of the pier being destroyed as Friday at dusk, not Thursday noon."

"Which aligns with the deputy's version," the woman adds.

"Why's this matter so much?" Jennifer Daniels asks the two of them.

"Because he says *he* did it," the man says.

"What, he have to pay for it or something?" Jennifer Daniels asks, not turning away to exhale, but not needing to. The breeze off the ice is enough.

"Our supervisor doesn't like reports with conflicting elements," the woman says, doing her eyes like "What can you do?" Bosses.

"He's not even a real deputy yet," Jennifer Daniels says about Deputy Tompkins, kind of confidentially. "He's still in his probationary period, I mean. And his hand, you saw it. It's a mummy hand."

"So," the man leads off, putting this together, "you're saying that a mark on his record, like—like wrecking a snowplow into the lake—"

"And destroying town property," the woman cuts in with a toler-ant grin.

"Wrecking a state snowplow," the man goes on. "You're saying that won't exactly help him become a *permanent* deputy?"

"You tell me," Jennifer Daniels says, looking from face to face.

"Not our concern," the man says for both of them.

"He's a good one, though, I think," Jennifer Daniels says. Then she shrugs, adds, "He wasn't always, but… he's a husband now. And a father. And if you lock him away—"

"Nobody said anything about jail time," the woman says.

"If you lock him away from the job he's… *taken* to," Jennifer Daniels says. "Then who's wearing the badge around here? With both our other sheriffs gone?"

"'Around here,'" the man repeats.

"Proofrock," the woman clarifies.

"Not our concern," the man reiterates.

"And if he's out submitting app-li-ca-tions," Jade goes on, stretching the word out like that, as if using the time it takes to think of what to say next, ". . . then, bam, he's not there for his daughter. His wife. And she needs him right now. So does Ad—so does his little girl."

"You're a friend of the family, I take it, Ms. Daniels?" the man asks.

"Small town," Jennifer Daniels answers back. "And, it's Jade."

"We just need to—" the man and the woman say in accidental unison, glancing over at each other in apology.

"*I* did it," Jennifer Daniels says then, crushing her cigarette out on her bandaged palm and then depositing it in the Styrofoam cup, her gauze smoking until she rubs it out with her fingers.

"*You* did it?" the man asks.

"Girl can't drive a truck, what?" Jennifer Daniels says to him, offering her wrists to be cuffed.

"You're just taking the fall for him," the woman says, her voice especially no-nonsense.

"Ask anybody," Jennifer Daniels says right back. "You can't trust me. I'm a bad bet. The worst bet."

"Someone does have to be responsible," the woman says to the man.

"It didn't just get there by itself," the man says back after considering, and so Jennifer Daniels is—after drilling her Styrofoam ashtray into the mounded snow—led away to the helicopter, and what I can't help but wonder is if, in the moment she claimed this act, she remembered the conditions of her parole: that she would destroy no city, county, state, or federal property for a period of six months, lest she serve the full term, with no trial, no takebacks.

Due to the cold and the elevation and the injunctions about limited traffic during the state's largest snow-removal effort to date, there was no media on hand to snap an iconic photograph of Jennifer Daniels—*Jade*—being perp-walked to that helicopter, Mr. Armitage. But I can tell you her newly long hair was lifted slightly in the updraft from the rotors starting up again, bouncy like you see in shampoo commercials, and that she shook her head harshly to Deputy Tompkins when he started to rush out to her, shook her head and thinned her lips and flashed her eyes at him to stay, to stop.

Perhaps this is the true cost of being what she would call a final girl?

You know the genre better than I do, of course.

I should say too that there is actually one photograph of this.

I snapped it on my phone. The light's poor, the composition happen-stance, but the focus is good—we daughters of Terra Nova always have the best phones.

In that snapshot, Jade is leaning forward to look past the woman holding her by the wrist. She's looking to the left, out across the lake, perhaps taking a snapshot of her own.

Please find on your porch, Mr. Armitage, a 3 x 5 glossy print of that.

It's tucked into the Styrofoam cup of ashes and butts I collected from beside the memorial bench that cold day in the snow.

Consider it your parting gift, along with what no

photograph could have captured: Jade shrugging free of the two state officials holding her by the upper arms, shaking free and stepping ahead, reaching her right arm back to her waistband. When she thrusts her right arm up in victory, what she's holding there for all the gods to see, for the whole world to know, for you to never have in your sacred collection, it's a hook. From the killer she killed. Because she's Jade fucking Daniels. And a thousand men like you can't even reach up to touch her combat boots.

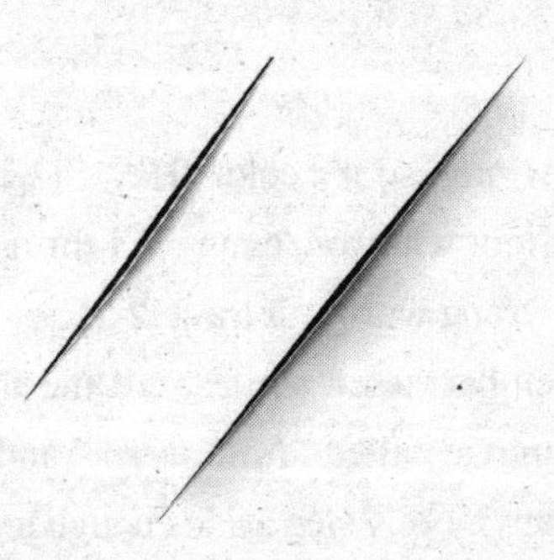

ACKNOWLEDGMENTS

I'm six years old. It's 1978. I'm either living at my grandparents' house five miles south of Stanton, Texas, or I'm there for a weekend, a week, the month, that year—I don't know. Their place was home base for my mom and my brothers and me. It was where we always fell back to. Back then you could stand on the porch at night and not see a single light in any direction. Just darkness, maybe a butane pump popping out there somewhere, and the coyotes yapping. The house was on a ten acre plot, and way at the corner of it, my uncle and his new wife were living in a little trailer. They were either still in high school or just out of it, and to a six-year-old kid, they were the most amazing people ever, just... titans on my landscape, able to do no wrong. I think I'm still trying to be my uncle from back then, even: down-at-heel boots, pearl snap shirts, faded jeans, shaggy hair, old trucks, a looking-away smile—Darren from *Mongrels*, pretty much. But also Gabe from *The Only Good Indians*.

Anyway, I'm sleeping on the floor of the living room one night when a knock comes on the door. I stay wrapped in my blanket, shuffle over all bleary-headed, and haul the door open. Standing there wrapped in their own blanket are my aunt and uncle. This is winter, so it's cold. "Hey, Stevie," they say, "we come sleep on the floor with you, maybe?" I shrug sure, but have to ask: "Why? What's wrong with your trailer?" They kind of look at each other then smile embarrassed smiles, tell me they just went to town and saw this movie called "*Halloween*," and now they can't sleep in their place anymore. I step aside enough to let them huddle past, into the house, and... you know those moments when your world is kind of crackling all around you like crumpled paper unfolding, so you can finally read what's on that page, what you didn't even know was there hiding, had been written all along? This is that, for me. It's my life going this direction, not that direction. I distinctly remember standing there while they huddle past in their blanket. I'm kind of sideways so I can hold the screen door open for them, and there's a breath or two after they've passed where I'm still standing there, where I'm looking out into the darkness of the pasture, and wondering what could possibly be scary enough to drive these two amazing people to come sleep on the cold floor with me? I've been looking into that darkness ever since, waiting for Dean Cundey to roll that big dimmer switch over just enough for me to see the contours of Michael Myers's pale face. All of which is to say thank you, Bruce and Tami, for going to the movies that night. For saying "*Halloween*" in that reverent, powerful, embarrassed way. Thank you for introducing me to slashers before I'd even ever heard that term.

But my aunt and uncle aren't the only ones I owe for introducing me to slasherkind. There's also my friend I grew up with, Brett Watkins. When we were twelve, I'm not sure I'd ever actually been to a movie theater, and didn't have any movie theaters on my horizons, either. We lived way out in the country, I wasn't driving yet, nobody in my house went to movies, so... that decided it. Brett had an older brother, though. This brother took him to see *The Terminator.* The week after that, in Brett's living room, he acted the whole movie out for me. I remember so well him dragging one leg to get the end right. Yes, Michael's the first slasher I sort of heard about, but that T-800 was the first sort-of slasher I ever saw. And I never forgot. I also owe Mr. Jerry Reed, though. Not for slashers, but for a certain name in *Reaper.* The song "Amos Moses" has a person in it—Doc Milsap—I've always heard as "Dark Mill South," and probably always will. Thanks also to Greg Greene, for asking me what story or two I considered to kind of be at the base of who I am as a writer. This was for his *Chthonica* podcast. The two stories I knee-jerked up were Mona Simpson's "Lawns" and Tony Earley's "The Prophet from Jupiter," neither of which I'd actually read for a few years. So I dove back in, kind of wanted to see who I might be as well, and one story turned out to be Jade in utero, and the other story's Indian Lake, right down to the dam, just proving I'm more thief than writer, really.

Chainsaw and *Reaper* also owe a lot to *The Watcher in the Woods*, the first horror movie I ever saw. Twenty-five or so years after watching it on a VCR rented from the gas station, I would publish a story called "Raphael" in *Cemetery Dance*—my first horror story. It's about a girl who goes missing years and years ago, but then comes back. Pretty much, it's *Watcher.* Just, the way I did it was that some boys throw this young girl into the lake, but instead of sinking, she lands on *top* of the water. Which is to say: I've been writing about Stacey Graves as long as I've been publishing horror, which really means I've been writing about Jade. Some characters are your best heart, aren't they? Jade's mine. Like her, I was a high school janitor. Like her, I was sent home over and over for my t-shirts. Like her, I used to try to color my hair. Like her, I was the only Indian at all the schools I went to. Like her, I was always getting hauled in to a cell, an interrogation room. Like her, I was really into blades, was always coming away cut.

And, talking Jade: Mr. Holmes. Which is to say: teachers I've had. The first one to thank is from what should have been my senior year. I was seventeen, day one at another new school. Government class. This teacher walks in, cases the place, sets her books down on the desk, sighs, then zeroes in on me way in the back, in a way that I kind of feel my throat swell a bit, because she's going to recognize me in some way, or's going to introduce me all around, plug me into this new place, I don't know, anything can happen, right? What she says once the room's quieted down, though, is for me to get my *greasy* head off her clean chalkboard. I lean forward like she wants, everyone sneaking looks back to me, logging me as that kid, and, after class, I walk out this teacher's door, down the hall, and out of high school forever. Which was wonderful research for writing Jade. So, thank you, government teacher. And, yes, I am that student who showed back up at the end of that semester to ace the final, just to prove to you I could, even if I was way past credit, or graduation. The next teacher is Dr. Jill Patterson. I'm a senior again, but this time at college, which I never even meant to go to—I'm meant to be driving tractor, chopping cotton. But, here I am in fiction workshop somehow, and I'm pretty much levitating in my seat, am reading everything I can get my hands on, and writing every minute of the day. I can't get enough of books, of writers, of reading. This is a world I didn't even know could be real. In class early in the semester, then, wanting to show off what-all I'd been packing into my head, I proudly say something about Yeats. Except, to the chorus of a few embarrassed-for-me chuckles, I pronounce his name *Yeets*, not "Yates." Jill—you probably don't remember this—instead of telling me to get my greasy head off your clean chalkboard, you just grinned to get your words right and said you're pretty sure it's pronounced the other way, Stephen, but, yes, it does *look* like "Yeets," and so, instead of walking out again, back to where I belong, I stick with this whole reading and writing thing until I've got my PhD like you, and am here, doing this, even using Yeats's "The Second Coming"—the poem I was halfway citing in workshop that day, via The Police—in this novel about a girl with a heart bigger than her body. Thank you, Jill. And thank you to my next writing teacher, William J. Cobb, for telling me about this new novel he'd just reviewed, *Galatea 2.2* by Richard Powers, which stuck with me enough that I named a background character "Galatea" in *Chainsaw*, and then, when I needed someone to write essays for *Reaper*—here she was, raising her hand politely but insistently, telling me, like that guy at the end of *Hoosiers*, that she's got this, Coach. Too, Bill? Every line I write, I hear your prose cadence under it. It's the only one I know. And thank you to my next writing teacher, Janet Burroway. Janet: one day in workshop you had us do an exercise on what lines we would and wouldn't cross in fiction. The novel I wrote as a result of that five-minute exercise was "All the Beautiful Sinners," but after a publisher used that title for a serial killer novel I'd done, I called this novel *Demon Theory*. There's a character in it, Nona, who knows all the horror trivia, a character I'd do again in *The Last Final Girl*, as Izzy Stratford… and then she finally looked up from the sink she'd been dyeing her hair in all along, saw herself in the mirror as she really is: Jade Daniels. I'm thinking I never find her without *Demon Theory*. Without you, Janet, asking us what lines we would and wouldn't cross. Thank you. But? Thank you too to Dean Fontenont and a Composition II instructor at Texas Tech whose name I've lost, for typing up my first-ever story, and submitting it for an award, getting this whole thing started.

And thanks to Thea Lucas, my great-granddad, Pop, for walking with me along fence lines the same way Hardy walks with Jade along the top of Glen Dam, never mind how old you were, how much it probably hurt you to walk out there with me.

Thank you to Adam Bradley, for guiding me through Tupac Shakur's catalogue, and life. Thanks to Larry McMurtry, for *Lonesome Dove*. Without a structuring device you use in there, that I'm stealing here, I never find my way through *Reaper*, I don't think. Thanks to Mike Flanagan's *Midnight Mass*, for a scene that told me how to do a key thing with Jade and Letha: just let them *talk*, dude. Thanks to Tim Sale and Jeph Loeb's *Batman: The Long Halloween* and Scott Turow's *Presumed Innocent*, for carving a path *Reaper* could follow. Thanks to Dorothy Allison's *Bastard Out of Carolina*, for carving another path, one with light at the end. Thanks to Layli Long Soldier, for her amazing poem "38." Thanks to Mackenzie Kiera, for reading *Reaper* I don't know how many times, helping me to shake it straight, and feeding me good ideas besides. Thanks to Jesse Lawrence again: you're always there for the early reads, man. Thanks to Jesse Peters, for cueing me in about the Morris Industrial School for Indians—this really helped the revision figure itself out. Thanks to the endless cans of Yerba Mate Pineapple-Coconut energy drinks I lived on for the ten weeks I wrote *Reaper*—you taste like suntan lotion, only, I can drink you and not die. Thanks to my local blood bank, which always lets me get away with another bag of…

not blood, I've got plenty of that (well), but what they call "tails": the ends of all the different-colored tape rolls they wind around your arm after donating. These tails hold the armrests together on my twenty-two-year-old possibly stolen office chair. Thank you to *The Empire Strikes Back* and *The Two Towers*; both of you were where I went when I was trying to navigate the middle installment of a trilogy. But thanks as well to Jerome Sable and Eli Batalion's short film *The Legend of Beaver Dam*. I go back to you whenever I need to remember to sing my heart out, and splash blood on every wall. Thanks to the *With Gourley and Rust* podcast, for doing episodes twice as long as the slashers themselves. That kind of enthusiasm is infectious. Thanks as well to Ryan Turek, for spreading the slasher gospel far and wide every chance you get.

And a special huge thank you to a certain bookseller at Mysterious Galaxy, one R.J. Crowther, Jr. You may not remember, Rob, but ten or twelve months ago I posted a screencap of... maybe it was one of the *Child's Plays*? I posted it just for the elk antler—it was a thing I was doing, a service I thought needed providing: documenting any and all elk racks in slashers. At which point you replied with *Silent Night, Deadly Night*, which I'd completely spaced on. But? Maybe a quarter into *Reaper* as I was, it wasn't too late: I reshaped the book from there on out, to account for Linnea Quigley's character's death on those antlers. And it kind of let everything lock into place in a way I hadn't even been suspicious of. I don't know what *Reaper* might look like, had you not chimed in, Rob. Thanks too, I guess, to Cream's Ginger Baker, for letting me use your name? I should have clocked that back-when, during *Chainsaw*, but I only heard it here in *Reaper*, when Jade was going down the hall to see her, and it was way too late to undo it at that point. Thanks too to that *Grease Live* production that somehow heartened me, while writing *Reaper.* Thank you to *Where the Red Fern Grows*, for what you do with that axe at the end of the story. Ever since fourth grade I've felt I could do something similar, if I really-really tried, so: that scar Jade sees in the door of the dam's control booth, in a book that comes out when I'm fifty-one. Thanks to @JeffMessineo, for help with terminology regarding a feather hatband. Thanks to Tyler Mahan Coe, of the *Cocaine & Rhinestones* podcast, for help with an Armitage-y part of *Reaper* that I think might be gone, now. But it's still sort of a strange attractor, I think, disturbing the narrative from a point just past the margins.

Thanks also to my daughter Kinsey, who interrupted me writing *Reaper* one afternoon with the best break ever: half a shredded-bison Indian taco from Tocabe, all the way over in Denver. It fueled me through a scene that was giving me no end of grief. Thanks also to my son Rane, for taking me to Gorehound's Playground up in Fort Collins. When I walked in there, I instantly knew I was standing in what Armitage wanted to build—or, no, what he had in his *heart.* So I ran home, wrote that, hadn't even realized how obviously it had been missing. But, novels are snowballs rolling across the landscape, aren't they? They pick this up, they pick that up too, and they just make it part of them. Or, that's the thief's excuse, anyway.

And, finally, thanks to everyone at Saga and Gallery and Simon & Schuster for believing in this trilogy. Sydney Morris and Kayleigh Webb and Bianca Ducasse for getting *Chainsaw* and *Reaper* out there. Jéla Lewter, for somehow keeping all the slightly different versions of *Reaper* stacked correctly. Lisa Litwack: yet another killer cover (can't wait to see the third). And of course Joe Monti, my editor: you were right, one hundred percent. Again. I'm not half the writer it maybe looks like I am without you pushing me to be better. Which is to say: Dark Mill South never becomes what he is now, without you telling me he's not quite there yet. And thanks to my superstar of an agent, BJ Robbins, for wrangling with me over *Reaper* for two or three months before we even gave it over to Joe. Used to? Used to there were all these long, winding interviews between Gal and Armitage, but you were right, BJ, and then Joe: there was a better way waiting in the wings, if I would just slow down for a moment, maybe look over there. A better Galatea.

And thanks finally, and always and forever, to my beautiful wife Nancy. I've told you the dream I had once, of how being dead wasn't actually death, it just meant you and me get to hold hands and roller-skate all through the college campus we met on, forever? Yeah, the reaper's coming for us all, there's nothing we can really do about that. But, if I do get to roller-skate into eternity holding your hand, then, there really isn't anything to be scared of, is there?

Here, take my hand. I want to be sure not to lose you.

Stephen Graham Jones
Boulder, CO
1 February – 10 April, 2021